OTTO PENZLER PRESENTS
AMERICAN MYSTERY CLASSICS

THE ADVENTURES OF ELLERY QUEEN

ELLERY QUEEN was a pen name created and shared by two cousins, Frederic Dannay (1905-1982) and Manfred B. Lee (1905-1971), as well as the name of their most famous detective. Born in Brooklyn, they spent forty-two years writing the greatest puzzle mysteries of their time, gaining the duo a reputation as the foremost American authors of the Golden Age "fair play" mystery.

Besides co-writing the Queen novels, Dannay founded *Ellery Queen's Mystery Magazine*, one of the most influential crime publications of all time. Although Dannay outlived his cousin by nine years, he retired the fictional Queen upon Lee's death.

OTTO PENZLER, the creator of American Mystery Classics, is also the founder of the Mysterious Press (1975); MysteriousPress.com (2011), an electronic-book publishing company; and New York City's Mysterious Bookshop (1979). He has won a Raven, the Ellery Queen Award, two Edgars (for the *Encyclopedia of Mystery and Detection*, 1977, and *The Lineup*, 2010), and lifetime achievement awards from NoirCon and *The Strand Magazine*. He has edited more than 70 anthologies and written extensively about mystery fiction.

THE ADVENTURES OF ELLERY QUEEN

ELLERY QUEEN

Introduction by
OTTO PENZLER

AMERICAN MYSTERY CLASSICS

Penzler Publishers
New York

Published in 2023 by Penzler Publishers
58 Warren Street, New York, NY 10007
penzlerpublishers.com

Distributed by W. W. Norton

Cover image: Andy Ross
Cover design: Mauricio Diaz

Paperback ISBN 978-1-61316-458-7
Hardcover ISBN 978-1-61316-457-0

Library of Congress Control Number: 2023908395

Printed in the United States of America

9 8 7 6 5 4 3 2 1

THE ADVENTURES OF ELLERY QUEEN

CONTENTS

INTRODUCTION

A USED paperback edition of *The Adventures of Ellery Queen* happened to be in the Mysterious Bookshop's spinner rack so I took it with me to reread before sitting down to write this little introduction. Two thoughts came to mind when I opened it.

First, I remember very clearly holding this very edition in my hands the first time I read it. It's not true of every book I've ever read, nor even of most, but it's not uncommon for me to recall the illustration on the cover of a paperback, or dust jacket, or the binding of a hardcover edition I read fifty or sixty years ago, or—gasp!—seventy. And, often, exactly where I was for at least part of the time—in bed (my favorite location), on the subway, in the library, at my grandmother's apartment—bringing back the surrounding sights and sounds. Maybe I can't quite remember what I had for dinner last night but I easily visualize hundreds of books that I read back in the days when I was inhaling four or five a week. As useful and handy as e-books are, they cannot replicate the sensations of a memorable cover, or the feel of a physical copy.

My second thought was about the nature of short story collections and the great publishing wisdom, passed from father to son, mother to daughter, is that no one likes anthologies (stories by a variety of authors) or collections (stories by a single author). I've always loved short fiction and these volumes were among the first I collected. In the early years of the Mysterious Press, most of the first dozen or so books it published were collections by Robert Bloch, Cornell Woolrich, Ross Macdonald, Stanley Ellin, Donald E. Westlake, Patricia Highsmith, and others.

On the copyright page of the Pocket Books edition of *The Adventures of Ellery Queen* the publisher very helpfully provided the publishing history of this title. Most readers can skip this part because it has nothing to do with how extraordinary the stories in this book are but, for that small coterie of people (nerds, like me) who finds these things fascinating, this is what I learned:

The first printing, courtesy of Frederick A. Stokes, was released on November 1, 1934. The hardcover reprint house Grosset & Dunlap issued its edition in July 1935; it went through four printings. The Mercury Bestseller Library, which reissued books in digest-size paperbacks, published an edition in February 1940; it had two printings. Triangle Books, noted for producing very cheap hardcover editions, then published it again in June 1940, followed by a second printing. The first Pocket Books edition was released in March 1941. The copy in my hands is dated September 1954—the twenty-second Pocket Books edition! (I don't know if there were further printings but it wouldn't be a major surprise.)

I ask you: Does this seem to suggest that short story collections don't sell? Granted, most compilations aren't as good as *The Adventures of Ellery Queen* and would be unlikely to have comparable success, but these statistics illustrate two points: 1—Short story collections have a wide and appreciative readership; 2—The overwhelming popularity of this particular book suggests you are in for a treat.

The eleven stories in this volume are the earliest short works to feature Queen as a detective and, to me, are among the very best of the author's fair-play mysteries. Much as Arthur Conan Doyle did when he produced his greatest Sherlock Holmes stories, each of these studies in detection has its title begin with "The Adventure of...," followed by a title that instantly pulls the reader in: "The Hanging Acrobat," "The One-Penny Black," "The Two-Headed Dog," "The Mad Tea Party." Who could resist?

So many of the elements that comprise the gestalt of Ellery Queen may be found in these short tales (strangely, compiled out of the chronological sequence of their initial publication, mainly in magazines): In "The African Traveler," there is the pedantry so prominent in the early novels, as well as the offering of alternate solutions; in "The Bearded Lady," the greatest practitioner of the dying clue is at the peak of his powers; the author's ability to find fresh variations of other works is evident in "The One-Penny Black" as it pays homage to Poe's "The Purloined Letter."

In what was doubtless an awkward decision, Ellery Queen selected *The Adventures of Ellery Queen* for a place in *Queen's Quorum*, a compendium of the 106 greatest works of detective fiction ever written. It would have been actionable had he not, as it almost certainly is the finest collection of Golden Age mysteries by an American.

Often called the Golden Age of the detective novel, the years between the two World Wars produced some of the most iconic names in the history of mystery. In England, the names Agatha

Christie and Dorothy L. Sayers continue to resonate to the present day. In America, there is one name that towers above the rest, and that is Ellery Queen.

That famous name was the brainchild of two Brooklyn-born cousins, Frederic Dannay (born Daniel Nathan, he changed his name to Frederic as a tribute to Chopin, with Dannay merely a combination of the first two syllables of his birth name) and Manfred B. Lee (born Manford Lepofsky). They wanted a simple nom de plume and had the brilliant stroke of inspiration to employ Ellery Queen as both their byline and as the name of their protagonist, reckoning that readers might forget one or the other but not both.

Dannay was a copywriter and art director for an advertising agency while Lee was writing publicity and advertising material for a motion picture company when they were attracted by a $7,500 prize offered by *McClure's* magazine in 1928; they were twenty-three years old.

They were informed that their submission, *The Roman Hat Mystery*, had won the contest but, before the book could be published or the prize money handed over, *McClure's* went bankrupt. Its assets were assumed by *Smart Set* magazine, which gave the prize to a different novel that it thought would have greater appeal to women. Frederick A. Stokes decided to publish *The Roman Hat Mystery* anyway, thus beginning one of the most successful mystery series in the history of the genre. Since the contest had required that books be submitted under pseudonyms, the simple but memorable Ellery Queen name, born out of necessity, became an icon.

The success of the novels got them Hollywood offers and they went to write for Columbia, Paramount, and MGM, though they never received any screen credits. The popular medium of radio also called to them and they wrote all the scripts for the successful *Ellery Queen* radio series for nine years from 1939 to 1948. In an innovative approach, they interrupted the narration so that Ellery could ask his guests—well-known personalities—to solve the case as they now had all the necessary clues. The theories almost invariably in vain, the program would then proceed, revealing the correct solution. The Queen character was also translated into a comic strip character and several television series starring Richard Hart, Lee Bowman, Hugh Marlowe, George Nader, Lee Philips, and, finally, Jim Hutton.

While Lee had no particular affection for mystery fiction, always hoping to become the Shakespeare of the twentieth century, Dannay had been interested in detective stories since his boyhood. He wanted to produce a magazine of quality mystery stories in all sub-genres and founded *Mystery* in 1933 but it failed after four issues when the publisher went bankrupt. However, after Dannay's long convalescence from a 1940 automobile accident that nearly took his life, he created *Ellery Queen's Mystery Magazine*; the first issue appeared in 1941 and remains the leading mystery fiction magazine in the world to the present day.

Although Dannay and Lee were lifelong collaborators on their novels and short stories, they had very different personalities and frequently disagreed, often vehemently, in what Lee once described as "a marriage made in hell." Dannay was a quiet, scholarly introvert, noted as a perfectionist. Lee was impulsive and assertive, given to explosiveness and earthy language. They remained steadfast in their refusal to divulge their working methodology, claiming that over their many years together they had tried every possible combination of their skills and talent to produce the best work they could. However, upon close examination of their letters and conversations with their friends and family, it eventually became clear that, in almost all instances, it was Dannay who created the extraordinary plots and Lee who brought them to life.

Each resented the other's ability, with Dannay once writing that he was aware that Lee regarded him as nothing more than "a clever contriver." Dannay's ingenious plots, fiendishly detailed with strict adherence to the notion of playing fair with readers, remain unrivalled by any mystery American author. Yet he did not have the literary skill to make characters plausible, settings visual, or dialogue resonant. Lee, on the other hand, with his dreams of writing important fiction, had no ability to invent stories, although he could improve his cousin's creations to make the characters come to life and the plots suspenseful and compelling.

The combined skills of the collaborators produced the memorable Ellery Queen figure, though in the early books he was clearly based on the best-selling Philo Vance character created by S.S. Van Dine. The Vance books had taken the country by storm in the 1920s so it was no great leap of imagination for Dannay and Lee to model their detective after him. In all candor, both Vance and the early Queen character were insufferable, showing off their supercilious attitude and pedantry at every possible opportunity.

When Queen made his debut in *The Roman Hat Mystery*, he was ostensibly an author but spends precious little time working at his career. He appears to have unlimited time to collect books and help his father, Inspector Richard Queen, solve cases. Although close to his father, the arrogant young man is often condescending to him as he loves to show off his erudition. As the series progresses (and as the appetite for Philo Vance diminished), Ellery becomes a far more realistic and likable character.

"Ellery Queen *is* the American detective story," as Anthony Boucher, the mystery reviewer for the *New York Times*, wrote, and it would be impossible for any reasonable person to disagree.

The American Mystery Classics series bring back into print the greatest authors and books of the Golden Age of the detective novel. Yes, they are available as e-books, but owning a physical copy of a masterwork by a favorite author is a different experience.

—OTTO PENZLER

FOREWORD

IN THE past your humble prefator has garnered a vicarious fame by acting as master of ceremonies, *entrepreneur*, and general buffer between Mr. Ellery Queen and his public; and has, indeed, been quite happy in the task. In serving in my customary capacity in this volume, however, I must confess that I stand in the shadow of my friend by courtesy only, drawn there by the old fascination and a certain irresistible tug of habit. For while in the past I have had my legitimate excuse—I was personally responsible, for instance, for the introduction of Ellery's cases to the reading public—I have no tittle of excuse for participation in the present. In fact, this whole thing has come as a surprise to me.

The first I knew about it Ellery called me up and said: "Look here J.J., you've been perfectly splendid about these things in the past—"

"What things?" I said

"Forewords and things. You see—"

"What *are* you talking about?"

"Well," said Ellery rather sheepishly, "I've been bitten by the bug, J.J. I'm rather afraid your job as official goad and prodder extraordinary has become outmoded. I was looking over some of my notes not that long ago—"

"Don't tell me," I cried, "you've unearthed some case I'm ignorant of!"

"Oodles of them. Fact is, there were so many I couldn't resist them. A few of them you know about. Remember Mason—Phineas Mason, of the Park Row firm?"

"Of course … By George! I sent him to you in the Shaw matter."

"Exactly. Then you went out of town or something—I don't believe you ever found out what happened. Well, that's one of them. I've already done a good deal of work and they'll be out in volume form very soon. Er—would you write a foreword, as usual?"

The truth of the matter is that I couldn't refuse Ellery, and he said that for various reasons it was impossible to turn the manuscript over to me; so in my travail I went to Sergeant Velie.

"Sergeant," I said pleadingly, "do you know anything about this book Ellery Queen's getting up?"

"What book?" growled the good Sergeant. He seemed suspicious. "He's always writing a book."

I realized that I couldn't even tell Velie what book it was. "There's something in it," I said hopefully, "about Mason and the Shaw case."

"Mason and the Shaw case…" Velie rubbed his steel jaw. "Oh, that one!" And he began to chuckle. "What a case that was!"

"Ah, then you do know something about it," I said with a sigh of relief. "Well, Sergeant, how would you like to write a little foreword for the volume? You know—for friendship's sake, and all that sort of thing."

"*Me?*" gasped Sergeant Velie, and he began to back away. "'Scuse me, Mr. McC—, I think the Inspector's waitin' for me."

The Inspector may have been waiting for Velie, but it was I who got there first. I found the old gentleman up to his ears in reports, and apparently in a high dudgeon about something appurtenant to his office. The moment did not seem propitious for the request, but I confess I was a desperate man, and I blurted it out without ceremony.

Inspector Queen put down his pen and sucked some snuff into his nostrils and leaned back in his chair. "Sit down, Mr. McC—," he said, not unkindly. "I want to talk to you like a Dutch uncle. I know you're a good friend of El's, and all that; but did it ever occur to you you're a sucker for a left jab?"

"A su—" It rather took the wind out of my sails. "I'm afraid I don't understand, Inspector."

"That's the trouble with my son's friends," sighed the old gentleman. "He hypnotizes 'em, or something. Don't you realize that for five or six years he's been victimizing you?"

"Victimizing me!"

"Exactly. He should have been a ward leader. Makin' you do all that work!"

"But it's been a pleasure, an—an honor," I protested, aghast.

The Inspector's frosty blue eyes twinkled. "That's the beauty of his technique," he said dryly. "Makes you work and like it, too. You're determined to keep on writing pretty little forewords for his books?"

"I don't think you get the point, Inspector," I began. "I'm asking you if *you* wouldn't be kind enough, under the circumstances—"

"Well, I've been trying to tell you," chuckled the old gentleman. "The answer is: I wouldn't. Honor's all yours." Then he added, with what I found to be a maddening thoughtfulness, "But they *were* pips, some of 'em."

I bit my nails. "What on earth am I to do? Ellery says this is rather a rush job—"

"Now, now, don't be stampeded," said the Inspector with a sort of pitying look. "I know just how you feel. El's been jumping me through hoops so long I'm kind of dizzy myself. Why don't you just scribble down that I wouldn't help you? Might give El a laugh, and it will fill a couple of pages."

And so here I am, grateful even for that suggestion. Ellery knows nothing of what I am doing—he's off somewhere in Minnesota tracking down a murderer who persists in removing the left forefinger of his victims—and I daresay he will complain at my lack of resourcefulness.

If there is one redeeming feature of the affair it is that I find myself in the pleasant and unaccustomed position—at least insofar as Ellery Queen's memoirs are concerned—of looking forward to a few nights of exciting reading. I suggest we indulge our pleasure together!

J. J. McC.

New York

THE ADVENTURES OF
ELLERY QUEEN

The Adventure of
THE AFRICAN TRAVELER

MR. ELLERY QUEEN, wrapped loosely in English tweeds and reflections, proceeded—in a manner of speaking—with effort along the eighth-floor corridor of the Arts Building, that sumptuous citadel of the University. The tweeds were pure Bond Street, for Ellery was ever the sartorial fellow; whereas the reflections were Americanese, Ellery's ears being filled with the peculiar patois of young male and female collegians, and he himself having been Harvard, 'Teen.

This, he observed severely to himself as he lanced his way with the ferrule of his stick through a brigade of yelling students, was higher education in New York! He sighed, his silver eyes tender behind the lenses of his *pince-nez;* for, possessing that acute faculty of observation so essential to his business of studying criminal phenomena, he could not help but note the tea-rose complexions, the saucy eyes, and the osier figures of various female students in his path. His own Alma Mater, he reflected gloomily, paragon of the educational virtues that it was, might have been better—far better—off had it besprinkled its muscular classes with nice-smelling co-eds like these—yes, indeed!

Shaking off these unprofessorial thoughts, Mr. Ellery Queen edged gingerly through a battalion of giggling girls and approached Room 824, his destination, with dignity.

He halted. A tall and handsome and fawn-eyed young woman was leaning against the closed door, so obviously lying in wait for him that he began, under the buckling tweeds, to experience a—good lord!—a trepidation. Leaning, in fact, on the little placard which read:

CRIMINOLOGY, APPLIED

MR. QUEEN

This was, of course, sacrilege. . . . The fawn-eyes looked up at him soulfully, with admiration, almost with reverence. What did a member of the faculty do in such a predicament? Ellery wondered with a muted groan. Ignore the female person, speak to her firmly—?

The decision was wrested from his hands and, so to speak, placed on his arm. The brigand grasped his left biceps with devotional vigor and said in fluty tones: "You're Mr. Ellery Queen, himself, aren't you?"

"I *knew* you were. You've the nicest eyes. Such a queer color. Oh, it's going to be *thrilling*, Mr. Queen!"

"I beg your pardon."

"Oh, I didn't say, did I?" The hand, which he observed with some astonishment was preposterously small, released his tingling biceps. She said sternly, as if in some way he had fallen in her estimation: "And you're the famous detective. Hmm. Another illusion blasted. . . . Old Icky sent me, of course."

"Old *Icky?*"

"You don't know even that. Heavens! Old Icky is Professor Ickthorpe, B.A., M.A., Ph.D., and goodness knows what else."

"Ah!" said Ellery. "I begin to understand."

"And high time, too," said the young woman severely. "Furthermore, Old Icky is my father, do you see. . . . " She became all at once very shy, or so Ellery reasoned, for the black lashes with their impossible sweep dropped suddenly to veil eyes of the ultimate brownness.

"I do see, Miss Ickthorpe." Ickthorpe! "I see all too clearly. Because Professor Ickthorpe—ah—inveigled me into giving this fantastic course, because you are Professor Ickthorpe's daughter, you think you may wheedle your way into my group. Fallacious reasoning," said Ellery, and planted his stick like a standard on the floor. "I think not. No."

Her slipper-toe joggled his stick unexpectedly, and he flailed wildly to keep from falling. "Do come off your perch, Mr. Queen. . . . There! That's settled. Shall we go in, Mr. Queen? Such a nice name."

"But—"

"Icky has arranged things, bless him."

"I refuse abso—"

"The Bursar has been paid his filthy lucre. I have my B.A., and I'm just dawdling about here working for my Master's. I'm really very intelligent. Oh, come on—don't be so professorish. You're much too nice a young man, and your *devastating* silv'ry eyes—"

"Oh, very well," said Ellery, suddenly pleased with himself. "Come along."

It was a small seminar room, containing a long table flanked with chairs. Two young men rose, rather respectfully, Ellery thought. They seemed surprised but not too depressed at the vision of Miss Ickthorpe, who was evidently a notorious character. One of them bounded forward and pumped Ellery's hand.

"Mr. Queen! I'm Burrows, John Burrows. Decent of you to pick me and Crane out of that terrific bunch of would-be manhunters." He was a nice young fellow, Ellery decided, with bright eyes and a thin intelligent face.

"Decent of your instructors and record, Burrows, I'd say. . . . And you're Walter Crane, of course?"

The second young man shook Ellery's hand decorously, as if it were a rite; he was tall, broad, and studious-looking in a pleasant way. "I am, sir. Degree in chemistry. I'm really interested in what you and the Professor are attempting to do."

"Splendid. Miss Ickthorpe—rather unexpectedly—is to be the fourth member of our little group," said Ellery. "Rather unexpectedly! Well, let's sit down and talk this over."

Crane and Burrows flung themselves into chairs, and the young woman seated herself demurely. Ellery threw hat and stick into a corner, clasped his hands on the bare table, and looked at the white ceiling. One must begin. . . . "This is all rather nonsensical, you know, and yet there's something solid in it. Professor Ickthorpe came to me some time ago with an idea. He had heard of my modest achievements in solving crimes by pure analysis, and he thought it might be interesting to develop the faculty of detection by deduction in young university students. I wasn't so sure, having been a university student myself."

"We're rather on the brainy side these days," said Miss Ickthorpe.

"Hmm. That remains to be seen," said Ellery dryly. "I suppose it's against the rules, but I can't think without tobacco. You may smoke, gentlemen. A cigarette, Miss Ickthorpe?"

She accepted one absently, furnished her own match, and kept looking at Ellery's eyes. "Field work, of course?" asked Crane, the chemist.

"Precisely." Ellery sprang to his feet. "Miss Ickthorpe, *please* pay attention. . . . If we're to do this at all, we must do it right. . . . Very well. We shall study crimes out of the current news—crimes, it goes without saying, which lend themselves to our particular brand of detection. We start from scratch, all of us—no preconceptions, understand. . . . You will work under my direction, and we shall see what happens."

Burrows' keen face glowed. "Theory? I mean—won't you give us any principles of attack first—classroom lectures?"

"To hell with principles. I beg your pardon, Miss Ickthorpe. . . . The only way to learn to swim, Burrows, is to get into the water. . . . There were sixty-three applicants for this confounded course. I wanted only two or three—too many would defeat my purpose; unwieldy, you know. I selected you, Crane, because you seem to have the analytical mind to a reasonable degree, and your scientific training has developed your sense of observation. You, Burrows, have a sound academic background and, evidently, an excellent top-piece." The two young men blushed. "As for you, Miss Ickthorpe," continued Ellery stiffly, "you selected yourself, so you'll have to take the consequences. Old Icky or no Old Icky, at the first sign of stupidity out you go."

"An Ickthorpe, sir, is never stupid."

"I hope—I sincerely hope—not. . . . Now, to cases. An hour ago, before I set out for the University, a flash came in over the Police Headquarters' wire. Most fortuitously, I thought, and we must be properly grateful. . . . Murder in the theatrical district—chap by the name of Spargo is the victim. A queer enough affair, I gathered, from the sketchy facts given over the tape. I've asked my father—Inspector Queen, you know—to leave the scene of the crime exactly as found. We go there at once."

"Bully!" cried Burrows. "To grips with Crime! This is going to be great. Shan't we have any trouble getting in, Mr. Queen?"

"None at all. I've arranged for each of you gentlemen to carry a special police pass, like my own; I'll get one for you later, Miss Ickthorpe. . . . Let me caution all of you to refrain from taking anything away from the scene of the crime—at least without consulting me first. And on no account allow yourselves to be pumped by reporters."

"A murder," said Miss Ickthorpe thoughtfully, with a sudden dampening of spirits.

"Aha! Squeamish already. Well, this affair will be a test-case for all of you. I want to see how your minds work in contact with the real thing. . . . Miss Ickthorpe, have you a hat or something?"

"Sir?"

"Duds, duds! You can't traipse in there this way, you know!"

"Oh!" she murmured, blushing. "Isn't a sport dress *au fait* at murders?" Ellery glared, and she added sweetly: "In my locker down the hall, Mr. Queen. I shan't be a moment."

Ellery jammed his hat on his head. "I shall meet the three of you in front of the Arts Building in five minutes. Five minutes, Miss Ickthorpe!" And, retrieving his stick, he stalked like any professor from the seminar room. All the way down the elevator, through the main corridor, on the marble steps outside, he breathed deeply. A remarkable day! he observed to the campus. A really remarkable day.

The Fenwick Hotel lay a few hundred yards from Times Square. Its lobby was boiling with policemen, detectives, reporters and, from their universal appearance of apprehension, guests.

Mountainous Sergeant Velie, Inspector Queen's right-hand man, was planted at the door, a cement barrier against curiosity-seekers. By his side stood a tall, worried-looking man dressed somberly in a blue serge suit, white linen, and black bow-tie.

"Mr. Williams, the hotel manager," said the Sergeant.

Williams shook hands. "Can't understand it. Terrible mess. You're with the police?"

Ellery nodded. His charges surrounded him like a royal guard—a rather timid royal guard, to be sure, for they pressed close to him as if for protection. There was something sinister in the atmosphere. Even the hotel clerks and attendants, uniformly dressed in gray—suits, ties, shirts—wore strained expressions, like stewards on a foundering ship.

"Nobody in or out, Mr. Queen," growled Sergeant Velie. "Inspector's orders. You're the first since the body was found. These people okay?"

"Yes. Dad's on the scene?"

"Upstairs, third floor, Room 317. Mostly quiet now."

Ellery leveled his stick. "Come along, young 'uns. And don't—" he added gently, "don't be so nervous. You'll become accustomed to this sort of thing. Keep your heads up."

They bobbed in unison, their eyes a little glassy. As they ascended in a policed elevator, Ellery observed that Miss Ickthorpe was trying very hard to appear professionally *blasé*. Ickthorpe indeed! This should take the starch out of her. . . . They walked down a hushed corridor to an open door. Inspector Queen, a small birdlike gray little man with sharp eyes remarkably like his son's, met them in the doorway.

Ellery, suppressing a snicker at the convulsive start of Miss Ickthorpe, who had darted one fearful glance into the death-room and then gasped for dear life, introduced the young people to the Inspector, shut the door behind his somewhat reluctant charges, and looked about the bedroom.

Lying on the drab carpet, arms outflung before him like a diver, lay a dead man. His head presented a curious appearance: as if some one had upset a bucket of thick red paint over him, clotting the brown hair and gushing over his shoulders. Miss Ickthorpe gave vent to a faint gurgle which certainly was not appreciation. Ellery observed with morbid satisfaction that her tiny hands were clenched and that her elfin face was whiter than the bed near which the dead man lay sprawled. Crane and Burrows were breathing hard.

"Miss Ickthorpe, Mr. Crane, Mr. Burrows—your first corpse," said Ellery briskly. "Now, dad, to work. How does it stand?"

Inspector Queen sighed. "Name is Oliver Spargo. Forty-two, separated from his wife two years ago. Mercantile traveler for a big drygoods exporting house. Returned from South Africa after a year's stay. Bad reputation with the natives in the outlying settlements—thrashed them, cheated them; in fact, was driven out of British Africa by a scandal. It was in the New York papers not long ago. . . . Registered at the Fenwick here for three days—same floor, by the way—then checked out to go to Chicago. Visiting relatives." The Inspector grunted, as if this were something justifiably punished by homicide. "Returned to New York this morning by plane. Checked in at 9:30. Didn't leave this room. At 11:30 he was found dead, just as you see him, by the colored maid on this floor, Agatha Robins."

"Leads?"

The old man shrugged. "Maybe—maybe not. We've looked this bird up. Pretty hard guy, from the reports, but sociable. No enemies, apparently; all his movements since his boat docked innocent and accounted for. *And* a lady-killer. Chucked his wife over before his last trip across, and took to his bosom a nice blonde gal. Fussed with her for a couple of months, and then skipped out—and *didn't* take her with him. We've had both women on the pan."

"Suspects?"

Inspector Queen stared moodily at the dead traveler. "Well, take your pick. He had one visitor this morning—the blonde lady I just mentioned. Name of Jane Terrill—no sign of occupation. Huh! She evidently read in the ship news of Spargo's arrival two weeks ago; hunted him up, and a week ago, while Spargo was in Chicago, called at the desk downstairs inquiring for him. She was told he was expected back this morning—he'd left word. She came in at 11:05 this a.m., was given his room-number, was taken up by the elevator-boy. Nobody remembers her leaving. But she says she knocked and there was no answer, so she went away and hasn't been back since. Never saw him— according to her story."

Miss Ickthorpe skirted the corpse with painful care, perched herself on the edge of the bed, opened her bag and began to powder her nose. "And the wife, Inspector Queen?" she murmured. Something sparkled in the depths of her fawn-brown eyes. Miss Ickthorpe, it was evident, had an idea and was taking heroic measures to suppress it.

"The wife?" snorted the Inspector. "God knows. She and Spargo separated, as I said, and she claims she didn't even know he'd come back from Africa. Says she was window-shopping this morning."

It was a small featureless hotel room, containing a bed, a

wardrobe closet, a bureau, a night-table, a desk, and a chair. A dummy fireplace with a gas-log; an open door which led to a bathroom—nothing more.

Ellery dropped to his knees beside the body, Crane and Burrows trooping after with set faces. The Inspector sat down and watched with a humorless grin. Ellery turned the body over; his hands explored the rigid members, stiff in *rigor mortis.*

"Crane, Burrows, Miss Ickthorpe," he said sharply. "Might as well begin now. Tell me what you see—Miss Ickthorpe, you first." She jumped from the bed and ran around the dead man; he felt her hot unsteady breath on the back of his neck. "Well, well? Don't you see *anything?* Good lord, there's enough here, I should think."

Miss Ickthorpe licked her red lips and said in a strangled voice: "He—he's dressed in lounging-robe, carpet-slippers and—yes, silk underwear beneath."

"Yes. And black silk socks and garters. And the robe and underwear bear the dealer's label: *Johnson's, Johannesburg, U.S.Afr.* What else?"

"A wrist-watch on his left wrist. I think"—she leaned over and with the shrinking tip of a finger nudged the dead arm—"Yes, the watch crystal is cracked. Why, it's set at 10:20!"

"Good," said Ellery in a soft voice. "Dad, did Prouty examine the cadaver?"

"Yes," said the Inspector in a resigned voice. "Spargo died some time between 11:00 and 11:30, Doc says. I figure—"

Miss Ickthorpe's eyes were shining. "Doesn't that mean—?"

"Now, now, Miss Ickthorpe, if you have an idea keep it to yourself. Don't leap at conclusions. That's enough for you. Well, Crane?"

The young chemist's brow was ridged. He pointed to the

watch, a large gaudy affair with a leather wrist-strap. "Man's watch. Concussion of fall stopped the works. Crease in leather strap at the second hole, where the prong now fits; but there's also a crease, a deeper one, at the third hole."

"That's really excellent, Crane. And?"

"Left hand splattered and splashed with dried blood. Left palm also shows stain, but fainter, as if he had grabbed something with his bloody hand and wiped most of the blood off. There ought to be something around here showing a red smudge from his clutching hand. . . ."

"Crane, I'm proud of you. Was anything found with a blood-smear on it, dad?"

The Inspector looked interested. "Good work, youngster. No, El, nothing at all. Not even a smear on the rug. Must be something the murderer took away."

"Now, Inspector," chuckled Ellery, "this isn't *your* examination. Burrows, can you add anything?"

Young Burrows swallowed rapidly. "Wounds on the head show he was struck with a heavy instrument many times. Disarranged rug probably indicates a struggle. And the face—"

"Ah! So you've noticed the face, eh? What about the face?"

"Freshly shaved. Talcum powder still on cheeks and chin. Don't you think we ought to examine the bathroom, Mr. Queen?"

Miss Ickthorpe said peevishly: "I noticed that, too, but you didn't give me a chance. . . . The powder *is* smoothly applied, isn't it? No streaks, no heavy spots."

Ellery sprang to his feet. "You'll be Sherlock Holmeses yet. . . . The weapon, dad?"

"A heavy stone hammer, crudely made—some kind of African curio, our expert says. Spargo must have had it in his bag—his trunk hasn't arrived yet from Chicago."

Ellery nodded; on the bed lay an open pigskin traveling-bag. Beside it, neatly laid out, was an evening outfit: tuxedo coat, trousers, and vest; stiff-bosomed shirt; studs and cufflinks; a clean wing-collar; black suspenders; a white silk handkerchief. Under the bed were two pairs of black shoes, one pair brogues, the other patent-leather. Ellery looked around; something, it seemed, disturbed him. On the chair near the bed lay a soiled shirt, a soiled pair of socks, and a soiled suit of underwear. None exhibited bloodstains. He paused thoughtfully.

"We took the hammer away. It was full of blood and hair," continued the Inspector. "No fingerprints anywhere. Handle anything you want—everything's been photographed and tested for prints."

Ellery began to puff at a cigarette. He noticed that Burrows and Crane were crouched over the dead man, occupied with the watch. He sauntered over, Miss Ickthorpe at his heels.

Burrows' thin face was shining as he looked up. "Here's something!" He had carefully removed the timepiece from Spargo's wrist and had pried open the back of the case. Ellery saw a roughly circular patch of fuzzy white paper glued to the inside of the case, as if something had been rather unsuccessfully torn away. Burrows leaped to his feet. "That gives *me* an idea," he announced. "Yes, sir." He studied the dead man's face intently.

"And you, Crane?" asked Ellery with interest. The young chemist had produced a small magnifying-glass from his pocket and was scrutinizing the watchworks.

Crane rose. "I'd rather not say now," he mumbled. "Mr. Queen, I'd like permission to take this watch to my laboratory."

Ellery looked at his father; the old man nodded. "Certainly, Crane. But be sure you return it. . . . Dad, you searched this room thoroughly, fireplace and all?"

The Inspector cackled suddenly. "I was wondering when you'd get to that. There's something almighty interesting in that fireplace." His face fell and rather grumpily he produced a snuffbox and pinched some crumbs into his nostrils. "Although I'll be hanged if I know what it means."

Ellery squinted at the fireplace, his lean shoulders squaring; the others crowded around. He squinted again, and knelt; behind the manufactured gas-log, in a tiny grate, there was a heap of ashes. Curious ashes indeed, patently not of wood, coal, or paper. Ellery poked about in the debris—and sucked in his breath. In a moment he had dug out of the ashes ten peculiar objects: eight flat pearl buttons and two metal things, one triangular in outline, eye-like, the other hook-like—both small and made of some cheap alloy. Two of the eight buttons were slightly larger than the rest. The buttons were ridged, and in the depression in each center were four thread-holes. All ten objects were charred by fire.

"And what do you make of that?" demanded the Inspector.

Ellery juggled the buttons thoughtfully. He did not reply directly. Instead, he said to his three pupils, in a grim voice: "You might think about these. . . . Dad, when was this fireplace last cleaned?"

"Early this morning by Agatha Robins, the mulatto maid. Some one checked out of this room at seven o'clock, and she cleaned up the place before Spargo got here. Fireplace was clean this morning, she says."

Ellery dropped buttons and metal objects on the night-table and went to the bed. He looked into the open traveling-bag; its interior was in a state of confusion. The bag contained three four-in-hand neckties, two clean white shirts, socks, underwear, and handkerchiefs. All the haberdashery, he noted,

bore the same dealer's tab—*Johnson's, Johannesburg, U.S.Afr.*
He seemed pleased, and proceeded to the wardrobe closet. It
contained merely a tweed traveling suit, a brown topcoat, and
a felt hat.

He closed the door with a satisfied bang. "You've observed everything?" he asked the two young men and the girl.

Crane and Burrows nodded, rather doubtfully. Miss Ickthorpe was barely listening; from the rapt expression on her face, she
might have been listening to the music of the spheres.

"Miss Ickthorpe!"

Miss Ickthorpe smiled dreamily. "Yes, Mr. Queen," she said
in a submissive little voice. Her large brown eyes began to rove.

Ellery grunted and strode to the bureau. Its top was bare. He
went through the drawers; they were empty. He started for the
desk, but the Inspector said: "Nothing there, son. He hadn't time
to stow anything away. Except for the bathroom, you've seen everything."

As if she had been awaiting the signal, Miss Ickthorpe dashed
for the bathroom. She seemed very anxious indeed to explore its
interior. Crane and Burrows hurried after her.

Ellery permitted them to examine the bathroom before him.
Miss Ickthorpe's hands flew over the objects on the rim of the
washbowl. There was a pigskin toilet-kit, open, draped over the
marble; an uncleansed razor; a still-damp shaving-brush; a tube
of shaving cream; a small can of talcum and a tube of tooth-
paste. To one side lay a celluloid shaving-brush container, its cap
on the open kit.

"Can't see a thing of interest here," said Burrows frankly. "You,
Walter?"

Crane shook his head. "Except that he must have just finished
shaving before he was murdered, not a thing."

Miss Ickthorpe wore a stern and faintly exultant look. "That's because, like all men, you're blinder'n bats. . . . *I've* seen enough."

They trooped by Ellery, rejoining the Inspector, who was talking with some one in the bedroom. Ellery chuckled to himself. He lifted the lid of a clothes-hamper; it was empty. Then he picked up the cap of the shaving-brush container. The cap came apart in his fingers, and he saw that a small circular pad fitted snugly inside. He chuckled again, cast a derisive glance at the triumphant back of the heroic Miss Ickthorpe outside, replaced cap and tube, and went back into the bedroom.

He found Williams, the hotel manager, accompanied by a policeman, talking heatedly to the Inspector. "We can't keep this up forever, Inspector Queen," Williams was saying. "Our guests are beginning to complain. The night-shift is due to go on soon, I've got to go home myself, and you're making us stay here all night, by George. After all—"

The old man said: "Pish!" and cocked an inquiring eye at his son. Ellery nodded. "Can't see any reason for not lifting the ban, dad. We've learned as much as we can. . . . You young people!" Three pairs of eager eyes focused on him; they were like three puppies on a leash. "Have you seen enough?" They nodded solemnly. "Anything else you want to know?"

Burrows said quickly: "I want a certain address."

Miss Ickthorpe paled. "Why, so do I! John, you mean thing!"

And Crane muttered, clutching Spargo's watch in his fist: "I want something, too—but I'll find it out right in this hotel!"

Ellery smoothed away a smile, shrugged, and said: "See Sergeant Velie downstairs—that Colossus we met at the door. He'll tell you anything you may want to know.

"Now, follow instructions. It's evident that the three of you have definite theories. I'll give you two hours in which to formu-

late them and pursue any investigations you may have in mind."
He consulted his watch. "At 6:30, meet me at my apartment
on West Eighty-seventh Street, and I'll try to rip your theories
apart. . . . Happy hunting!"

He grinned dismissal. They scrambled for the door, Miss Ickthorpe's turban slightly awry, her elbows working vigorously to
clear the way.

"And now," said Ellery in a totally different voice when they
had disappeared down the corridor, "come here a moment, dad. I
want to talk to you alone."

At 6:30 that evening Mr. Ellery Queen presided at his own
table, watching three young faces bursting with sternly repressed
news. The remains of a dinner, barely touched, strewed the cloth.

Miss Ickthorpe had somehow contrived, in the interval between her dismissal and her appearance at the Queens' apartment, to change her gown; she was now attired in something
lacy and soft, which set off—as she obviously was aware—the
whiteness of her throat, the brownness of her eyes, and the pink-
ness of her cheeks. The young men were preoccupied with their
coffee-cups.

"Now, class," chuckled Ellery, "recitations." They brightened,
sat straighter and moistened their lips. "You've had, each of you,
about two hours in which to crystallize the results of your first
investigation. Whatever happens, I can't take credit, since so far
I've taught you nothing. But by the end of this little confabu-
lation, I'll have a rough idea of just what material I'm working
with."

"Yes, sir," said Miss Ickthorpe.

"John—we may as well discard formality—what's *your* theory?"

Burrows said slowly: "I've more than a theory, Mr. Queen. I've
the solution!"

"*A* solution, John. Don't be too cocky. And what," said Ellery, "is this solution of yours?"

Burrows drew a breath from the depths of his boots. "The clue that led to my solution was Spargo's wrist-watch." Crane and the girl started. Ellery blew smoke and said encouragingly: "Go on."

"The two creases on the leather strap," replied Burrows, "were significant. As Spargo wore the watch, the prong was caught in the second hole, so that there was a crease *across* the second hole. Yet a deeper crease appeared across the *third* hole. Conclusion: the watch was habitually worn by a person with a smaller wrist. In other words, the watch was not Spargo's!"

"Bravo," said Ellery softly. "Bravo."

"Why, then, was Spargo wearing some one else's watch? For a very good reason, I maintain. The doctor had said Spargo died between 11:00 and 11:30. Yet the watch-hands had apparently stopped at 10:20. The answer to this discrepancy? That the murderer, finding no watch on Spargo, took her own watch, cracked the crystal and stopped the works, then set the hands at 10:20 and strapped it about Spargo's dead wrist. This would seem to establish the time of death at 10:20 and would give the murderer an opportunity to provide an alibi for that time, when all the while the murder actually occurred about 11:20. How's that?"

Miss Ickthorpe said tartly: "You say 'her.' But it's a man's watch, John—you forget that."

Burrows grinned. "A woman can own a man's watch, can't she? Now whose watch was it? Easy. In the back of the case there was a circular patch of fuzzy paper, as if something had been ripped out. What made of paper is usually pasted in the back of a watch? A photograph. Why was it taken out? Obviously, because the murderer's face was in that photograph. . . . In the last two hours I followed this lead. I visited my suspect on a reportorial pretext and managed to get a look at a photograph-album she has. There I found one photograph with a circular patch cut out. From the rest of the photo it was clear that the missing circle contained the heads of a man and a woman. My case was complete!"

"Perfectly amazing," murmured Ellery. "And this murderess of yours is—?"

"Spargo's wife! . . . Motive—hate, or revenge, or thwarted love, or something."

Miss Ickthorpe sniffed, and Crane shook his head. "Well," said Ellery, "we seem to be in disagreement. Nevertheless a very interesting analysis, John. . . . Walter, what's yours?"

Crane hunched his broad shoulders. "I agree with Johnny that the watch did not belong to Spargo, that the murderer set the hands at 10:20 to provide an alibi; but I disagree as to the identity of the criminal. I also worked on the watch as the main clue. But with a vastly different approach.

"Look here." He brought out the gaudy timepiece and tapped its cracked crystal deliberately. "Here's something you people may not know. Watches, so to speak, breathe. That is, contact with warm flesh causes the air inside to expand and force its way out through the minute cracks and holes of the case and crystal. When the watch is laid aside, the air cools and contracts, and dust-bearing air is sucked into the interior."

"I always said I should have studied science," said Ellery. "That's a new trick, Walter. Continue."

"To put it specifically, a baker's watch will be found to contain flour-dust. A bricklayer's watch will collect brick-dust." Crane's voice rose triumphantly. "D'you know what I found in this watch? Tiny particles of a woman's face-powder!"

Miss Ickthorpe frowned. Crane continued in a deep voice:

"And a very special kind of face-powder it is, Mr. Queen. Kind used only by women of certain complexions. What complexions? Negro brown! The powder came from a mulatto woman's purse! I've questioned her, checked her vanity-case, and although she denies it, I say that Spargo's murderess is Agatha Robins, the mulatto maid who 'found' the body!"

Ellery whistled gently. "Good work, Walter, splendid work. And of course from your standpoint she would deny being the owner of the watch anyway. That clears something up for *me*. . . . But motive?"

Crane looked uncomfortable. "Well, I know it sounds fantastic, but a sort of voodoo vengeance—reversion to racial type—Spargo had been cruel to African natives . . . it was in the papers. . . ."

Ellery shaded his eyes to conceal their twinkle. Then he turned to Miss Ickthorpe, who was tapping her cup nervously, squirming in her chair, and exhibiting other signs of impatience. "And now," he said, "we come to the star recitation. What have you to offer, Miss Ickthorpe? You've been simply saturated with a theory all afternoon. Out with it."

She compressed her lips, "You boys think you're clever. You, too, Mr. Queen—you especially. . . . Oh, I'll admit John and Walter have shown superficial traces of intelligence. . . ."

"*Will* you be explicit, Miss Ickthorpe?"

She tossed her head. "Very well. The watch had nothing to do with the crime at all!"

The boys gaped, and Ellery tapped his palms gently together. "*Very* good. I agree with you. Explain, please."

Her brown eyes burned, and her cheeks were very pink. "Simple!" she said with a sniff. "Spargo had arrived from Chicago only two hours before his murder. He had been in Chicago for a week and a half. Then for a week and a half he had been living *by Chicago time*. And, since Chicago time is *one hour earlier* than New York time, it merely means that *nobody* set the hands back; that they were standing at 10:20 when he fell dead, because he'd neglected to set his watch ahead on arriving in New York this morning!"

Crane muttered something in his throat, and Burrows flushed a deep crimson. Ellery looked sad. "I'm afraid the laurels so far go to Miss Ickthorpe, gentlemen. That happens to be correct. Anything else?"

"Naturally. I know the murderer, and it isn't Spargo's wife or that outlandish mulatto maid," she said exasperatingly. "Follow me. . . . Oh, this is so easy! . . . We all saw that the powder on Spargo's dead face had been applied very smoothly. From the condition of his cheeks and the shaving things in the bathroom it was evident that he'd shaved just before being murdered. But how does a man apply powder after shaving? How do *you* powder your face, Mr. Queen?" she shot at him rather tenderly.

Ellery looked startled. "With my fingers, of course." Crane and Burrows nodded.

"Exactly!" chortled Miss Ickthorpe. "And what happens? *I* know, because I'm a very observant person and, besides, Old Icky shaves every morning and I can't *help* noticing when he kisses me good-morning. Applied with the fingers on cheeks still slightly moist, the powder goes on in streaks, smudgy, heavier in some spots than others. But look at *my* face!" They looked, with varying expressions of appreciation. "You don't see powder streaks on *my* face, do you? Of course not! And why? Because I'm a woman, and a woman uses a powder-puff, and there isn't a single powder-puff in Spargo's bedroom or bathroom!"

Ellery smiled—almost with relief. "Then you suggest, Miss

Ickthorpe, that the last person with Spargo, presumably his murderess, was a woman who watched him shave and then, with endearment perhaps, took out her own powder-puff and dabbed it over his face—only to bash him over the head with the stone hammer a few minutes later?"

"Well—yes, although I didn't think of it *that* way.... But—yes! And psychology points to the specific woman, too, Mr. Queen. A man's wife would never think of such an—an amorous proceeding. But a man's mistress would, and I say that Spargo's lady-love, Jane Terrill, whom I visited only an hour ago and who denies having powdered Spargo's face—she would!—killed him."

Ellery sighed. He rose and twitched his cigarette-stub into the fireplace. They were watching him, and each other, with expectancy. "Aside," he began, "from complimenting you, Miss Ickthorpe, on the acuteness of your knowledge of mistresses"—she uttered an outraged little gasp—"I want to say this before going ahead. The three of you have proved very ingenious, very alert; I'm more pleased than I can say. I do think we're going to have a cracking good class. Good work, all of you!"

"But, Mr. Queen," protested Burrows, "which one of us is right? Each one of us has given a different solution."

Ellery waved his hand. "Right? A detail, theoretically. The point is you've done splendid work—sharp observation, a rudimentary but promising linking of cause and effect. As for the case itself, I regret to say—you're all wrong!"

Miss Ickthorpe clenched her tiny fist. "I *knew* you'd say that! I think you're horrid. And I *still* think I'm right."

"There, gentlemen, is an extraordinary example of feminine psychology," grinned Ellery. "Now attend, all of you.

"You're all wrong for the simple reason that each of you has taken just one line of attack, one clue, one chain of reasoning, and completely ignored the other elements of the problem. You, John, say it's Spargo's wife, merely because her photograph-album contains a picture from which a circular patch with two heads has been cut away. That this might have been sheer coincidence apparently never occurred to you.

"You, Walter, came nearer the truth when you satisfactorily established the ownership of the watch as the mulatto maid's. But suppose Maid Robins had accidentally dropped the watch in Spargo's room at the hotel during his first visit there, and he had found it and taken it to Chicago with him? That's what probably happened. The mere fact that he wore her watch doesn't make her his murderess.

"You, Miss Ickthorpe, explained away the watch business with the difference-in-time element, but you overlooked an important item. Your entire solution depends on the presence in Spargo's room of a powder-puff. Willing to believe that no puff remained on the scene of the crime, because it suited your theory, you made a cursory search and promptly concluded no puff was there. But a puff *is* there! Had you investigated the cap of the celluloid tube in which Spargo kept his shaving-brush, you would have found a circular pad of powder-puff which toilet-article manufacturers in this effeminate age provide for men's traveling-kits."

Miss Ickthorpe said nothing; she seemed actually embarrassed.

"Now for the proper solution," said Ellery, mercifully looking away. "All three of you, amazingly enough, postulate a woman as the criminal. Yet it was apparent to me, after my examination of the premises, that the murderer *must have been a man.*"

"A man!" they echoed in chorus.

"Exactly. Why did none of you consider the significance of those eight buttons and the two metal clips?" He smiled. "Probably because again they didn't fit your preconceived theories. But *everything* must fit in a solution. . . . Enough of scolding. You'll do better next time.

"Six small pearl buttons, flat, and two slightly larger ones, found in a heap of ashes distinctly not of wood, coal, or paper. There is only one common article which possesses these characteristics—a man's shirt. A man's shirt, the six buttons from the front, the two larger ones from the cuffs, the debris from the linen or broadcloth. Some one, then, had burned a man's shirt in the grate, forgetting that the buttons would not be consumed.

"The metal objects, like a large hook and eye? A shirt suggests haberdashery, the hook and eye suggests only one thing—one of the cheap bow-ties which are purchased ready-tied, so that you do not have to make the bow yourself."

They were watching his lips like kindergarten children. "You, Crane, observed that Spargo's bloody left hand had clutched something, most of the blood coming off the palm. But nothing smudged with blood had been found. . . . A man's shirt and tie had been burned. . . . Inference: In the struggle with the murderer, after he had already been hit on the head and was streaming blood, Spargo had clutched his assailant's collar and tie, staining them. Borne out too by the signs of struggle in the room.

"Spargo dead, his own collar and tie wet with blood, what could the murderer do? Let me attack it this way: The murderer must have been from one of three classes of people: a rank outsider, or a guest at the hotel, or an employee of the hotel. What had he done? He had burned his shirt and tie. But if he had been an outsider, he could have turned up his coat-collar, concealing the stains long enough to get out of the hotel—no necessity, then, to burn shirt and tie when time was precious. Were he one of the hotel guests, he could have done the same thing while he went to his own room. Then he must have been an employee.

"Confirmation? Yes. As an employee he would be forced to remain in the hotel, on duty, constantly being seen. What could he do? Well, he had to change his shirt and tie. Spargo's bag was open—shirt inside. He rummaged through—you saw the confusion in the bag—and changed. Leave his shirt? No, it might be traced to him. So, boys and girls, burning was inevitable. . . .

"The tie? You recall that, while Spargo had laid out his evening-clothes on the bed, there was no bow-tie there, in the bag, or anywhere else in the room. Obviously, then, the murderer took the bow-tie of the tuxedo outfit, and burned his own bow-tie with the shirt."

Miss Ickthorpe sighed, and Crane and Burrows shook their heads a little dazedly. "I knew, then, that the murderer was an employee of the hotel, a man, and that he was wearing Spargo's shirt and black or white bow-tie, probably black. But all the employees of the hotel wear gray shirts and gray ties, as we observed on entering the Fenwick. Except"—Ellery inhaled the smoke of his cigarette—"except one man. Surely you noticed the difference in his attire? . . . And so, when you left on your various errands, I suggested to my father that this man be examined—he seemed the best possibility. And, sure enough, we found on him a shirt and bow-tie bearing Johannesburg labels like those we had observed on Spargo's other haberdashery. I knew we should find this proof, for Spargo had spent a whole year in South Africa, and since most of his clothes had been purchased there, it was reasonable to expect that the stolen shirt and tie had been, too."

"Then the case was finished when we were just beginning," said Burrows ruefully.

"But—who?" demanded Crane in bewilderment.

Ellery blew a great cloud. "We got a confession out of him in three minutes. Spargo, that gentle creature, had years before stolen this man's wife, and then thrown her over. When Spargo registered at the Fenwick two weeks ago, this man recognized him and decided to revenge him elf. He's at the Tombs right now—Williams, the hotel manager!"

There was a little silence. Burrows bobbed his head back and forth. "We've got a lot to learn," he said. "I can see that."

"Check," muttered Crane. "I'm going to like this course."

Ellery pshaw-pshawed. Nevertheless, he turned to Miss Ickthorpe who by all precedent should be moved to contribute to the general spirit of approbation. But Miss Ickthorpe's thoughts were far away. "Do you know," she said, her brown eyes misty, "you've never asked me my first name, Mr. Queen?"

The Adventure of
THE HANGING ACROBAT

LONG, LONG ago in the Incubation Period of Man—long before booking agents, five-a-days, theatrical boarding houses, subway circuits, and *Variety*—when Megatherium roamed the trees, when Broadway was going through its First Glacial Period, and when the first vaudeville show was planned by the first lop-eared, low-browed, hairy impresario, it was decreed: "The acrobat shall be first."

Why the acrobat should be first no one ever explained; but that this was a dubious honor every one on the bill—including the acrobat—realized only too well. For it was recognized even then, in the infancy of Show Business, that the first shall be last in the applause of the audience. And all through the ages, in courts and courtyards and feeble theatres, it was the acrobat—whether he was called buffoon, *farceur,* merry-andrew, tumbler, mountebank, Harlequin, or *punchinello*—who was thrown, first among his fellow mimes, to the lions of entertainment to whet their appetites for the more luscious feasts to come. So that to this day their muscular miracles are performed hard on the overture's last wall-shaking blare, performed with a simple resignation that speaks well for the mildness and resilience of the whole acrobatic tribe.

Hugo Brinkerhof knew nothing of the whimsical background of his profession. All he knew was that his father and mother had been acrobats before him with a traveling show in Germany, that he possessed huge smooth muscles with sap and spring and strength in them, and that nothing gave him more satisfaction than the sight of a glittering trapeze. With his trapeze and his Myra, and the indulgent applause of audiences from Seattle to Okeechobee, he was well content.

Now Hugo was very proud of Myra, a small wiry handsome woman with the agility of a cat and something of the cat's sleepy green eyes. He had met her in the office of Bregman, the booker, and the sluggish heart under his magnificent chest had told him that this was his fate and his woman. It was Myra who had renamed the act "Atlas & Co." when they had married between the third and fourth shows in Indianapolis. It was Myra who had fought tooth and nail for better billing. It was Myra who had conceived and perfected the dazzling pinwheel of their finale. It was Myra's shapely little body and Myra's lithe gyrations on the high trapeze and Myra's sleepy smile that had made Atlas & Co. an "acrobatic divertissement acclaimed from coast to coast," had earned them a pungent paragraph in *Variety*, and had brought them with other topnotchers on the Bregman string to the Big Circuit.

That every one loved his Myra mighty Brinkerhof, the Atlas, knew with a swelling of his chest. Who could resist her? There had been that baritone with the dancing act in Boston, the revue comedian in Newark, the tap-dancer in Buffalo, the *adagio* in

THE HANGING ACROBAT · 29

Washington. Now there were others—Tex Crosby, the Crooning Cowboy (Songs & Patter); the Great Gordi (successor to Houdini); Sailor Sam, the low comic. They had all been on the same bill together now for weeks, and they all loved sleepy-eyed Myra, and big Atlas smiled his indulgent smile and thrilled in his stupid, stolid way to their admiration. For was not his Myra the finest female acrobat in the world and the most lovely creature in creation? And now Myra was dead.

It was Brinkerhof himself, with a gaunt suffering look about him that mild Spring night, who had given the alarm. It was five o'clock in the morning and his Myra had not come home to their theatrical boarding-house room on Forty-seventh Street. He had stayed behind with his wife after the last performance in the Metropole Theatre at Columbus Circle to try out a new trick. They had rehearsed and then he had dressed in haste, leaving her in their joint dressing-room. He had had an appointment with Bregman, the booker, to discuss terms of a new contract. He had promised to meet her back at their lodgings. But when he had returned—*ach!* no Myra. He had hurried back to the theatre; it was locked up for the night. And all the long night he had waited. . . .

"Prob'ly out bummin', buddy," the desk-lieutenant at the West Forty-seventh Street station had said with a yawn. "Go home and sleep it off."

But Brinkerhof had been vehement, with many gestures. "She never haf this done before. I haf telephoned it the theatre, too, but there iss no answer. Captain, find her, please!"

"These heinies," sighed the lieutenant to a lounging detective. "All right, Baldy, see what you can do. If she's piffed in a joint somewhere, give this big hunk a clout on the jaw."

So Baldy and the pale giant had gone to see what they could do, and they had found the Metropole Theatre locked, as Brinkerhof had said, and it was almost six in the morning and dawn was coming up across the Park and Baldy had dragged Brinkerhof into an all-night restaurant for a mug of coffee. And they had waited around the theatre until seven, when old Perk the stage-door man and timer had come in, and he had opened the theatre for them, and they had gone back-stage to the dressing-room of Atlas & Co. and found Myra hanging from one of the sprinkler-pipes with a dirty old rope, thick as a hawser, around her pretty neck.

And Atlas had sat down like the dumb hunk he was and put his shaggy head between his hands and stared at the hanging body of his wife with the silent grief of some Norse god crushed to earth.

When Mr. Ellery Queen pushed through the chattering crowd of reporters and detectives backstage and convinced Sergeant Velie through the door of the dressing-room that he was indeed who he was, he found his father the Inspector holding court in the stuffy little room before a gang of nervous theatrical people. It was only nine o'clock and Ellery was grumbling through his teeth at the unconscionable inconsiderateness of murderers. But neither the burly Sergeant nor little Inspector Queen was impressed with his grumblings to the point of lending ear; and indeed the grumblings ceased after he had taken one swift look at what still hung from the sprinkler-pipe.

Brinkerhof sat red-eyed and huge and collapsed in the chair before his wife's dressing-table. "I haf told you everything," he muttered. "We rehearsed the new trick. It was then an appointment with Mr. Bregman. I went." A fat hard-eyed man, Bregman the broker, nodded curtly. "Undt that's all. Who—why—I do not know."

In a bass *sotto voce* Sergeant Velie recited the sparse facts. Ellery took another look at the dead woman. Her stiff muscles of thigh and leg bulged in *rigor mortis* beneath the tough thin silk of her flesh tights. Her green eyes were widely open. And she swayed a little in a faint dance of death. Ellery looked away and at the people.

Baldy the precinct man was there, flushed with his sudden popularity with the newspaper boys. A tall thin man who looked like Gary Cooper rolled a cigarette beside Bregman—Tex Crosby, the cowboy-crooner; and he leaned against the grime-smeared wall and eyed the Great Gordi—in person—with flinty dislike. Gordi had a hawk's beak and sleek black mustachios and long olive fingers and black eyes, and he said nothing. Little Sam, the comedian, had purple pouches under his tired eyes and he looked badly in need of a drink. But Joe Kelly, the house-manager, did not, for he smelled like a brewery and kept mumbling something drunken and obscene beneath his breath.

"How long you been married, Brinkerhof?" growled the Inspector.

"Two years. *Ja.* In Indianapolis that was, *Herr Inspector.*"

"Was she ever married before?"

"*Nein.*"

"You?"

"*Nein.*"

"Did she or you have any enemies?"

"*Gott, nein!*"

"Happy, were you?"

"Like two doves we was," muttered Brinkerhof.

Ellery strolled over to the corpse and stared up. Her ropy-veined wrists were jammed behind her back, bound with a filthy rouge-stained towel, as were her ankles. Her feet dangled a yard from the floor. A battered stepladder leaned against one of the walls, folded up; a man standing upon it, he mused, could easily have reached the sprinkler-pipe, flung the rope over it, and hauled up the light body.

"The stepladder was found against the wall there?" he murmured to the Sergeant, who had come up behind him and was staring with interest at the dead woman.

"Yep. It's always kept out near the switchboard light panel.

"No suicide, then," said Ellery. "At least that's something."

"Nice figger, ain't she?" said the Sergeant admiringly.

"Velie, you're a ghoul. . . . This *is* a pretty problem."

The dirty rope seemed to fascinate him. It had been wound tightly about the woman's throat twice, in parallel strands, and concealed her flesh like the iron necklace of a Ubangi woman. A huge knot had been fashioned beneath her right ear, and another knot held the rope to the pipe above.

"Where does this rope come from?" he said abruptly.

"From around an old trunk we found backstage, Mr. Queen. Trunk's been here for years. In the prop-room. Nothin' in it; some trouper left it. Want to see it?"

"I'll take your word for it, Sergeant. Property room, eh?" He sauntered back to the door to look the people over again.

Brinkerhof was mumbling something about how happy he and Myra had been, and what he would do to the *verdammte Teufel* who had wrung his pretty Myra's neck. His huge hands opened and closed convulsively. "Joost like a flower she was," he said. "Joost like a flower."

"Nuts," snapped Joe Kelly, the house-manager, weaving on his feet like a punch-drunk fighter. "She was a floozy, Inspector. You ask *me*," and he leered at Inspector Queen.

"Floo-zie?" said Brinkerhof with difficulty, getting to his feet. "What iss that?"

Sam, the comic, blinked his puffy little eyes rapidly and said in a hoarse voice: "You're crazy, Kelly, crazy. Wha'd'ye want to say that for? He's pickled, Chief."

"Pickled, am I?" screamed Kelly, livid. "Aw right, you as' *him*, then!" and he pointed a wavering finger at the tall thin man.

"What is this?" crooned the Inspector, his eyes bright. "Get together, gentlemen. You mean, Kelly, that Mrs. Brinkerhof was playing around with Crosby here?"

Brinkerhof made a sound like a baffled gorilla and lunged forward. His long arms were curved flails and he made for the cowboy's throat with the unswervable fury of an animal. Sergeant Velie grabbed his wrist and twisted it up behind the vast back, and Baldy jumped in and clung to the giant's other arm. He swayed there, struggling and never taking his eyes from the tall thin man, who had not stirred but who had gone very pale.

"Take him away," snapped the Inspector to Sergeant Velie. "Turn him over to a couple of the boys and keep him outside till he calms down." They hustled the hoarsely breathing acrobat out of the room. "Now, Crosby, spill it."

"Nothin' to spill," drawled the cowboy, but his drawl was a little breathless and his eyes were narrowed to wary slits. "I'm Texas an' I don't scare easy, Mister Cop. He's just a squarehead. An' as for that pie-eyed sawback over there"—he stared malevolently at Kelly—"he better learn to keep his trap shut."

"He's been two-timin' the hunk!" screeched Kelly. "Don't b'lieve him, Chief! That sassy little tramp got what was comin' to her, I tell y'! She's been pullin' the wool over the hunk's eyes all the way from Chi to Beantown!"

"You've said enough," said the Great Gordi quietly. "Can't you see the man's drunk, Inspector, and not responsible? Myra was—companionable. She may have taken a drink or two with Crosby or myself on the sly once or twice—Brinkerhof didn't like her to, so she never drank in front of him—but that's all."

"Just friendly, hey?" murmured the Inspector. "Well, who's lying? If you know anything solid, Kelly, come out with it."

"I know what I know," sneered the manager. "An' when it comes to that, Chief, the Great Gordi could tell you somethin' about the little bum. Ought to be able to! He swiped her from Crosby only a couple o' weeks ago."

"Quiet, both of you," snapped the old gentleman as the Texan and the dark mustachioed man stirred. "And how could you know that, Kelly?"

The dead woman swayed faintly, dancing her noiseless dance.

"I heard Tex there bawl Gordi out only the other day," said Kelly thickly, "for makin' the snatch. An' I saw Gordi grapplin' with her in the wings on'y yest'day. How's 'at? Reg'lar wrestler, Gordi. Can he clinch!"

Nobody said anything. The tall Texan's fingers whitened as he glared at the drunken man, and Gordi the magician did nothing at all but breathe. Then the door opened and two men came in—Dr. Prouty, Assistant Medical Examiner, and a big shambling man with a seared face.

Everybody relaxed. The Inspector said: "High time, Doc. Don't touch her, though, till Bradford can take a look at that knot up there. Go on, Braddy; on the pipe. Use the ladder."

The shambling man took the stepladder and set it up and climbed beside the dangling body and looked at the knot behind the woman's ear and the knot at the top of the pipe. Dr. Prouty pinched the woman's legs.

Ellery sighed and began to prowl. Nobody paid any attention to him; they were all pallidly intent upon the two men near the body.

Something disturbed him; he did not know what, could not put his finger precisely upon the root of the disturbance. Perhaps it was a feeling in the air, an aura of tension about the silent dangling woman in tights. But it made him restless. He had the feeling. . .

He found the loaded revolver in the top drawer of the woman's dressing-table—a shiny little pearl-handled .22 with the initials *MB* on the butt. And his eyes narrowed and he glanced at his father, and his father nodded. So he prowled some more. And then he stopped short, his gray eyes suspicious.

On the rickety wooden table in the center of the room lay a long sharp nickel-plated letter-opener among a clutter of odds and ends. He picked it up carefully and squinted along its glittering length in the light. But there was no sign of blood.

He put it down and continued to prowl.

And the very next thing he noticed was the cheap battered gas-burner on the floor at the other side of the room. Its pipe fitted snugly over a gas outlet in the wall, but the gas-tap had been turned off. He felt the little burner; it was stone-cold.

So he went to the closet with the oddest feeling of inevitability. And sure enough, just inside the open door of the closet lay a wooden box full of carpenter's tools, with a heavy steel hammer prominently on top. There was a mess of shavings on the floor near the box, and the edge of the closet-door was unpainted and virgin-fresh from a plane.

His eyes were very sharp now, and deeply concerned. He went quickly to the Inspector's side and murmured: "The revolver. The woman's?"

"Yes."

"Recent acquisition?"

"No. Brinkerhof bought it for her soon after they were married. For protection, he said."

"Poor protection, I should say," shrugged Ellery, glancing at the Headquarters men. The shambling red-faced man had just lumbered off the ladder with an expression of immense surprise. Sergeant Velie, who had returned, was mounting the ladder with a pen-knife clutched in his big fingers. Dr. Prouty waited expectantly below. The Sergeant began sawing at the rope tied to the sprinkler-pipe.

"What's that box of tools doing in the closet?" continued Ellery, without removing his gaze from the dead woman.

"Stage carpenter was in here yesterday fixing the door—it had warped or something. Union rules are strict, so he quit the job unfinished. What of it?"

"Everything," said Ellery, "of it." The Great Gordi was quietly watching his mouth; Ellery seemed not to notice. The little comedian, Sam, was shrunken in a corner, eyes popping at the Sergeant. And the Texan was smoking without enjoyment, not looking at any one or anything. "Simply everything. It's one of the most remarkable things I've ever run across."

The Inspector looked bewildered. "But, El, for cripe's sake—remarkable? I don't see—"

"You should," said Ellery impatiently. "A child should. And yet it's astounding, when you come to think of it. Here's a room with four dandy weapons in it—a loaded revolver, a letter-cutter, a gas-burner, and a hammer. And yet the murderer deliberately trussed the woman with the towels, deliberately left this room, deliberately crossed the stage to the property room, unwound that rusty old rope from a worthless trunk discarded years ago by some nameless actor, carried the rope and the ladder from beside the switchboard back to this room, used the ladder to sling the rope over the pipe and fasten the knot, and strung the woman up."

"Well, but—"

"Well, but why?" cried Ellery. "Why? Why did the murderer ignore the four simple, easy, handy methods of murder here—shooting, stabbing, asphyxiation, bludgeoning—and go to all that extra trouble to *hang* her?"

Dr. Prouty was kneeling beside the dead woman, whom the Sergeant had deposited with a thump on the dirty floor.

The red-faced man shambled over and said: "It's got me, Inspector."

"What's got you?" snapped Inspector Queen.

"This knot." His thick red fingers held a length of knotted rope. "The one behind her ear is just ordinary; even clumsy for the job of breakin' her neck." He shook his head. "But this one, the one that was tied around the pipe—well, sir, it's got me."

"An unfamiliar knot?" said Ellery slowly, puzzling over its complicated convolutions.

"New to me, Mr. Queen. All the years I been expertin' on knots for the Department I never seen one like that. Ain't a sailor's knot, I can tell you that; and it ain't Western."

"Might be the work of an amateur," muttered the Inspector, pulling the rope through his fingers. "A knot that just happened."

The expert shook his head. "No, sir, I wouldn't say that at all. It's some kind of variation. Not an accident. Whoever tied that knew his knots."

Bradford shambled off and Dr. Prouty looked up from his work. "Hell, I can't do anything here," he snapped. "I'll have to take this body over to the Morgue and work on it there. The boys are waiting outside."

"When'd she kick off, Doc?" demanded the Inspector, frowning.

"About midnight last night. Can't tell closer than that. She died, of course, of suffocation."

"Well, give us a report. Probably nothing, but it never hurts. Thomas, get that doorman in here."

When Dr. Prouty and the Morgue men had gone with the body and Sergeant Velie had hauled in old Perk, the stagedoor man and watchman, the Inspector growled: "What time'd you lock up last night, Mister?"

Old Perk was hoarse with nervousness. "Honest t' Gawd, Inspector, I didn't mean nothin' by it. On'y Mr. Kelly here'd fire me if he knew. I was that sleepy—"

"What's this?" said the Inspector softly.

"Myra told me after the last show last night she an' Atlas were gonna rehearse a new stunt. I didn't wanna wait aroun', y'see," the old man whined, "so seein' as nob'dy else was in the house that late, the cleanin' women gone an' all, I locked up everything but the stage door an' I say to Myra an' Atlas, I says: 'When ye leave, folks,' I says, 'jest slam the stage door.' An' I went home."

"Rats," said the Inspector irritably. "Now we'll never know who could have come in and who didn't. Anybody could have sneaked back without being seen or waited around in hiding until—" He bit his lip. "You men there, where'd you all go after the show last night?"

The three actors started simultaneously. It was the Great Gordi who spoke first, in his soft smooth voice that was now uneasy. "I went directly to my rooming house and to bed."

"Anybody see you come in? You live in the same hole as Brinkerhof?"

The magician shrugged, "No one saw me. Yes, I do."

"You, Texas?"

The cowboy drawled: "I moseyed round to a speak somewhere an' got drunk."

"What speak?"

"Dunno. I was primed. Woke up in my room this mornin' with a head."

"You boys sure are in a tough spot," said the Inspector sarcastically. "Can't even fix good alibis for yourself. Well, how about you, Mr. Comedian?"

The comic said eagerly: "Oh, I can prove where I was, Inspector. I went around to a joint I know an' can get twenny people to swear to it."

"What time?"

"Round midnight."

The Inspector snorted and said: "Beat it. But hang around. I'll be wanting you boys, maybe. Take 'em away, Thomas, before I lose my temper."

Long, long ago—when, it will be recalled, Megatherium roamed the trees—the same lop-eared impresario who said: "The acrobat shall be first," also laid down the dictum that: "The show must go on," and for as little reason. Accidents might happen, the juvenile might run off with the female lion-tamer, the ingénue might be howling drunk, the lady in the fifth row, right, might have chosen the theatre to be the scene of her monthly attack of epilepsy, fire might break out in Dressing Room A, but the show must go on. Not even a rare juicy homicide may annul the sacred dictum. The show must go on despite hell, high water, drunken managers named Kelly, and The Fantastic Affair of the Hanging Acrobat.

So it was not strange that when the Metropole began to fill with its dribble of early patrons there was no sign that a woman had been slain the night before within its gaudy walls and that police and detectives roved its backstage with suspicious, if baffled, eyes.

The murder was just an incident to Show Business. It would rate two columns in *Variety*.

Inspector Richard Queen chafed in the hard seat in the fifteenth row while Ellery sat beside him sunk in thought. Stranger than everything had been Ellery's insistence that they remain to witness the performance. There was a motion picture to sit through—a film which, bitterly, the Inspector pointed out he had seen—a newsreel, an animated cartoon. . . .

It was while "Coming Attractions" were flitting over the screen that Ellery rose and said: "Let's go backstage. There's something—" He did not finish.

They passed behind the dusty boxes on the right and went backstage through the iron door guarded by a uniformed officer. The vast bare reaches of the stage and wings were oppressed with an unusual silence. Manager Kelly, rather the worse for wear, sat on a broken chair near the light panel and gnawed his unsteady fingers. None of the vaudeville actors was in evidence.

"Kelly," said Ellery abruptly, "is there anything like a pair of field glasses in the house?"

The Irishman gaped. "What the hell would you be wantin' *them* for?"

"Please."

Kelly fingered a passing stagehand, who vanished and reappeared shortly with the desired binoculars. The Inspector grunted: "So what?"

Ellery adjusted them to his eyes. "I don't know," he said, shrugging. "It's just a hunch."

There was a burst of music from the pit: the Overture.

"*Poet and Peasant*," snarled the Inspector. "Don't they ever get anything new?"

But Ellery said nothing. He merely waited, binoculars ready, eyes fixed on the now footlighted stage. And it was only when the last blare had died away, and grudging splatters of applause came from the orchestra, and the announcement cards read: "Atlas & Co.," that the Inspector lost something of his irritability and even became interested. For when the curtains slithered up there was Atlas himself, bowing and smiling, his immense body impressive in flesh tights; and there beside him stood a tall smiling woman with golden hair and at least one golden tooth which flashed in the footlights. And she too wore flesh tights. For Brinkerhof with the mildness and resilience of all acrobats had insisted on taking his regular turn, and Bregman the booker had sent him another partner, and the two strangers had spent an hour rehearsing their intimate embraces and clutches and swingings and nuzzlings before the first performance. The show must go on.

Atlas and the golden woman went through an intricate series of tumbles and equilibristic maneuvers. The orchestra played brassy music. Trapezes dived stageward. Simple swings. Somersaults in the air. The drummer rolled and smashed his cymbal.

Ellery made no move to use the binoculars. He and the Inspector and Kelly stood in the wings, and none of them said anything, although Kelly was breathing hard like a man who has just come out of deep water for air. A queer little figure materialized beside them; Ellery turned his head slowly. But it was only Sailor Sam, the low comic, rigged out in a naval uniform three sizes too large for his skinny little frame, his face daubed liberally with greasepaint. He kept watching Atlas & Co. without expression.

"Good, ain't he?" he said at last in a small voice.

No one replied. But Ellery turned to the manager and whispered: "Kelly, keep your eyes open for—" and his voice sank so low neither the comedian nor Inspector Queen could hear what he said. Kelly looked puzzled; his bloodshot eyes opened a little wider; but he nodded and swallowed, riveting his gaze upon the whirling figures on the stage.

And when it was all over and the orchestra was executing the usual *crescendo sustenuto* and Atlas was bowing and smiling and the woman was curtseying and showing her gold tooth and the curtain dropped swiftly, Ellery glanced at Kelly. But Kelly shook his head.

The announcement cards changed. "Sailor Sam." There was a burst of fresh fast music, and the little man in the oversize naval uniform grinned three times, as if trying it out, drew a deep breath, and scuttled out upon the stage to sprawl full-length with his gnomish face jutting over the footlights to the accompaniment of surprised laughter from the darkness below.

They watched from the wings, silent.

The comedian had a clever routine. Not only was he a travesty upon all sailormen, but he was a travesty upon all sailormen in their cups. He drooled and staggered and was silent and then chattered suddenly, and he described a mythical voyage and fell all over himself climbing an imaginary mast and fell silent again to go into a pantomime that rocked the house.

The Inspector said grudgingly: "Why, he's as good as Jimmy Barton any day, with that drunk routine of his."

"Just a slob," said Kelly out of the corner of his mouth.

Sailor Sam made his exit by the complicated expedient of swimming off the stage. He stood in the wings, panting, his face streaming perspiration. He ran out for a bow. They thundered for more. He vanished. He reappeared. He vanished again. There was a stubborn look on his pixie face.

"Sam!" hissed Kelly. "F'r cripe's sake, Sam, give 'em 'at encore rope number. F'r cripe's sake, Sam—"

"Rope number?" said Ellery quietly.

The comedian licked his lips. Then his shoulders drooped and he slithered out onto the stage again. There was a shout of laughter and the house quieted at once. Sam scrambled to his feet, weaving and blinking blearily.

"'Hoy there!" he howled suddenly. "Gimme rope!"

A *papier-mâché* cigar three feet long dropped to the stage from the opposite wings. Laughter. "Naw! Rope! Rope!" the little man screamed, dancing up and down.

A blackish rope snaked down from the flies. Miraculously it coiled over his scrawny shoulders. He struggled with it. He scrambled after its tarred ends. He executed fantastic flying leaps. And always the tarred ends eluded him, and constantly he became more and more enmeshed in the black coils as he wrestled with the rope.

The gallery broke down. The man *was* funny; even Kelly's dour face lightened, and the Inspector was frankly grinning. Then it was over and two stagehands darted out of the wings and pulled the comedian off the stage, now a helpless bundle trussed in rope. His face under the paint was chalk-white. He extricated himself easily enough from the coils.

"Good boy," chuckled the Inspector. "That was fine!"

Sam muttered something and trudged away to his dressing-room. The black rope lay where it had fallen. Ellery glanced at it once, and then turned his attention back to the stage. The music had changed. A startlingly beautiful tenor voice rang through the theatre. The orchestra was playing softly *Home on the Range*. The curtain rose on Tex Crosby.

The tall thin man was dressed in gaudiest stage-cowboy costume. And yet he wore it with an air of authority. The pearl-butted six-shooters protruding from his holsters did not seem out of place. His big white sombrero shaded a gaunt Western face. His legs were a little bowed. The man was real.

He sang Western songs, told a few funny stories in his soft Texan drawl, and all the while his long-fingered hands were busy with a lariat. He made the lariat live. From the moment the curtain rose upon his lanky figure the lariat was in motion, and it did not subside through the jokes: the patter, even the final song, which was inevitably *The Last Round-Up*.

"Tinhorn Will Rogers," sneered Kelly, blinking his bloodshot eyes.

For the first time Ellery raised the binoculars. When the Tex-

THE HANGING ACROBAT · 45

an had taken his last bow Ellery glanced inquiringly at the manager. Kelly shook his head.

The Great Gordi made his entrance in a clap of thunder, a flash of lightning, and a black Satanic cloak, faced with red. There was something impressive about his very charlatanism. His black eyes glittered and his mustache-points quivered above his lips and his beak jutted like an eagle's; and meanwhile neither his hands nor his mouth kept still.

The magician had a smooth effortless patter which kept his audience amused and diverted their attention from the fluent mysteries of his hands. There was nothing startling in his routine, but it was a polished performance that fascinated. He performed seeming miracles with cards. His sleight-of-hand with coins and handkerchiefs was, to the layman, amazing. His evening clothes apparently concealed scores of wonders.

They watched with a mounting tension while he went through his bag of tricks. For the first time Ellery noticed, with a faint start, that Brinkerhof, still in tights, was crouched in the opposite wings. The big man's eyes were fixed upon the magician's face. They ignored the flashing fingers, the swift movements of the black-clad body. Only the face . . . In Brinkerhof's eyes was neither rage nor venom; just watchfulness. What was the matter with the man? Ellery reflected that it was just as well that Gordi was unconscious of the acrobat's scrutiny; those subtle hands might not operate so fluidly.

Despite the tension the magician's act seemed interminable. There were tricks with odd-looking pieces of apparatus manipulated from backstage by assistants. The house was with him, completely in his grasp.

"Good show," said the Inspector in a surprised voice. "This is darned good vaudeville."

"It'll get by," muttered Kelly. There was something queer on his face. He too was watching intently.

And suddenly something went wrong on the stage. The orchestra seemed bewildered. Gordi had concluded a trick, bowed, and stepped into the wings near the watching men. Not even the curtain was prepared. The orchestra had swung into another piece. The conductor's head was jerking from side to side in a panicky, inquiring manner.

"What's the matter?" demanded the Inspector.

Kelly snarled: "He's left out his last trick. Good hunch, Mr. Queen. . . . Hey, ham!" he growled to the magician, "finish your act, damn you! While they're still clappin'!"

Gordi was very pale. He did not turn; they could see only his left cheek and the rigidity of his back. Nor did he reply. Instead, with all the reluctance of a tyro, he slowly stepped back onto the stage. From the other side Brinkerhof watched. And this time Gordi, with a convulsive start, saw him.

"What's coming off here?" said the Inspector softly, as alert as a wren.

Ellery swung the glasses to his eyes.

A trapeze hurtled stageward from the flies—a simple steel bar suspended from two slender strands. A smooth yellow rope, very new in appearance, accompanied it from above, falling to the stage.

The magician worked very, very, painfully slowly. The house was silent. Even the music had stopped.

Gordi grasped the rope and did something with it; his back concealed what he was doing; then he swung about and held up his left hand. Tied with an enormous and complicated knot to his left wrist was the end of the yellow rope. He picked up the other end and leaped a little, securing the trapeze. At the level of his chest he steadied it and turned again so that he concealed what he was doing, and when he swung about once more they saw that the rope's other end was now knotted in the same way about the steel bar of the trapeze. He raised his right hand in signal and the drummer began a long roll.

Instantly the trapeze began to rise, and they saw that the rope was only four feet long. As the bar rose, Gordi's lithe body rose with it, suspended from the bar by the full length of the rope attached to his wrist. The trapeze came to a stop when the magician's feet were two yards from the stage.

Ellery squinted carefully through the powerful lenses. Across the stage Brinkerhof crouched.

Gordi now began to squirm and kick and jump in the air, indicating in pantomime that he was securely tied to the trapeze and that not even the heavy weight of his suspended body could undo the knots; in fact, was tightening them.

"It's a good trick," muttered Kelly. "In a second a special drop'll come down, an' in eight seconds it'll go up again and there he'll be on the stage, with the rope on the floor."

Gordi cried in a muffled voice: "Ready!"

But at the same instant Ellery said to Kelly: "*Quick!* Drop the curtain! This instant. Signal those men in the flies, Kelly!"

Kelly leaped into action. He shouted something unintelligible and after a second of hesitation the main curtain dropped. The house was dumb with astonishment; they thought it was part of the trick. Gordi began to struggle frantically, reaching up the trapeze with his free hand.

"Lower that trapeze!" roared Ellery on the cut-off stage now, waving his arms at the staring men above. "Lower it! *Gordi, don't move!*"

The trapeze came down with a thud. Gordi sprawled on the stage, his mouth working. Ellery leaped upon him, an open blade in hand. He cut quickly, savagely, at the rope. It parted, its torn end dangling from the trapeze.

"You may get up now," said Ellery, panting a little. "It's the knot I wanted to see, *Signor* Gordi."

They crowded around Ellery and the fallen man, who seemed incapable of rising. He sat on the stage, his mouth still working, naked fear in his eyes. Brinkerhof was there, his muscular biceps rigid. Crosby, Sailor Sam, Sergeant Velie, Kelly, Bregman. . . .

The Inspector stared at the knot on the trapeze. Then he slowly took from his pocket a short length of the dirty old rope which had hanged Myra Brinkerhof. The knot was there. He placed it beside the knot on the trapeze.

They were identical.

"Well, Gordi," said the Inspector wearily, "I guess it's all up with you. Get up, man. I'm holding you for murder, and anything you say—"

Without a sound Brinkerhof, the mighty Atlas, sprang upon the man on the floor, big hands on Gordi's throat. It took the combined efforts of the Texan, Sergeant Velie, and Manager Kelly to tear the acrobat off.

Gordi gasped, holding his throat: "I didn't do it, I tell you! I'm innocent! Yes, we had—we lived together. I loved her. But why should I kill her? I didn't do it. For God's sake—"

"*Schwein,*" growled Atlas, his chest heaving.

Sergeant Velie tugged at Gordi's collar. "Come on, come on there. . . ."

Ellery drawled: "Very pretty. My apologies, Mr. Gordi. Of course you didn't do it."

A shocked silence fell. From behind the heavy curtain voices—loud voices—came. The feature picture had been flashed on the screen.

"Didn't—do—it?" muttered Brinkerhof.

"But the knots, El," began the Inspector in a bewildered voice.

"Precisely. The knots." In defiance of fire regulations Ellery lit a cigarette and puffed thoughtfully. "The hanging of Myra Brinkerhof has bothered me from the beginning. Why was she *hanged?* In preference to one of four other methods of committing murder which were simpler, more expedient, easier of accomplishment, and offered no extra work, as hanging did? The point is that if the murderer chose the hard way, the complicated way, the roundabout way of killing her, then he chose that way *deliberately.*"

Gordi was staring with his mouth open. Kelly was ashen pale.

"But why," murmured Ellery, "did he choose hanging deliberately? Obviously, because hanging offered the murderer some peculiar advantage not offered by any of the other four methods. Well, what advantage could hanging conceivably offer that shooting, stabbing, gassing, or hammering to death could not? To put it another way, what is characteristic of hanging that is not characteristic of shooting and the rest? Only one thing. *The use of a rope.*"

"Well, but I still don't see—" frowned the Inspector.

"Oh, it's clear enough, dad. There's something about the rope that made the murderer use it in preference to the other methods. But what's the outstanding significance of this particular rope—the rope used to hang Myra Brinkerhof? *Its knot*—its peculiar knot, so peculiar that not even the Department's expert could identify it. In other words, the use of that knot was like the leaving of a fingerprint. Whose knot is it? Gordi's, the magician's—and, I suspect, his exclusively."

"I can't understand it," cried Gordi. "Nobody knew my knot. It's one I developed myself—"Then he bit his lip and fell silent.

"Exactly the point. I realize that stage-magicians have developed knot-making to a remarkable degree. Wasn't it Houdini who—?"

"The Davenport brothers, too," muttered the magician. "My knot is a variation on one of their creations."

"Quite so," drawled Ellery. "So I say, had Mr. Gordi wanted to kill Myra Brinkerhof, would he have deliberately chosen *the single method that incriminated him,* and him alone? Certainly not if he were reasonably intelligent. Did he tie his distinctive knot, then, from sheer habit, subconsciously? Conceivable, but then why had he chosen hanging in the first place, when those four easier methods were nearer to his hand?" Ellery slapped the magician's back. "So, I say—our apologies, Gordi. The answer is very patently that you're being framed by some one who deliberately chose the hanging-plus-knot method to implicate you in a crime you're innocent of."

"But he says nobody else knew his confounded knot," growled the Inspector. "If what you say is true, El, somebody must have learned it on the sly."

"Very plausible," murmured Ellery. "Any suggestions, *Signor?*"

The magician got slowly to his feet, brushing his dress-suit off. Brinkerhof gaped stupidly at him, at Ellery.

"I don't know," said Gordi, very pale. "I thought no one knew. Not even my technical assistants. But then we've all been travelling on the same bill for weeks. I suppose if some one wanted to. . ."

"I see," said Ellery thoughtfully. "So there's a dead end, eh?"

"Dead beginning," snapped his father. "And thanks, my son, for the assistance. *You're* a help!"

"I tell you very frankly," said Ellery the next day in his father's office, "*I* don't know what it's all about. The only thing I'm sure of is Gordi's innocence. The murderer knew very well that somebody would notice the unusual knot Gordi uses in his rope-escape illusion. As for motive—"

"Listen," snarled the Inspector, thoroughly out of temper, "I can see through glass the same way you can. They all had motive. Crosby kicked over by the dame, Gordi . . . Did you know that this little comedian was sniffin' around Myra's skirts the last couple of weeks? Trying his darnedest to make her. And Kelly's had monkey business with her, too, on a former appearance at the Metropole."

"Don't doubt it," said Ellery sombrely. "The call of the flesh. She was an alluring little trick, at that. Real old Boccaccio melodrama, with the stupid husband playing cuckold—"

The door opened and Dr. Prouty, Assistant Medical Examiner, stumped in looking annoyed. He dropped into a chair and clumped his feet on the Inspector's desk. "Guess what?" he said.

"I'm a rotten guesser," said the old gentleman sourly.

"Little surprise for you gentlemen. For me, too. The woman wasn't hanged."

"What!" cried the Queens, together.

"Fact. She was dead when she was swung up." Dr. Prouty squinted at his ragged cigar.

"Well, I'll be eternally damned," said Ellery softly. He sprang from his chair and shook the physician's shoulder. "Prouty, for heaven's sake, don't look so smug! What killed her? Gun, gas, knife, poison—"

"Fingers."

"Fingers?"

Dr. Prouty shrugged. "No question about it. When I took that dirty hemp off her lovely neck I found the distinct marks of fingers on the skin. It was a tight rope, and all that, but there were the marks, gentlemen. She was choked to death by a man's hands and then strung up—why, *I* don't know."

"Well," said Ellery. "Well," he said again, and straightened. "*Very* interesting. I begin to scent the proverbial rodent. Tell us more, good leech."

"Certainly is queer," muttered the Inspector, sucking his mustache.

"Something even queerer," drawled Dr. Prouty. "You boys have seen choked stiffs plenty. What's the characteristic of the fingermarks?"

Ellery was watching him intently. "Characteristic?" He frowned. "Don't know what you mean—Oh!" His gray eyes glittered. "Don't tell me. . . . The usual marks point upward, thumbs toward the chin."

"Smart lad. Well, these marks don't. They all point *downward*."

Ellery stared for a long moment. Then he seized Dr. Prouty's limp hand and shook it violently. "Eureka! Prouty, old sock, you're the answer to a logician's prayer! Dad, come on!"

"What is this?" scowled the Inspector. "You're too fast for me. Come where?"

"To the Metropole. Urgent affairs. If my watch is honest," Ellery said quickly, "we're just in time to witness another performance. And I'll show you why our friend the murderer not only

didn't shoot, stab, asphyxiate, or hammer little Myra into Kingdom Come, but didn't hang her either!"

Ellery's watch, however, was dishonest. When they reached
the metropole it was noon, and the feature picture was still
showing. They hurried backstage in search of Kelly.

"Kelly or this old man they call Perk, the caretaker," Ellery
murmured, hurrying his father down the dark side-aisle. "Just
one question. . . ."

A patrolman let them through. They found backstage deserted except for Brinkerhof and his new partner, who were
stolidly rehearsing what was apparently a new trick. The trapeze was down and the big man was hanging from it by his
powerful legs, a rubber bit in his mouth. Below him, twirling
like a top, spun the tall blonde, the other end of the bit in her
mouth.

Kelly appeared from somewhere and Ellery said: "Oh, Kelly.
Are all the others in?"

Kelly was drunk again. He wobbled and said vaguely: "Oh,
sure. Sure."

"Gather the clans in Myra's dressing-room. We've still a little
time. Question's unnecessary, dad. I should have known without—"

The Inspector threw up his hands.

Kelly scratched his chin and staggered off. "Hey, Atlash," he
called wearily. "Stop Atlash-ing an' come on." He swayed off toward the dressing-rooms.

"But, El," groaned the Inspector, "I don't understand—"

"It's perfectly childish in its simplicity," said Ellery, "now that
I've seen what I suspected was the case. Come along, sire; don't
crab the act."

When they were assembled in the dead woman's cubbyhole Ellery leaned against the dressing-table, looked at the sprinkler-pipe, and said: "One of you might as well own up . . . you see, I know who killed the little—er—lady."

"You know that?" said Brinkerhof hoarsely. "Who is—" He stopped and glared at the others, his stupid eyes roving.

But no one else said anything.

Ellery sighed. "Very well, then, you force me to wax eloquent, even reminiscent. Yesterday I posed the question: Why should Myra Brinkerhof have been hanged in preference to one of four handier methods? And I said, in demonstrating Mr. Gordi's innocence, that the reason was that hanging permitted the use of a rope and consequently of Gordi's identifiable knot." He brandished his forefinger. "But I forgot an additional possibility. If you find a woman with a rope around her neck who has died of strangulation, you assume it was the rope that strangled her. I completely overlooked the fact that hanging, in permitting use of a rope, also accomplishes the important objective of *concealing the neck.* But why should Myra's neck have been concealed? By a rope? Because a rope is not the only way of strangling a victim, because a victim can be *choked* to death by fingers, because choking to death leaves marks on the neck, and because the choker didn't want the police to know there *were* fingermarks on Myra's neck. He thought that the tight strands of the rope would not only conceal the fingermarks but would obliterate them as well—sheer ignorance, of course, since in death such marks are ineradicable. But that is what he thought, and that *primarily* is why he chose hanging for Myra when she was already dead. The leaving of Gordi's knot to implicate him was only a secondary reason for the selection of rope."

"But, El," cried the Inspector, "that's nutty. Suppose he did choke the woman to death. I can't see that he'd be incriminating himself by leaving fingermarks on her neck. You can't match fingermarks—"

"Quite true," drawled Ellery, "but you *can* observe that fingermarks are on the neck *the wrong way*. For these point, not upward, but downward."

And still no one said anything, and there was silence for a space in the room with the heavily breathing men.

"For you see, gentlemen," continued Ellery sharply, "when Myra was choked she was choked *upside down*. But how is this possible? Only if one of two conditions existed. Either at the time she was choked she was hanging head down above her murderer, or—"

Brinkerhof said stupidly: "*Ja.* I did it. *Ja.* I did it." He said it over and over, like a phonograph with its needle grooved.

A woman's voice from the amplifier said: "But I love you, darling, love you, love you, love you. . ."

Brinkerhof's eyes flamed and he took a short step toward the Great Gordi. "Yesterday I say to Myra: 'Myra, tonight we rehearse the new trick.' After the second show I see Myra undt that *schweinhund* kissing undt kissing behind the scenery. I hear them talk. They haf been fooling me. I plan. I will kill her. When we rehearse. So I kill her." He buried his face in his hands and began to sob without sound. It was horrible; and Gordi seemed transfixed with its horror.

And Brinkerhof muttered: "Then I see the marks on her throat. They are upside down. I know that iss bad. So I take the rope undt I cover up the marks. Then I hang her, with the *schwein's* knot, that she had once told me he had shown to her—"

He stopped. Gordi said hoarsely, "Good God. I didn't remember—"

"Take him away," said the Inspector in a small dry voice to the policeman at the door.

"It was all so clear," explained Ellery a little later, over coffee. "Either the woman was hanging head down above her murderer, or her murderer was hanging head down above the woman. One squeeze of those powerful paws. . ." He shivered. "It had to be an acrobat, you see. And when I remembered that Brinkerhof himself had said they had been rehearsing a new trick—" He stopped and smoked thoughtfully.

"Poor guy," muttered the Inspector. "He's not a bad sort, just dumb. Well, she got what was coming to her."

"Dear, dear," drawled Ellery. "Philosophy, Inspector? I'm really not interested in the moral aspects of crime. I'm more annoyed at this case than anything."

"Annoyed?" said the Inspector with a sniff. "You look mighty smug to me."

"Do I? But I really am. I'm annoyed at the shocking unimaginativeness of our newspaper friends."

"Well, well," said the Inspector with a sigh of resignation. "I'll bite. What's the gag?"

Ellery grinned. "Not one of the reporters who covered this case saw the perfectly obvious headline. You see, they forgot that one of the cast is named—of all things, dear God!—Gordi."

"Headline?" frowned the Inspector.

"Oh, lord. How could they have escaped casting me in the role of Alexander and calling this The Affair of the Gordian Knot?"

The Adventure of
THE ONE-PENNY BLACK

"ACH!" SAID old Uneker. "It iss a terrible t'ing, Mr. Quveen, a terrible t'ing, like I vass saying. Vat iss New York coming to? Dey come into my store—*polizei*, undt bleedings, undt whackings on de headt. . . . Diss iss vunuff my oldest customers, Mr. Quveen. He too hass hadt exberiences. . . . Mr. Hazlitt, Mr. Quveen. . . . Mr. Quveen iss dot famous detectiff feller you read aboudt in de papers, Mr. Hazlitt. Inspector Richardt Quveen's son."

Ellery Queen laughed, uncoiled his length from old Uneker's counter, and shook the man's hand. "Another victim of our crime wave, Mr. Hazlitt? Unky's been regaling me with a feast of a whopping bloody tale."

"So you're Ellery Queen," said the frail little fellow; he wore a pair of thick-lensed goggles and there was a smell of suburbs about him. "This *is* luck! Yes, I've been robbed."

Ellery looked incredulously about old Uneker's book-shop. "Not *here?*" Uneker was tucked away on a side street in mid-Manhattan, squeezed between the British Bootery and

Mme. Carolyne's, and it was just about the last place in the world you would have expected thieves to choose as the scene of a crime.

"Nah," said Hazlitt. "Might have saved the price of a book if it had. No, it happened last night about ten o'clock. I'd just left my office on Forty-fifth Street—I'd worked late—and I was walking crosstown. Chap stopped me on the street and asked for a light. The street was pretty dark and deserted, and I didn't like the fellow's manner, but I saw no harm in lending him a packet of matches. While I was digging it out, though, I noticed he was eyeing the book under my arm. Sort of trying to read the title."

"What book was it?" asked Ellery eagerly. Books were his private passion.

Hazlitt shrugged. "Nothing remarkable. That best-selling non-fiction thing, *Europe in Chaos;* I'm in the export line and I like to keep up to date on international conditions. Anyway, this chap lit his cigarette, returned the matches, mumbled his thanks, and I began to walk on. Next thing I knew something walloped me on the back of my head and everything went black. I seem to remember falling. When I came to, I was lying in the gutter, my hat and glasses were on the stones, and my head felt like a baked potato. Naturally thought I'd been robbed; I had a lot of cash about me, and I was wearing a pair of diamond cuff-links. But—"

"But, of course," said Ellery with a grin, "the only thing that was taken was *Europe in Chaos.* Perfect, Mr. Hazlitt! A fascinating little problem. Can you describe your assailant?"

"He had a heavy mustache and dark-tinted glasses of some kind. That's all. I—"

"He? He can describe not'ing," said old Uneker sourly. "He iss like all you Americans—blindt, a *dummkopf.* But de book,

Mr. Quveen—de book! Vhy should any von vant to steal a book like dot?"

"And that isn't all," said Hazlitt. "When I got home last night—I live in East Orange, New Jersey—I found my house broken into! And what do you think had been stolen, Mr. Queen?"

Ellery's lean face beamed. "I'm no crystal-gazer; but if there's any consistency in crime, I should imagine another book had been stolen."

"Right! And it was my second copy of *Europe in Chaos!*"

"Now you do interest me," said Ellery, in quite a different tone. "How did you come to have two, Mr. Hazlitt?"

"I bought another copy from Uneker two days ago to give to a friend of mine. I'd left it on top of my bookcase. It was gone. Window was open—it had been forced and there were smudges of hands on the sill. Plain case of housebreaking. And although there's plenty of valuable stuff in my place—silver and things—nothing else had been taken. I reported it at once to the East Orange police, but they just tramped about the place, gave me funny looks, and finally went away. I suppose they thought I was crazy."

"Were any other books missing?"

"No, just that one."

"I really don't see. . ." Ellery took off his *pince-nez* eyeglasses and began to polish the lenses thoughtfully. "Could it have been the same man? Would he have had time to get out to East Orange and burglarize your house before you got there last night?"

"Yes. When I picked myself out of the gutter I reported the assault to a cop, and he took me down to a nearby station-house, and they asked me a lot of questions. He would have had plenty of time—I didn't get home until one o'clock in the morning."

"I think, Unky," said Ellery, "that the story *you* told me begins to have point. If you'll excuse me, Mr. Hazlitt, I'll be on my way. *Auf wiedersehen!*"

Ellery left old Uneker's little shop and went downtown to Center Street. He climbed the steps of Police Headquarters, nodded amiably to a desk lieutenant, and made for his father's office. The Inspector was out. Ellery twiddled with an ebony figurine of Bertillon on his father's desk, mused deeply, then went out and began to hunt for Sergeant Velie, the Inspector's chief-of-operations. He found the mammoth in the Press Room, bawling curses at a reporter.

"Velie," said Ellery, "stop playing bad man and get me some information. Two days ago there was an unsuccessful man-hunt on Forty-ninth Street, between Fifth and Sixth Avenues. The chase ended in a little bookshop owned by a friend of mine named Uneker. Local officer was in on it. Uneker told me the story, but I want less colored details. Get me the precinct report like a good fellow, will you?"

Sergeant Velie waggled his big black jaws, glared at the reporter, and thundered off. Ten minutes later he came back with a sheet of paper, and Ellery read it with absorption.

The facts seemed bald enough. Two days before, at the noon hour, a hatless, coatless man with a bloody face had rushed out of the office-building three doors from old Uneker's bookshop, shouting: "Help! Police!" Patrolman McCallum had run up, and the man yelled that he had been robbed of a valuable postage-stamp—"My one-penny black!" he kept shouting. "My one-penny black!"—and that the thief, black-mustached and wearing heavy blue-tinted spectacles, had just escaped. McCallum had noticed a man of this description a few minutes before, acting peculiarly, enter the nearby bookshop. Followed by the screaming stamp-dealer, he dashed into old Uneker's place with drawn revolver. Had a man with black mustaches and blue-tinted spectacles come into the shop within the past few minutes? "*Ja*—he?" said old Uneker. "Sure, he iss still here." Where? In the back-room looking at some books. McCallum and the bleeding man rushed into Uneker's back-room; it was empty. A door leading to the alley from the back-room was open; the man had escaped, apparently having been scared off by the noisy entrance of the policeman and the victim a moment before. McCallum had immediately searched the neighborhood; the thief had vanished.

The officer then took the complainant's statement. He was, he said, Friederich Ulm, dealer in rare postage stamps. His office was in a tenth-floor room in the building three doors away—the office of his brother Albert, his partner, and himself. He had been exhibiting some valuable items to an invited group of three stamp-collectors. Two of them had gone away. Ulm happened to turn his back; and the third, the man with the black mustache and blue-tinted glasses, who had introduced himself as Avery Beninson, had swooped on him swiftly from behind and struck at his head with a short iron bar as Ulm twisted back. The blow had cut open Ulm's cheekbone and felled him, half-stunned; and then with the utmost coolness the thief had used the same iron bar (which, said the report, from its description was probably a "jimmy") to pry open the lid of a glass-topped cabinet in which a choice collection of stamps was kept. He had snatched from a leather box in the cabinet an extremely high-priced item—"the Queen Victoria one-penny black"—and had then dashed out, locking the door behind him. It had taken the assaulted dealer several minutes to open the door and follow. McCallum went with Ulm to the office, examined the rifled cabinet, took the names and addresses of the three collectors who had been present that morning—with particular note of "Avery Beninson"—scribbled his report, and departed.

The names of the other two collectors were John Hinchman and J. S. Peters. A detective attached to the precinct had visited each in turn and had then gone to the address of Beninson. Beninson, who presumably had been the man with black mustaches and blue-tinted spectacles, was ignorant of the entire affair; and his physical appearance did not tally with the description of Ulm's assailant. He had received no invitation from the Ulm brothers, he said, to attend the private sale. Yes, he had had an employee, a man with black mustaches and tinted glasses, for two weeks—this man had answered Beninson's advertisement for an assistant to take charge of the collector's private stamp-albums, had proved satisfactory, and had suddenly, without explanation or notice, disappeared after two weeks' service. He had disappeared, the detective noted, on the morning of the Ulms' sale.

All attempts to trace this mysterious assistant, who had called himself William Planck, were unsuccessful. The man had vanished among New York City's millions.

Nor was this the end of the story. For the day after the theft old Uneker himself had reported to the precinct detective a queer tale. The previous night—the night of the Ulm theft—said Uneker, he had left his shop for a late dinner; his night-clerk had remained on duty. A man had entered the shop, had asked to see *Europe in Chaos,* and had then to the night-clerk's astonishment purchased all copies of the book in stock—seven. The man who had made this extraordinary purchase wore black mustaches and blue-tinted spectacles!

"Sort of nuts, ain't it?" growled Sergeant Velie.

"Not at all," smiled Ellery. "In fact, I believe it has a very simple explanation."

"And that ain't the half of it. One of the boys told me just now of a new angle on the case. Two minor robberies were reported from local precincts last night. One was uptown in the Bronx; a man named Hornell said his apartment was broken into during the night, and what do you think? Copy of *Europe in Chaos* which Hornell had bought in this guy Uneker's store was stolen! Nothin' else. Bought it two days ago. Then a dame named Janet Meakins from Greenwich Village had *her* flat robbed the same night. Thief had taken her copy of *Europe in Chaos*—she'd bought it from Uneker the afternoon before. Screwy, hey?"

"Not at all, Velie. Use your wits." Ellery clapped his hat on his head. "Come along, you Colossus; I want to speak to old Unky again."

They left Headquarters and went uptown.

"Unky," said Ellery, patting the little old bookseller's bald pate affectionately, "how many copies of *Europe in Chaos* did you have in stock at the time the thief escaped from your back-room?"

"Eleffen."

"Yet only seven were in stock that same evening when the thief returned to buy them," murmured Ellery. "Therefore, four copies had been sold between the noon-hour two days ago and the dinner-hour. So! Unky, do you keep a record of your customers?"

"*Ach,* yes! De few who buy," said old Uneker sadly. "I addt to my mailing-lisdt. You vant to see?"

"There is nothing I crave more ardently at the moment."

Uneker led them to the rear of the shop and through a door into the musty back-room from whose alley-door the thief had escaped two days before. Off this room there was a partitioned cubicle littered with papers, files and old books. The old book-seller opened a ponderous ledger and, wetting his ancient fore-finger, began to slap pages over. "You vant to know de four who boughdt *Europe in Chaos* dot afternoon?"

Uneker hooked a pair of greenish-silver spectacles over his ears and began to read in a singsong voice. "Mr. Hazlitt—dot's the gentleman you met, Mr. Quveen. *He* boughdt his second copy, de vun dot vass robbed from his house. . . . Den dere vass Mr. Hornell, an oldt customer. Den a Miss Janet Meakins—*ach!* dese Anglo-Saxon names. *Schrecklich!* Undt de fourt' vun vass Mr. Chester Singermann, uff t'ree-tvelf East Siggsty-fift' Street. Und dot's all."

"Bless your orderly old Teutonic soul," said Ellery. "Velie, cast those Cyclopean peepers of yours this way." There was a door from the cubicle which, from its location, led out into the al-ley at the rear, like the door in the back-room. Ellery bent over the lock; it was splintered away from the wood. He opened the door; the outer piece was scratched and mutilated. Velie nodded. "Forced," he growled. "This guy's a regular Houdini."

Old Uneker was goggle-eyed. "Broken!" he shrilled. "Budt dot door iss neffer used! I didn't notice not'ing, undt de detectiff—"

"Shocking work, Velie, on the part of the local man," said Ellery. "Unky, has anything been stolen?" Old Uneker flew to an antiquated bookcase; it was neatly tiered with volumes. He un-locked the case with anguished fingers, rummaging like an aged terrier. Then he heaved a vast sigh. "*Nein,*" he said. "Dose rare vons . . . Not'ing stole."

"I congratulate you. One thing more," said Ellery briskly. "Your mailing-list—does it have the business as well as private addresses of your customers?" Uneker nodded. "Better and better. Ta-ta, Unky. You may have a finished story to relate to your other customers after all. Come along, Velie; we're going to visit Mr. Chester Singermann."

They left the bookshop, walked over to Fifth Avenue and turned north, heading uptown. "Plain as the nose on your face," said Ellery, stretching his long stride to match Velie's. "And that's pretty plain, Sergeant."

"Still looks nutty to me, Mr. Queen."

"On the contrary, we are faced with a strictly logical set of facts. Our thief stole a valuable stamp. He dodged into Uneker's bookshop, contrived to get into the back-room. He heard the officer and Friederich Ulm enter, and got busy thinking. If he were caught with the stamp on his person . . . You see, Velie, the only explanation that will make consistent the business of the subsequent thefts of the same book—a book not valuable in itself—is that the thief, Planck, slipped the stamp between the pages of one of the volumes on a shelf while he was in the back-room—it happened by accident to be a copy of *Europe in Chaos,* one of a number kept in stock on the shelf—and made his escape immediately thereafter. But he still had the problem of regaining possession of the stamp—what did Ulm call it?—the 'one-penny black,' whatever *that* may be. So that night he came back, watched for old Uneker to leave the shop, then went in and bought from the clerk all copies of *Europe in Chaos* in the place. He got seven. The stamp was not in any one of the seven he purchased, otherwise why did he later steal others which had been bought that afternoon? So far, so good. Not finding the stamp in any of the seven, then, he returned, broke into Unky's little office during the night—witness the shattered lock—from the alley, and looked up in Unky's Dickensian ledger the names and addresses of those who had bought copies of the book during that afternoon. The next night he robbed Hazlitt; Planck evidently followed him from his office. Planck saw at once that he had made a mistake; the condition of the weeks-old book would have told him that this wasn't a book purchased only the day before. So he hurried out to East Orange, knowing Hazlitt's private as well as business address, and stole Hazlitt's recently purchased copy. No luck there either, so he feloniously visited Hornell and Janet Meakins, stealing their copies. Now, there is still one purchaser unaccounted for, which is why we are calling upon Singermann. For if Planck was unsuccessful in his theft of Hornell's and Miss Meakins' books, he will inevitably visit Singermann, and we want to beat our wily thief to it if possible."

Chester Singermann, they found, was a young student living with his parents in a battered old apartment-house flat. Yes, he still had his copy of *Europe in Chaos*—needed it for supplementary reading in political economy—and he produced it. Ellery went through it carefully, page for page; there was no trace of the missing stamp.

"Mr. Singermann, did you find an old postage-stamp between the leaves of this volume?" asked Ellery.

The student shook his head. "I haven't even opened it, sir. Stamp? What issue? I've got a little collection of my own, you know."

"It doesn't matter," said Ellery hastily, who had heard of the maniacal enthusiasm of stamp-collectors, and he and Velie beat a precipitate retreat.

"It's quite evident," explained Ellery to the Sergeant, "that our slippery Planck found the stamp in either Hornell's copy or Miss Meakins'. Which robbery was first in point of time, Velie?"

"Seem to remember that this Meakins woman was robbed second."

"Then the one-penny black was in her copy. . . . Here's that office-building. Let's pay a little visit to Mr. Friederich Ulm."

Number 1026 on the tenth floor of the building bore a black legend on its frosted-glass door:

ULM

Dealers in

Old & Rare Stamps

Ellery and Sergeant Velie went in and found themselves in a large office. The walls were covered with glass cases in which, separately mounted, could be seen hundreds of canceled and uncanceled postage stamps. Several special cabinets on tables contained, evidently, more valuable items. The place was cluttered; it had a musty air astonishingly like that of old Uneker's bookshop.

Three men looked up. One, from a crisscrossed plaster on his cheekbone, was apparently Friederich Ulm himself, a tall gaunt old German with sparse hair and the fanatic look of the confirmed collector. The second man was just as tall and gaunt and old; he wore a green eye-shade and bore a striking resemblance to Ulm, although from his nervous movements and shaky hands he must have been much older. The third man was a little fellow, quite stout, with an expressionless face.

Ellery introduced himself and Sergeant Velie; and the third man picked up his ears. "Not *the* Ellery Queen?" he said, waddling forward. "I'm Heffley, investigator for the insurance people. Glad to meet you." He pumped Ellery's hand with vigor. "These gentlemen are the Ulm brothers, who own this place. Friederich and Albert. Mr. Albert Ulm was out of the office at the time of the sale and robbery. Too bad; might have nabbed the thief."

Friederich Ulm broke into an excited gabble of German. Ellery listened with a smile, nodding at every fourth word. "I see, Mr. Ulm. The situation, then, was this: you sent invitations by mail to three well-known collectors to attend a special exhibition of rare stamps—object, sale. Three men called on you two mornings ago, purporting to be Messrs. Hinchman, Peters, and Beninson. Hinchman and Peters you knew by sight, but Beninson you did not. Very well. Several items were purchased by the first two collectors. The man you thought was Beninson lingered behind, struck you—yes, yes, I know all that. Let me see the rifled cabinet, please."

The brothers led him to a table in the center of the office. On it there was a flat cabinet, with a lid of ordinary thin glass framed by a narrow rectangle of wood. Under the glass reposed a number of mounted stamps, lying nakedly on a field of black satin. In the center of the satin lay a leather case, open; its white lining had been denuded of its stamp. Where the lid of the cabinet had been wrenched open there were the unmistakable marks of a "jimmy," four in number. The catch was snapped and broken.

"Amatchoor," said Sergeant Velie with a snort. "You could damn near force that locked lid up with your fingers."

Ellery's sharp eyes were absorbed in what lay before him. "Mr. Ulm," he said, turning to the wounded dealer, "the stamp you call 'the one-penny black' was in this open leather box?"

"Yes, Mr. Queen. But the leather box was closed when the thief forced open the cabinet."

"Then how did he know so unerringly what to steal?" Friederich Ulm touched his cheek tenderly. "The stamps in this cabinet were not for sale; they're the cream of our collection; every stamp in this case is worth hundreds. But when the three men were here we naturally talked about the rarer items, and I opened this cabinet to show them our very valuable stamps. So the thief saw the one-penny black. He was a collector, Mr.

Queen, or he wouldn't have chosen that particular stamp to steal. It has a funny history."

"Heavens!" said Ellery. "Do these things have histories?"

Heffley, the man from the insurance company, laughed. "And how! Mr. Friederich and Mr. Albert Ulm are well known to the trade for owning two of the most unique stamps ever issued, both identical. The one-penny black, as it is called by collectors, is a British stamp first issued in 1840; there are lots of them around, and even an uncanceled one is worth only seventeen and a half dollars in American money. But the two in the possession of these gentlemen are worth thirty thousand dollars a piece, Mr. Queen—that's what makes the theft so dog-gone serious. In fact, my company is heavily involved, since the stamps are both insured for their full value."

"Thirty thousand dollars!" groaned Ellery. "That's a lot of money for a little piece of dirty paper. Why are they so valuable?"

Albert Ulm nervously pulled his green shade lower over his eyes. "Because both of ours were actually initialed by Queen Victoria, that's why. Sir Rowland Hill, the man who created and founded the standard penny-postage system in England in 1839, was responsible for the issue of the one-penny black. Her Majesty was so delighted—England, like other countries, had had a great deal of trouble working out a successful postage system— that she autographed the first two stamps off the press and gave them to the designer—I don't recall his name. Her autograph made them immensely valuable. My brother and I were lucky to get our hands on the only two in existence."

"Where's the twin? I'd like to take a peep at a stamp worth a queen's ransom."

The brothers bustled to a large safe looming in a corner of the office. They came back, Albert carrying a leather case as if it were a consignment of golden bullion, and Friederich anxiously holding his elbow, as if he were a squad of armed guards detailed to protect the consignment. Ellery turned the thing over in his fingers; it felt thick and stiff. It was an average-sized stamp rectangle, imperforate, bordered with a black design, and containing an engraving in profile view of Queen Victoria's head—all done in tones of black. On the lighter portion of the face appeared two tiny initials in faded black ink—V. R.

"They're both exactly alike," said Friederich Ulm. "Even to the initials."

"Very interesting," said Ellery, returning the case. The brothers scurried back, placed the stamp in a drawer of the safe, and locked the safe with painful care. "You closed the cabinet, of course, after your three visitors looked over the stamps inside?"

"Oh, yes," said Friederich Ulm. "I closed the case of the one-penny black itself, and then I locked the cabinet."

"And did you send the three invitations yourself? I noticed you have no typewriter here."

"We use a public stenographer in Room 1102 for all our correspondence, Mr. Queen."

Ellery thanked the dealers gravely, waved to the insurance man, nudged Sergeant Velie's meaty ribs, and the two men left the office. In Room 1102 they found a sharp featured young woman. Sergeant Velie flashed his badge, and Ellery was soon reading carbon copies of the three Ulm invitations. He took note of the names and addresses, and the two men left.

They visited the collector named John Hinchman first. Hinchman was a thick-set old man with white hair and gimlet eyes; He was brusque and uncommunicative. Yes, he had been present in the Ulms' office two mornings before. Yes, he knew Peters. No, he'd never met Beninson before. The one-penny black? Of course. Every collector knew of the valuable twin stamps owned by the Ulm brothers; those little scraps of paper bearing the initials of a queen were famous in stampdom. The theft? Bosh! He, Hinchman, knew nothing of Beninson, or whoever it was that impersonated Beninson. He, Hinchman, had left before the thief. He, Hinchman, furthermore didn't care two raps in Hades who stole the stamp; all he wanted was to be let strictly alone.

Sergeant Velie exhibited certain animal signs of hostility; but Ellery grinned, sank his strong fingers into the muscle of the Sergeant's arm, and herded him out of Hinchman's house. They took the subway uptown.

J. S. Peters, they found, was a middle-aged man, tall and thin and yellow as Chinese sealing-wax. He seemed anxious to be of assistance. Yes, he and Hinchman had left the Ulms' office together, before the third man. He had never seen the third man before, although he had heard of Beninson from other collectors. Yes, he knew all about the one-penny blacks, had even tried to buy one of them from Friederich Ulm two years before; but the Ulms had refused to sell.

"Philately," said Ellery outside to Sergeant Velie, whose honest face looked pained at the word, "is a curious hobby. It seems to afflict its victims with a species of mania. I don't doubt these stamp-collecting fellows would murder each other for one of the things."

The Sergeant was wrinkling his nose. "How's she look now?" he asked rather anxiously.

"Velie," replied Ellery, "she looks swell—and different."

They found Avery Beninson in an old brownstone house near the River; he was a mild-mannered and courteous host.

"No, I never did see that invitation," Beninson said. "You see, I hired this man who called himself William Planck, and he took care of my collection and the bulky mail all serious collectors have. The man knew stamps, all right. For two weeks he was invaluable to me. He must have intercepted the Ulms' invitation. He saw his chance to get into their office, went there, said he was Avery Beninson. . ." The collector shrugged. "It was quite simple, I suppose, for an unscrupulous man."

"Of course, you haven't had word from him since the morning of the theft?"

"Naturally not. He made his haul and lit out."

"Just what did he do for you, Mr. Beninson?"

"The ordinary routine of the philatelic assistant—assorting, cataloguing, mounting, answering correspondence. He lived here with me for the two weeks he was in my employ." Beninson grinned deprecatingly. "You see, I'm a bachelor—live in this big shack all alone. I was really glad of his company, although he *was* a queer one."

"A queer one?"

"Well," said Beninson, "he was a retiring sort of creature. Had very few personal belongings, and I found those gone two days ago. He didn't seem to like people, either. He always went to his own room when friends of mine or collectors called, as if he didn't want to mix with company."

"Then there isn't any one else who might be able to supplement description of him?"

"Unfortunately, no. He was a fairly tall man, well advanced in age, I should say. But then his dark glasses and heavy black mustache would make him stand out anywhere."

Ellery sprawled his long figure over the chair, slumping on his spine. "I'm most interested in the man's habits, Mr. Beninson.

Individual idiosyncrasies are often the innocent means by which criminals are apprehended, as the good Sergeant here will tell you. Please think hard. Didn't the man exhibit any oddities of habit?"

Beninson pursed his lips with anxious concentration. His face brightened. "By George, yes! He was a snuff-taker."

Ellery and Sergeant Velie looked at each other. "That's interesting," said Ellery with a smile. "So is my father—Inspector Queen, you know—and I've had the dubious pleasure of watching a snuff-taker's gyrations ever since my childhood. Planck inhaled snuff regularly?"

"I shouldn't say that exactly, Mr. Queen," replied Beninson with a frown. "In fact, in the two weeks he was with me I saw him take snuff only once, and I invariably spent all day with him working in this room. It was last week; I happened to go out for a few moments, and when I returned I saw him holding a carved little box, sniffing from a pinch of something between his fingers. He put the box away quickly, as if he didn't want me to see it—although I didn't care, lord knows, so long as he didn't smoke in here. I've had one fire from a careless assistant's cigarette, and I don't want another."

Ellery's face had come alive. He sat up straight and began to finger his *pince-nez* eyeglasses studiously. "You didn't know the man's address, I suppose?" he asked slowly.

"No, I did not. I'm afraid I took him on without the proper precautions." The collector sighed. "I'm fortunate that he didn't steal anything from me. My collection is worth a lot of money."

"No doubt," said Ellery in a pleasant voice. He rose. "May I use your telephone, Mr. Beninson?"

"Surely."

Ellery consulted a telephone directory and made several calls, speaking in tones so low that neither Beninson nor Sergeant Velie could hear what he was saying. When he put down the instrument he said: "If you can spare a half-hour, Mr. Beninson, I'd like to have you take a little jaunt with us downtown."

Beninson seemed astonished; but he smiled, said: "I'd be delighted," and reached for his coat.

Ellery commandeered a taxicab outside, and the three men were driven to Forty-ninth Street. He excused himself when they got out before the little bookshop, hurried inside, and came out after a moment with old Uneker, who locked his door with shaking fingers.

In the Ulm brother's office they found Heffley, the insurance man, and Hazlitt, Uneker's customer, waiting for them. "Glad you could come," said Ellery cheerfully to both men. "Good afternoon, Mr. Ulm. A little conference, and I think we'll have this business cleared up to the Queen's taste. Ha, ha!"

Friederich Ulm scratched his head; Albert Ulm, sitting in a corner with his hatchet-knees jack-knifed, his green shade over his eyes, nodded.

"We'll have to wait," said Ellery. "I've asked Mr. Peters and Mr. Hinchman to come, too. Suppose we sit down?"

They were silent for the most part, and not a little uneasy. No one spoke as Ellery strolled about the office, examining the rare stamps in their wall-cases with open curiosity, whistling softly to himself. Sergeant Velie eyed him doubtfully. Then the door opened, and Hinchman and Peters appeared together. They stopped short at the threshold, looked at each other, shrugged, and walked in. Hinchman was scowling.

"What's the idea, Mr. Queen?" he said. "I'm a busy man."

"A not unique condition," smiled Ellery. "Ah, Mr. Peters, good day. Introductions, I think, are not entirely called for . . . Sit down, gentlemen!" he said in a sharper voice, and they sat down.

The door opened and a small, gray, birdlike little man peered in at them. Sergeant Velie looked astounded, and Ellery nodded gaily. "Come in, dad, come in! You're just in time for the first act."

Inspector Richard Queen cocked his little squirrel's head, looked at the assembled company shrewdly, and closed the door behind him. "What the devil is the idea of the call, son?"

"Nothing very exciting. Not a murder, or anything in your line. But it may interest you. Gentlemen, Inspector Queen."

The Inspector grunted, sat down, took out his old brown snuff-box, and inhaled with the voluptuous gasp of long practice.

Ellery stood serenely in the hub of the circle of chairs, looking down at curious faces. "The theft of the one-penny black, as you inveterate stamp-fiends call it," he began, "presented a not uninteresting problem. I say 'presented' advisedly. For the case is solved."

"Is this that business of the stamp robbery I was hearing about down at Headquarters?" asked the Inspector.

"Yes."

"Solved?" asked Beninson. "I don't think I understand, Mr. Queen. Have you found Planck?"

Ellery waved his arm negligently. "I was never too sanguine of catching Mr. William Planck, as such. You see, he wore tinted spectacles and black mustachios. Now, any one familiar with the science of crime-detection will tell you that the average person identifies faces by superficial details. A black mustache catches the eye. Tinted glasses impress the memory. In fact, Mr. Hazlitt here, who from Uneker's description is a man of poor observational powers, recalled even after seeing his assailant in dim street-light that the man wore a black mustache and tinted glasses. But this is all fundamental and not even particularly smart. It was reasonable to assume that Planck wanted these special facial characteristics to be remembered. I was convinced that he had disguised himself, that the mustache was probably a false one, and that ordinarily he does not wear tinted glasses."

They all nodded.

"This was the first and simplest of the three psychological sign-posts to the culprit." Ellery smiled and turned suddenly to the Inspector. "Dad, you're an old snuff-addict. How many times a day do you stuff that unholy brown dust up your nostrils?"

The Inspector blinked. "Oh, every half-hour or so. Sometimes as often as you smoke cigarettes."

"Precisely. Now, Mr. Beninson told me that in the two weeks during which Planck stayed at his house, and despite the fact that Mr. Beninson worked side by side with the man every day, he saw Planck take snuff only *once*. Please observe that here we have a most enlightening and suggestive fact."

From the blankness of their faces it was apparent that, far from seeing light, their minds on this point were in total darkness. There was one exception—the Inspector; he nodded, shifted in his chair, and coolly began to study the faces about him.

Ellery lit a cigarette. "Very well," he said, expelling little puffs of smoke, "there you have the second psychological factor. The third was this: Planck, in a fairly public place, bashes Mr. Friederich Ulm over the face with the robust intention of stealing a valuable stamp. Any thief under the circumstances would desire speed above all things. Mr. Ulm was only half-stunned—he might come to and make an outcry; a customer might walk in; Mr. Albert Ulm might return unexpectedly—"

"Just a moment, son," said the Inspector. "I understand there are two of the stamp thingamajigs in existence. I'd like to see the one that's still here."

Ellery nodded. "Would one of you gentlemen please get the stamp?"

Friederich Ulm rose, pottered over to the safe, tinkered with the dials, opened the steel door, fussed about the interior a moment, and came back with the leather case containing the second one-penny black. The Inspector examined the thick little scrap curiously; a thirty-thousand-dollar bit of old paper was as awesome to him as to Ellery.

He almost dropped it when he heard Ellery say to Sergeant Velie: "Sergeant, may I borrow your revolver?"

Velie's massive jaw see-sawed as he fumbled in his hip pocket and produced a long-barreled police revolver. Ellery took it and hefted it thoughtfully. Then his fingers closed about the butt and he walked over to the rifled cabinet in the middle of the room.

"Please observe, gentlemen—to expand my third point—that in order to open this cabinet Planck used an iron bar; and that in prying up the lid he found it necessary to insert the bar between the lid and the front wall four times, as the four marks under the lid indicate.

"Now, as you can see, the cabinet is covered with thin glass. Moreover, it was locked, and the one-penny black was in this closed leather case inside. Planck stood about here, I should judge, and mark that the iron bar was in his hand. What would you gentlemen expect a thief, working against time, to do under these circumstances?"

They stared. The Inspector's mouth tightened; and a grin began to spread over the expanse of Sergeant Velie's face.

"But it's so clear," said Ellery. "Visualize it. I'm Planck. The revolver in my hand is an iron 'jimmy.' I'm standing over the cabinet. . ." His eyes gleamed behind the *pince-nez*, and he raised the revolver high over his head. And then, deliberately, he began to bring the steel barrel down on the thin sheeting of glass atop the cabinet. There was a scream from Albert Ulm, and Friederich Ulm half-rose, glaring. Ellery's hand stopped a half-inch from the glass.

"Don't break that glass, you fool!" shouted the green-shaded dealer. "You'll only—"

He leaped forward and stood before the cabinet, trembling arms outspread as if to protect the case and its contents. Ellery grinned and prodded the man's palpitating belly with the muzzle of the revolver. "I'm glad you stopped me, Mr. Ulm. Put your hands up. Quickly!"

"Why—why, what do you mean?" gasped Albert Ulm, raising his arms with frantic rapidity.

"I mean," said Ellery gently, "that you're William Planck, and that brother Friederich is your accomplice!"

The brothers Ulm sat trembling in their chairs, and Sergeant Velie stood over them with a nasty smile. Albert Ulm had gone to pieces; he was quivering like an aspen-leaf in high wind.

"A very simple, almost an elementary, series of deductions," Ellery was saying. "Point three first. Why did the thief, instead of taking the most logical course of smashing the glass with the iron bar, choose to waste precious minutes using a 'jimmy' four times to force open the lid? *Obviously to protect the other stamps in the cabinet which lay open to possible injury,* as Mr. Albert Ulm has just graphically pointed out. And who had the greatest concern in protecting these other stamps—Hinchman, Peter, Beninson, even the mythical Planck himself? Of course not. Only the Ulm brothers, owners of the stamps."

Old Uneker began to chuckle; he nudged the Inspector. "See? Didn't I say he vass smardt? Now me—me, I'd neffer t'ink of dot."

"And why didn't Planck steal these other stamps in the cabinet? You would expect a thief to do that. Planck did not. But if the *Herren* Ulm were the thieves, the theft of the other stamps became pointless."

"How about that snuff business, Mr. Queen?" asked Peters.

"Yes. The conclusion is plain from the fact that Planck apparently indulged only once during the days he worked with Mr. Beninson. Since snuff-addicts partake freely and often, Planck wasn't a snuff-addict. Then it wasn't snuff he inhaled that day. What else is sniffed in a similar manner? Well—drugs in powder form—heroin! What are the characteristics of a heroin-addict? Nervous drawn appearance; gauntness, almost emaciation; and most important, tell-tale eyes, the pupils of which contract under influence of the drug. Then here was another explanation for the tinted glasses Planck wore. They served a double purpose—as an easily recognizable disguise, and also to conceal his eyes, which would give his vice-addiction away! But when I observed that Mr. Albert Ulm—" Ellery went over to the cowering man and ripped the green eye-shade away, revealing two stark, pin-point pupils—"wore this shade, it was a psychological confirmation of his identity as Planck."

"Yes, but that business of stealing all those books," said Hazlitt.

"Part of a very pretty and rather far-fetched plot," said Ellery. "With Albert Ulm the disguised thief, Friederich Ulm, who exhibited the wound on his cheek, must have been an accomplice. Then with the Ulm brothers the thieves, the entire business of the books was a blind. The attack on Friederich, the ruse of the bookstore escape, the trail of the minor robberies of copies of

Europe in Chaos—a cleverly planned series of incidents to authenticate the fact that there was an outside thief, to convince the police and the insurance company that the stamp actually was stolen when it was not. Object, of course, to collect the insurance without parting with the stamp. These men are fanatical collectors."

Heffley wriggled his fat little body uncomfortably. "That's all very nice, Mr. Queen, but where the deuce is that stamp they stole from themselves? Where'd they hide it?"

"I thought long and earnestly about that, Heffley. For while my trio of deductions were psychological indications of guilt, the discovery of the stolen stamp in the Ulms' possession would be evidential proof." The Inspector was turning the second stamp over mechanically. "I said to myself," Ellery went on, "in a reconsideration of the problem: what would be the most likely hiding-place for the stamp? And then I remembered that the two stamps were identical, even the initials of the good Queen being in the same place. So I said to myself: if I were Messrs. Ulm, I should hide that stamp—like the character in Edgar Allan Poe's famous tale—in the most obvious place. And what is the most obvious place?"

Ellery sighed and returned the unused revolver to Sergeant Velie. "Dad," he remarked to the Inspector, who started guiltily, "I think that if you allow one of the philatelists in our company to examine the second one-penny black in your fingers, you'll find that the *first* has been pasted with non-injurious rubber cement precisely over the second!"

The Adventure of
THE BEARDED LADY

MR. PHINEAS MASON, attorney-at-law—of the richly, almost indigestibly respectable firm of *Dowling, Mason & Coolidge,* 40 Park Row—was a very un-Phineaslike gentleman with a chunky nose and wrinkle-bedded eyes which had seen thirty years of harassing American litigation and looked as if they had seen a hundred. He sat stiffly in the lap of a chauffeur-driven limousine, his mouth making interesting sounds.

"And now," he said in an angry voice, "there's actually been murder done. I can't imagine what the world is coming to."

Mr. Ellery Queen, watching the world rush by in a glaring Long Island sunlight, mused that life was like a Spanish wench: full of surprises, none of them delicate and all of them stimulating. Since he was a monastic who led a riotous mental existence, he liked life that way; and since he was also a detective—an appellation he cordially detested—he got life that way. Nevertheless, he did not vocalize his reflections: Mr. Phineas Mason did not appear the sort who would appreciate fleshly metaphor.

He drawled: "The world's all right; the trouble is the people in it. Suppose you tell me what you can about these curious Shaws. After all, you know, I shan't be too heartily received by your local Long Island constabulary; and since I foresee difficulties, I should like to be forearmed as well."

Mason frowned. "But McC. assured me—"

"Oh, bother J. J.! He has vicarious delusions of grandeur. Let me warn you now, Mr. Mason, that I shall probably be a dismal flop. I don't go about pulling murderers out of my hat. And with your cossacks trampling the evidence—"

"I warned them," said Mason fretfully. "I spoke to Captain Murch myself when he telephoned this morning to inform me of the crime." He made a sour face. "They won't even move the body, Mr. Queen. I wield—ah—a little local influence, you see."

"Indeed," said Ellery, adjusting his *pince-nez;* and he sighed. "Very well, Mr. Mason. Proceed with the dreary details."

"It was my partner, Coolidge," began the attorney in a pained voice, "who originally handled Shaw's affairs. John A. Shaw, the millionaire. Before your time, I daresay. Shaw's first wife died in childbirth in 1895. The child—Agatha; she's a divorcee now, with a son of eight—of course survived her mother; and there was one previous child, named after his father. John's forty-five now. . . . At any rate, old John Shaw remarried soon after his first wife's death, and then shortly after his second marriage died himself. This second wife, Maria Paine Shaw, survived her husband by a little more than thirty years. She died only a month ago."

"A plethora of mortalities," murmured Ellery, lighting a cigarette. "So far, Mr. Mason, a prosaic tale. And what has the Shaw history to do—"

"Patience," sighed Mason. "Now old John Shaw bequeathed

his entire fortune to this second wife, Maria. The two children, John and Agatha, got nothing, not even trusts; I suppose old Shaw trusted Maria to take care of them."

"I scent the usual story," yawned Ellery. "She didn't? No go between stepmother and acquired progeny?"

The lawyer wiped his brow. "It was horrible. They fought for thirty years like—like savages. I will say, in extenuation of Mrs. Shaw's conduct, that she had provocation. John's always been a shiftless, unreliable beggar: disrespectful, profligate, quite vicious. Nevertheless she's treated him well in money matters. As I said, he's forty-five now; and he hasn't done a lick of work in his life. He's a drunkard, too."

"Sounds charming. And Sister Agatha, the divorcee?"

"A feminine edition of her brother. She married a fortune-hunter as worthless as herself; when he found out she was penniless he deserted her and Mrs. Shaw managed to get her a quiet divorce. She took Agatha and her boy, Peter, into her house and they've been living there ever since, at daggers' points. Please forgive the—ah—brutality of the characterizations; I want you to know these people as they are."

"We're almost intimate already," chuckled Ellery.

"John and Agatha," continued Mason, biting the head of his cane, "have been living for only one event—their stepmother's death. So that they might inherit, of course. Until a certain occurrence a few months ago Mrs. Shaw's will provided generously for them. But when that happened—"

Mr. Ellery Queen narrowed his gray eyes. "You mean—?"

"It's complicated," sighed the lawyer. "Three months ago there was an attempt on the part of some one in the household to poison the old lady!"

"Ah!"

"The attempt was unsuccessful only because Dr. Arlen—Dr. Terence Arlen is the full name—had suspected such a possibility for years and had kept his eyes open. The cyanide—it was put in her tea—didn't reach Mrs. Shaw, but killed a house-cat. None of us, of course, knew who had made the poisoning attempt. But after that Mrs. Shaw changed her will."

"Now," muttered Ellery, "I *am* enthralled. Arlen, eh? That creates a fascinating mess. Tell me about Arlen, please."

"Rather mysterious old man with two passions: devotion to Mrs. Shaw and a hobby of painting. Quite an artist, too, though I know little about such things. He lived in the Shaw house about twenty years. Medico Mrs. Shaw picked up somewhere; I think only she knew his story, and he's always been silent about his past. She put him on a generous salary to live in the house and act as the family physician; I suspect it was rather because she anticipated what her stepchildren might attempt. And then too it's always seemed to me that Arlen accepted this unusual arrangement so tractably in order to pass out of—ah—circulation."

They were silent for some time. The chauffeur swung the car off the main artery into a narrow macadam road Mason breathed heavily.

"I suppose you're satisfied," murmured Ellery at last through a fat smoke ring, "that Mrs. Shaw died a month ago of natural causes?"

"Heavens, yes!" cried Mason. "Dr. Arlen wouldn't trust his own judgment, we were so careful; he had several specialists in, before and after her death. But she died of the last of a series of heart-attacks; she was an old woman, you know. Something-thrombosis, they called it." Mason looked gloomy. "Well, you can understand Mrs. Shaw's natural reaction to the poisoning episode. 'If they're so depraved,' she told me shortly after, 'that they'd attempt my *life*, they don't deserve any consideration at my *hands*.' And she had me draw up a new will, cutting both of them off without a cent."

"There's an epigram," chuckled Ellery, "worthy of a better cause."

Mason tapped on the glass. "Faster, Burroughs." The car jolted ahead. "In looking about for a beneficiary, Mrs. Shaw finally remembered that there was some one to whom she could leave the Shaw fortune without feeling that she was casting it to the winds. Old John Shaw had had an elder brother, Morton, a widower with two grown children. The brothers quarrelled violently and Morton moved to England. He lost most of his money there; his two children, Edith and Percy, were left to shift for themselves when he committed suicide."

"These Shaws seem to have a penchant for violence."

"I suppose it's in the blood. Well, Edith and Percy both had talent of a sort, I understand, and they went on the London stage in a brother-and-sister music-hall act, managing well enough. Mrs. Shaw decided to leave her money to this Edith, her niece. I made inquiries by correspondence and discovered that Edith Shaw was now Mrs. Edythe Royce, a childless widow of many years' standing. On Mrs. Shaw's decease I cabled her and she crossed by the next boat. According to Mrs. Royce, Percy—her brother—was killed in an automobile accident on the Continent a few months before; so she had no ties whatever."

"And the will—specifically?"

"It's rather queer," sighed Mason. "The Shaw estate was enormous at one time, but the depression whittled it down to about three hundred thousand dollars. Mrs. Shaw left her niece two

hundred thousand outright. The remainder, to his astonishment,"
and Mason paused and eyed his tall young companion with a
curious fixity, "was put in trust for Dr. Arlen."

"Arlen!"

"He was not to touch the principal, but was to receive the income from it for the remainder of his life. Interesting, eh?"

"That's putting it mildly. By the way, Mr. Mason, I'm a suspicious bird. This Mrs. Royce—you're satisfied she *is* a Shaw?"

The lawyer started; then he shook his head. "No, no, Queen,
that's the wrong tack. There can be absolutely no question about
it. In the first place she possesses the marked facial characteristics of the Shaws; you'll see for yourself; although I will say
that she's rather—well, rather a character, rather a character! She
came armed with intimate possessions of her father, Morton
Shaw; and I myself, in company with Coolidge, questioned her
closely on her arrival. She convinced us utterly, from her knowledge of *minutiae* about her father's life and Edith Shaw's childhood in America—knowledge impossible for an outsider to have
acquired—that she *is* Edith Shaw. We were more than cautious,
I assure you; especially since neither John nor Agatha had seen
her since childhood."

"Just a thought." Ellery leaned forward. "And what was to be
the disposition of Arlen's hundred-thousand-dollar trust on Arlen's death?"

The lawyer gazed grimly at the two rows of prim poplars
flanking a manicured driveway on which the limousine was now
noiselessly treading. "It was to be equally divided between John
and Agatha," he said in a careful voice. The car rolled to a stop
under a coldly white *porte-cochère.*

"I see," said Ellery. For it was Dr. Terence Arlen who had
been murdered.

A county trooper escorted them through high Colonial halls into a remote and silent wing of the ample old house, up a staircase to a dim cool corridor patrolled by a nervous man with a bull neck.

"Oh, Mr. Mason," he said eagerly, coming forward. "We've been waiting for you. This is Mr. Queen?" His tone changed from unguent haste to abrasive suspicion.

"Yes, yes. Murch of the county detectives, Mr. Queen. You've left everything intact, Murch?"

The detective grunted and stepped aside. Ellery found himself in the study of what appeared to be a two-room suite; beyond an open door he could see the white counterpane of a bird's-eye-maple four-poster. A hole at some remote period had been hacked through the ceiling and covered with glass, admitting sunlight and converting the room into a sky-light studio. The trivia of a painter's paraphernalia lay in confusion about the room, overpowering the few medical implements. There were easels, paint-boxes, a small dais, carelessly draped smocks, a profusion of daubs in oils and water-colors on the walls.

A little man was kneeling beside the outstretched figure of the dead doctor—a long brittle figure frozen in death, capped with curiously lambent silver hair. The wound was frank and deep: the delicately chased haft of a stiletto protruded from the man's heart. There was very little blood.

Murch snapped: "Well, Doc, anything else?"

The little man rose and put his instruments away. "Died instantly from the stab-wound. Frontal blow, as you see. He tried to dodge at the last instant, I should say, but wasn't quick enough." He nodded and reached for his hat and quietly went out.

Ellery shivered a little. The studio was silent, and the corridor was silent, and the wing was silent; the whole house was crushed under the weight of a terrific silence that was almost uncanny. There was something indescribably evil in the air. . . . He shook his shoulders impatiently. "The stiletto, Captain Murch. Have you identified it?"

"Belonged to Arlen. Always right here on this table."

"No possibility of suicide, I suppose."

"Not a chance, Doc said."

Mr. Phineas Mason made a retching sound. "If you want me, Queen—" He stumbled from the room, awakening dismal echoes.

The corpse was swathed in a paint-smudged smock above pajamas; in the stiff right hand a paint-brush, its hairs-stained jet-black, was still clutched. A color-splashed palette had fallen face down on the floor near him. . . . Ellery did not raise his eyes from the stiletto. "Florentine, I suppose. Tell me what you've learned so far, Captain," he said absently. "I mean about the crime itself."

"Damned little," growled the detective. "Doc says he was killed about two in the morning—about eight hours ago. His body was found at seven this a.m. by a woman named Krutch, a nurse in the house here for a couple of years. Nice wench, by God! Nobody's got an alibi for the time of the murder, because according to their yarns they were all sleeping, and they all sleep separately. That's about the size of it."

"Precious little, to be sure," murmured Ellery. "By the way, Captain, was it Dr. Arlen's custom to paint in the wee hours?"

"Seems so. I thought of that, too. But he was a queer old cuss and when he was hot on something he'd work for twenty-four hours at a clip."

"Do the others sleep in this wing?"

"Nope. Not even the servants. Seems Arlen liked privacy, and whatever he liked the old dame—Mrs. Shaw, who kicked off a month ago—said 'jake' to." Murch went to the doorway and snapped: "Miss Krutch."

She came slowly out of Dr. Arlen's bedroom—a tall fair young woman who had been weeping. She was in nurse's uniform and there was nothing in common between her name and her appearance. In fact, as Ellery observed with appreciation, she was a distinctly attractive young woman with curves in precisely the right places. Miss Krutch, despite her tears, was the first ray of sunshine he had encountered in the big old house.

"Tell Mr. Queen what you told me," directed Murch curtly.

"But there's so little," she quavered. "I was up before seven, as usual. My room's in the main wing, but there's a storeroom here for linen and things. . . . As I passed I—I saw Dr. Arlen lying on the floor, with the knife sticking up—The door was open and the light was on. I screamed. No one heard me. This is so far away. . . . I screamed and screamed and then Mr. Shaw came running, and Miss Shaw. Th-that's all."

"Did any of you touch the body, Miss Krutch?"

"Oh, no, sir!" She shivered.

"I see," said Ellery, and raised his eyes from the dead man to the easel above, casually, and looked away. And then instantly he looked back, his nerves tingling. Murch watched him with a sneer.

"How," jeered Murch, "d'ye like that, *Mr.* Queen?"

Ellery sprang forward. A smaller easel near the large one supported a picture. It was a cheap "processed" oil painting, a commercial copy of Rembrandt's famous self-portrait group, *The Artist and His Wife*. Rembrandt himself sat in the foreground, and his wife stood in the background. The canvas on the large easel was a half-finished replica of this painting. Both figures had been completely sketched in by Dr. Arlen and brush work begun: the lusty smiling mustached artist in his gayly plumed hat, his left arm about the waist of his Dutch-garbed wife. *And on the woman's chin there was painted a beard.*

Ellery gaped from the processed picture to Dr. Aden's copy. But the one showed a woman's smooth chin, and the other— the doctor's—a squarish, expertly stroked black beard. And yet it had been daubed in hastily, as if the old painter had been working against time.

"Good heavens!" exclaimed Ellery, glaring. "That's insane!"

"Think so?, said Murch blandly. "Me, I don't know. I've got a notion about it." He growled at Miss Krutch: "Beat it," and she fled from the studio, her long legs twinkling.

Ellery shook his head dazedly and sank into a chair, fumbling for a cigarette. "That's a new wrinkle to me, Captain. First time I've ever encountered in a homicide an example of the beard-and-mustache school of art—you've seen the pencilled hair on the faces of men and women in billboard advertisements? It's—" And then his eyes narrowed as something leaped into them and he said abruptly: "Is Miss Agatha Shaw's boy—that Peter—in the house?"

Murch, smiling secretly as if he were enjoying a huge jest, went to the hallway door and roared something. Ellery got out of the chair and ran across the room and returned with one of the smocks, which he flung over the dead man's body.

A small boy with frightened yet inquisitive eyes came slowly into the room, followed by one of the most remarkable creatures Ellery had ever seen. This apparition was a large stout woman of perhaps sixty, with lined rugged features—so heavy they were almost wattled—painted, bedaubed, and varnished with an astounding cosmetic technique. Her lips, gross as they were, were shaped by rouge into a perfect and obscene Cupid's-bow; her eyebrows had been tweezed to incredible thinness; round rosy spots punctuated her sagging cheeks; and the whole rough heavy skin was floury with white powder.

But her costume was even more amazing than her face. For she was rigged out in Victorian style—a tight-waisted garment, almost bustle-hipped, full wide skirts that reached to her thick ankles, a deep and shiny bosom, and an elaborate boned lace choker-collar. . . . And then Ellery remembered that, since this must be Edythe Shaw Royce, there was at least a partial explanation for her eccentric appearance: she was an old woman, she came from England, and she was no doubt still basking in the vanished glow of her girlhood theatrical days.

"Mrs. Royce," said Murch mockingly, "*and* Peter."

"How d'ye do," muttered Ellery, tearing his eyes away. "Uh—Peter."

The boy, a sharp-featured and skinny little creature, sucked his dirty forefinger and stared.

"Peter!" said Mrs. Royce severely. Her voice was quite in tune with her appearance: deep and husky and slightly cracked. Even her hair, Ellery noted with a wince, was nostalgic—a precise deep brown, frankly dyed. Here was one female, at least, who did not mean to yield to old age without a determined struggle, he thought. "'He's frightened. Peter!"

"Ma'am," mumbled Peter, still staring.

"Peter," said Ellery, "look at that picture." Peter did so, reluctantly. "Did you put that beard on the face of the lady in the picture, Peter?"

Peter shrank against Mrs. Royce's voluminous skirts. "N-no!"

"Curious, isn't it?" said Mrs. Royce cheerfully. "I was remarking about that to Captain Burch—Murch only this morning.

I'm sure Peter wouldn't have drawn the beard on *that* one. He'd learned his lesson, hadn't you, Peter?" Ellery remarked with alarm that the extraordinary woman kept screwing her right eyebrow up and drawing it deeply down, as if there were something in her eye that bothered her.

"Ah," said Ellery. "Lesson?"

"You see," went on Mrs. Royce, continuing her ocular gymnastics with unconscious vigor, "it was only yesterday that Peter's mother caught him drawing a beard with chalk on one of Dr. Arlen's paintings in Peter's bedroom. Dr. Arlen gave him a round hiding, I'm afraid, and himself removed the chalk-marks. Dear Agatha was *so* angry with poor Dr. Arlen. So you didn't do it, did you, Peter?"

"Naw," said Peter, who had become fascinated by the bulging smock on the floor.

"Dr. Arlen, eh?" muttered Ellery. "Thank you," and he began to pace up and down as Mrs. Royce took Peter by the arm and firmly removed him from the studio. A formidable lady, he thought, with her vigorous room-shaking tread. And he recalled that she wore flat-heeled shoes and had, from the ugly swelling of the leather, great bunions.

"Come on," said Murch suddenly, going to the door.

"Where?"

"Downstairs." The detective signalled a trooper to guard the studio and led the way. "I want to show you," he said as they made for the main part of the house, "the reason for the beard on that dame-in-the-picture's jaw."

"Indeed?" murmured Ellery, and said nothing more. Murch paused in the doorway of a pale Colonial living-room and jerked his head.

Ellery looked in. A hollow-chested, cadaverous man in baggy tweeds sat slumped in a Cogswell chair staring at an empty glass in his hand, which was shaking. His eyes were yellow-balled and shot with blood, and his loose skin was a web of red veins.

"That," said Murch contemptuously and yet with a certain triumph, "is Mr. John Shaw."

Ellery noted that Shaw possessed the same heavy features, the same fat lips and rock-hewn nose, as the wonderful Mrs. Royce, his cousin; and for that matter, as the dour and annoyed-looking old pirate in the portrait over the fireplace who was presumably his father.

And Ellery also noted that on Mr. John Shaw's unsteady chin there was a bedraggled, pointed beard.

Mr. Mason, a bit greenish about the jowls, was waiting for them in a sombre reception-room. "Well?" he asked in a whisper, like a supplicant before the Cumæan Sibyl.

"Captain Murch," murmured Ellery, "has a theory."

The detective scowled. "Plain as day. It's John Shaw. It's my hunch Dr. Arlen painted that beard as a clue to his killer. The only one around here with a beard is Shaw. It ain't evidence, I admit, but it's something to work on. And believe you me," he said with a snap of his brown teeth, "I'm going to work on it!"

"John," said Mason slowly. "He certainly had motive. And yet I find it difficult to. . ." His shrewd eyes flickered. "Beard? What beard?"

"There's a beard painted on the chin of a female face upstairs," drawled Ellery, "the face being on a Rembrandt Arlen was copying at the time he was murdered. That the good doctor painted the beard himself is quite evident. It's expertly stroked, done in black oils, and in his death hand there's still the brush tipped with black oils. There isn't any one else in the house who paints, is there?"

"No," said Mason uncomfortably.

"*Voilà.*"

"But even if Arlen did such a—a mad thing," objected the lawyer, "how do you know it was just before he was attacked?"

"Aw," growled Murch, "when the hell else would it be?"

"Now, now, Captain," murmured Ellery, "let's be scientific. There's a perfectly good answer to your question, Mr. Mason. First, we all agree that Dr. Arlen couldn't have painted the beard *after* he was attacked; he died instantly. Therefore he must have painted it before he was attacked. The question is: How long before? Well, why did Arlen paint the beard at all?"

"Murch says as a clue to his murderer," muttered Mason. "But such a—a fantastic legacy to the police! It looks deucedly odd."

"What's odd about it?"

"Well, for heaven's sake," exploded Mason, "if he wanted to leave a clue to his murderer, why didn't he write the murderer's name on the canvas? He had the brush in his hand. . ."

"Precisely," murmured Ellery. "A very good question, Mr. Mason. Well, why didn't he? If he was alone—that is, if he was *anticipating* his murder—he certainly would have left us a written record of his concrete suspicions. The fact that he left no such record shows that he didn't anticipate his murder before the appearance of his murderer. Therefore he painted the beard *while his murderer was present.* But now we find an explanation for the painted beard as a clue. With his murderer present, he *couldn't* paint the name; the murderer would have noticed it and destroyed it. Arlen was forced, then, to adopt a subtle means: leave a clue that would escape his killer's attention. Since he was painting at the time, he used a painter's means. Even if his murderer noticed it, he probably ascribed it to Arlen's nervousness; although the chances are he didn't notice it."

Murch stirred. "Say, listen—"

"But a beard on a woman's face," groaned the lawyer. "I tell you—"

"Oh," said Ellery dreamily, "Dr. Arlen had a precedent."

"Precedent?"

"Yes; we've found, Captain Murch and I, that young Peter in his divine innocence had chalked a beard and mustache on one of Dr. Arlen's daubs which hangs in Peter's bedroom. This was only yesterday. Dr. Arlen whaled the tar out of him for this horrible crime *vers l'art,* no doubt justifiably. But Peter's beard-scrawl must have stuck in the doctor's mind; threshing about wildly in his mind while his murderer talked to him, or threatened him, the beard business popped out at him. Apparently he felt that it told a story, because he used it. And there, of course, is the rub."

"I still say it's all perfectly asinine," grunted Mason.

"Not asinine," said Ellery. "Interesting. He painted a beard on the chin of Rembrandt's wife. Why Rembrandt's wife, in the name of all that's wonderful?—a woman dead more than two centuries! These Shaws aren't remote descendants. . ."

"Nuts," said Murch distinctly.

"Nuts," said Ellery, "is a satisfactory word under the circumstances, Captain. Then a grim jest? Hardly. But if it wasn't Dr. Arlen's grisly notion of a joke, what under heaven was it? What did Arlen mean to convey?"

"If it wasn't so ridiculous," muttered the lawyer, "I'd say he was pointing to—Peter."

"Nuts and double-nuts," said Murch, "begging your pardon, Mr. Mason. The kid's the only one, I guess, that's got a real alibi.

It seems his mother's nervous about him and she always keeps his door locked from the outside. I found it that way myself this morning. And he couldn't have got out through the window."

"Well, well," sighed Mason, "I'm sure I'm all at sea. John, eh. . . . What do *you* think, Mr. Queen?"

"Much as I loathe argument," said Ellery, "I can't agree with Brother Murch."

"Oh, yeah?" jeered Murch. "I suppose you've got reasons?"

"I suppose," said Ellery, "I have; not the least impressive of which is the dissimilar shapes of the real and painted beards."

The detective glowered. "Well, if he didn't mean John Shaw by it, what the hell did he mean?"

Ellery shrugged. "If we knew that, my dear Captain, we should know everything."

"Well," snarled Murch, "I think it's spinach, and I'm going to haul Mr. John Shaw down to county headquarters and pump the old bastard till I *find* it's spinach."

"I shouldn't do that, Murch," said Ellery quickly. "If only for—"

"I know my duty," said the detective with a black look, and he stamped out of the reception-room.

John Shaw, who was quietly drunk, did not even protest when Murch shoved him into the squad car. Followed by the county morgue-truck bearing Dr. Arlen's body, Murch vanished with his prey.

Ellery took a hungry turn about the room, frowning. The lawyer sat in a crouch, gnawing his fingernails. And again the room, and the house, and the very air were charged with silence, an ominous silence.

"Look here," said Ellery sharply, "there's something in this business you haven't told me yet, Mr. Mason."

The lawyer jumped, and then sank back biting his lips. "He's such a worrisome creature," said a cheerful voice from the doorway and they both turned, startled, to find Mrs. Royce beaming in at them. She came in with the stride of a grenadier, her bosom joggling. And she sat down by Mason's side and with daintiness lifted her capacious skirts with both hands a bit above each fat knee. "I know what's troubling you, Mr. Mason!" The lawyer cleared his throat hastily. "I assure you—"

"Nonsense! I've excellent eyes. Mason, you haven't introduced this nice young man." Mason mumbled something placative. "Queen, is it? Charmed, Mr. Queen. First sample of reasonably attractive American I've seen since my arrival. I can appreciate a handsome man; I was on the London stage for many years. And really," she thundered in her formidable baritone, "I wasn't so ill-looking myself!"

"I'm sure of that," murmured Ellery. "But what—"

"Mason's afraid for me," said Mrs. Royce with a girlish simper. "A most conscientious barrister! He's simply petrified with fear that whoever did for poor Dr. Arlen will select me as his next victim. And *I* tell him now, as I told him a few moments ago when you were upstairs with that dreadful Murch person, that for one thing I shan't be such an easy victim—" Ellery could well believe *that*—"and for another I don't believe either John or Agatha, which is what's in Mason's mind—don't deny it, Mason!—was responsible for Dr. Arlen's death."

"I never—" began the lawyer feebly.

"Hmm," said Ellery. "What's *your* theory, Mrs. Royce?"

"Some one out of Arlen's past," boomed the lady with a click of her jaws as a punctuation mark. "I understand he came here twenty years ago under most mysterious circumstances. He may have murdered somebody, and that somebody's brother or some one has returned to avenge—"

"Ingenious," grinned Ellery. "As tenable as Murch's, Mr. Mason."

The lady sniffed. "He'll release Cousin John soon enough," she said complacently. "John's stupid enough under ordinary circumstances, you know, but when he's drunk—! There's no evidence, is there? A cigarette, if you please, Mr. Queen."

Ellery hastened to offer his case. Mrs. Royce selected a cigarette with a vast paw, smiled roguishly as Ellery held a match, and then withdrew the cigarette and blew smoke, crossing her legs as she did so. She smoked almost in the Russian fashion, cupping her hand about the cigarette instead of holding it between two fingers. A remarkable woman! "Why are you so afraid for Mrs. Royce?" he drawled.

"Well—" Mason hesitated, torn between discretion and desire. "There may have been a double motive for killing Dr. Arlen, you see. That is," he added hurriedly, "*if* Agatha or John had anything to do—"

"Double motive?"

"One, of course, is the conversion of the hundred thousand to Mrs. Shaw's stepchildren, as I told you. The other . . . Well, there is a proviso in connection with the bequest to Dr. Arlen. In return for offering him a home and income for the rest of his life, he was to continue to attend to the medical needs of the family, you see, with *special* attention to Mrs. Royce."

"Poor Aunt Maria," said Mrs. Royce with a tidal sigh. "She must have been a dear, dear person."

"I'm afraid I don't quite follow, Mr. Mason."

"I've a copy of the will in my pocket." The lawyer fished for a crackling document. "Here it is. 'And in particular to conduct monthly medical examinations of my niece, Edith Shaw—or more frequently if Dr. Arlen should deem it necessary—to insure her continued good health; a provision, (mark this, Queen!) '*a provision I am sure my stepchildren will appreciate.*'"

"A cynical addendum," nodded Ellery, blinking a little. "Mrs. Shaw placed on her trusted leech the responsibility for keeping you healthy, Mrs. Royce, suspecting that her dearly beloved stepchildren might be tempted to—er—tamper with your life. But why should they?"

For the first time something like terror invaded Mrs. Royce's massive face. She set her jaw and said, a trifle tremulously: "N-nonsense. I can't believe—Do you think it's possible they've already tr—"

"You don't feel ill, Mrs. Royce?" cried Mason, alarmed.

Under the heavy coating of powder her coarse skin was muddily pale. "No, I—Dr. Arlen was supposed to examine me for the first time tomorrow. Oh, if it's . . . The food—"

"Poison was tried three months ago," quavered the lawyer. "On Mrs. Shaw, Queen, as I told you. Good God. Mrs. Royce, you'll have to be careful!"

"Come, come," snapped Ellery. "What's the point? Why should the Shaws want to poison Mrs. Royce, Mason?"

"Because," said Mason in a trembling voice, "in the event of Mrs. Royce's demise her estate is to revert to the original estate; which would automatically mean to John and Agatha." He mopped his brow.

Ellery heaved himself out of the chair and took another hungry turn about the sombre room. Mrs. Royce's right eyebrow suddenly began to go up and down with nervousness.

"This needs thinking over," he said abruptly; and there was something queer in his eyes that made both of them stare at him with uneasiness. "I'll stay the night, Mr. Mason, if Mrs. Royce has no objection."

"Do," whispered Mrs. Royce in a tremble; and this time she was afraid, very plainly afraid. And over the room settled an impalpable dust, like a distant sign of approaching villainy. "Do you think they'll actually *try*. . . ?"

"It is entirely," said Ellery dryly, "within the realm of possibility."

The day passed in a timeless haze. Unaccountably, no one came; the telephone was silent; and there was no word from Murch, so that John Shaw's fate remained obscure. Mason sat in a miserable heap on the front porch, a cigar cold in his mouth, rocking himself like a weazened old doll. Mrs. Royce retired, subdued, to her quarters. Peter was off somewhere in the gardens tormenting a dog; occasionally Miss Krutch's tearful voice reprimanded him ineffectually.

To Mr. Ellery Queen it was a painful, puzzling, and irritatingly evil time. He prowled the rambling mansion, a lost soul, smoking tasteless cigarettes and thinking. . . . That a blanket of menace hung over this house his nerves convinced him. It took all his willpower to keep his body from springing about at unheard sounds; moreover, his mind was distracted and he could not think clearly. A murderer was abroad; and this was a house of violent people.

He shivered and darted a look over his shoulder and shrugged and bent his mind fiercely to the problem at hand. . . . And after hours his thoughts grew calmer and began to range themselves in orderly rows, until it was evident that there was a beginning and an end. He grew quiet.

He smiled a little as he stopped a tiptoeing maid and inquired the location of Miss Agatha Shaw's room. Miss Shaw had wrapped herself thus far in a mantle of invisibility. It was most curious. A sense of rising drama excited him a little. . . .

A tinny female voice responded to his knock, and he opened the door to find a feminine Shaw as bony and unlovely as the masculine edition curled in a hard knot on a *chaise-longue,* staring balefully out the window. Her négligé was adorned with boa feathers and there were varicose veins on her swollen naked legs.

"Well," she said acidly, without turning. "What do you want?"

"My name," murmured Ellery, "is Queen, and Mr. Mason has called me in to help settle your—ah—difficulties."

She twisted her skinny neck slowly. "I've heard all about you, What do you want me to do, kiss you? I suppose it was you who instigated John's arrest. You're fools, the pack of you!"

"To the contrary, it was your worthy Captain Murch's exclusive idea to take your brother in custody, Miss Shaw. He's not formally arrested, you know. Even so, I advised strongly against it."

She sniffed, but she uncoiled the knot and drew her shapeless legs beneath her wrapper in a sudden consciousness of femininity. "Then sit down, Mr. Queen. I'll help all I can."

"On the other hand," smiled Ellery, seating himself in a gilt and Gallic atrocity, "don't blame Murch overly, Miss Shaw. There's a powerful case against your brother, you know."

"And me!"

"And," said Ellery regretfully, "you."

She raised her thin arms and cried: "Oh, how I hate this

damned, damned house, that damned woman! She's the cause of all our trouble. Some day she's likely to get—"

"I suppose you're referring to Mrs. Royce. But aren't you being unfair? From Mason's story it's quite evident that there was no ghost of coercion when your stepmother willed your father's fortune to Mrs. Royce. They had never met, never corresponded, and your cousin was three thousand miles away. It's awkward for you, no doubt, but scarcely Mrs. Royce's fault."

"Fair! Who cares about fairness? She's taken our money away from us. And now we've got to stay here and—and be *fed* by her. It's intolerable, I tell you! She'll be here at least two years—trust her for that, the painted old hussy!—and all that time. . ."

"I'm afraid I don't understand. Two years?"

"That *woman's* will," snarled Miss Shaw, "provided that this precious cousin of ours come to live here and preside as mistress for a minimum of two years. That was her revenge, the despicable old witch! Whatever father saw in her . . . To 'provide a home for John and Agatha,' she said in the will, 'until they find a permanent solution of their problems.' How d'ye like that? I'll never forget those words. Our 'problems'! Oh, every time I think—" She bit her lip, eyeing him sidewise with a sudden caution.

Ellery sighed and went to the door. "Indeed? And if something should—er—drive, Mrs. Royce from the house before the expiration of the required period?"

"We'd get the money, of course," she flashed with bitter triumph; her thin dark skin was greenish. "If something should happen—"

"I trust," said Ellery dryly, "that nothing will." He closed the door and stood for a moment gnawing his fingers, and then he smiled rather grimly and went downstairs to a telephone.

John Shaw returned with his escort at ten that night. His chest was hollower, his fingers shakier, his eyes bloodier; and he was sober. Murch looked like a thundercloud. The cadaverous man went into the living-room and made for a full decanter. He drank alone, with steady mechanical determination. No one disturbed him.

"Nothing," growled Murch to Ellery and Mason.

At twelve the house was asleep.

The first alarm was sounded by Miss Krutch. It was almost one when she ran down the upper corridor screaming at the top of her voice: "Fire! Fire! Fire!" Thick smoke was curling about her slender ankles and the moonlight shining through the corridor-window behind her silhouetted her long plump trembling shanks through the thin nightgown.

The corridor erupted, boiled over. Doors crashed open, dishevelled heads protruded, questions were shrieked, dry throats choked over the bitter smoke. Mr. Phineas Mason, looking a thousand years old without his teeth, fled in a cotton nightshirt toward the staircase. Murch came pounding up the stairs, followed by a bleary, bewildered John Shaw. Scrawny Agatha in silk pajamas staggered down the hall with Peter, howling at the top of his lusty voice, in her arms. Two servants scuttled downstairs like frantic rats.

But Mr. Ellery Queen stood still outside the door of his room and looked quietly about, as if searching for some one.

"Murch," he said in a calm, penetrating voice. The detective ran up. "The fire!" he cried wildly. "Where the hell's the fire?"

"Have you seen Mrs. Royce?"

"Mrs. Royce? Hell, no!" He ran back up the hall, and Ellery

followed on his heels, thoughtfully. Murch tried the knob of a door; the door was locked. "God, she may be asleep, or overcome by—"

"Well, then," said Ellery through his teeth as he stepped back, "stop yowling and help me break this door down. We don't want her frying in her own lard, you know."

In the darkness, in the evil smoke, they hurled themselves at the door. . . . At the fourth assault it splintered off its hinges and Ellery sprang through. An electric torch in his hand flung its powerful beam about the room, wavered. . . . Something struck it from Ellery's hand, and it splintered on the floor. The next moment Ellery was fighting for his life.

His adversary was a brawny, panting demon with muscular fingers that sought his throat. He wriggled about, coolly, seeking an armhold. Behind him Murch was yelling: "Mrs. Royce! It's only us!"

Something sharp and cold flicked over Ellery's cheek and left a burning line. Ellery found a naked arm. He twisted, hard, and there was a clatter as steel fell to the floor. Then Murch came to his senses and jumped in. A county trooper blundered in, fumbling with his electric torch. . . . Ellery's fist drove in, hard, to a fat stomach. Fingers relaxed from his throat. The trooper found the electric switch. . . .

Mrs. Royce, trembling violently, lay on the floor beneath the two men. On a chair nearby lay, in a mountain of Victorian clothing, a very odd and solid-looking contraption that might have been a rubber *brassière*. And something was wrong with her hair; she seemed to have been partially scalped.

Ellery cursed softly and yanked. Her scalp came away in a piece, revealing a pink gray-fringed skull.

"She's a man!" screamed Murch.

"Thus," said Ellery grimly, holding Mrs. Royce's throat firmly with one hand and with the other dabbing at his bloody cheek, "vindicating the powers of thought."

"I still don't understand," complained Mason the next morning, as the chauffeur drove him and Ellery back to the city, "how you guessed, Queen."

Ellery raised his eyebrows. "Guessed? My dear Mason, that's considered an insult at the Queen Hearth. There was no guesswork whatever involved. Matter of pure reasoning. And a neat job, too," he added reflectively, touching the thin scar on his cheek.

"Come, come, Queen," smiled the lawyer, "I've never really believed McC.'s panegyrics on what he calls your uncanny ability to put two and two together; and though I'm not unintelligent and my legal training gives me a mental advantage over the layman and I've just been treated presumably to a demonstration of your—er—powers, I'll be blessed if I yet believe."

"A skeptic, eh?" said Ellery, wincing at the pain in his cheek. "Well, then, let's start where I started—with the beard Dr. Arlen painted on the face of Rembrandt's wife just before he was attacked. We've agreed that he deliberately painted in the beard to leave a clue to his murderer. What could he have meant? He was not pointing to a *specific* woman, using the beard just as an attention-getter; for the woman in the painting was the wife of Rembrandt, a historical figure and as far as our *personæ* went an utter unknown. Nor could Arlen have meant to point to a woman with a beard *literally;* for this would have meant a freak, and there were no freaks involved. Nor was he pointing to a bearded man, for there was *a man's face* on the painting which he left untouched; had he meant to point to a bearded man as his murderer that is, to John Shaw—he would have painted the beard on Rembrandt's beardless face. Besides, Shaw's is a vandyke, a pointed beard; and the beard Arlen painted was squarish in shape. . . . You see how exhaustive it is possible to be, Mason."

"Go on," said the lawyer intently.

"The only possible conclusion, then, all others having been eliminated, was that Arlen meant the beard *merely to indicate masculinity,* since facial hair is one of the few exclusively masculine characteristics left to our sex by dear, dear Woman. In other words, by painting a beard on a woman's face—any woman's face, mark—Dr. Arlen was virtually saying: 'My murderer is a person who seems to be a woman but is really a man.'"

"Well, I'll be damned!" gasped Mason.

"No doubt," nodded Ellery. "Now, 'a person who seems to be a woman but is really a man' suggests, surely, impersonation. The only actual stranger at the house was Mrs. Royce. Neither John nor Agatha could be impersonators, since they were both well-known to Dr. Arlen as well as to you; Arlen had examined them periodically, in fact, for years as the personal physician of the household. As for Miss Krutch, aside from her unquestionable femininity—a ravishing young woman, my dear Mason—she could not possibly have had motive to be an impersonator.

"Now, since Mrs. Royce seemed the likeliest possibility, I thought over the infinitesimal phenomena I had observed connected with her person—that is, appearance and movements. I was amazed to find a vast number of remarkable confirmations!"

"Confirmations?" echoed Mason, frowning.

"Ah, Mason, that's the trouble with skeptics: they're so easily confounded. Of course! Lips constitute a strong difference between the sexes: Mrs. Royce's were shaped meticulously into a perfect Cupid's-bow with lipstick. Suspicious in an old woman. The general overuse of cosmetics, particularly the heavy application of face powder: *very* suspicious, when you consider that overpowdering is not common among genteel old ladies and also that a man's skin, no matter how closely and frequently shaved, is undisguisably coarser.

"Clothes? Really potent confirmation. Why on earth that outlandish Victorian get-up? Here was presumably a woman who had been on the stage, presumably a woman of the world, a sophisticate. And yet she wore those horrible doodads of the '90s. Why? Obviously, to swathe and disguise a padded figure—impossible with woman's thin, scanty, and clinging modern garments. And the collar—ah, the collar! That was his inspiration. A choker, you'll recall, concealing the entire neck? But since a prominent Adam's-apple is an inescapable heritage of the male, a choker-collar becomes virtually a necessity in a female impersonation. Then the baritone voice, the vigorous movements, the mannish stride, the flat shoes. . . . The shoes were especially illuminating. Not only were they flat, but they showed signs of great bunions—and a man wearing woman's shoes, no matter how large, might well be expected to grow those painful excrescences."

"Even if I grant all that," objected Mason, "still they're generalities at best, might even be coincidences when you're arguing from a conclusion. Is that all?" He seemed disappointed.

"By no means," drawled Ellery. "These were, as you say, the generalities. But your cunning Mrs. Royce was addicted to three habits which are exclusively masculine, without argument. For one thing, when she sat down on my second sight of her she elevated her skirts at the knees with both hands; that is, one to each knee. Now that's precisely what a man does when he sits down: raises his trousers; to prevent, I suppose, their bagging at the knees."

"But—"

"Wait. Did you notice the way she screwed up her right eyebrow constantly, raising it far up and then drawing it far down? What could this have been motivated by except the lifelong use of a monocle? And a monocle is masculine. . . . And finally, her peculiar habit, in removing a cigarette from her lips, of cupping her hand about it rather than withdrawing it between the forefinger and middle finger, as most cigarette-smokers do. But the cupping gesture is precisely the result of *pipe-smoking*, for a man cups his hands about the bowl of a pipe in taking it out of his mouth. Man again. When I balanced these three specific factors on the same side of the scale as those generalities, I felt certain Mrs. Royce was a male.

"What male? Well that was simplest of all. You had told me, for one thing, that when you and your partner Collidge quizzed her she had shown a minute knowledge of Shaw history and specifically of Edith Shaw's history. On top of that, it took histrionic ability to carry off this female impersonation. Then there was the monocle deduction—England, surely? And the strong family resemblance. So I knew that 'Mrs. Royce,' being a Shaw undoubtedly, and an English Shaw to boot, was the other Shaw of the Morton side of the family—that is, Edith Shaw's brother Percy!"

"But she—he, I mean," cried Mason, "had told me Percy Shaw died a few months ago in Europe in an automobile accident!"

"Dear, dear," said Ellery sadly, "and a lawyer, too. She lied, that's all!—I mean 'he,' confound it. Your legal letter was addressed to Edith Shaw, and Percy received it, since they probably shared the same establishment. If he received it, it was rather obvious, wasn't it, that it was Edith Shaw who must have died shortly before; and that Percy had seized the opportunity to gain a fortune for himself by impersonating her?"

"But why," demanded Mason, puzzled, "did he kill Dr. Arlen? He had nothing to gain—Arlen's money was destined for Shaw's cousins, not for Percy Shaw. Do you mean there was some past connection—"

"Not at all," murmured Ellery. "Why look for past connections when the motive's slick and shiny at hand? If Mrs. Royce was a man, the motive was at once apparent. Under the terms of Mrs. Shaw's will Arlen was periodically to examine the family, with particular attention to Mrs. Royce. And Agatha Shaw told me yesterday that Mrs. Royce was constrained by will to remain in the house for two years. Obviously, then, the only way Percy Shaw could avert the cataclysm of being examined by Dr. Arlen and his disguise penetrated—for a doctor would have seen the truth instantly on examination, of course—was to kill Arlen. Simple, *nein?*"

"But the beard Arlen drew—that meant he *had* seen through it?"

"Not unaided. What probably happened was that the impostor, knowing the first physical examination impended, went to Dr. Arlen the other night to strike a bargain, revealing himself as a man. Arlen, an honest man, refused to be bribed. He must have been painting at the time and, thinking fast, unable to rouse the house because he was so far away from the others, unable to paint his assailant's name because 'Mrs. Royce' would see it and destroy it, thought of Peter's beard, made the lightning connection, and calmly painted it while 'Mrs. Royce' talked to him. Then he was stabbed."

"And the previous poisoning attempt on Mrs. Shaw?"

"That," said Ellery, "undoubtedly lies between John and Agatha."

Mason was silent, and for some time they rode in peace. Then the lawyer stirred, and sighed, and said: "Well, all things considered, I suppose you should thank Providence. Without concrete evidence—your reasoning was unsupported by legal evidence, you realize that, of course, Queen—you could scarcely have accused Mrs. Royce of being a man, could you? Had you been wrong, what a beautiful suit she could have brought against you! That fire last night was an act of God."

"I am," said Ellery calmly, "above all, my dear Mason, a man of free will. I appreciate acts of God when they occur, but I don't sit around waiting for them. Consequently. . ."

"You mean—" gasped Mason, opening his mouth wide.

"A telephone call, a hurried trip by Sergeant Velie, and smoke-bombs were the *materia* for breaking into Mrs. Royce's room in the dead of night," said Ellery comfortably. "By the way, you don't by any chance know the permanent address of—ah—Miss Krutch?"

The Adventure of
THE THREE LAME MEN

WHEN ELLERY QUEEN walked into the bedroom, with its low ash-gray bed and its tinted walls and angular furniture and chromium gewgaws, he found his father the Inspector yammering at a frightened colored girl whose face looked like liverwurst with two red-brown marbles stuck into it.

Sergeant Velie leaned his impossible shoulders against the delicate gray door and said: "Look out for that rug, Mr. Queen."

It was a pastel-gray rug, unbordered; all around it lay a gleaming frame of polished hardwood floor. The rug was tracked with muddy footprints and on the waxed hardwood between the rug and an open window across the room there was a straight scratchy bruise tapering from a wide scab to a thin vanishing line, like a furrow on ice.

He clucked and shook his head. "Shocking, Velie, really revolting. Tramping mud and snow all over this feminine fairyland!"

"Who, me? Listen, Mr. Queen, we found those prints here."

"Ah," said Ellery. "And the scratch?"

"That, too."

He shivered in his ulster; the room was chilly with a snowy cold that swept through the open window from the white night outside. A velvet-and-steel chair beside the bed was draped with the cobwebs of a woman's chemise and *brassière*.

The Inspector said peevishly: "'Lo, son. This is something in your line. Fancy. . . . All right, Thomas. Take her away, but keep her on ice."

Sergeant Velie steered the Negress clear of the evidence on the rug and pushed her past the gray door into the living-room, which was filled with smoke and laughing men. Then he closed the door.

Ellery sat down on the furry zibeline bedspread and pulled out a cigarette, and the Inspector sneezed three times over his snuff. "Queer set-up," he said thoughtfully, wiping his nose. "The legmen outside'll tell it in headlines. Park Avenue love-nest, beautiful ex-chorine—they're always beautiful—prominent clubman, a snatch. . . . The old bellywash, made to order for the tabs. And yet—"

"You know," said Ellery plaintively, "sometimes I think you give me credit for a sort of psychomancy. What is this, a *séance?* Murder, you say? Who was murdered? Who's been snatched? Whose love-nest? What's it all about? All I know is that some one from Headquarters 'phoned me a few minutes ago to hurry down here."

"I left word for you with the Lieutenant at the desk." The Inspector skirted the rug and pattered across the glistening floor. He slithered and teetered, and regained his balance. "Damn these slippery floors! . . . Have a look for yourself." He flung open the door of a wall-closet.

Something quiet was sitting on the floor of the closet, head hidden by hanging garments, slim long naked legs drawn up, tied at the ankles with a pair of silk stockings.

Ellery stared down with sharp impersonal eyes. It was a dead woman sitting there so quietly, on the floor of the closet, dressed in a shimmering kimono and stark naked underneath. He stooped and held aside the concealing garments. Her head hung on her breast and ash-blonde hair was tumbled over her face. Beneath the hair he saw a cloth which covered her mouth, nose, and eyes tightly. Her hands were out of sight behind her.

He straightened, raising his eyebrows.

"Smothered by the gag," said the Inspector in a matter-of-fact voice. "Looks as if whoever pulled this snatch tied her up and gagged her to get her out of the way."

"Forgetting," murmured Ellery, craning about, "that in order to continue living in this sorry world one must breathe. Quite so. . . . Her name?"

"Lily Divine," said Inspector Queen grimly.

"No! The Divine Lily?" His gray eyes glittered. "I thought she was out of circulation."

"She was. Left Jaffee's *Scandals* a few years ago, or was kicked out—I never did get it straight. Some man involved—they were hitched. It lasted three months. Then he divorced her. Since then she's been the belle of Park Avenue—traveled up and down the big street till there isn't a doorman or elevator-boy who doesn't know her. *Or* a renting agent."

"God's gift to the realtors. *Demi-mondaine,* eh?"

"That's one name for it."

Ellery's eyes for the third time strayed to the open window, one of three in the bedroom; the other two were shut. It was the only window in the room which gave on a fire-escape. "And who's the wealthy incumbent?"

"Come again?"

"Who's been paying for *this* playground?"

"Oh! Now that's interesting." The old gentleman kicked the closet-door shut and went to the fire-escape window. "Guess."

"Come, come, dad! I'm the world's poorest guesser."

"Joseph E. Sherman!"

"Ah. The banking chap?"

"That's the one." The Inspector sighed and continued with some bitterness: "That's the hell of having money. You begin to crave expensive toys. Who'd have thought it of the great J. E. ? Straitlaced as they come, got a nice wife and a grown daughter, everything in the world money can buy; goes to church regularly—and means it. . . . " He stared out the window onto the snow-covered fire-escape. The snow was silver in the moonlight. "And here he is in this mess."

Sergeant Velie's back heaved and he whirled in some surprise. A chatter of men's pleading voices burst into the bedroom. A woman was backing in, saying: "No. Please, I—I can't say anything, really. I don't know—"

Velie leaped, thrust her aside, growled: "Lay off, you eggs," and slammed the door in the newspapermen's faces.

The woman faced about and said: "Hello?" in a surprised voice.

She was very young, no more than eighteen; but there was maturity in her full figure and something tired and wise in her pretty little face. She wore a mink coat and a mink toque.

"And who might you be?" asked the Inspector softly, coming forward.

Her lashes swept down and up. The surprise showed on her

face. She was looking for some one, something. Then she said rapidly: "I'm Rosanne Sherman. Where's my father, please?"

The Inspector grimaced. "This isn't the place for you, Miss Sherman. There's a dead woman in the closet—"

"Oh. So that's where—" She caught her breath a little, her liquid eyes pouncing upon the closet-door. "But where's my father?"

"Sit down, please," said Ellery. The girl obeyed quickly.

"He's gone, Miss Sherman," said the Inspector in a soothing voice. "I'm afraid we've bad news for you and your mother. Kidnaped—"

"Kidnaped!" She looked about in a sick daze. "Kidnaped? But this—this apartment, this woman. . ."

"You'll have to know," said Ellery. "Or perhaps you know already?"

She said with difficulty: "He's been living with her."

"Your mother knew?" snapped the Inspector.

"I—I don't know."

"How do *you* know?"

"You just know those—those things," she said dully.

There was a breath of silence. The Inspector looked at her with veiled keenness and went back to the window. "Your mother's coming?"

"Yes. I—I couldn't wait. She's coming with Bill—I mean with Mr. Kittering, father's . . . one of the vice-presidents at the bank."

There was another silence. Ellery ground his cigarette out in a writhing ashtray and, apologetically, went to the rug and stooped for a sharp look. Without raising his eyes he said: "What's the story, dad? Miss Sherman may as well know. Perhaps she can be of assistance."

"Yes, yes," she said eagerly. "Perhaps I can."

The Inspector rocked on his heels, eyeing the dim ceiling.

"About two hours ago—around 7:30—Sherman came into the lobby downstairs. Doorman saw him. Seemed as usual. Elevator-boy took him up here to the sixth floor, saw him—" he hesitated—"fish out his key and open the front door to this apartment. That's the last of him. Nobody else came; at least not through the front way."

"There's another entrance into the building?"

"More'n one. Tradesmen's entrance in the basement, from the rear. Also the emergency stairway. *And* the fire-escape here." He thumbed the window behind him. "Anyway, about a half-hour ago this colored girl I was talking to when you came in—she's the Divine woman's maid—came back and. . ."

They ignored the girl. She sat very still, listening. From time to time her eyes went to the closet-door. Ellery frowned. "Came back from where?"

"Lily had given her a couple of hours off. Always did, the shine said, when she expected—uh—Sherman. Anyway, she came back. Front door was locked. She used her key but couldn't get in. It had not only been locked but bolted from the inside with one of those bolt-and-chain thinga-majigs. She called out but couldn't get any answer. So she called the super—"

"I know, I know," said Ellery impatiently. "Dilly-dallied, and finally they broke the door down. I saw it when I came in. They found the Divine woman in the closet?"

"Hold your horses, will you? Didn't find any such thing—*they* didn't. They forced the bedroom door—"

"Oh," said Ellery in a strange voice. "This door was locked, too?"

"Yes. They looked in. Room seemed kind of upset. And they saw these muddy tracks on the rug." Rosanne Sherman looked at the rug. Then she closed her eyes and leaned back, her pale lips quivering. "The super's a smart Swede and called a cop without touching anything. The cop found the body and here we are. . . . The note was pinned on the bed."

"Note?"

"Note?" murmured Miss Sherman, opening her eyes.

Ellery took a sheet of dainty paper from the Inspector's fingers. He read aloud: "J. E. Sherman is in our hands and will be released on payment of fifty grand according to instructions to come. Police, lay off. You will find the woman, unharmed, in the closet." The message had been scrawled in block letters and was unsigned.

"They used her own paper and pencil," grunted the Inspector. "Nice refined note."

"Restrained. There's a sort of grim elegance about it," murmured Ellery. He returned the note and again his eyes lingered upon the window overlooking the fire-escape. "Unharmed, eh?"

The girl said quietly: "There was a note before this, too. About a week ago. I found father reading it one night. He tried to hide it but I—I made him let me see it. A threatening note. Demanded twenty-five thousand dollars at once for 'protection.' It said if he didn't pay it they would—would. . ."

"Kill him?"

"Kidnap him. And ask for fifty." Then all at once her reserve vanished and she sprang from the chair; eyes blazing. "Why don't you *do* something?" she cried. "They may be torturing him, murdering him. . . ." She sank back, sobbing.

"Now, now," said the Inspector. "Keep cool, Miss Sherman. You've got your mother to think of."

"It will kill mother," she sobbed. "You should have seen her face—"

"Miss Sherman," murmured Ellery, "where is this first note?"

She raised her head. "He burned it. He said not to tell mother. He said it was from some crank, and didn't mean anything. He laughed it off."

Ellery shook his head dolefully and looked at the open window again. "If the bedroom door—" he mumbled. He stopped and went to the door. Sergeant Velie silently stepped aside. The door had no keyhole. On the bedroom side there was a knob which, on being turned, operated a hidden bolt which locked the door. He nodded absently. "Bolted from the bedroom side. Hmm. . . . So they got out through the window."

"That's right."

It was a small window, the lower pane raised as far as it would go. On the sill perched a window-box filled with churned, loose earth and the desiccated stalks of dead geraniums. The box covered the entire sill and was a foot high, leaving little more than two feet of open space above it. And it was immovable, built into the sill of the narrow window. Ellery blinked and leaned out, scrutinizing the iron-slatted floor of the fire-escape. Its snow-covered surface was pitted with clean crisp footprints, and only footprints; elsewhere the snow was virgin smooth. Mingled footprints, he saw, pattered downward and upward on the iron steps leading toward the alley below. He glanced down; as far as he could see the steps bore the same crisp prints. Beneath the ledge outside, coming to the edge of the sill, the snow had piled up in a drift, which was undisturbed.

"Now," said the Inspector imperturbably, "take another look at the rug."

Ellery drew back his tingling head. He knew very well what story the rug told. Three different pairs of men's shoes had desecrated the rich grayness of the rug with wet muddy prints. All three pairs were of large shoes, but the first had acutely pointed tips, the second blunter tips, and the third square bulldog tips. The prints pointed in all directions, and the rug was scuffed and wrinkled, as if there had been a struggle.

Ellery's thin nostrils began to oscillate. "You mean," he said slowly, "that there's something peculiar about these footprints, of course."

"Smart lad," chuckled the Inspector. "That's why I said there was something fancy about this case. The experts have been looking at these prints and the ones outside. What's your diagnosis?"

"The right shoes show lighter impressions uniformly," muttered Ellery, "especially the right heels. In most cases the right heelprints don't show at all."

"Right. *All three of the birds who pulled this job were lame.*"

Ellery puffed at another cigarette. "Nonsense."

"Hey?"

"I don't believe it. It's—it's impossible."

"And that from you," grinned the old gentleman. "Not only lame, but all three of 'em lame on the right foot."

"Impossible, I tell you!" snapped Ellery.

The girl gaped. The Inspector raised his bushy brows. "The best print men in the Department say it's not only not impossible, but it happened."

"I don't care what they say. Three limping men." Ellery scowled. "I—"

Sergeant Velie opened the door swiftly. There was a commotion outside. Thick cigarette smoke drifted into the bedroom out of a bedlam of shouting voices. A small woman and a tall athletic man were struggling in the center of a group of reporters, like honeypots attacked by flies. The Sergeant scattered the men with a rush, roaring at the top of his voice.

"Come in, come in," said the Inspector gently, closing the

door. The woman looked at the girl, who had risen; then they fell into each other's arms, crying as if their hearts were breaking.

"Hello, Kittering," said Ellery awkwardly.

The tall man, lines of worry incised in his hard cheeks, muttered: "Hullo, Queen. Rough, eh? Poor old J. E. And this damned woman—"

"You know each other?" said the Inspector with glittering eyes.

"We've met at a club or two," drawled Ellery.

Kittering was still a young man, still well-conditioned. Bachelor, wealthy man-about-town, he was a familiar New York figure. His photograph was constantly turning up in rotogravure sections; he was a polo player, he bred pedigreed dogs, he owned a racing yawl. He paced up and down with the restless vitality of a caged animal, avoiding the sobbing women.

All at once the room was full of voices—the Inspector's, Rosanne's, Mrs. Sherman's. Ellery, at the open window, heard them through a haze of thought, while the Inspector in a sympathetic voice explained the situation. Kittering continued to patrol the polished floor; his feet were sure as a cat's.

Mrs. Sherman sank into the velvet-and-steel chair. Tears streaked her soft face, but she was no longer crying. She was perhaps forty, although she seemed younger. There was something gracious, even queenly, in her manner; a dignity and tempered beauty not even pain could destroy. "I've known about Joe's affair with this woman," she said in a low voice, "for some time." She pressed her daughter's hand. "Yes, Ro, I have. I—I never said anything. Bill—" she glanced at the tall man. "Bill knew, too. Didn't you, Bill?" A spasm of pain crossed her face.

Kittering looked uncomfortable. "Well, I suppose so," he said in a savage tone. "But Joe didn't mean anything by it, Enid. You know that—"

"No," said Mrs. Sherman gravely, "he never did. He's been good to me, to Rosanne, to all of us. It's just that he—he's weak."

"There have been others, Mrs. Sherman?" asked the Inspector.

"Yes. . . . I always knew. A woman can tell. Once—" her gloved hands clenched—"once he knew I knew. He was ashamed of himself, prostrate, h-humble." She paused. "He promised it would never happen again. But it did. I knew it would. He just couldn't help himself. But he always came back to me, you see. He always loved just me, you see." She spoke as if she were trying to explain things, not to them, but to herself.

The girl shook her head angrily; she took one of her mother's hands. Kittering said in a low voice: "Now, Enid. Now. It—Well, it doesn't help. It's all beside the point, anyway." He leveled his cool eyes at the Inspector. "How about the kidnaping, Inspector? That's the vital thing. Do you think they mean business?"

"What do you think?" said the Inspector grimly.

Mrs. Sherman rose suddenly. "Oh, Bill, we *must* get Joe back!" she cried. "Pay what they ask. Anything—"

The Inspector shrugged. "You'll have to talk to the Commissioner, Mrs. Sherman. I personally can't—"

"Nonsense, man. You can't put any bars in our way," snarled Kittering. "These men are criminals. They won't stop at anything. Joe's life means more—"

"Now, now," said Ellery mildly, coming forward. "This discussion is getting us precisely nowhere. Kittering, what's the state of Mr. Sherman's finances?"

"Finances?" Kittering glared. "Sound as a dollar."

"No troubles of any kind?"

"No. See here, Queen, what are you hinting at?" The man's eyes flamed.

"*Tch, tch,*" said Ellery. "Keep your shirt on, old fellow. You say you knew about Mr. Sherman's relationship with Lily Divine. Did he know you knew?"

Kittering's eyes fell. "Yes," he muttered. "I told him he was playing with fire. I knew no good would come of it, that he'd get into some sort of scrape over her. She had underworld connections at one time—" He stopped, jaw dropping. "By George!" he bellowed. "Queen! Inspector! That's it!"

"What's it?" said the Inspector. For some reason he seemed amused.

"Bill! What's struck you?" cried Rosanne, springing to his side.

"Just came over me, Ro," said Kittering swiftly. He paced up and down. "Yes, that must be it. Underworld—of course. Inspector, d'ye know who used to be that woman's lover?"

"Certainly," smiled the Inspector. "Mac McKee."

"The gangster!" whispered Mrs. Sherman, horror in her eyes.

"Then you knew." Kittering flushed. "Well, why don't you do something? Don't you see? McKee must have engineered this job!"

"Dad," said Ellery coldly. "Why didn't you tell me? McKee got a finger in this pie?"

"Didn't get the chance. I've got the boys out rounding him up now." The old man shook his head. "I'm not promising anything, Mrs. Sherman. He may be perfectly innocent. Or if he's guilty he'll have a good alibi. He's a slick article. We'll have to feel our way. Now why don't you good people go home and leave these things to us?" He continued quickly: "Kittering, take the ladies home. We'll keep you informed from this end. There's time, you know. We still have to hear from them about how to send the ransom-money. It isn't as bad as it might be. I—"

"I think we'll stay here," said Mrs. Sherman quietly.

"Enid—" said Kittering.

The door banged against Velie's back and two uniformed men came in with a covered basket. The women paled and crept into a corner. Kittering went with them, pleading. They all kept their eyes averted from the closet.

"How about this man McKee?" said Ellery in a low voice to his father, as the Morgue men tugged at something in the closet. "How hot is that angle?"

"Hot enough, son. I've known all along, of course, about the fact that Lily'd lived with Mac a couple of years ago. But tonight when I questioned the telephone operator on duty downstairs before you came I found out something."

"He called her this evening?" said Ellery sharply.

"She called him. A little before eight. Asked the operator to get her a number—a number which we know leads to McKee's mob headquarters. The 'phone girl's nosy and she listened in. Heard Lily speak to a man she called 'Mac,' asked him to come to her apartment here on the double-quick. Seemed upset about something, the operator says."

"Did McKee come?"

"Doorman says no. But then there are those other entrances."

Ellery's brow wriggled. "Yes, yes, but if Lily Divine called him at eight, how could he have—"

The Inspector chuckled. "I've got my own ideas about that."

The Morgue men dumped something in the basket that landed with a thud. Mrs. Sherman looked faint, and Kittering was supporting her, speaking in a low urgent voice. Ellery flashed a glance at them and whispered: "Those prints in the snow on the fire-escape and iron steps; are they of the same shoes that made the prints on the rug here?"

"What's eating you?" demanded the Inspector. "Sure."

"Did Sherman keep clothes here?"

"My dear son," said the Inspector plaintively, "do I have to tell you the facts of life all over again? Of course he did!"

"Shoes?"

"We've checked all that. All his shoes are here, and they're all the same size, and none of 'em matches any of the prints on the rug or in the snow. That's how we know three men pulled this job. None of these prints belonged to Sherman; his shoes were dry."

"How do you know?"

"We found his wet rubbers in the foyer."

"Does Sherman limp?"

The Inspector said reproachfully: "Now how the hell should I know?" The Morgue men stooped, grasped the handles attached to the basket fore and aft, and stolidly trudged from the room. "Mrs. Sherman, does your husband limp?"

The woman, in a tremble, sat down again. "Limp? No."

"He's never limped?"

"No."

"Any one of your or his acquaintance limp?"

"Of course not!" growled Kittering. "What sort of hocus-pocus are you up to this time? How about getting after this cowardly thug McKee?"

"I think you'd better go now," said the Inspector evenly. "All of you. This has gone far enough."

"Just a moment," said Ellery. "I must get these facts straight. Do the prints on the fire-escape show the characteristic lameness, too?"

"Sure. Say, what are you driving at?"

"I'm sure I don't know," said Ellery irritably. "I'm just annoyed. Three lame men . . . Mrs. Sherman, isn't your husband rather a big man?"

"Big?" She seemed dazed. "Very. Six feet three. He weighs two-fifty."

Ellery nodded with a sort of restless satisfaction. He whispered to his father: "Aren't any of Sherman's prints in the snow?"

"No. He must have been carried. Probably knocked on the head."

"The scratch," said a deep voice over the Inspector's shoulder.

"Oh, it's you, Thomas. What d'ye mean, the scratch?"

"Well, sir," rumbled Sergeant Velie, eyes agleam with the vastness of his inspiration, "he was dragged, see? Scratch there on the waxed floor goes from the rug to the window. So he was dragged to the window, then they h'isted him and slung him through and carried him down. That's an areaway down there. Must 'a' got up that way, too. Surprised these two tootsies billin' and cooin', tied up the frail and gagged her, socked Sherman on the head, dragged him to—"

"Heard you the first time," growled the Inspector. "That scratch has been pretty well fixed. Made by a shoe-heel, the boys say. Well, what are we wasting time for? Oh, yes, there's one thing more."

Kittering broke in stiffly: "Inspector. We're going. We rely upon you to—"

"Yes, yes," snapped Ellery. "Hold on a moment like a good chap, Kittering. What's that you were saying, dad? I have a notion—"

A hoarse yell hurled them at the bedroom door. Velie tore it open. In the living-room filled with men two detectives were grappling with a huge man in a camel's-hair overcoat. Smoky lights flashed all over the room as cameras clicked and photographers, delirious over their good fortune, worked madly. Two other men, snarling but cautious, were pinned against the wall by other detectives.

"What's this?" said the Inspector pleasantly from the doorway. The noise ceased and the huge man stopped fighting. Sanity flooded back into his eyes. "McKee!" drawled the old gentleman. "Well, well. This isn't like you, Mac. Fighting! I'm ashamed of you. All right, boys. Let go. He'll be good now."

The man twitched his immense shoulders viciously and the detectives fell back, panting. "This a plant?" he growled.

"We'll go now," said Rosanne in a small voice.

"Not yet, my dear," smiled the Inspector, without turning. "Come in, Mac. Thomas, close that door. You men there," he barked, "keep McKee's boy-friends company."

They all returned to the bedroom. The big man was watchful. He had heavy batrachian lids, and his mouth was loose and fat. But his jaw was vast, and there was cunning in his eyes. The Sherman women shrank back against Kittering, who was pale. For a moment naked animal cruelty had glittered in the gunman's eyes. But he was uneasy, too.

"Know what you were picked up for, Mac?" said the Inspector, stepping close to the giant and staring up into the cruel eyes.

"You're off your nut, Inspector," rumbled McKee. Then his eyes swept over the Shermans, Kittering, Ellery, the rug, the open window, the open door of the closet. "I wasn't picked up. I came here myself and those flatfeet of yours just ganged me."

"Oh, I see," said the old man softly. "Just walked in for a friendly call, hey? To see Lily?"

Velie hovered expectantly behind the man; they were of a

height and breadth. But McKee was very quiet. "Suppose I was? What of it? Where is she? What's happened here?"

"Don't you know?"

"What the hell! Would I ask you if I knew?"

"Good boy," chuckled the Inspector. "Still the slickest hood in the big time. Ever see these people before, Mac?"

McKee's eyes flickered over Kittering and the two women. "No."

"Know who they are?"

"Ain't had the pleasure."

"That's Mrs. Sherman, and her daughter, and Mr. Kittering, a business associate of Joseph E. Sherman's."

"So what?"

"So what, he asks," murmured the Inspector. "Listen, you lunk!" he snarled suddenly, glaring up. "Lily's been given the works, and J. E. Sherman's been snatched. That mean anything to you?"

A faint pallor crept under the top skin of the big man's swarthy face. His tongue wet his lips, once. "Lily got it?" he muttered. "Here?" He looked around, as if for her body.

"Yes, here. Smothered to death. I admit it's not your usual technique, Mac; a little refined for you. But the snatch is right up your alley—"

The big man drew himself in, like a Galápagos turtle. His shoulders hunched in ridges of fat and muscle, and his eyes almost vanished. "If you think I had anything to do with this job, Inspector, you're nuts. Why, my alibi—"

"You dirty killer," said Kittering dully. McKee whirled, snatching at something beneath his coat under the armpit. Then he caught himself and relaxed. "Where's Joe Sherman?" Kittering sprang and, so suddenly that neither Sergeant Velie nor

Ellery could intervene, lashed out at McKee's jaw. It was a solid smack, like wet meat slapping a sidewalk; and McKee staggered, blinking. But he made no move to retaliate. Only his eyes burned; burned at Kittering like a fuse. Rosanne and Enid Sherman grasped Kittering's arms, crying. Ellery swore beneath his breath, and Sergeant Velie stepped between the two men.

"That'll be just about enough," said Inspector Queen curtly, "Off with you, Kittering. You, too, Mrs. Sherman; and the girl." And in an almost inaudible voice he said to Kittering: "That sock was a mistake, young man. Beat it!"

Kittering dropped his arms, sighing. The two women led him, speechless, from the bedroom. They were swallowed up in the deluge of clamoring men outside.

McKee's arms quivered and his eyes burned at the gray door. He said something very softly to himself, his lips barely moving.

"Lily 'phoned you tonight, didn't she?" rapped the Inspector. The gunman licked his lips cautiously. "Oh. Yeah. That's right." "Why? What'd she want?"

"I don't know."

"She asked you to come over?"

"Yeah."

"You once lived with Lily, didn't you?"

"You tell me. You know all the answers."

"She 'phoned you at eight tonight?"

"Yeah."

The Inspector said craftily: "And here it is about ten. Take you two hours to come down from the Bronx?"

"Somethin' held me up."

"You knew Sherman?"

"Heard of him."

"Did you know Lily was living with him?"

McKee shrugged. "Oh, hell, Inspector, you've got nothin' on me. Sure I knew, but what of it? I was washed up with that broad years ago. When she 'phoned tonight I thought she might 'a' been in some kind of trouble, so for old times' sake I thought I'd ankle down here and see what was up. That's all."

"I think," said Ellery mildly, "that you had better take your shoes off, McKee."

The gunman gaped. "*What?*"

"Off with your shoes," said Ellery in a patient voice. "In another age it would have been a different part of your anatomy. Velie, please get the shoes of the two—er—gentlemen who accompanied Mr. McKee."

Velie went out. McKee, like a blind bull, looked at the rug, and the muddy tracks, and then he cursed and snatched a guilty glance at his own gargantuan feet. Without a word he sat down in the velvet-and-steel chair and unlaced his oxfords, which were streaked with damp mud.

"That's a good idea, El," said the Inspector approvingly, stepping back.

Velie returned bearing two pairs of wet shoes to the accompaniment of a burst of derisive laughter from the men in the living-room. Ellery went to work in silence. After a time he looked up, handed the big shoes back to McKee and the others to Velie, who left the room again.

"No dice, hey?" sneered McKee, lacing up his shoes. "I told you you birds were cockeyed."

"Does either of the two men outside limp, Velie?" asked Ellery when the Sergeant returned.

"No, sir."

Ellery stepped back, tapping a cigarette on his thumbnail; and

McKee, with an ugly laugh, rose to go. "Just a second, Mac," said the Inspector. "I'm holding you."

"You're *what?*"

"Holding you on suspicion," said the old man evenly. "You and Lily Divine were working a game of Sherman. You put the woman up to playing Sherman on his weak side, getting him under her thumb." McKee glared, his face livid. "Tonight you came over, with the trap set; double-crossed Lily, putting her away to shut her up; left the note and beat it with Sherman. What d'ye say to that?"

"I say to hell with it! How about the tracks on the rug there? You saw yourself they didn't fit!"

"Clever," said the Inspector. "You wore different shoes."

"Nuts. How about Lily's call to me at eight? I heard somebody outside say she kicked off around that time. If she called me up—"

"That was smart, too. You were here all the time. You made her put in that call while you stood over her, just to establish an alibi."

McKee grinned. "Go ahead and prove it," he said shortly. He turned on his heel and walked out. Velie followed him.

"And how about the limping tracks?" murmured Ellery, when the door was shut. "Eh, gentle sire? Did he and his minions fake the limp, too?"

"Why not?" The Inspector tugged his mustache irritably.

"An unanswerable question, I admit." Ellery shrugged. "Look here. You were going to tell me before that there was something else. What?"

"Oh, that! Something's missing from this room."

Ellery glared. "Missing? Why in thunder didn't you say so before?"

"But—"

"Too much," muttered Ellery feverishly. "That would be too much. Don't tell me it was a valise? A suitcase? Something of the sort?"

The Inspector looked faintly astonished. "For the lord's sake, El! How did you guess? The colored wench says an alligator handbag, empty, belonging to the Divine woman, is gone. She saw it in the closet only an hour before Lily sent her out. There's nothing else missing."

"Sweet, sweet. Tra, la! We're going somewhere. The colored lady . . . Ah, Velie, there you are. Be a good chap and haul her in here, will you?"

Velie brought the Negress in. She looked sick. Ellery pounced upon her. "When was this floor waxed last?"

"Huh?" Her eyes grew enormous, and the Inspector started. "W-why, jest t'day."

"When today?"

"'Safternoon, suh. I did it myse'f."

"Good enough, I suppose," he muttered impatiently. "All right, all right. That's all, young woman. Take her away, Sergeant."

"But, El—" protested the Inspector.

"Very pretty," Ellery continued to mutter, "very pretty indeed. But, damn it all, there's a piece missing. Without it. . ." He bit his lip.

"Say, listen," said the Inspector slowly, "what have you got, son?"

"Everything—and nothing."

"Bah! How about Sherman?"

"Follow Mrs. Sherman's wishes in the matter. Sherman's safety is the prime consideration. After that—we'll see."

"All right," said the Inspector with drooping resignation. "But I can't understand—"

"Three lame men," sighed Ellery. "Very interesting. *Very* interesting."

Joseph E. Sherman sat in an armchair in Inspector Richard Queen's office in Centre Street and told his story in a cracked voice. A police radio car had picked him up—dirty, disheveled, dazed—in Pelham an hour before. For a time he was incoherent, kept asking brokenly for his wife and daughter. He seemed half-starved, and his eyes were red and staring, as if for days he had gone without sleep. It was three days after the discovery of Lily Divine's body and the kidnapers' note. The police had not interfered. A third note had come in the post to Mrs. Sherman the day after the murder—an untraceable note in the same disguised block capitals, reiterating the demand for $50,000 and assigning a clever rendezvous for the delivery of the ransom. Kittering had raised the cash and acted as intermediary. The money had been paid the day before. And today here was Sherman, his immense bulk shaking with nerves and fatigue.

"What happened, Mr. Sherman? Who were they? Tell us the whole story," the Inspector urged gently. The man had been fortified with food and whisky, but he continued to shiver as if he had a chill.

"My wife—" he mumbled.

"Yes, yes, Mr. Sherman. She's all right. We've sent for her."

Sergeant Velie opened the door. Sherman tottered to his feet, cried out vaguely, and fell into his wife's arms. Rosanne wept and clung to his hand. Kittering was with them; he retreated to the background, stonily watching. No one said anything.

"That woman—" Sherman muttered at last.

Enid Sherman put her fingers on his lips. "Not another word, Joe. I—I understand. Thank God you're back." She turned on the

Inspector, eyes brimming with tears. "Can't we take my husband home now, Inspector? He's so—so. . ."

"We must know what happened, Mrs. Sherman."

The banker glanced nervously at Kittering. "Bill, old man. . ." He sank back into the armchair, clutching his wife's hand. His tremendous body filled the chair. "I'll tell you what I know, Inspector," he said in a low voice. "I'm tired. I don't know much." A police stenographer was scribbling beside the desk. Ellery stood by the window, frowning and gnawing his lips. "I—went to—her apartment that night. As usual. She was acting funny—"

"Yes," said the Inspector encouragingly. "By the way, did you know she was an old flame of Mac McKee's, the gangster?"

"Not at first." Sherman's shoulders sagged. "When I found out, I was already hopelessly— embroiled. I would never have ventured into. . ." Mrs. Sherman pressed his hand, and he gave her a slow queer grateful look. "While we were—together," he went on very softly, "the front doorbell rang. She went out to answer it. I waited. Perhaps I was a little afraid—of being—well, caught. Then . . . I don't know what happened. A hand clamped over my eyes—"

"Man's or woman's?" snapped Ellery.

His bloodshot eyes shifted. "I—I don't know. Then a rag of some kind was jammed against my nose—it smelled sweet, sickening. I struggled, but it did no good. That's all I know. Everything went blank. I must have been chloroformed."

"Chloroformed!" They all turned, startled, upon Ellery. He was staring at Sherman with a wild light in his eyes. "Mr. Sherman," he said slowly, coming forward, "do you mean to say you were *hors de combat* through the rest of it? Unconscious?"

"Yes," said Sherman, blinking.

Ellery straightened. "Indeed," he said in a strange voice. "The missing piece at last." And he went back to the window to stare out.

"The missing piece?" faltered the banker.

"Let's get this over with," said Kittering harshly. "Joe's in no condition—"

Sherman passed a trembling hand over his mouth. "When I woke up I was sick. My eyes were bound. I was tied up. I didn't know where I was. No one came near me. Once, though, some one fed me. Then—God knows how much later—I was carried out somewhere and later I knew I was in a car. They pushed me out on a road somewhere. When I came to I realized I had been untied. I took the rag from my eyes. . . . You know the rest."

There was a silence. The Inspector clicked his teeth together and said pettishly: "Do you mean to say, then, you can't identify any of your kidnapers, Mr. Sherman? How about their voices? Anything, man, to give us a lead!"

The banker's shoulders sagged lower. "Nothing," he muttered. "Can't I go now?"

"Hold on," said Ellery. "There's no other information you can give us?"

"Eh? No."

Ellery scowled. "There's nothing about this you're concealing, Mr. Sherman? You'd rather drop the whole matter, I take it?"

"Nothing. . . . Yes, drop it," mumbled Sherman. "Drop it entirely."

"I'm afraid," murmured Ellery, "that that's impossible. Because, you see, Mr. Sherman, I know who kidnaped you and murdered Lily Divine."

"You *know?*" whispered Rosanne. The banker sat like stone, and Kittering took a short step forward and stopped.

"Knowledge is a tricky thing," said Ellery, "but within human limitations—I know." He thrust a cigarette into his mouth and his eyebrows twitched. Sergeant Velie, at the door, took his hands out of his pockets and looked about expectantly. "A very odd affair, you see. This won't take long, and it may prove—interesting."

"But, Ellery—" frowned the Inspector.

"Please, dad. Consider that gash on the waxed floor. Your experts maintained that it was made by the heel of a shoe. The good Sergeant here pointed out that since it was made by a shoe-heel, then clearly it denoted Mr. Sherman's being dragged toward the window by his assailants."

"Well, what of it?" said the Inspector sharply. The Shermans sat dumb and fascinated; and Kittering did not stir.

Ellery drawled: "Everything of it. It occurred to me then and there that our good Sergeant had been in error." Velie's face fell. "If a body is being dragged, with sufficient force to cause shoe-marks on a freshly waxed floor, then there should be *two* scratches, you see; because even a child knows that the usual complement of feet in bipeds is two, not one. So I said to myself: 'Whatever this mark on the floor means, it was certainly not caused by dragging.'"

"What then?" growled the old gentleman.

"Well," smiled Ellery, "if the mark was made by a shoe-heel, and yet not by the shoe-heel of a man being dragged, then the only sensible alternative is that *some one slipped on the floor*, you see. You yourself, dad, slipped and almost fell the other night. Have we any confirmation?"

"What's this, a lesson in logic?" said Kittering gruffly. "You take an odd time, Queen, to go oratorical."

"Quiet, Kittering," said the Inspector. "Confirmation?"

"The three lame men," said Ellery gently.

"The three lame men!"

"Precisely. We had definite evidences of lameness, of limping, in the footprints. Considerably bolstering the slip-on-the-floor, theory. The person who slipped either sprained an ankle or suffered some leg injury, not necessarily serious but painful enough to cause a temporary lameness. You see that?"

"I'm going home," said Rosanne suddenly. Her cheeks were scarlet.

Ellery said quickly: "Sit down, Miss Sherman. Now we have three sets of limping prints, all of different pairs of shoes. That this fact was utterly incredible, dad, I tried to point out to you. Did three men, or even two, slip and fall and go lame in that bedroom? Ridiculous. For one thing, there was only one scratch on the floor; for another, the exact triplication of a phenomenon—three limping right feet—shows falsity, not truth."

"You mean," said Mrs. Sherman with a puzzled frown, "that there weren't three men who kidnaped my husband, Mr. Queen?"

"Exactly," drawled Ellery. "I say that the argument shows that one man, the one who slipped on the floor, was responsible for all three different sets of limping footprints. How? Obviously, by using three different pairs of shoes."

"But what happened to the shoes, El?"

"They weren't found. So the limper must have taken them away with him. Any corroboration? Yes; *one of Lily Divine's bags was missing.*" Ellery's gray eyes hardened. "The crux of the matter is, of course, the answer to the question: Why did the limper go to the trouble of falsifying the trail, of planting three sets of apparently different footprints? The answer again must be apparent: to make the kidnaping look like the work of more than one person—specifically, of three. This suggests a gang, surely?

Inversely, then, the limper is probably not a gangster at all. But aside from that we have now reached the point where we may say that our limper, a lone wolf, was the murderer of Lily Divine and the kidnaper of Mr. Sherman!"

No one said anything. Sergeant Velie's hands opened and closed tentatively.

Ellery sighed. "The window and the fire-escape tell most of the rest of the story. With the bedroom door found bolted from the inside, then the kidnaper got away through the only window in the room giving upon the fire-escape. The window is small, and on its sill there is an immovable window-box. The window-box reduces the size of the window opening by at least one-third, leaving about two feet of space vertically for possible exit.

"Now Mr. Sherman here is a giant of a man—well over six feet tall and weighing two hundred and fifty pounds. How would the limper get Mr. Sherman's unconscious body through that small window-space? Sling it over his shoulder and climb through? A palpable absurdity, under the circumstances; certainly the most difficult method, and it probably would not even occur to him. But even if it had, he would have found the method unsuccessful. There are only two other ways to get out with the body: one would be to climb out first, leaving the body hanging over the window-box to be accessible from outside, and then pull the body out onto the fire-escape. But he didn't use this method; nowhere did the snow on the fire-escape or directly below the window-sill show a sign of disturbance such as would have been made by a heavy body resting even partly in it. The remaining method would be to push the body out first, and then climb out after it. But here the same objection holds: there was no impression of a body in the snow; only footprints."

The Inspector blinked. "But I don't see—"

"I didn't either, for some time," said Ellery. His face was like stone now. "The immediate conclusion was unquestionably that *an unconscious body was not taken out of the window!*"

Joseph E. Sherman got to his feet with a hoarse cry. His splotched cheeks were furrowed with tears. "All right!" he shouted. "I did it! I planned the whole thing. I wrote the first note to myself and all the others. I brought the three pairs of shoes into the apartment at odd times in the past two weeks, under cover, and hid them there. The night—the other night when I'd—I'd done it I used the earth in the window-box to muddy the bottoms of the shoes. I killed her to make it look like a kidnaping of myself, killed her because she was bleeding me, the slut! She's been hammering at me to divorce Enid and marry her. *Marry* her! I couldn't stand it. I was trapped. My position. . ."

Mrs. Sherman was staring at her husband with the glazed dullness of a dying animal. "But I knew—" she whispered.

He grew calmer. He said quietly: "I knew you knew, Enid darling. But I went crazy."

The Inspector said, with pity in his eyes: "Take him away, Thomas."

"But you must have known the whole story right there on the scene," complained the Inspector with some asperity an hour later, when the sordid business of Sherman's commitment had been finished.

Ellery shook his head sombrely. "No. The apex of my argument couldn't be arrived at until I knew definitely whether Sherman had been unconscious or not. That's why I recommended paying the ransom and getting the man to come back. I wanted to hear his story. When he said he'd been chloroformed in the apartment, my case was complete. Because I knew that no unconscious body was carried or dragged through the window. Sherman was lying, then, when he said that he had been chloroformed. In other words, there was no kidnaping. If there was no kidnaping, then obviously it was Sherman who had slipped on the floor, who limped, who had faked a kidnaping of himself to cover up the fact that he had murdered Lily Divine, concocting a plot by which he hoped to foster the illusion that a gang had kidnaped him and killed the woman incidentally. His slip on the floor was pure accident; he probably didn't realize that the tracks he was leaving would show the limping characteristics."

They sat in silence for a while, Ellery smoking and the Inspector staring out his iron-barred window. Then the old gentleman sighed. "I feel sorry for her."

"For whom?" said Ellery absently.

"Mrs. Sherman."

Ellery shrugged. "You always were a sentimentalist. But perhaps the most extraordinary thing about this case is its moral."

"Moral?"

"The moral that even a hardened criminal tells the truth sometimes. Lily called McKee, probably to get McKee to apply the well-known pressure to Sherman after Sherman refused to marry her. McKee was delayed, and he walked into the arms of the police. But he told the truth throughout. . . . So suppose," drawled Ellery, "you call up the Tombs—a detail you've forgotten in the excitement—and get poor old Mac his well-earned release."

The Adventure of
THE INVISIBLE LOVER

ROGER BOWEN was thirty, blue-eyed, and white. He was taller than most, laughed a little more readily, spoke English with an apologetic Harvard accent, drank an occasional cocktail, smoked more cigarettes than were good for him, was very thoughtful of his only living relative—an elderly aunt living, chiefly upon his bounty, in San Francisco—and balanced his reading between Sabatini and Shaw. And he practised what law there was to practise in the town of Corsica, N. Y. (population 745), where he had been born, stolen apples from old man Carter's orchard, swum raw in Major's Creek, and sparked with Iris Scott of Saturday nights on the veranda of the Corsica Pavilion (two bands, continuous dancing).

To listen to his acquaintances, who comprised one hundred percent of the population of Corsica, he was a "prince," a "real good boy," "no darned highbrow," and a "reg'lar guy." To listen to his friends—who for the most part shared the same residence, Michael Scott's boarding house on Jasmine Street off Main—

there was no jollier, kindlier, gentler, more inoffensive young man in the length and breadth of the land.

Within a half-hour of his arrival in Corsica from New York, Mr. Ellery Queen was able to gauge the temper of the Corsican populace concerning its most talked-of citizen. He learned something from a Mr. Klaus, the grocer on Main Street, a juicy morsel from a nameless urchin playing marbles in the road near the County Courthouse, and a good deal from one Mrs. Parkins, wife of the Corsican postmaster. He learned least of all from Mr. Roger Bowen himself, who seemed a decent enough sort, and quite plainly hurt and bewildered.

And as he left the county jail and headed for the boarding house and Roger Bowen's inner circle of friends, who were responsible for his hurried journey from Manhattan, it struck Mr. Ellery Queen that it was uncommonly curious such a paragon of all the virtues should be lying disconsolately on a cot in a dingy iron-barred cell awaiting trial on a charge of murder in the first degree.

"Now, now," said Mr. Ellery Queen after a space, rocking gently back and forth on the rose-curtained porch, "surely it can't be as black as all that? From all I've heard about young Bowen—"

Father Anthony clasped his bony hands tightly. "I baptized Roger myself," he said in a trembling voice. "It isn't possible, Mr. Queen. I baptized him! And he has told me he did not shoot McGovern. I believe him; he wouldn't lie to me. And yet . . . John Graham, the biggest lawyer in the county, who is defending Roger, Mr. Queen, says it's one of the worst circumstantial cases he has ever seen."

"For that matter," growled towering Michael Scott, snapping his suspenders over his burly breast, "the boy says so himself.

Hell, I wouldn't believe it even if Roger confessed! Beggin' your pardon, Father."

"All I say," snapped Mrs. Gandy from her wheel-chair, "any one says Roger Bowen shot that sneaky, black-haired devil from New York is a fool. Suppose Roger was in his room, alone, the night it happened? A person has the right to go to sleep, hasn't he? And how on earth would there be a witness to *that,* hey, Mr. Queen? The poor child's no flibbertigibbet, like some I know!"

"No alibi," sighed Ellery.

"Makes it bad," grumbled Pringle, chief of police of Corsica, a very fat and brawny old man. "Makes it downright bad. Better if he'd *had* some one with him that night. Not," he added hastily at Mrs. Gandy's outraged glare, "that Roger would, ye understand. But when I heard about that there, now, fight he'd had with Mc-Govern—"

"Oh," said Ellery softly. "They came to blows? There were threats?"

"Not exactly blows, Mr. Queen," said Father Anthony, wincing. "But they did quarrel. It was the same evening: McGovern was shot about midnight, and Roger had words with him only an hour or so before. As a matter of fact, sir, it wasn't the first time. They had quarreled violently on several previous occasions. Enough to establish motive to the District Attorney's satisfaction."

"But the slug," growled Michael Scott. "The slug!"

"Yes," said Dr. Dodd, a short mousy intelligent-looking man; he spoke unhappily. "I'm county coroner as well as local undertaker, you see, Mr. Queen, and it was my duty to examine that bullet when I dug it out of McGovern's body on autopsy. When Pringle held Roger on suspicion and got hold of the boy's gun, we naturally compared the bore-marks. . . ."

"Bore-marks?" drawled Ellery. "Really!" He inspected Chief Pringle and Coroner Dodd with rather grudging admiration.

"Oh, we didn't trust our own judgment in the matter," said the coroner hastily, "although under my microscope it did look. . . . It was all very nasty, Mr. Queen, but duty's duty, and an officer of the law has his oath to uphold. We sent it to New York, with the gun, for examination by a ballistics expert. His report came back confirming our findings. What were we to do? Pringle arrested Roger."

"Sometimes," said Father Anthony quietly, "there is a higher duty, Samuel."

The coroner looked miserable. Ellery said: "Does Bowen have a license to carry firearms?"

"Yep," muttered the fat policeman. "Lot of folks up this way do. Good huntin' in the hills yonder. It's a .38 did the job, all right—Roger's .38. Colt automatic, and a dandy, too."

"Is he a good shot?"

"I'll say he is!" exclaimed Scott. "That boy can shoot." His hard face lengthened. "I ought to know. I've got six pieces of shrapnel in my left leg right now where a Heinie shell came after me in Belleau."

"Excellent shot," faltered the coroner. "We've often gone rabbit-hunting together, and I've seen him pot a running target at fifty yards with his Colt. He won't use a rifle; too tame for real sport, he says."

"But what does Mr. Bowen say to all this?" demanded Ellery, squinting at the smoke of his cigarette. "He wouldn't talk to me at all."

"Roger," murmured Father Anthony, "says no. He did not kill McGovern, he says. That's enough for me."

"But scarcely for the District Attorney, eh?" Ellery sighed

again. "Then, since his automatic was used, it logically follows that—granted he's telling the truth—some one stole it from him and replaced it secretly after the murder?"

The men looked at one another uncomfortably, and Father Anthony smiled a faint proud smile. Then Scott growled: "Damnedest thing. Graham—that's our lawyer—Graham he says to Roger: 'Listen, young man. It's absolutely necessary for you to testify that the gun could have been stolen from you. Your life may depend on it,' and all that. And what do you think that young fool says? 'No,' he says, 'that's not the truth, Mr. Graham. Nobody did steal my gun. I'm a light sleeper,' he says, 'and the bureau with the gun in it is right next my bed. And I'd bolted my door that night. Nobody could have got in and taken it. So,' he says, 'I'm not going to testify to any such thing!'"

Ellery expelled smoke in a whistle. "Our hero, eh? That's—" He shrugged. "Now, this—ah—series of quarrels. If I understand correctly, it concerned—"

"Iris Scott," said a cool voice from the screen-door. "No don't get up, Mr. Queen! Oh, it's quite all right, father. I'm of age, and there's no point in keeping from Mr. Queen what the whole town knows anyway." Her voice stopped and caught on something. "What do you want to know, Mr. Queen?"

Mr. Queen, it was to be feared, was temporarily incapable of coherent speech. He was on his feet, gaping like a lout in a museum. If he had found a perfect diamond winking in the dust of Corsica's Main Street he could not have been more flabbergasted. Beauty anywhere is a rarity; in Corsica it was a miracle. So this is Iris Scott, he thought. Well named, O Michael! She was fresh and soft and handsomely made, and dewy and delicate as the flower itself. Strange soil to spring from! Her queerly wide black eyes held him fascinated, and he lost himself in her loveliness. In the gloom of the doorway she stood alone, a thing of beauty. It was joy just to look at her. If there was seductiveness in her, it was the unconscious lure of perfection—the swoop of an eyebrow, the curve of lips, the poise of a sculptured breast.

And so Mr. Ellery Queen understood why it was possible for such a paragon as Roger Bowen to be facing the electric chair. Even if he himself had been blind to her beauty, the men on the porch would have made him see. Dodd was regarding her quietly, with remote and humble worship. Pringle stared at her with vast thirst—yes, even Pringle, that enormous fat old man. And Father Anthony's aged eyes were proud, and a little sad. But in Michael Scott's eyes there was only the fierce jubilance of possession. This was Circe and Vesta in one, and she might move a man to murder as easily as a poet to lyric ecstasy.

"Well!" he said at last, drawing a deep breath. "Pleasant surprise. Sit down, Miss Scott, while I collect my wits. McGovern was an admirer of yours?"

Her heels made little clackings on the porch. "Yes," she said in a subdued voice, staring at the ivory hands in her lap. "You might call it that. And I—I liked him. He was different. An artist from New York. He'd come up to Corsica about six months ago to paint our famous hills. He knew so much, he'd travelled in France and Germany and England, so many celebrities were his friends. . . . We're almost peasants here, Mr. Queen. I never m-met any one like him."

"Sneaky devil," hissed Mrs. Gandy, her thin features contorted.

"Forgive me," smiled Ellery. "Did you love him?"

A bee buzzed about Pringle's hairy ears, and he angrily slapped at it. She said: "I—It's—Now that he's dead, no.

Death—somehow—makes a difference. Perhaps I—saw him in his true colors."

"But you spent a lot of time with him—alive?"

"Yes, Mr. Queen."

There was a small silence, and then Michael Scott said heavily: "I don't interfere in my daughter's affairs; see? She's got her own life to live. But I never cottoned to McGovern myself. He was a four-flusher with a smooth line, and plenty tough. I wouldn't trust him from here to there. I told Iris, but she wouldn't listen. Like a girl, she sort of went off her nut. He hung around longer than he'd expected—owed me," grimly, "five weeks' rent. Why the hell wouldn't he hang around? Why wouldn't anything in pants?"

"There," drawled Ellery, "is the perfect rhetorical question. And Roger Bowen, Miss Scott?"

"We—we've grown up together," said Iris in the same low voice. And she tossed her head suddenly. "It's always been so *settled*. I suppose I've resented that. And then his interference. He was simply furious about Mr. McGovern. Once, several weeks ago, Roger threatened to kill him. We all heard him; they—they were arguing in the parlor there, and we were sitting on the porch here. . . ."

There was another silence, and then Ellery said gently: "And do you think young Roger shot this city-slicker, Miss Scott?"

She raised her devastating eyes to his. "No! I'll never believe that. Not Roger. He was angry, that's all. He didn't mean what he said." And then she choked and to their horror began to sob. Michael Scott grew brick-red, and Father Anthony looked distressed. The others winced. "I-I'm sorry," she said.

"And who do you think did?" asked Ellery softly.

"Mr. Queen, I don't know."

"Any one?" They shook their heads. "Well, I believe, Pringle, you mentioned something about McGovern's room having been left precisely as you found it the night of the murder. . . . By the way, what happened to his body?"

"Well," said the coroner, "we held it after the autopsy for inquest, of course, and tried to find some relative to claim the body. But McGovern apparently was alone in the world, and not even a friend stepped forward. He left nothing except a few possessions in his New York studio. I fixed him up myself, and we buried him in the New Corsican Cemetery with the proceeds."

"Here's the key," wheezed the policeman, struggling to his feet. "I got to go on down to Lower Village. Dodd'll tell you everything you want to know. I hope—" He stopped helplessly, and then waddled off the porch. "Comin', padre?" he muttered without turning.

"Yes," said Father Anthony. "Mr. Queen . . . Anything at all, you understand—" His thin shoulders drooped as he slowly followed Pringle down the cement walk.

"If you'll excuse us, Mrs. Gandy?" murmured Ellery.

"Who found the body?" he demanded as they trudged upstairs in the cool semi-darkness of the house.

"I did," sighed the coroner. "I've been boarding with Michael for twelve years. Ever since Mrs. Scott died. Just a couple of old bachelors, eh, Michael?" They both sighed. "It was on that terribly stormy night three weeks ago—thundered and rained, remember? I'd been reading in my room—it was about midnight—and I started for the bathroom down the hall upstairs before going to bed. I passed McGovern's room; the door was open and the light was on. He was sitting in the chair, facing the door." The coroner shrugged. "I saw at once he was dead. Shot through the heart. The blood on his pajamas . . . I roused Michael at once. Iris heard us and came, too." They paused at the head of the stairs. Ellery heard the girl catch her breath, and Scott was panting.

"Had he been dead long?" he asked, making for a closed door indicated by the coroner's forefinger.

"Just a few minutes; his body was still warm. He died instantly."

"I presume the storm prevented any one from hearing the shot—there was only one wound, I suppose?" Dr. Dodd nodded. "Well, here we are." Ellery fitted the key Pringle had given him into the lock, and twisted it. Then he pushed open the door. No one said anything.

The room was flooded with sunlight; it looked as innocent of violence as a newborn baby. It was a very large room, shaped exactly like Ellery's own. And it was furnished exactly like Ellery's. The bed was identical, and it stood in a similar position between two windows; the table and rush-bottomed, cane-backed chair in the middle of the room might have come from Ellery's room; the rug, the bureau, the highboy . . . Hmm! There *was* a difference.

He murmured: "Are all your rooms furnished exactly alike?"

Scott raised his tufted brows. "Sure. When I went into this business and changed the shack into a rooming house, I bought up a lot of stuff from a bankrupt place in Albany. All the same stuff. All these rooms up here are the same. Why?"

"No special reason. It's interesting, that's all." Ellery leaned against the jamb and took out a cigarette, searching the scene meanwhile with his restless gray eyes. There was no faintest sign of a struggle. Directly before the doorway were the table and cane-backed chair, and the chair faced the door. In a straight line with the door and chair on the far side of the room stood an old-fashioned highboy against the wall. His eyes narrowed again. Without turning, he said: "That highboy. In my room it's between the two windows."

He heard the girl's soft breathing behind him. "Why . . . father! The highboy wasn't there when—when Mr. McGovern was alive!"

"That's funny," muttered Scott in astonishment.

"But on the night of the murder was the highboy where it is now?"

"Why—yes, it was," said Iris in a puzzled way.

"Certainly. I remember now," said the coroner, frowning.

"Good," drawled Ellery, pushing away from the door. "Something to work on." He strode over to the highboy, stooped and tugged at it until he had pulled it back from the wall. He knelt behind it and went over the wall, inch by inch, intently. And then he stopped. He had found a peculiar dent in the plaster about a foot from the wainscoting. It was no more than a quarter of an inch in diameter, was roughly circular, and was impressed perhaps a sixteenth of an inch into the wall. A fragment of plaster had fallen away; he found it on the floor.

When he rose he wore an air of disappointment. He returned to the doorway. "Nothing much. You're sure nothing's been disturbed since the night of the murder?"

"I'll vouch for that," said Scott.

"Hmm. By the way, I see some of McGovern's personal belongings are still here. Did Pringle search this room thoroughly on the night of the murder, Dr. Dodd?"

"Oh, yes."

"But he didn't find anything," growled Scott.

"You're positive? Nothing at all?"

"Why, we were all here when he was looking, Mr. Queen!"

Ellery smiled, examining the room with a peculiar zest. "No offense, Mr. Scott. Well! I think I'll go to my own room and mull over this baffling business for a bit. I'll keep this key, Doctor."

"Of course. Anything you want, you know—"

"Not now, at any rate. Where will you be if something comes up?"

"At my undertaking parlors on Main Street."

"Good." And rather vaguely and wearily Ellery smiled again and turned the key in the lock and trudged down the hall.

He found his room cool and soothing, and he lay back on the bed with his hands crossed beneath his aching head, thinking. The house was quiet enough. Outside one of his windows a robin chirped and a bee zoomed; that was all. Past the fluttering curtains came the sweet-scented wind from the hills.

Once he heard Iris' light step in the hall outside; and again the rumble of Michael Scott's voice downstairs.

He lay smoking for perhaps twenty minutes; and then all at once he sprang from the bed and darted to the door. Opening it to a crack, he listened. . . . All clear. So he quietly stepped out into the hall and tip-toed to the locked door of the dead man's room, and unlocked it, and went in, and turned the key again behind him.

"If there's any sense in this misbegotten world—" he muttered, stopped, and hurried to the cane-chair in which McGovern had been sitting when he died. He knelt and closely examined the solid crisscrossing mesh of cane making up the back of the chair. But there was nothing wrong with it.

Frowning, he got to his feet and began to prowl. He prowled the length and breadth of the room, stooped over like an old hunchback, his underlip thrust forward and his eyes straining.

He even sprawled full length on the floor to grope beneath pieces of furniture; and he made a tour under the bed like a sapper in No Man's Land. But when his inspection of the floor was completed, he was empty-handed. He brushed the dust from his clothes with a grimace.

It was as he was replacing the contents of the waste-basket, disconsolately, that his face lit up. "Lord! If it's possible that—" He left the room, locking the door again, and made a quick and cautious reconnaissance up and down the hall, listening. Apparently he was alone. So, noiselessly and quite without a feeling of guilt, he began room by room to search the sleeping quarters.

It was in the cane-chair of the fourth room he investigated that he found what his deductions had led him to believe he might find. And the room belonged to the person to whom he had even beforehand vaguely glimpsed it as belonging.

Very careful to leave the room precisely as he had found it, Mr. Ellery Queen returned to his own quarters, bathed his face and hands, adjusted his necktie, brushed his clothes again, and with a dreamy smile went downstairs.

Finding Mrs. Gandy and Michael Scott occupied on the porch playing a desultory game of two-handed whist, Ellery chuckled silently and made his way to the rear of the lower floor. He discovered Iris in a vast cavern of a kitchen, busy stirring something pungently savory over a huge stove. The heat had carmined her cheeks, she wore a crisp white apron, and altogether, she looked delectable.

"Well, Mr. Queen?" she asked anxiously, dropping her ladle and facing him with grave, begging eyes.

"Do you love him as much as that?" sighed Ellery, drinking in her loveliness. "Lucky Roger! Iris, my child—you see, I'm being very fatherly, although I assure you my soul is in the proverbial torment—we progress. Yes, indeed. I think I may tell you that young Lothario faces a rosier prospect than he faced this morning. Yes, yes, we have made strides."

"You mean you—he—Oh, Mr. Queen!"

Ellery sat down in a gleaming kitchen chair, filched a sugared cookie from a platter on the porcelain table, munched it, swallowed, looked critical, smiled, and took another. "Yours? Delicious. A veritable Lucrece, b'gad! Or is it Penelope I'm thinking of? Yes, I mean just that, honey. If this is a sample of your cooking—"

"Baking." She rushed forward suddenly and to his stupefaction clutched at his hand and pulled it to her breast. "Oh, Mr. Queen, if you only could—would—I never knew I—I loved him so much until just—just now. . . . In jail!" She shuddered. "I'll do anything—anything—"

Ellery blinked, loosened his collar, tried to look nonchalant, and then gently disengaged his hand. "Now, now, my dear, I know you would. But don't ever do that to me again. It makes me feel like God. Whew!" He swabbed his brow. "Now, listen, beautiful. Listen hard. There *is* something you can do."

"Anything!" Her face glowed into his.

He rose and began to stride around the spotless floor. "Am I right in supposing that your Samuel Dodd's very faithful to his office?"

She stared. "Sam Dodd? What on earth—He takes his job seriously, if that's what you mean."

"I thought so. It complicates matters." He smiled grimly. "However, we must face reality, mustn't we? My dear young goddess, than whom no lovelier creature ever graced the sour earth, you're going to vamp your Dr. Sam Dodd to within an inch of his officious life tonight. Or didn't you know that?"

Anger flashed from her black eyes. "Mr. Queen!"

"Tut-tut, although it's most becoming. I'm not suggesting anything—er—drastic, my child. Another cookie is called for." He helped himself to two. "Can you get him to take you to the movies tonight? His being in the house here makes matters difficult, and I've got to have him out of the way or he's liable to call out the State Militia to stop me."

"I can make Sam Dodd do anything I want," said the goddess very coolly, the blush leaving her cheeks, "but I don't understand why."

"Because," mumbled Ellery over another cake, "I say so, dear heart. I'm going to trample over his authority tonight, you see. There's something I must get done, and without the proper hocus-pocus of papers and things it's distinctly illegal, if not criminal. Dodd could help, but if I'm any judge of character he won't; and so if he doesn't know anything about it neither he nor I will have anything on the well-known conscience."

She measured him impersonally, and he felt uncomfortable under those level eyes. "Will it help Roger?"

"And," said Ellery fervently, "how!"

"Then I'll do it." And she lowered her eyes suddenly and began to fuss with her apron. "And now if you'll please get out of my kitchen, Mr. Ellery Queen, I've some dinner to make. And I think"—she fled to the stove and took up the ladle—"you're very wonderful."

Mr. Ellery Queen gulped, flushed, and beat a hasty retreat.

When he pushed open the screen-door he found Mrs. Gandy gone, and Scott sitting silent with Father Anthony on the porch. "The very men," he said cheerily. "Where's the afflicted Mrs. Gandy? By the way, how does she negotiate those stairs in that wheel-chair?"

"Doesn't. She's got a room on the lower floor," said Scott. "Well, Mr. Queen?" His eyes were haggard.

Father Anthony was regarding him with steadfast gravity.

Ellery's face turned bleak of a sudden. He sat down and drew his rocker close to theirs. "Father," he said quietly, "something informs me that you serve—honestly serve—a higher law than man's."

The old priest studied him for a moment. "I know little of law, Mr. Queen. I serve two masters—Christ and the souls He died for."

Ellery considered this in silence. Then he said: "Mr. Scott, you mentioned before that you had gone through Belleau Wood. Death, then, holds no terrors for you."

The burly man's hard eyes bored into Ellery's. "Listen, Mr. Queen, I saw my best friend torn in half before me. I had to pick his guts off my hands. No, I'm not scared of all hell; I've been there."

"Very good," said Ellery softly. "Very good indeed. Aramis, Porthos, and—if I may presume—D'Artagnan. A little cock-eyed, but it will serve. Father, Mr. Scott," and the priest and the burly father of Iris stared at his lips, "will you help me open a grave tonight?"

The eve of St. Walpurga was months dead, but the witch-es danced that night nevertheless. They danced in the shadows flung by the dark moon over the crazy hillside; they squealed and screeched in the wind over the mute, waiting graves.

Mr. Ellery Queen felt uncommonly glad that he was one of three that night. The cemetery lay on the outskirts of Corsica, ringed in iron and bordered with capering trees. An icy breeze blew death over their heads. The gravestones glimmered on the breast of the hillside like dead men's bones polished clean and white by the winds. An angry, furry black cloud hid half the moon, and the trees wept restlessly. No, it was not difficult to imagine that witches danced.

They walked in silence, instinctively keeping together. It was Father Anthony who braved the spirits, breasting the agitated air like a tall ship in the van, his vestments flapping and snapping. His face was dark and grave, but unruffled. Ellery and Michael Scott struggled behind under the weight of spades, picks, ropes, and a large bulky bundle. On all the moving, whispering, shadow-infested hillside they were the only living beings.

They found McGovern's grave in virgin soil, a little away from the main colony of headstones. It was a lonely spot high on the hill, a vulture's roost. Earth still raw made a mound above the dead man, and there was only a scrawny stick to mark the clay that lay there. Still in silence, and with drawn faces, the two men set to work with their picks while Father Anthony kept the vigil above them. The moon swam in and out maddeningly.

When the hard earth had been loosened, they cast aside the picks and attacked the soil with their spades. Both wore old overalls over their clothes.

"Now I know," muttered Ellery, resting a moment by the mounting pile of earth beside the grave, "what it feels like to be a ghoul. Father, I'm thankful you're along. I'm cursed with too much imagination."

"There is nothing to be afraid of, my son," said the old priest in a little bitter murmur. "These are only dead men."

Ellery shivered. Scott growled: "Let's get goin'!"

And so at last their spades struck hollowly upon wood.

How they managed it Ellery never clearly remembered. It was titans' work, and long before it was finished he was drenched with perspiration which stung like icicles under the cold fingers of the wind. He felt disembodied, a phantom in a nightmare. Scott labored in isolated silence, performing prodigies, while Ellery panted beside him and Father Anthony looked somberly on. And then Ellery realized that he was hauling upon two ropes on one side of the pit, and that old Scott was pulling on their other ends opposite him. Something long and black-clotted and heavy came precariously up from the depths, swaying as if it had life. One last heave, and it thumped over the side, to Ellery's horror overturning. He sank to the ground, squatting on his hams and fumbling for a cigarette.

"I—need—a—breather," he muttered, and puffed desperately. Scott leaned calmly on his spade. Only Father Anthony went to the pine box, and tugged until it righted itself, and with slow tender hands began to pry off the lid.

Ellery watched the old man, fascinated; and then he sprang to his feet, hurled his cigarette away, cursed himself beneath his breath, and snatched the pick from the priest's hands. A single powerful wrench, the lid screeched up. . . .

Scott set his muscular mouth and stepped, forward. He pulled canvas gloves on his hands. Then he bent over the dead man. Father Anthony stepped back, closing his tired eyes. And Ellery feverishly unwrapped the bulky bundle he had carried all the way from Jasmine Street, disclosing a huge tripod-camera borrowed surreptitiously from the editor of the *Corsica Call.* He fumbled with something.

"Is it there?" he croaked. "Mr. Scott, is it there?"

The burly man said clearly: "Mr. Queen, it's there."

"Only one?"

"Only one."

"Turn him over." And, after a while, Ellery said: "Is it there?"

And Scott said: "Yes."

"Only one?"

"Yes."

"Where I said it would be?"

"Yes."

And Ellery raised something high above his head, directing the eye of the camera with his other hand upon what lay in the mud-coated coffin and made a convulsive fist, and something blue as witchfire flashed to the accompaniment of a reverberating boom, lighting up the hillside momentarily like a flare in purgatory.

And Ellery paused in his labors and leaned on his spade and said: "Let me tell you a story." Michael Scott worked on relentlessly, his broad back writhing with his exertions. Father Anthony sat on the rewrapped camera-bundle and cupped his old face in his hands.

"Let me tell you," said Ellery tonelessly, "a story of remarkable cleverness that was thwarted by . . . There is a God, Father.

"When I discovered that the highboy in McGovern's room was out of its customary position, apparently moved to its new place some time within the general period of the murder, I saw that it was possible the murderer himself had so moved it. If he had, there must have been a reason for the action. I pushed aside the highboy and found on the wall behind it a foot or so from the wainscoting a small circular impression in the plaster. This dent and the highboy before it were in a direct line with two objects: the cane-chair facing the door in which McGovern had presumably been sitting when he was shot, and the doorway where the murderer must have been standing when he squeezed the trigger. Coincidence? It did not seem likely.

"I saw at once that the dent was just such a dent as might have been made by a bullet—a spent bullet, since the depression was so shallow. It was also evident that since the murderer must have been standing, and the victim sitting—being shot through the heart besides—then the dent on the wall several yards behind the chair would appear, if it was caused by a bullet fired by the murderer, just about where I found it, the line of fire being generally downward."

The clods thumped and bumped on the box.

"Now it was also evident," said Ellery in a strange voice, gripping the spade, "that had the spent bullet been one which had passed through McGovern's body there should be a hole in the cane-meshed back of McGovern's chair. I examined the chair; there was no bullet-hole. Then it was possible the bullet which had made the dent in the wall had not passed through McGovern's body but had gone wild; in other words, that two shots had been fired that stormy, noisy night, the one which lodged in the body and the one which caused the dent. But no mention had been made of second bullet having been found in the room, despite unanimous testimony that the room had been thoroughly searched. I myself inspected every inch of that floor without success. But if a second bullet was not there, then it must have, been taken away by the murderer at the same time he moved the highboy over to conceal the dent the bullet had made." He paused and gloomily eyed the filling grave. "But why should the murderer take away one bullet and leave the vital one to be found—the one in the victim's body? It did not make sense. On the other hand, its alternative did make sense. That there never had been two bullets at all; *that only one bullet had been fired."*

The hillside quivered in shadow as the witches danced.

"I worked," continued Ellery wearily, "on this theory. If only one bullet had been fired, then it was that bullet which had killed McGovern, piercing his heart and emerging from his back, penetrating the cane of the chair-back, and winging on across the room to strike the wall where I found the dent; falling, spent, to the floor below. Then why didn't McGovern's chair show a bullet-hole? It could only be because it was *not* McGovern's chair. The murderer had done one thing to conceal the fact that the bullet had emerged from the body: he had moved the highboy. Why not another? So he must have exchanged chairs. All your rooms, Mr. Scott, are identically furnished; he dragged McGovern's chair to his own room and brought his own chair to replace McGovern's. All my deductions up to this point would be demonstrated correct if I could find a cane-backed chair with a hole in its back—a hole where a hole should be, just at the place where a bullet would penetrate if it had gone through the heart of some one sitting in the chair. And find it I did—in the room of some one in your house, Mr. Scott."

The ugly raw earth was level with the hillside now; only a little heap was left. Father Anthony watched his friend with veiled and anguished eyes; and for an instant the black cloud draped the moon and they were in darkness.

"Why," muttered Ellery, "should the murderer want to conceal the fact that a spent bullet existed? There could be only one reason: he did not wish the bullet found and examined. But a bullet *was* found and examined." The cloud edged off angrily, and the moon glowered at them again. "Then the bullet which *was* found must have been *the wrong one!"*

At last it was done: the mound loomed, round and dark and smooth, in the moonlight. Father Anthony absently reached for the small wooden grave-marker and thrust it into the mound. Michael Scott rose to his full height, wiping his brow.

"The wrong bullet?" he said hoarsely.

"The wrong bullet. For what did that bullet's being found accomplish? It directly involved Roger Bowen as the murderer; it was a bullet demonstrably from Bowen's .38 automatic. But if it was the wrong bullet, then Bowen was being framed by some one who, unable by reason of Bowen's nightly vigilance to get hold of Bowen's automatic, but possessing *a spent bullet which had already been fired* from Bowen's automatic, was able after the murder to switch Bowen's—as it were—innocent bullet for the one actually used to kill McGovern!" Ellery's voice rose stridently. "The bullet from the murderer's gun wouldn't show the telltale bore-markings of Bowen's gun, naturally. Had the murderer left his own bullet to be found, tests would have shown that it didn't come from Bowen's .38 and would have instantly defeated the frame-up. So the murderer had to take away the real, the lethal, bullet, conceal the dent in the wall, change cane-back chairs."

"But why," demanded Scott in a strangled growl, "didn't the damn' fool leave the chair there and let the dent be found? Why didn't he just take away his own bullet and drop Bowen's on the floor in its place? That would have been the easiest thing to do. And then he wouldn't have had to cover up the fact that the slug had gone clear through the body."

"A good question," said Ellery softly. "Why, indeed? If he didn't do it that way, then it must have been that he couldn't do it that way. He didn't have on him at the time of the murder the spent bullet he had stolen from Bowen; he'd left it somewhere where he couldn't get it on the spur of the moment."

"Then he didn't expect the bullet would go clear through the body," cried Scott, waving his huge arms so that their shadows slashed across McGovern's ugly grave. "And he must have expected to be able to substitute Bowen's bullet for the real slug *afterwards,* after the killing, after the police examination, after. . ."

"That's it," murmured Ellery, "exactly. That—" He stopped. A ghost in diaphanous white garments was floating up the hillside toward them, skimming the dark earth. Father Anthony rose, and he looked taller than a man should look. Ellery gripped his spade.

But Michael Scott called harshly: "Iris! What—"

She flung herself wildly at Ellery. "Mr. Queen!" she gasped. "They're—they're coming! They found out—some one saw you and father and Father Anthony come this way with the spades. . . . Pringle came for Sam Dodd. . . . I ran—"

"Thank you, Iris," said Ellery gently. "Among your other virtues you number courage, too." But he made no move to go.

"Let's roll," muttered Michael Scott. "I don't want—"

"Is it a crime," murmured Ellery, "to seek communion with the blessed dead? No, I wait."

Two dots appeared, became dancing dolls, loomed larger, scrambled frantically up the slope. The first was large and fat, and something winked dully in his hand. Behind him struggled a small white-faced man.

"Michael!" snarled Chief Pringle, waving his revolver. "Father! You, there, Queen! What the hell d'ye call this? Are ye all out of your minds? Diggin' up graves!"

"Thank God," panted the coroner. "We're not too late. They haven't dug—" He eyed the mound, the tools gratefully. "Mr. Queen, you know it's against the law to—"

"Chief Pringle," said Ellery regretfully, stepping forward and fixing the coroner with his gray eyes, "you will arrest this man for the deliberate murder of McGovern and the frame-up of Roger Bowen."

The porch was in purple shadow; the moon had long since set and Corsica was asleep; only Iris' white gown glimmered a little, and Michael Scott's pipe glowed fretfully.

"Sam Dodd," he mumbled. "Why, I've known Sam Dodd—"

"Oh, Father!" moaned Iris, and groped for the hand of Father Anthony in the rocker beside her.

"It had to be Dodd, you know," said Ellery wearily; his feet were on the railing. "You put your finger on the precise point, Mr. Scott, when you said that the murderer must have expected to be able to make the substitution later, and that he hadn't expected that the bullet he fired would pass clear through McGovern's body. For who could have switched bullets had the bullet remained in McGovern's body, as the murderer expected it to remain before he fired? Only Dodd, the coroner, who makes the autopsy which is mandatory in a murder. Who could have continued to keep unknown the fact that the bullet had passed through McGovern's body? Only Dodd, the undertaker, who prepared the body for burial. Who actually stated that the bullet was *in* the body? Only Dodd, who performed the autopsy; if he were innocent why should he have lied? Who introduced Bowen's bullet in evidence? Only Dodd, who claimed to have recovered it from the heart of the dead man." Iris sobbed a little. "Were there confirmations? Plenty. Dodd lived in this house, and therefore he had access to McGovern's room that night. Dodd 'found' the body; therefore he could have done everything that was necessary without interference. Dodd as coroner set the time of death; he could have said it was a little later than it actually was to cover up the time he consumed in moving the highboy and switching chairs. Dodd by his own admission had often gone out rabbit-hunting with Roger Bowen; therefore he could easily have secured a spent bullet from Bowen's automatic, a bullet which Bowen had fired but which had missed its target. Dodd, being a coroner, was professionally minded; it took a professional mind to think of bore-marks. Dodd, being a coroner, was ballistically minded and had a microscope to check bore-marks. . . . Then I had proofs. It was in Dodd's room I found the cane-chair with the hole in its back. And, most important, I knew that if McGovern's body on exhumation showed one bullet-wound in the chest and one exit-hole in the back, then I had complete proof that Dodd had lied in his official report and that my whole chain of reasoning was correct. We dug up the body and there was the exit-hole. My photographs will send Dodd to the chair."

"And God, my son?" said Father Anthony quietly from the darkness.

Ellery sighed. "I prefer to think that it was some such Agency that made the bullet Dodd fired completely pierce McGovern's body. Had it lodged in McGovern's heart, as Dodd had every reason to expect it would, there would have been no dent in the wall, no hole in the chair, and therefore no reason to exhume the body. Dodd would have produced Bowen's bullet after autopsy, claiming it was the one he 'dug out,' as he did claim, and Bowen would have been a very unlucky young man."

"But Sam Dodd!" cried Iris, hiding her face in her hands. "I've known him so long, since I was a little girl. He's always been so quiet, so gentle, so—so. . ."

Ellery rose and his shoes creaked on the black porch. He bent over the glimmer of her and cupped her chin in his hand

and stared down with the most whimsical yearning into her all-but-invisible face. "Beauty like yours, my dear, is a dangerous gift. Your gentle Sam Dodd killed McGovern to rid himself of one rival and framed Roger Bowen for the murder to rid himself of the other, you see."

"Rival?" gasped Iris.

"Rival, hell!" growled Scott.

"Your eyes, my son," whispered Father Anthony, "are good."

"Hope springs not only eternal but lethal," said Ellery softly. "Sam Dodd loves you."

The Adventure of
THE TEAKWOOD CASE

THE WOODY, leathery, homely living room of the Queens' apartment on West Eighty-seventh Street in New York City had seen queerer visitors than Mr. Seaman Carter, but surely none quite so ill at ease.

"Really, Mr. Carter," said Ellery Queen with amusement, stretching his long legs nearer the fireplace, "you've been wretchedly misinformed. I'm not a detective at all, you know. My father is the sleuth of this family! Officially I've no more right to investigate a crime than you have."

"But that's exactly the point, Mr. Queen!" wheezed Carter with a vast rolling of his porphyry eyes. "We don't *want* the police. We want *unofficial* advice. We want *you*, Mr. Queen, to clear up these devilish robberies *sub rosa*—ahem!—so to speak; or I shouldn't have come. The Gothic Arms can't afford the notoriety, my dear, dear Mr. Queen. We're an exclusive development catering to the best people—"

"Pshaw, Mr. Carter," said Ellery between lazy puffs of the inevitable cigarette, "go to the police. You've had five robberies in as many months. All of jewels, all filched from different tenants on different floors. And now this latest theft two days ago—a diamond necklace from the bedroom wall-safe of a Mrs. Mallorie, an invalid and one of your oldest tenants. . . ."

"Mrs. Mallorie!" Carter shuddered with the sinuous ripplings of an octopus in motion. "She's an old woman. She went into hysterics—a terrible person, Mr. Queen. Insists on calling in the police, informing the insurance company. . . . We're at our wits' end."

"It seems to me," said Ellery, fixing his sharp eyes on the man's lumpy cheeks, which were quivering, "that you'll be in the devil of a sweet mess, Mr. Carter, if you don't get official help at once. You're making an extraordinary fuss about very small potatoes."

The telephone-bell rang and Djuna, the Queens' boy-of-all-work, slipped into the bedroom to answer it. He popped his small gypsy head out of the doorway almost at once. "For you, Mr. Ellery. Dad Queen is on the wire and he's hopping."

"Excuse me," said Ellery, abruptly, and went into the bedroom.

When he came out all amusement had fled from his lean features. He had divested his tall body of the battered old dressing-gown and was fully attired for the street.

"You'll be interested to learn, no doubt," he said in a flat voice, "that once more fact has outdone fiction, Mr. Carter. I've been treated to the spectacle of an amazing coincidence. On which floor did you say Mrs. Mallorie's apartment lies?"

Mr. Seaman Carter shook like the damp flanks of a grumbling volcano; his little eyes became glassy. "My God!" he screeched, dragging himself to his feet. "What happened now? Mrs. Mallorie occupies Apartment F on the sixteenth floor!"

"I'm delighted to hear it. Well, Mr. Carter, your laudable effort to smother legitimate news has failed, and you have enlisted my poor services. Except that we are *en route* to the scene of a crime more serious than theft. My father, Inspector Queen, informs me that a man in Apartment H on the sixteenth floor of the Gothic Arms has been found foully done in. In a word, he's been murdered."

An express elevator took Ellery and the Superintendent to the sixteenth floor. They emerged on the west corridor of the building. A central corridor bisected the hall in which they found themselves, and at its end could be seen the bronze doors of the elevator on the east corridor. Carter, his globular carcass trembling like gelatinous ooze, led the way toward the right. They came to a door before which stood a whistling detective. The door, marked with a gilded *H,* was closed. Carter opened it and they went in.

They were in a small foyer, through the open door of which they could see into a large room filled with men. Ellery brushed by a uniformed officer, nodded to his father—a small bird-like creature with gray plumage and bright little eyes—and stared down at a still figure in an armchair beside a small table in the center of the room.

"Strangled?"

"Yes," said Inspector Queen. "And who's this with you, Ellery?"

"Mr. Seaman Carter, Superintendent of the building." Ellery idly explained the purpose of Carter's visit; his eyes were roving.

"Carter, who's this dead man?" demanded the Inspector. "No one here seems to know."

Carter shifted, from one elephantine foot to the other. "Who?" he babbled. "Who? Why, isn't it Mr. Lubbock?"

A foppish young man in morning coat dotted with a *bouton-*

nière coughed hesitantly. They turned to stare at him. "It's not Lubbock, Mr. Carter," he lisped. "Though it does look like him from the back." His simpering lips were pale with fear.

"Who's *that?*" asked Ellery.

"Fullis, my assistant," muttered the Superintendent. "Heavens, Fullis, you're right at that." He pushed around the armchair for a better view of the body.

A trim tall man with a ruddy complexion came briskly into the room. He was carrying a black bag. Carter addressed him as Dr. Eustace. The physician set his bag down by the chair and proceeded to examine the dead man. Dr. Eustace was the house physician.

Ellery drew the Inspector aside. "Anything?" he asked in low tones.

The Inspector gasped over a generous noseful of snuff. "Nothing. A complete mystery. Body was found by accident about an hour or so ago. A woman from Apartment C across the central corridor came in here to see John Lubbock, who lives alone in this two-room suite. At least, that's what *she* says." He moved his head slightly in the direction of a platinum-haired young woman, whose tears had played havoc with the careful lacquer on her face; she was sitting forlornly across the room guarded by a policeman. "She's Billy Harms, the ingénue of that punk comedy at the Roman Theater. Managed to squeeze out of her the information that she's been Lubbock's playmate for a couple of months; her maid tells me—thank God for maids!—that she and Lubbock had a lovers' battle a few weeks ago. Seems he won't pay her rent any more, and I guess the market on sugar-daddies has gone 'way down."

"Lovely people," said Ellery. "And?"

"She walked herself plump in here—seems it was sort of

dim; only a small light in the lamp on the table—thought this chap was asleep, shook him, saw he wasn't Lubbock and that he was dead. . . . The old story. She screamed and a lot of people ran in—neighbors. Over there." Ellery saw five people huddled near Billy Harms' chair. "They all live on this floor. That elderly couple—Mr. and Mrs. Orkins, Apartment A across the hall. The sour-faced mutt next to the Orkinses is a jeweler, Benjamin Schley—Apartment B. Those other two people are Mr. and Mrs. Forrester—he's got some kind of soft job with the city; they're in Apartment D, next to Billy Harms."

"Get anything out of them?"

"Not a lead." The Inspector bit off the end of a gray hair from his mustache. "Lubbock left here this morning and hasn't been seen since. He's a man-about-town, it seems, and he's been pretty gay with the ladies. Understand from one of the house-maids that he's been playing around with Mrs. Forrester, too—kind of pretty, isn't she? But there doesn't seem to be any connection with the others." He shrugged. "Had a few feelers out already—Lubbock has no business and nobody seems to know his source of income. Anyway, it's not Lubbock we're interested in right now, although we're trying to locate him. Got Hagstrom on the job. But none of the people employed here can say who this feller is that was choked. Never saw him before, they say; and there's nothing in his effects to show who he is."

Dr. Eustace signaled the Inspector; he had risen from his inspection of the corpse. The Queens moved back toward the chair. "What's the dope, Doctor?" asked the Inspector.

"Strangled to death from behind," replied the physician, "a little more than an hour ago. That's really all I can tell, sir."

"That's a help, that is."

Ellery strolled over to the little table by the dead man's chair.

The contents of the man's clothes had been dumped there. A worn cheap wallet containing fifty-seven dollars; a few coins; a small automatic; a single Yale key; a New York evening newspaper; a crumpled program of the Roman Theater; the torn half of a Roman Theater ticket, dated that very day; two soiled handkerchiefs; a stiff new packet of matches, its flap bearing the imprint of the Gothic Arms; a glistening green cigarette package, half of the tin-foil and blue seal at the top torn away. The package contained four cigarettes, although it was apparently a fresh one and retained its full shape.

A meagre enough grist on the surface.

Ellery picked up the small key. "Have you identified this?" he asked the Inspector.

"Yes. It's the key to this apartment."

"A duplicate?"

Mr. Seaman Carter took it from Ellery's hand with slippery fingers, fumbled with it, consulted with lisping Fullis, and returned it to Ellery. "That's the original, Mr. Queen," he quavered. "Not the duplicate."

Ellery flung the key on the table; his sharp eyes began to prowl. He spied a small metal waste-basket beneath the table, and dug it out. It was clean and empty except for a crumpled ball of tin-foil and blue paper, and a crushed cellophane wrapper. Ellery at once matched his finds to the package of cigarettes; he smoothed out the silver-and-blue scrap and discovered that it exactly fitted the hole torn in the top of the package.

The Inspector smiled at his look of concentration. "Don't get excited, sonny boy. He walked in the lobby downstairs from the street about an hour and a half ago, and bought that pack of butts at the desk; got the matches there, too, of course. Then he came upstairs. Elevatorman let him off at this floor, and that's the last any one saw of him."

"Except his murderer," said Ellery with a frown. "And yet . . . Did you look into this package, dad?"

"No. Why?"

"If you had, you would have seen that there are only four cigarettes here. And that, I believe, is significant."

He said nothing more and commenced a leisurely amble about the room. It was large, rich, and furnished with a dilettante's taste. But Ellery was not interested in John Lubbock's interior decorations at the moment; he was looking for ash-trays. He saw several scattered about, of different shapes and sizes; all of them were perfectly clean. His eyes lowered to the floor, and leveled again as if they had not found what they were seeking. "Does that lead to the bedroom?" he asked, pointing to a door at the southeast corner of the room. The Inspector nodded, and Ellery crossed the room and disappeared through the doorway.

A group of newcomers—a police-photographer, a fingerprint man, the Assistant Medical Examiner of New York County— invaded the living room as Ellery left; he could hear dull booms from flashlights and the crackling insistence of the Inspector as the old man began to requestion the tenants of the sixteenth floor.

Ellery looked about the bedroom. The bed was a canopied affair, ornate with silk and tassels; there was a lush Chinese rug on the floor; and the furniture and fripperies made his simple eyes ache. He looked for exits. There were three doors—the one he had just opened from the living room; one to his right, which on investigation he found opened out on the west corridor; and one to his left. He tried the knob of this door; it was locked, but there was a key in the keyhole. He unlocked the door and found himself looking into a room devoid of furniture, architecturally the counterpart of Lubbock's bedroom. Further investigation revealed an empty living room and a bare foyer. This, as he could see, was Apartment G; obviously unoccupied. All doors leading into Apartment G, as he discovered at once, were unlocked.

Ellery sighed, returned to Lubbock's bedroom, and turned the key in the lock, leaving it there. On impulse he paused to take out his handkerchief and wipe the knob clean. Then he proceeded directly to a wardrobe and began to rummage through the pockets of the numerous men's garments hanging on a rack inside—there were coats, suits, hats in profusion. He went through a curious routine; he seemed to be interested in nothing but crumbs. He turned pockets inside out and examined the sediment in the crevices. "No tobacco grains," he murmured to himself. "Interesting—but where the deuce does it get me?"

Then he carefully restored all pockets and garments to their original condition, closed the wardrobe, and went to the west corridor door. He opened it, stepped out, and hurried down the corridor to the front door of Lubbock's suite. He caught sight of the photographer, the fingerprint man, Sergeant Velie, and the tall, lank, saturnine figure of Dr. Prouty, Assistant Medical Examiner, standing near the elevators engaged in amiable conversation.

Nodding to the detective on guard before Apartment H—the man was still whistling—Ellery entered the foyer and repeated his odd examination of pockets in all the garments hanging in the foyer-closet; a fruitless quest, to judge from his expression.

Raised voices from the living room made him close the closet-door with a little snap. He heard his father say: "You'd better pull yourself together, Mr. Lubbock."

Ellery hurried into the living room. The neighbors had left, or had been sent to their apartments under guard. Of the original cast of the drama, only Mr. Seaman Carter and Dr. Eustace remained. But there was a newcomer—a small, slender, sunken-cheeked dandy with sandy hair and blue eyes whose well-scraped jaws wabbled ludicrously as he stared down at the dead man.

"Who's this?" asked Ellery pleasantly.

The man turned, looked at him without intelligence and twisted his head back toward the corpse.

"Mr. John Lubbock," said the Inspector. "Tenant of this apartment. He's just been found—Hagstrom brought him in. *And* we've identified the lad in the chair."

Ellery studied John Lubbock's face. "Relative of yours, Mr. Lubbock? There's a distinct resemblance."

"Yes," said Lubbock hoarsely, coming to life. "He's—he was my brother. I—he got into town from Guatemala this morning; he was an engineer and we hadn't seen each other for three years. Looked me up at one of my clubs. I had an appointment, gave him the key to my apartment, and he said he'd take in a matinée and meet me here late this afternoon. And here I find him—" He squared his shoulders, sucked in his breath, and sanity crept back into his marbly blue eyes. "It's beyond my comprehension."

"Mr. Lubbock," said the Inspector, "did your brother have any enemies?"

The sandy-haired man gripped the edge of the table. "I don't know," he said helplessly. "Harry never wrote me anything—anything like that."

Ellery said: "Mr. Lubbock, I want you to examine these things on the table. They are the contents of your brother's pockets. Is anything missing that should be here?"

The dilettante looked at the table. He shook his head. "I really wouldn't know," he said.

Ellery touched his arm. "*Are you certain his cigarette-case isn't missing, Mr. Lubbock?*"

Lubbock started, and something like curiosity came into his dull eyes. As for the Inspector, he was petrified with astonishment.

"Cigarette-case? What's this about a cigarette-case, Ellery? We haven't found any such thing!"

"Precisely the point," said Ellery gently. "Well, Mr. Lubbock?"

Lubbock moistened his dry lips. "Now that you mention it—yes," he said with, an effort. "Though how in God's name you knew is more than I can see. Why, I forgot it myself! Before Harry left the States for Central America three years ago he showed me two cigarette-cases, exactly alike." He fumbled in the inner breast-pocket of his jacket and brought out a shallow dull-black case, intricately inset with an Oriental design in silver, one tiny sliver of which was missing from its groove.

Ellery opened the case, which contained half a dozen cigarettes, with shining eyes; a rabid worshiper of the weed himself, cigarette-cases were one of Ellery's cherished passions.

"A friend of Harry's," continued Lubbock wearily, "sent the two cases to him from Bangkok. Finest teak wood in the world comes from the East Indies, you know. Harry gave one of them to me, and I've had it ever since. But how did you know, Mr. Queen, that—"

Ellery snapped the lid down and returned the case to Lubbock. He was smiling. "It's our business to know things, although really my knowledge isn't the least bit mysterious."

Lubbock was stowing the case carefully away in his breast-pocket—quite as if it were a treasure—when there came a mutter of voices from the foyer and two white-clad internes marched in. The Inspector nodded; they unrolled their stretcher, hauled the dead man out of the armchair, dumped him unceremoniously upon the canvas, covered him with a blanket, and marched out toting their burden as if it were a side of fresh-killed beef. John Lubbock clutched the edge of the table again, his pale face grew paler, he gulped, retched, and began to slip to the floor.

"Here! You, Eustace! Doc Prouty, out there! Quick!" cried the Inspector as he and Ellery lunged forward and caught the fainting man. Dr. Eustace opened his bag as Dr. Prouty dashed in. Lubbock muttered thickly: "Guess it was—too much—for me—seeing them take—Poor Harry . . . Give me a sedative—something—brace me up."

Dr. Prouty snorted and went right out again. Dr. Eustace produced a bottle and thrust it beneath Lubbock's nostrils. They quivered and Lubbock grinned faintly. "Here," said Ellery, pulling out his own cigarette-case. "Have a smoke. Do your nerves good." But Lubbock shook his head and pushed the pellet away. "I'll—be all right," he gasped, struggling erect. "Sorry."

Ellery said to Superintendent Carter, who stood like a blind rhinoceros near the table, perspiration pouring down his face: "Please send up the maid who cleans this suite, Mr. Carter. At once."

The fat man nodded eagerly and waddled out of the living room as fast as his jelly legs could carry him. Sergeant Velie, strolling in, scowled at Carter with disgust. Ellery glanced at his father, jerked his head toward the foyer, and the old man said: "You stay here and rest up a bit, Mr. Lubbock; we'll be back shortly."

Ellery and the Inspector went out into the foyer, and Ellery very softly closed the door to the living room.

"What the devil's up now?" growled the Inspector.

Ellery smiled and said: "Wait." He put his hands behind his back and began to stroll about.

A trim little colored girl in black regalia hurried up to the apartment door, her face an alarming violet.

"Ah," said Ellery. "Come in. You're the maid who cleans this suite regularly?"

"Yes, suh!"

"You cleaned it this morning as usual?"

"Yes, suh!"

"And were there any ashes in the ashtrays?"

"No, suh! Nevuh is in Mistuh Lubbock's apa'tment 'ceptin' when he's had comp'ny."

"You're positive of that?"

"Cross mah haht, suh!"

The girl retreated hastily. The Inspector said: "I'll be jiggered."

Ellery had dropped his cloak of insouciance; he drew his father's slender little body closer. "Listen. The maid's testimony was all we needed. Delicate situation, O venerable ancestor. Follow my reasoning.

"The package of cigarettes from Harry Lubbock's pocket: a fresh package, observe, confirmed by the fact that he purchased it just before coming up here, by the scrap, of perfectly fitting tin-foil and blue paper from the basket, by the cellophane wrapper, and by the uncrushed condition of the package itself. Harry Lubbock came up here to wait for his brother. He sat down in the armchair, his back to the foyer door. He didn't smoke; no ashes anywhere; no cigarette-stubs. Yet despite the fact that this was a new package, we find only *four* cigarettes inside. What happened to the other sixteen, since there are twenty to the pack? First possibility is that his murderer took them away, stealing

THE TEAKWOOD CASE · 179

them from the package. Psychologically rotten—can't visualize a murderer taking fresh cigarettes from his victim's package. Second possibility: that Lubbock himself opened the package before the arrival of the murderer *in order to fill a cigarette-case.* This would explain the peculiar number of missing cigarettes; many cigarette-cases hold sixteen. Yes, I was convinced that the sixteen missing cigarettes had been placed by Harry Lubbock, the engineer, in his case. But where was the case? Obviously, since it's gone, the murderer took it away." The Inspector chewed upon that, then nodded. "Good! Now where are we? The cigarettes themselves, being brand new, couldn't have been the object of the theft. Then the *case* must have been the object of the theft!"

Inspector Queen pursed his old lips. "Why? There certainly isn't a hidden spring or compartment in that case. It's not thick enough to conceal a Chinaman's breath in the wood itself."

"Don't know, sire, don't know. Haven't the faintest notion *why*. But it's so.

"Now as to John Lubbock. Three psychological indications. . . . But I'll give them to you more graphically. Maid's testimony: no ashes in this apartment, ever, *except* after guests. Sign of a non-smoker? *Oui, papa.* John Lubbock half faints, asks for a sedative, and *refuses* the cigarette I offer him! Sign of a non-smoker? Decidedly; in moments of emotional stress a smoker by habit falls back on the weed—it's the nicotine-addict's nerve soother. And third: there isn't a shred of tobacco in any pocket of any garment in John Lubbock's closets! Ever examine my coat-pocket? There's always tobacco in small grains lurking in the crevices. None in John Lubbock's clothes. Sign of a non-smoker? You answer."

"All right," said the Inspector softly. "He doesn't indulge.

Then why in tunket does he carry a cigarette-case with ciga-rettes in it?"

"Precisely!" cried Ellery. "We've deduced that a cigarette-case was probably stolen from the murdered man. Since John Lub-bock isn't a smoker and carries a cigarette-case . . . you see? It's almost tenable—it *is* tenable, by thunder—to say that the case John showed us was his murdered brother's!"

"And that would make him Harry Lubbock's killer," muttered the Inspector. "But there weren't sixteen cigarettes in it, El. And the six that *were* there are of a different brand."

"Pie. Naturally our friend the dilettante would ditch the ones his engineer-brother had bought and substitute not only a dif-ferent number but a different kind. I don't say this is conclusive. But at the moment the wind blows his way quite stiffly. If he's the murderer of his own brother then his story of *two* teakwood cases is a fabrication, composed on the spur of the moment to explain his possession of the teakwood case should there be a search."

The Queens turned swiftly at a knock on the foyer-door. But it was only Dr. Eustace. He came out, leaving the door to the living room ajar. "Sorry to disturb you," he said in gruff apology. "But I've got to see my other patients."

"You'd better be available, Doctor," said the Inspector in a clear grim voice. "We've just decided to take John Lubbock down to Headquarters for a little talk, and we'll need your rou-tine testimony, too."

"Lubbock?" Dr. Eustace stared, then shrugged. "Well, I sup-pose it's none of my business. I'll be either in my office on the mezzanine floor or I'll leave word at the desk. Ready when you are, Inspector." He nodded and went out.

"Don't scare him," suggested Ellery, as the Inspector made a move toward the living room. "My logic may be wetter than Triton's beard."

When they opened the door to the living room they found Sergeant Velie alone, sitting in the dead man's chair, feet propped on the table. "Where's Lubbock?" asked Ellery swiftly.

Velie yawned; his mouth was a red cavern fringed with enamel. "Went into the bedroom a coupla minutes ago," he rumbled. "Didn't see any harm in it myself." He pointed to the bedroom door, which was closed.

"Oh, you gigantic idiot!" cried Ellery, dashing across the room. He tore open the bedroom door. The bedroom was empty.

The Inspector yelled to his men in the corridor, Sergeant Velie flushed a wine-red and leaped to his feet. . . . The alarm was sounded; men began to comb the halls; the elderly Orkinses poked their white heads out of Apartment A; Billy Harms flew into the central corridor in a lacy chemise; an old witch of a woman in a wheelchair propelled herself from the front door of Apartment F and sent two cursing detectives sprawling with her clumsy manipulation of the conveyance. The scene was like a farcically rapid motion-picture reel.

Ellery wasted no time bewailing Sergeant Velie's unexpected stupidity. From the detective in the west corridor, he discovered that John Lubbock had not emerged from the western door of his bedroom. Ellery ran back to the eastern door, the door which led into the vacant suite. The key which he had left sticking in the door was gone. Gently, without touching the head of the knob, he tried to twist the bolt-bar. It refused to budge; the door was locked.

"The east corridor!" he yelled. "Door's open there!" and led the pack out of Lubbock's apartment, around the corner through the central corridor, up the east corridor and through the unlocked door into the bedroom of empty Apartment G. They tumbled through the doorway—and stopped.

John Lubbock lay sprawled on the floor, without hat or overcoat, fixed in the unmistakable contortions of violent death. Lubbock had been strangled!

At the instant of discovery Ellery had opened his mouth and gasped like a drowning man; the suspect himself murdered! So he sidled toward Sergeant Velie near the bedroom door—the door which communicated with Lubbock's own bedroom—and effaced himself.

His eyes went to this door and quickly narrowed. The key which he had last seen sticking in the lock on the Apartment H side was now in the lock of Apartment G. He fingered it thoughtfully, then slipped out of the room.

He went into the central corridor, found the fingerprint expert, and took him back through Lubbock's bedroom to the door between the two apartments. "See what you can get out of this doorknob," he said. The expert went to work. Ellery watched anxiously. Under the man's ministrations several clear fingerprints appeared in white powder on the black stone of the knob. A photographer came in and snapped a picture of the fingerprints.

They repaired to the vacant bedroom of Apartment G. The physicians had completed their task and were discussing something in low tones with Inspector Queen, Ellery pointed to John Lubbock's dead fingers.

When the expert rose from the dusty floor he flourished a white card with ten inked fingerprints. He went to the door, unlocked it, and compared the dead man's prints with those on the knob of Lubbock's bedroom. "Okay," he said. "The stiff's mitts were on this knob."

Ellery sighed.

He knelt beside John Lubbock's body, which looked as if it had turned to stone in the midst of a fierce struggle, and explored the inside breast-pocket of Lubbock's coat.

Ellery looked thoughtfully at the teakwood case. "I owe an abject apology to the shade of our man-about-town. There *are* two cases, as he said. . . . For this *isn't* the one he showed us a few moments ago!"

The Inspector gaped. Where they had formerly observed in the silverwork of the teakwood case a groove whose sliver of metal was missing, the ornamental design on the case in Ellery's hand was unbroken, perfect.

"The inferences are plain," said Ellery. "Whoever killed John Lubbock did it for the teakwood case in his breast pocket. Everything is clear now. When the murderer strangled John Lubbock in this room, he stole John's case from John's body. The murderer then put into the case he had stolen from *Harry's* body—the first brother—six cigarettes of the same brand John's case contained, and then placed *Harry's* case with these six cigarettes on John's body, where we found it—in order to make us believe it was still John's case. Clever, but defeated by the fact that John's case had a sliver missing from the design whereas the engineer's had not. The murderer probably didn't notice the difference."

Ellery turned to the others; he held up his hand and they fell silent. "Ladies and gentlemen, the murderer's exceeded himself. He's done. I ask you to be attentive while I go over the ground and point out . . . Mr. Carter, stop shaking. I have every reason to believe that your executive worries are over."

Ellery stood at the feet of the dead man, his lean face expressionless. They watched him with stupid eyes. The detectives at the door retreated in response to Ellery's signal; and the Orkinses, Billy Harms in a négligé, the acid-faced jeweler Schley, Mr. and Mrs. Forrester of Apartment D, and even Mrs. Mallorie in her wheel-chair, crowded into the room.

"Certain lines of reasoning are inevitable," said Ellery, in a dry lecture-voice; he looked at none of them, seeming to be addressing the congested veins in John Lubbock's dead neck. "The only object taken from the first victim's dead body was the teakwood case. This means that the teakwood case was the object of the first murder. Now John Lubbock, the second victim, has been murdered; *his* teakwood case has been taken, and the first one put on his body. Conclusion: The only one who could have switched cases is the one who stole the first victim's case—the murderer. Therefore, both Harry and John Lubbock were strangled by the same hand. Two crimes and one culprit. Fundamental reasoning.

"Why was Harry Lubbock murdered? Simply because the murderer *mistook* him for his brother John, and did not discover the error until after he strangled his victim and examined the first teakwood case. It was the wrong one!

"The murderer's error is understandable. The first victim was choked from behind; superficially the engineer bore a resemblance to his brother John; no doubt the murderer was unaware that there were two Lubbocks. In other words, the engineer's case, the case on the floor, had nothing intrinsically to do with the crimes."

He leaned forward. "But mark this. Neither teakwood case *in itself* could have concealed anything—a hidden compartment, for example; then the cases were sought by the murderer not for themselves but for *what they contained*. What do cigarette-cases contain? What did both cases contain? Only cigarettes. But why should a man commit murder for cigarettes? Obviously, not for the pellets themselves. But if something had been *hidden* in those cigarettes—if they had been doctored, if tobacco had been removed from them and something secreted inside, and the ends tamped up with tobacco again . . . then we arrive at a concrete inference."

Ellery straightened and drew a deep breath. "You're Mrs. Mallorie, I take it?" he asked the invalid in the wheel-chair.

"I am!" she replied.

"Only two days ago you were parted from a diamond necklace. How large were the stones?"

"Like small peas," shrilled Mrs. Mallorie. "Worth twenty thousand dollars, the lot of 'em."

"Like small peas. Hmm. A housewifely description, Mrs. Mallorie." Ellery smiled. "We progress. I postulated John Lubbock's cigarettes as the hiding-place of something valuable . . . Mrs. Mallorie's rather expensive peas, ladies and gentlemen!"

They buzzed and peep-peeped like fowls in a barnyard. Ellery silenced them: "Yes, we have arrived at the point where it is indicated that your neighbor John Lubbock was not only a dilettante but a jewel thief as well!"

"Mr. Lubbock!" wheezed Seaman Carter in a shocked voice.

"Exactly. Inspector Queen has not been able to discover our man-about-town's source of income. A gigolo? Gigolos do not pay for ladies' apartments; the shoe is rather on the other foot. Ah, but the jewels! Here, then, is a minor mystery solved." Billy Harms stretched her white neck like an ostrich and sniffed. "But note that John Lubbock was murdered for those diamond-concealing cigarettes," Ellery continued. "Who could have known that he had those diamonds—moreover, in such a fantastic hiding-place? Surely none but an accomplice. In other words, when we lay hands on the murderer of Harry and John Lubbock we shall have found John Lubbock's partner-in-thievery."

The vague relief they had all exhibited gave way again to fear. No one stirred. Mrs. Mallorie was glaring at John Lubbock's purple face with the utmost malevolence. Ellery smiled again—a very playful and annoying smile. "Now," he said softly, "for the last act of our little drama: the details of the second murder. Jimmy," he said to the Headquarters fingerprint expert, "what did you find in your search?"

"This dead man on the floor had his fingers on the other side of this door—the side where his bedroom is."

"Thank you. Now it happens, ladies and gentlemen, that just before John Lubbock was murdered I had myself wiped the knob of his bedroom door—the door that leads into this vacant apartment—clean of all fingerprints. This means that Lubbock himself, when he went into his bedroom a few moments ago, put his fingers on the knob. This means that he deliberately opened the door in order to enter this vacant apartment. Was John Lubbock trying to escape? No; he did not don hat or overcoat, for one thing; for another, he could not hope to get far; and even if he did, escape would certainly tar him with the brush of suspicion that he had murdered his brother—and he, of course, was innocent, since he himself has been murdered. Then why did he go into this vacant apartment?

"I was talking with the Inspector some minutes ago in the foyer of Lubbock's apartment next door. At that time we had reason to believe John guilty of his brother's murder. I had myself shut the door to the living room so that he should not overhear. But when Dr. Eustace came out to visit his other patients in the building, unfortunately he left the door ajar, and it was at that moment that the Inspector, no doubt unaware that the door was open, said distinctly that we were intending to take John Lubbock down to Headquarters 'for a talk'—obviously, to search him and put him on the grid. The harm was done. Sergeant Velie, you were in the living room with Lubbock at that time. Did *you* hear the Inspector make that remark?"

"I did that," muttered the Sergeant, digging his heels into the floor. "I guess he did, too. Only a minute later he said he wanted to go into the bedroom for something."

"Q. E. D.," murmured Ellery. "Lubbock, hearing that he was about to be taken to Police Headquarters, thought rapidly. The stolen diamonds were imbedded in the cigarettes in his teakwood case; a thorough search would certainly reveal them. He must rid himself of those cigarettes! So now we know why he went into the vacant apartment—not to escape, but to hide the cigarettes somewhere until he could regain possession of them later. Naturally, he intended to return.

"But how could the murderer possibly anticipate John Lubbock's instantaneous decision to dispose of the jewels in this vacant apartment, the only immediately available hiding-place? *Only if the murderer, too, had heard the Inspector's remark about taking Lubbock to Headquarters, had realized that Lubbock had also heard, had foreseen what Lubbock would instantly have to do.*"

Ellery smiled wickedly and leaned forward; his long fingers were curved in a predatory hook; his body was tense. "Only five people overheard the Inspector's remark," he snapped. "The Inspector himself, I, Sergeant Velie, the late John Lubbock, and—"

Billy Harms screamed, and old Mrs. Mallorie screeched like a wounded parrot. Some one had plunged toward the door to the east corridor, bellowing and scattering people aside like a maddened bull-elephant, like a Malay running amuck, like an ancient Norseman in a berserker rage. . . . Sergeant Velie flung his two hundred and fifty pounds of muscle forward; there was a wild mix-up, the thudding of the Sergeant's chunky fists, clouds of dust. . . . Ellery stood quietly waiting. The Inspector, who had observed Sergeant Velie in action on many former occasions, merely sighed.

"A double-crossing villain as well as a twofold murderer," said Ellery at last when the Sergeant had hammered his adversary into red pulp. "He wanted not only to get rid of John Lubbock, his accomplice, the only human being who knew his guilt as a thief and suspected no doubt his guilt as a murderer, but also to have Mrs. Mallorie's jewels all for himself. Dad, you will find the diamonds either on his person, in his bag, or somewhere about his quarters. The problem," said Ellery, lighting a cigarette and inhaling gratefully under the stony stares of his audience, "was after all a simple one, one which admitted of a strictly logical attack. The facts themselves pointed to that man on the floor as the only possible culprit."

The man writhing in Sergeant Velie's inexorable grip was Dr. Eustace.

The Adventure of
"THE TWO-HEADED DOG"

As THE lowslung Duesenberg hummed along the murk-
dusted road between rows of stripped and silent trees, something
in the salty wind which moaned over the tall slender man at the
wheel on its journey across Martha's Vineyard, Cape Cod's heel,
and Buzzards Bay stirred him. Many a traveler on that modern road had quivered to the slap of the Atlantic winds, prickled
with molecules of spray, responding uneasily to the dim wind-
call of some ancestor's sea-poisoned blood. But it was neither
blood nor nostalgia which stirred the man in the open car. The
wind, which was ululating like a banshee, held no charm for him,
and the tingling spray no pleasure. His skin was crawling, it was
true, but only because his coat was thin, the October wind cold,
the spray distinctly discomforting, and the bare nightfall outside
New Bedford indefinably grim and peopled with shadows.

Shivering behind the big wheel, he switched on his head-
lights. An antiqued sign sprang whitely into view some yards
ahead and he slowed down to read it. It swung creaking to and

fro in the wind, hinged on scabrous iron, and it flaunted a fearsome monstrosity with two heads whose *genus* had apparently eluded even the obscure wielder of the paints. Below the monster run the legend:

"THE TWO-HEADED DOG"
(Cap'n Hosey's Rest)
Rooms—$2 And Up
Permanent—Transient
Auto-Campers Accommodated
In Clean Modern Cabins
Drive In

"Even Cerberus would make an acceptable host tonight," thought the traveler with a wry smile, and he swung the car into a gravelly driveway lined with trees, soon bringing the machine to rest before a high white house crisply painted, its green shutters clear as eyeshades. The inn sprawled over considerable territory, he saw, examining the angular structure in the glare of floodlights over the clearing. Around both sides ran car-lanes, and dimly toward the sides going rearwards he made out small cabins and a large outbuilding which was apparently a garage. There was a smack of old New England about the inn, disagreeably leavened with the modern cabins on its flanks. The huge old ship's lantern creaking and gleaming in battered brass above the front door somehow lost its savor.

"Might be worse, I suppose," he grumbled, leaning on his klaxon. "Hybrid!" The unearthly racket caused the heavy-timbered door to pop open almost instantly. A young woman in a reefer that contrived to look rakish appeared under the brass lantern.

"Ah," sighed the traveler, "the farmer's daughter. No, I'm in the wrong county. Could this be Cap'n Hosey? My dear skipper, is it possible for a sore and weary wayfarer to secure food and shelter this wretched night? That portrait of a misbegotten Cerberus painted on the sign yonder wasn't too alluring."

"We're in the business, if that's what you mean," said the young woman crisply, in a cultured voice. "And I'm *not* Cap'n Hosey; I'm his daughter. Jump out. I'll have your—" she regarded the dusty old Duesenberg with a sniff and grinned—"your equipage taken round to the garage."

The man crawled out onto the gravel, shivering, and from nowhere appeared a shambling oil-smeared creature in dungarees who silently climbed into the car.

"Take her around, Isaac," directed the young woman. "Luggage?"

"I lost it somewhere between here and Davy Jones' Locker," groaned the tall young man. "No, by St. Elmo, here it is!" He chuckled and plucked a battered suitcase out of the car. "Proceed, Charon, and treat my steed well. . . . Ah! Is that codfish polluting the vigorous air? I might have known."

"We're rather full up," said the young woman curtly. "Can't give you a room in the inn. You'll have to take a cabin. We've got just one left."

He halted under the flickering ship's lantern and said in a stern voice: "I can't say I care for your atmosphere, Miss Hosey. Do you keep ghosts for pets? I've felt clammy fingers groping about my neck all the way from Duxbury. Dinner?"

She was a very young and pretty miss, he saw, with russet hair and windblown lips. Also, she was angry. "Look here—"

"Tut, tut," he said mildly, "mustn't beshrew the guests, my dear. I should have said 'supper,' I suppose. It's always supper, isn't it?"

Her lips relaxed suddenly. "Oh, all right. You're erratic but—

nice. I do resent that crack about our 'misbegotten Cerberus,' though. Didn't Cerberus have two heads? I'll admit the art is dubious—"

"Erudition in New Bedford? My dear, Cerberus has had three heads, and fifty heads, and a hundred heads on various literary excursions, but I've never heard of his having had two."

"Darn," said Cap'n Hosey's daughter. "I was minoring in Greek at the time and I did think it *was* two. Won't you come in?"

They entered a large smoky room filled with chattering people—tourists, he saw at once, wincing—and some very lovely old furniture decidedly the worse for irreverent wear. A desk in the brass-cuspidor-and-leaky-pen tradition graced one corner of the room, presided over by a tall gaunt red-cheeked old man with white hair, frosty blue eyes, and a mildly benevolent expression. He wore a faded blue coat with brass buttons.

"This," said the young woman demurely, as the traveler dropped his suitcase on the linoleum-covered floor, "is Cap'n Hosey, the ancient mariner."

"Delighted to meet you, Captain Hosey," murmured the tall young man. "That's familiar for Hosea, I take it?"

"Ye k'n have it," chuckled the proprietor, extending a large and horny hand. "Howdy-do. Ye've met my daughter Jenny? I heard ye two jawin' outside. Don't pay no 'tention to Jenny, sir; she's eddicated, she is, an' that makes her a mite sharp, like the feller said when he was honin' his jackknife. Radcliffe, ye betcha," he said proudly.

Jenny turned very red. The young man said: "How charming; I must look into the Greek curriculum there," and reached for the register. He signed his name with weary fingers. "And now, if I may have a facial and manual rinse and a ton of supper?"

Jenny consulted the register, and her eyes widened and she exclaimed: "Why, don't tell me you're the—"

"Such," sighed Mr. Ellery Queen, "is fame. Don't tell *me* there's a murder in the vicinity—although I will say the environment is peculiarly conducive to tragedy. Quite Hardyesque, in fact. I've been running away from murders. Just saddled my faithful Rosinante and galloped off into New England, hoping for surcease."

"You *are* the Ellery Queen, though, who goes about solving—"

"Silence," he whispered fiercely. "No. I'm young Davy, Prince of Wales, and Papa George has permitted me to go gallivantin' incognito. For heaven's sake, Jenny, use discretion. All those people are listening."

"Queen, hey?" boomed Cap'n Hosey, beaming. "Well, well. I've heard tell of ye, young man. Proud to have ye. Jenny, ye go tell Martha to scramble up some vittles fer Mr. Queen. We'll mess down in th' taproom. Meanwhile, if ye'll come with me—"

"We?" said Ellery weakly.

"Well," grinned Cap'n Hosey, "we don't git such folks as th' usual thing, Mr. Queen. Now what was that last case I was readin' about. . . ?"

In a brass-and-wooden room downstairs redolent of hops and fish Mr. Ellery Queen found himself the focus of numerous respectful and excited eyes. He blessed his gods privately that they possessed the delicacy to permit him to eat in comparative peace. There were oysters, and codfish cakes, and broiled mackerel, and foamy lager, and airy apple pie and coffee. He stuffed himself with a will and actually began to feel better. Outside the winds might howl and the ghosts wander, but here it was warm and cheerful and even companionable.

They were a curious company. Cap'n Hosey had apparently gathered the cream of his cronies for the honor of staring at the famous visitor from New York. There was a man named Barker, a traveling salesman "in hardware"; as he said: "Mechanics' and building tools, Mr. Queen, cement, quicklime, household wares, *et cetera* and so forth." He was a tall needle-thin man with sharp eyes and the glib tongue of the professional itinerant. He smoked long cheroots as emaciated as himself.

Then there was a chubby man named Heiman, with heavy pitted glistening features and a cast in one eye that contrived to give him a droll expression. Heiman, it appeared, was "in drygoods," and he and Barker from their cheerful raillery were boon companions, their itineraries crossing each other every three months or so when they were—as Heiman put it—"on the road"; for both covered the southern New England territory for their respective establishments.

The third of Cap'n Hosey's intimates needed only the costume to be Long John Silver in the flesh. There was something piratical in the cut of his jib; he possessed besides the traditional cold blue eyes—Ellery gulped down a slithery Cotuit instinctively when he first saw it—a pegleg; and his speech was bristly with the argot of the sea.

"So ye're the great d'tective," rumbled the peglegged pirate, whose name was Captain Rye, when Ellery had washed down the last delectable morsel of pie with the last warm drop of coffee. "Can't say I ever heard o' ye."

"Shush, Bull," growled Cap'n Hosey.

"No, no," said Ellery comfortably, lighting a cigarette. "That's refreshing candor. Cap'n Hosey, I like your place."

Jenny said: "Mr. Queen's been wondering about the name of the inn, father. That work-of-art over the bar inspired it, Mr. Queen. Relic of father's past."

Ellery noticed for the first time that a faded, seamy, and weatherworn wood-carving was nailed over the bar. It was a three-dimensional projection of the painted monstrosity swinging over the road—a remotely canine bust with two remotely canine heads branching off a single hairy neck.

"Figgerhead of my granddaddy's three-master," boomed Cap'n Hosey from behind stupefying clouds of clay-pipe smoke. "The whaler *Cerb'rus*. When we opened this here place Jenny she thought that was too high-a-mighty a handle. So she named it *Th' Two-Headed Dog*. Pretty, ain't it?"

"Speakin' about dogs," said Heiman in his piping voice, "tell Mr. Queen about that business happened here three months ago, Cap'n Hosey."

"Hell, yes," cried Barker. "Tell Mr. Queen about that, Cap'n." His Adam's apple bobbed eagerly as he turned to Ellery. "One of the most interesting things ever happened to the old coot, I guess, Mr. Queen. Haw-haw! Near turned the place inside out."

"Dogs?" murmured Ellery.

"Jee-rusalem!" roared Cap'n Hosey. "Clean fergot 'bout it. Reg'lar crime, Mr. Queen. Took th' wind slap out o' *my* sails. Happened—let's see, now. . ."

"July," said Barker promptly. "I remember Heiman and I were both here then on our regular summer trip."

"God, what a night that was!" muttered chubby Heiman. "Makes my skin creep to think of it."

An odd silence fell over the company, and Ellery regarded them one by one with curiosity. There was a queer unease on the clean fresh face of Jenny, and even Captain Rye had become subdued.

"Well," said Cap'n Hosey at last in a low tone, "'twas round 'bout this time o' month, I sh'd say. Ter'ble dirty weather, Mr. Queen, that night. Stormed all over this end o' th' coast. Rainin' an' thunderin' to beat hell. One o' th' worst summer squalls I rec'lect. Well, sir, we was all settin' upstairs nice an' cozy, when Isaac—that's th' swab does my odd jobs—Isaac, he hollers in from outside there's a customer jest hove in with a car wantin' vittles and lodgin' fer th' night."

"Will you ever forget that—that hideous little creature?" shuddered Jenny.

"Who's spinnin' this yarn, Jenny?" demanded Cap'n Hosey. "Anyways, we was full up, like t'night—jest one cabin empty. This man comes in shakin' off th' wet; he was rigged out in a cross 'tween a sou'wester an' a rubber tire; an' he takes th' vacant cabin fer th' night."

"But the dog," sighed Ellery.

"I'm comin' to that, Mr. Queen. Well, sir, he was a runt— sawed-off lubber, with scared lamps on 'm ye c'd see a league off, *an'* he was nervous."

"Craps, he was nervous," muttered Heiman. "Couldn't look you in the eye. About fifty, I'd say; looked like some kind of clerk, I remember thinkin'."

"Except for the chin-whiskers," said Barker ominously. "Red, they were, and you didn't have to be a detective to see right off they were phony."

"Disguised, eh?" said Ellery, stifling a yawn.

"Yes, sir," said Cap'n Hosey. "Anyways, he reg'sters under th' name o' Morse—John Morse—gobbles up a mess o' slum downstairs, an' Jenny shows 'm to th' cabin, with Isaac convoyin' 'em. Tell Mr. Queen what happened, Jenny."

"He was horrible," said Jenny in a shaky voice. "He wouldn't let Isaac touch the car—insisted on driving it around to the garage himself. Then he made me point out the cabin; wouldn't let me take him there. I did, and he—he swore at me in a tired sort of way, b-but savagely, Mr. Queen. I felt he was dangerous. So I went off, and Isaac too. But I watched; and I saw him sneak back to the garage. He stayed there for some time. When he came out he went into the cabin and locked the door; I heard him lock it." She paused, and for the moment the most curious tension crackled in the smoky air. Ellery, unaccountably, no longer felt sleepy. "Then I—I went into the garage. . ."

"What sort of car was it?"

"An old Dodge, I think, with side-curtains tightly drawn. But he'd been so mysterious about it—" She gulped and smiled wanly. "I got into the garage and put my hand on the nearest curtain. Curiosity killed a cat, and it almost got me a very badly bitten hand."

"Ah, there was a dog in the car?"

"Yes." She shuddered suddenly. "I'd left, the garage-door open. When lightning flashed I could . . . It flashed. Something bit into the rubber curtain and I jerked my hand away just in time. I almost screamed. I heard him—it growl; low, rumbling, animal." They were very quiet now. "In the lightning a black muzzle poked out of a hole in the curtain and I saw two savage eyes. It was a dog, a big dog. Then I heard a noise outside and there was the—the little man with the red beard. He glared at me and shouted something. I ran."

"Naturally," murmured Ellery. "Can't say I'm overfond of the more brutal canines myself. A sign of the effete times, I daresay. And?"

"Ain't a hound been whelped," growled Captain Rye, "can't be mastered. Whippin' does it. I mind I had a big brute once, mastiff he was—"

"Stow it, Bull," said Cap'n Hosey testily. "Ye wa'n't here, so what d'ye know 'bout it? Takes more'n jest dog to scare my Jenny. I tell ye that there wa'n't no or'n'ry mutt!"

"Oh, Captain Rye wasn't stopping at the inn then?" said Ellery.

"Naw. Hove in 'bout two-three weeks after. Anyways, that ain't th' real part o' the yarn. When Jenny come back we nat'rally talked 'bout this swab, an'—'twas real funny—we all agreed we'd seen his ugly map some'eres b'fore."

"Indeed?" murmured Ellery. "All of you?"

"Well, I knew I'd seen his pan somewhere," muttered the dry-goods salesman, "and so had Barker. Later, when the two—"

"Haul up!" roared Cap'n Hosey. "'M I tellin' this yarn or ain't I? Well, we went t' bed. Jenny 'n' me, we bunk in our own quarters in th' little shack back o' th' garage; 'n' Barker 'n' Heiman, here, they had cabins that night; bunch o' school-marms 'd took up jest 'bout all th' room there was. Well, sir, we took a look at this Morse's cabin on th' way out, but it was darker'n a Chinee Lazaret. Then round 'bout three-four in th' mornin' it happened."

"By the way," said Ellery, "had you investigated the car before you turned in?"

"Sure did," said Cap'n Hosey grimly. "Ain't no hound this side o' hell I'm skeered on. But he wa'n't in th' car. Dog-stink was, though. This Morse must 'a' taken-th' dog to his cabin after he caught Jenny pokin' round where she had no bus'ness pokin'."

"The man was a criminal, I suppose," sighed Ellery.

"How'd you know?" cried Barker, opening his eyes.

"Tut, tut," said Ellery modestly, and inwardly groaned.

"He were a crim'nal, all right," said Cap'n Hosey emphatically. "Wait till I tell ye. Early mornin'—'twas still dark—Isaac comes a-poundin' on th' door an' when I opens it there's Isaac, nekkid under a reefer, with two hard-lookin' customers drippin' rain. Still squally, 'twas. Make a long story short, they was d'tectives lookin' fer this here Morse. They showed me a picture, an' o' course I reco'nized him right off even though in th' snap he was clean-shaved. They knew he'd been sportin' a fake red beard, an' that he was travelin' with a dog—big police dog—that he'd owned b'fore he skipped with th' jool. He'd lived in a suburb outside Chicawgo some'eres an' neighbors'd said they'd see him walkin' out with a dog every once in a while."

"Here, here," said Ellery, sitting up alertly. "Do you mean to say that was John Gillette, the little lapidary who stole the Cormorant diamond from Shapley's in Chicago last May?"

"That's him!" shouted Heiman, blinking his lid rapidly over the eye with the cast. "Gillette!"

"I remember reading about the case when the theft occurred," said Ellery thoughtfully, "although I never followed it through. Go on."

"He'd worked in Shapley's for twenty years," sighed Jenny, "always quiet and honest and efficient. A stonecutter. Then he was tempted and stole the Cormorant and disappeared."

"Worth a hundred grand," muttered Barker.

"A hund'ed grand!" exclaimed Captain Rye suddenly, stamping his pegleg on the stone floor. And he sank back and shoved his pipe into his mouth.

"Heap o' money," nodded Cap'n Hosey. "These d'tectives'd follered Gillette's trail all over creation, al'ays jest missin' 'm. But th' dog give 'm away finally. He'd been seen up Dedham way with th' dog. Lot o' this we found out fr'm them fellers later. Anyways, I shows 'em th' cabin an' they busts in. Nothin' doin'. He'd heard 'em or kep' an eye open, most likely, an' skipped."

"Hmm," said Ellery. "He didn't take the car?"

"Couldn't," said Cap'n Hosey grimly. "Skeered to take th' chance. Th' garage is too near where I bunked an' where th' d'tectives was jawin' with me. He must of got away through th' woods o' th' cabins. Them fellers was wild. In th' rain there wa'n't no tracks t' foller. Got away clean. Prob'ly stole a launch or had one hid down in th' Harbor an' headed either fer Narragansett Bay or ducked round to th' Vineyard. Never did find 'm."

"Did he leave anything behind besides the car?" murmured Ellery. "Personal belongings? The diamond?"

"The hell he did," snorted Barker. "What do you think he is—a fool? He skipped clean, like Cap'n Hosey says."

"Except," said Jenny, "for the dog."

"Seems a persistent brute, at any rate," chuckled Ellery. "You mean he left the police dog behind? You found him?"

"Th' d'tectives found th' mutt," scowled Cap'n Hosey. "When they busted into th' cabin there was a big heavy chain attached to th' grate o' th' fireplace. Jest the double chain. No dog. They found th' dog fifty yards off in th' woods, dead."

"Dead? How? What do you mean?" asked Ellery swiftly.

"Bashed over th' skull. An' an ugly brute she was, too. Female. All blood an' mud. Th' d'tectives said Gillette'd done it th' last minute to git rid o' her. She was gittin' too dangerous t' tote around. They took th' carkiss away."

"Well," smiled Ellery, "it must have been a hectic time, Captain. I don't think poor Jenny's over it yet."

The young woman shivered. "I'll not forget that hideous little b-bug as long as I live. And then—"

"Oh, there's something else? By the way, what happened to the car and the chain?"

"D'tectives took 'em away," rumbled Cap'n Hosey.

"I suppose," said Ellery, "there's no doubt they *were* detectives?"

They were all startled at that. Barker exclaimed: "Sure they were, Mr. Queen! Why, reporters were here from as far as Boston, and those dicks posed for pictures and everything!"

"Just a vagrant thought," said Ellery mildly. "You said: 'And then—' Jenny. And then what?"

There was an awkward silence. Barker and Heiman looked puzzled, but the two old seamen and Jenny turned pale.

"What's the matter?" shrilled Heiman, rolling his eyes.

"Well," muttered Cap'n Hosey, "I s'pose it's all foolishness an' sech, but that cabin ain't been th' same since—since that night, ye see."

"Say," chuckled Barker, "I have to sleep in that cabin tonight, Cap'n. What d'ye mean—not the same?"

Jenny said uneasily: "Oh, it's ridiculous, as father says, but the most extraordinary things have been happening there, Mr. Queen, since that night in July. J-just as if a—a ghost were prowling around."

"Ghost!" Heiman went white and shrank back, visibly affected.

"Now, now," said Ellery with a smile. "Surely that's overheated imagination, Jenny? I thought ghosts are indigenous only to old English castles."

"Ye may scoff all ye want," said Captain Rye darkly, "but I

once seen a ghost with me own eyes. 'Twas off Hatteras in th' winter o' '93—"

"Dry up, Bull," said Cap'n Hosey irritably. "I'm a God-fearin' man, Mr. Queen, an' I ain't skeered o' th' toughest spook ever walked a midnight sea. But—well, it's mighty queer." He shook his head as a gust of wind rattled down the chimney and stirred the ashes in the fireplace. "Mighty queer," he repeated slowly. "Had that cabin occypied a couple o' times since that night, an' everybody tells me they hear funny sounds there."

Barker guffawed. "G'on! You're kidding, Cap'n!"

"Ain't doin' no sech thing. You tell 'em, Jenny."

"I—I tried it one night myself," said Jenny in a low voice. "I think I'm reasonably intelligent, Mr. Queen. They're two-room cabins, and the complaints had said the sounds came from the—the living room while they were trying to sleep in the bedroom. The night I stayed in that cabin I—well, I heard it, too."

"Sounds?" frowned Ellery. "What kind of sounds?"

"Oh," she hesitated, shrugging helplessly, "cries. Moans, mutters, whimpers, slithery noises, patters, scrapings—I can't really describe them, but they," she shivered, "they didn't sound—human. There was such a variety of them! As—as if it was a congress of ghosts." She smiled at Ellery's cynical eyebrows. "I suppose you think I'm a fool. But I tell you—hearing those muffled, stealthy, inhuman sounds . . . well, they get you, Mr. Queen."

"Did you investigate the—ah—scene of the visitation while these sounds were being produced?" asked Ellery dryly.

She gulped. "I took one peek. It was dark, though, and I couldn't see a thing. The sounds stopped the minute I opened the door."

"And did they continue afterward?"

"I didn't wait to see, Mr. Queen," she said with a tremulous grin. "I ducked out of the bedroom window and ran for dear life."

"Hmm," said Barker, narrowing his shrewd eyes. "I always did say this part of the country produced more imagination to the square inch than a trunkful of fiction. Well, no goldarned sounds are going to keep *me* up. And if they happen I'll find out what made 'em or know the reason why!"

"I'll exchange cabins with you, Mr. Barker," murmured Ellery. "I've always felt the most poignant fear of—and the most insatiable curiosity about—ghosts. Never met one, I suppose. What say? Shall we trade?"

"Hell, no," chuckled Barker, rising. "You see, I'm prob'ly the world's greatest disbeliever in spirits, Mr. Queen. I've got a sweet little .32 Colt"—he grinned in a mirthless way—"I'm in hardware, you see—and I never heard of a spook yet that liked the taste of bullets. I'm goin' to bed."

"Well," sighed Ellery, "if you insist. Too bad. I'd love to have met a wraith—all clanky with chains and dripping foul seaweed. . . . Think I'll turn in myself. By the way, this cabin which had been occupied by Gillette is the only one in which your ghost has walked, Cap'n Hosey?"

"Only one, yep," said the innkeeper gloomily.

"And have sounds been heard while the cabin's been unoccupied?"

"Nope. We watched a couple o' nights, too, but nothin' happened."

"Curious." Ellery sucked a fingernail thoughtfully for a moment. "Well! If Miss Jenny and these gentlemen will excuse me?"

"Here," said Heiman hurriedly, bouncing out of the chair. "I'm not goin' to cross that backyard alone. . . . W-wait for baby!"

The rear of the inn was a desolate place. As they emerged from the backstairs leading from the taproom its cold desolation struck them like a physical blow. Ellery could hear Heiman breathing hoarsely, as if he had run far and fast. There was a livid moon, and it lit up his companions' faces: Heiman's was drawn, fearful; Barker's amused and a trifle wary. The cabins were for the most part black and silent; it was late.

They walked shoulder to shoulder across the sandy terrain, instinctively keeping together. The wind kept up an incessant angry hissing through the dark trees beyond the cabins.

"Night," muttered Heiman suddenly and darted across to one of the cabins. They heard him scuttle inside and lock the door. Then the rattles of windows came to their ears as the chubby salesman closed them hastily; and a square of yellow brilliance sprang up as he flooded his quarters with ghost-dispelling light.

"I guess it's got Heiman, all right," laughed Barker, shrugging his bony shoulders. "Well, Mr. Queen, here's where the spook hangs out. D'y'ever hear anything so nutty? These old sailors are all the same—superstitious as hell. I'm surprised at Jenny, though; she's an educated girl."

"Are you sure you shouldn't like me to—" began Ellery.

"Naw. I'll be all right. I've got a quart of rye in one of my sample trunks that's the best little ghost-chaser y'ever saw." Barker chuckled deep in his throat. "Well, nighty-night, Mr. Queen. Sleep tight and don't let the spooks bite!" He sauntered to his cabin, squared his shoulders, whistled a rather dreary tune, and disappeared. A moment later the light flashed on and his thin long figure appeared at the front window and pulled down the shade.

"Whistling," thought Ellery grimly, "in the dark. At that, the man has intestines." He shrugged and flicked his cigarette away. It was no concern of his; some natural phenomenon, no doubt—wind sobbing down a chimney shaft, the scratchings of a mouse, the rattle of a loose window-pane; and there was a ghost. Tomorrow he would be well out of it, headed for Newport and the home of his friend. . . . He flattened against the door of his cabin.

Some one was standing in the shadow of the inn's back door, watching.

Ellery crouched and slipped along the walls of the cabins toward the inn—crept like a cat upon the motionless watcher before he realized how ridiculous his stealth was. When he caught himself up, swearing, it was too late. The watcher had spied him. It was Isaac, the man-of-all work.

"Out for a breath of air?" asked Ellery lightly, fumbling for another cigarette. The man did not reply. Ellery said: "Uh—by the way, Isaac, if I may use the familiar—when a cabin is unoccupied are the windows closed?"

The broad bowed shoulders twitched contemptuously. "Yep."

"Locked?"

"Nope." The man answered in a heavy rumble, like aged thunder. He stepped out of the shadow and gripped Ellery's arm so tightly that the cigarette fell out of his hand. "I harkened to yer scoffin' an' sneerin' in th' taproom. An' I says to ye: Scoff not an' sin not. There're more things in heav'n 'n' earth, Horaysheeo, th'n 're drempt of in yer philos'phy. Amen!" And Isaac turned and vanished.

Ellery stared at the empty shadows with puzzled, angry eyes. An innkeeper's daughter who had studied Greek; a shambling countryman who quoted Shakespeare! What the deuce was going on here, anyway? Then he cursed himself for a meddling, imaginative fool and strode back to his cabin. And yet, despite

himself, he shivered at the slash of the wind; and his scalp prickled at a perfectly natural night-sound from the silent woods.

Something cried out in the distance—faintly, desperately, a
lost soul. It cried again. And again. And again.

Mr. Ellery Queen found himself sitting up in bed, covered
with perspiration, listening with all the power of his ears. The
cabin bedroom, the black world outside, were profoundly quiet.
Had it been a dream?

He sat listening for minutes that were hours. Then, in the dark,
he fumbled for his watch. The luminous dials glowed at 1:25.

Something in the very silence made him get out of bed, slip
into his clothes, and go to the door of the cabin. The clearing
was a pit of darkness; the moon had long since set. The wind had
died somewhere in the lost hours and the air, while cold, was
still. Cries . . . A conviction grew within him that they had come
from Barker's cabin.

His shoes crunched loudly on the stiff earth as he went to
Barker's front door and knocked. There was no answer. He
knocked again.

A man's deep, curiously strained voice said behind him: "So ye
heard it, too, Mr. Queen?" He whirled to find old Cap'n Hosey,
in pants and slippers and a huge sweater, at his shoulder.

"Then it wasn't my imagination," muttered Ellery. He knocked
again, and there was still no answer. Trying the door, he found it
locked. He looked at Cap'n Hosey, and Cap'n Hosey looked at
him. Then, without speaking, the old man led the way around
the cabin to the back, facing the woods. The rear window to
Barker's living room stood open, although the shade was down.
Cap'n Hosey poked it aside and directed a flashlight into the
thick blackness of the room. They caught their breaths, sharply.

The lank figure of Barker, dressed in pajamas and bathrobe, slippers on his skinny naked feet, lay on the rug in the center of the room—contorted like an open jacknife in the ghastly, unmistakable attitude of violent death.

How the others knew no one thought of asking. Death wings its way swiftly into human consciousness. When Ellery rose from his knees beside the dead man he found Jenny, Isaac, and Heiman crowded in the doorway; Cap'n Hosey had opened the door. Behind them peered the vulturous face of Captain Rye. They were all in various stages of undress.

"Dead only a few minutes," murmured Ellery, looking down at the sprawled body. "Those cries we heard must have been his death-cries." He lit a cigarette and went to the window and leaned against the sill and stood there, drooping and watchful as he smoked. No one said anything, and no one moved. Barker was dead. A matter of hours before he had been alive, laughing and breathing and joking. And now he was dead. It was a curious thing.

It was a curious thing, too, that except for a very small area on the rug with the dead man as its nucleus, nothing in the room had been disturbed. In one corner stood two big trunks, both open, with various heavy drawers; they contained samples of Barker's wares. The furniture stood neatly and sedately about. Only the rug around Barker's body was scuffed and wrinkled, as if there had been a struggle at precisely that spot. One bit of wreckage not native to the room lay a few feet away: a flashlight, its glass and bulb shattered.

The dead man lay partly on his back. His eyes were wide open and staring with an unearthly intensity of horror and fear. His fingers clutched the loose collar of his pajama-coat, quite as if some one had been strangling him. But he had not been strangled; he had bled to death. For his throat, fully revealed by the painful backward stretching of his head, had been ripped and slashed raggedly, grotesquely, at the jugular vein, and his hands and coat and the rug were smeared with his still liquid blood.

"Good God," choked Heiman; he covered his face with his hands and began to sob. Captain Rye pulled him roughly outside, growling something at him; they heard the chubby man stumble off to his cabin.

Ellery flipped his cigarette out the window past the shade, which they had raised on climbing into the room, and went to Barker's sample trunks. He pulled out all the drawers. But nothing was there that should not have been there, and the hammers and saws and chisels and electrical supplies and samples of cement and lime and plaster were ranged in neat unviolated rows. Finding no evidence of disturbance in either trunk, he went quietly into the bedroom. He returned soon enough, looking thoughtful.

"What—what d'ye do in a case like this?" croaked Cap'n Hosey. His weatherbeaten face was the color of wet ashes.

"And what do you think about your ghost now, Mr. Queen?" giggled Jenny; her face was convulsed with horror. "G-ghosts . . . Oh, my God!"

"Now, now, pull yourself together," murmured Ellery. "Why, notify the local authorities, naturally, Captain. In fact, I advise very prompt action. The murder occurred only a matter of minutes ago. The murderer must still be in the vicinity—"

"Oh, he is, is he?" growled Captain Rye, stepping crookedly into the room on his pegleg. "Well, Hosey, what in time ye waitin' fer?"

"I—" The old man shook his head in a daze.

"The murderer got out through the back window," said Ellery

softly. "Probably hard on my first knock at the front door. He took the weapon with him, dripping blood. There are a few bloodstains on the sill here pointing to that." There was the most curious note in his voice: a compound of mockery and uncertainty.

Cap'n Hosey departed, heavily. Captain Rye hesitated and then stumped off after his friend. Isaac stood dumbly staring at the corpse. But there was a freshet of color in Jenny's young cheeks and her eyes reflected a returning sanity.

"What sort of weapon, Mr. Queen," she demanded in a small but steady voice, "do you think capable of inflicting such a frightful wound?"

Ellery started. "Eh?" Then he smiled. "There," he said dryly, "is a question indeed. Sharp and yet jagged. A vicious, lethal instrument. It suggests certain *outré* possibilities." Her eyes went wide, and he shrugged. "This is a curious case. I'm half-disposed to believe—"

"But you know nothing whatever about Mr. Barker!"

"Knowledge, my dear," he remarked gravely, "is the antidote to fear, as Emerson has pointed out. Moreover, it needs no catalyst." He paused. "Miss Jenny. This isn't going to be pleasant. Why don't you return to your own quarters? Isaac can stay and help me."

"You're going to—?" Terror glittered in her eyes again.

"There's something I must see. Please go." She sighed rather strangely and turned and went away. Isaac, a motionless hulk, still stared at the corpse. "Now, Isaac," said Ellery briskly, "stop gaping and help me with him. I want him moved out of the way."

The man stirred. "I told ye—" he began harshly, and then clamped his lips shut. He looked almost surly as he shambled forward. They raised the fast-chilling body without words and carried it into the bedroom. When they returned Isaac pulled out a lump of stiff brown stuff and bit off a piece. He chewed slowly, without enjoyment.

"Nothing missing, nothing stolen, so far as I can tell," muttered Ellery, half to himself. "That's a good sign. A very good sign indeed." Isaac stared at him without expression. Ellery shook his head and went to the middle of the room. He got to his knees and examined the rug in the area on which Barker's body had rested. There was a fairly smooth piece where the body had lain, surrounded like an island by the ripples of the disturbed rug. His eyes narrowed. Was it possible . . . He bent forward in some excitement, studying the rug fiercely. By God, it was!

"Isaac!" The countryman lumbered over. "What the devil caused this?" Ellery pointed. The nap of the rug where the corpse had sprawled was quite worn away. On examination it had a curiously scratched appearance, as if it had been subjected to a long and persistent scraping process. It was the only part of the rug, as he could see plainly enough, which was rubbed in that manner.

"Dunno," said Isaac phlegmatically.

"Who cleans these cabins?" snapped Ellery.

"Me."

"Have you ever noticed that spot before—that worn spot?"

"Cal'late."

"When, man, when? When'd you first begin to notice it?"

"Wall—round 'bout th' middle o' summer, I guess."

Ellery sprang to his feet. "*Banzai!* Better than my fondest hopes. That clinches it!" Isaac stared at him as if Ellery had suddenly gone mad. "The others," mumbled Ellery, "were mere speculations, stabs in the dark. This—" He smacked his lips together. "Look here, man. Is there a weapon on the premises somewhere? Revolver? Shotgun? Anything?"

Isaac grunted: "Wall, Cap'n Hosey's got an ol' shooter some'eres."

"Get it. See that it's oiled, loaded, ready for business. For God's sake, man, hurry! And—oh, yes, Isaac. Tell everybody to keep away from here. *Keep away!* No noise. No disturbance. Except the police. Do you understand?"

"I cal'late," muttered Isaac, and was gone.

For the first time something like fear leaped into Ellery's eyes. He twisted toward the window, took a step, stopped, shook his head, and hurried to the fireplace. There he found a heavy iron poker. Gripping it nervously, he ran into the bedroom and half-closed the door. He remained completely quiet until he heard Isaac's heavy step outside. Then he dashed through the living-room, snatched a big old-fashioned revolver from the man's hand, sent him packing, made sure the weapon was loaded and cocked, and returned to the living room. But now he acted with more assurance. He knelt by the telltale spot on the rug, placed the revolver near his foot, and swiftly hauled up the rug until the bare wooden floor was revealed. He scanned this closely for some time. Then he replaced the rug and took up the revolver again.

He met them at the door fifteen minutes later with his finger at his lips. They were three husky, hatchet-faced New Englanders with drawn revolvers. Curious heads were poking out of lighted cabins all about.

"Oh, the idiots!" groaned Ellery. "Reassure those people, blast 'em. You're the law here?" he whispered to the leading stranger.

"Yep. Benson's my name," growled the man. "I met your daddy once—"

"Never mind that now. Make those people put out their lights and keep absolutely quiet; d'ye understand?" One of the officers darted away. "Now come inside, and for the love of heaven don't make any noise."

"But where's the body of this drummer?" demanded the New Bedford man.

"In the bedroom. He'll keep," rasped Ellery. "Come on, man, for God's sake." He herded them into the living room, shut the door with caution, got them into an alcove, snapped off the light. . . . The room blinked out, vanished.

"Have your weapons ready," whispered Ellery. "How much do you know about this business?"

"Well, Cap'n Hosey told me over the 'phone about Barker, and those damn funny noises—" muttered Benson.

"Good." Ellery crouched a little, his eyes fixed on the exact center of the room, although he could see nothing. "In a few moments, if my deductions are correct, you'll meet—the murderer of Barker."

The two men drew in their breaths. "By God," breathed Benson, "I don't see—How—"

"Quiet, man!"

They waited for an eternity. There were no sounds whatever. Then Ellery felt one of the officers behind him stir uneasily and mutter something beneath his breath. After that the silence was ear-splitting. He realized suddenly that the palm of his hand around the butt of the big revolver was wet; he wiped it off noiselessly against his thigh. His eyes did not waver from the invisible center of the black room.

How long they huddled there none of them could say. But after eons they became conscious of . . . something in the room. They had not actually heard a physical sound. A negation of sound, and yet it was louder than thunder. Something, some one, in the center of the room. . .

They almost gasped. A weird, snivelling, moaning cry, barely audible, accompanied by mysterious scratchy sounds like the scraping of ice, came to their ears.

The nervous officer behind Ellery lost control of himself. He uttered a fearful squeal.

"You damned fool!" shouted Ellery, and instantly fired. He fired again, and again, trying to trace the intruder's invisible career in the room. The place became sulphurous with stink; they coughed in the smoke. Then there was one long gurgling shriek like nothing human. Ellery darted like lightning to the switch and snapped it on.

The room was empty. But a trail of fresh copious blood led raggedly to the open window, and the shade was still flapping. Benson cursed and vaulted through, followed by his man.

Simultaneously the door clattered open and staring eyes glared in. Cap'n Hosey, Jenny, Isaac. . . . "Come in, come in," said Ellery wearily. "There's a badly wounded murderer in the woods now, and it's only a question of time. He can't get away." He sank into the nearest chair and fumbled for a cigarette, his eyes shadowed with strain.

"But who—What—"

Ellery waved a listless hand. "It was simple enough. But queer; damnably queer. I can't recall a queerer case."

"You know *who*—" began Jenny in a breathless voice.

"Certainly. And what I don't know I can piece together. But there's something to be done before I. . ." He rose. "Jenny, do you think you can withstand another shock?"

She blanched. "What do you mean, Mr. Queen?"

"I daresay you can. Cap'n Hosey, lend a hand, please." He went to one of Barker's sample trunks and extracted a couple of chisels and an ax. Cap'n Hosey glared at the unknown. "Come, come,

Captain, there's no danger now. Jerk that rug away. I'm going to show you something." Ellery handed him a chisel when the old man had complied. "Pry up the nails holding these floor-boards together. Might's well do a neat job; there's no sense in ruining your floor utterly." He went to work with the second chisel at the opposite end of the board. They labored in silence for some time with chisels and ax, and finally loosened the boards.

"Stand back," said Ellery quietly, and he stooped and began to remove them one by one. . . . Jenny uttered an involuntary shriek and buried her face against her father's broad chest.

Beneath the floor, on the stony earth supporting the cabin, lay a horrible, shapeless, vaguely human mass, whitish in hue. Bones protruded here and there.

"You see lying here," croaked Ellery, "the remains of John Gillette, the jewel-thief."

"G-Gillette!" stuttered Cap'n Hosey, glaring into the hole.

"Murdered," sighed Ellery, "by your friend Barker three months ago."

He took a long scarf from one of the tables and flung it over the gap in the floor. "You see," he murmured in the stupefied silence, "when Gillette came here that night in July and asked for a cabin, while you all thought he looked vaguely familiar, Barker actually recognized him from having seen his photograph in the papers, no doubt. Barker himself was occupying a cabin that night. He knew Gillette had the Cormorant diamond. When everything was quiet he managed to get into this place and murdered Gillette. Since he carried all the hardware his heart could desire, *plus quicklime,* he pried up the boards under this rug, deposited Gillette's body there, poured the lime over it to destroy the flesh quickly and prevent the discovery of the body from an odor of putrefaction, nailed down the boards again. . . . There's more to it, of course. It all fitted nicely once I had deduced the identity of the murderer. It had to be."

"But," gulped Cap'n Hosey in a sick voice, "how'd ye *know*, Mr. Queen? An' who—"

"There were several pointers. Then I found something which clinched my vaguely glimpsed theory. I'll start from the clincher to make it more easily digestible." Ellery reached for the back-flung rug and pulled it out so that the curiously worn area was visible. "You see that? Nowhere on the rug except at this precise spot does such a strangely worn area appear. And mark, too, that it was on this precise spot that Barker was attacked and killed, since nowhere except closely about this spot was the rug wrinkled and scuffed; indicating that this must have been the vortex of a short struggle. . . . Any idea what might have caused such a peculiar wearing away of your rug, Captain?"

"Well," mumbled the old man, "it looks kinda scratchy, like as if—"

Benson's voice came from beyond the open window. It held a note of supreme disbelief. "We got him, Mr. Queen. He died out in the woods."

They flocked to the window. Below, on the cold earth, re-vealed in the harsh glare of Benson's flash, lay a huge male police dog. His coat was rough and dirty and matted with burrs, and on his head was the cicatrix of a terrible wound, as if he had long before been struck violently over the head. His body was punc-tured in two places by fresh bullet-holes from Ellery's revolver; but the blood on the snarling muzzle was already dry.

"You see," said Ellery wearily, a little later, "it struck me at once that the worn spot looked scratchy—that is, *as if it had been scratched at* and thus rubbed away. The scratchy nature of the erosion suggested an animal; probably a dog, for of all domesticated animals the dog is the most inveterate scratcher. In other words, a dog had visited this room at various times during the summer nights and scratched away on the rug at this spot."

"But how could you be sure?" protested Jenny.

"Not by that alone. But there were confirmations. The sounds, for example, of your 'ghost.' From the way you described them they might easily have been canine sounds; in fact, you yourself said they were 'inhuman.' I believe you said 'moans, mutters, whimpers, slithery noises, patters, scrapings.' Moans and mutters and whimpers—surely a dog in pain or grief, if you're on the track of a dog already? Slithery noises, patters—a dog prowling about. Scrapings—a dog scratching . . . in this case, at the rug. I felt it was significant." He sighed. "Then there was the matter of the *occasions* your ghost selected for his visitations to the cabin. As far as any one could tell, he never came when the cabin was unoccupied. And yet that is when you would expect a marauder to come. Why did he come only when some one was in the cabin? Well, Isaac told me that in empty cabins the windows are kept closed—not locked, merely closed. But a *human* marauder wouldn't be stopped by a closed window; wouldn't be stopped, when it comes to that, even by a locked window. Again the suggestion of an animal, you see. He was able to get in only when one of the windows was *open;* he could get in therefore only at such times as the cabin was occupied and its occupants *left* the living-room window open."

"By Godfrey!" muttered Cap'n Hosey.

"There were other confirmations, too. There had been evidence of one police dog in this case, a female. It had come here with Gillette. Yet when the Chicago detectives burst into the cabin and found Gillette apparently gone (which was what Barker relied on), they found indirect evidence—had they realized it—not of one dog but of *two*. For there was the heavy *double* chain. Why a double chain? Wouldn't one heavy chain be enough for even the most powerful dog? So there was another confirmation of an extra dog, a live dog—confirmation that Gillette really had had two all the time, although no one knew of the existence of the second; that when Miss Jenny tried to peer into Gillette's car in the garage there was still another dog behind the one that tried to bite her hand; that Gillette, fearing the dogs would betray him, then took them both into his cabin and chained them there. They were helpless while Barker murdered the thief. He must have battered the heads of the two dogs—perhaps with this very iron poker—thinking he was killing them both. Any barks or growls they may have uttered were quite swallowed up in the noise of the rain and thunder that night, as were the sounds of Barker's hammering down the boards afterward. Barker then must have dragged the two dogs' bodies out into the woods, reasoning that it would be assumed Gillette had killed them. But the male was not dead, only badly stunned—you saw the terrible scar on his head, which is what permitted me to reconstruct Barker's activity against the animals. The male recovered and slunk off. You see, the double chain, the storm that night, the wound—they tell a remarkably clear story."

"But why—" began Heiman, who had crept into the cabin a moment before.

Ellery shrugged. "There are lots of whys. Incidentally, the wound itself on Barker's throat confirmed my theory of a dog—a ragged slashing above the jugular. That's a dog's method of killing. But why, I asked myself, had the dog remained invisibly in the neighborhood, as he must have—prowling the woods, wild, wolfish, existing on small game or refuse? Why had he persisted in returning to this cabin and scratching on the rug—of all things? There could be only one answer. Something he loved was *below that rug,* at that exact spot. Not the female dog, probably his mate—she was dead and had been taken away. Then his master. But his master was Gillette. Was it possible, then, that Gillette had not made his escape, but was under the floor? It was the only answer; and if he was under the floor he was dead. After that it was easy. Barker wanted this cabin tonight badly. He went to the rug, stooped over to lift it. The dog was watching, sprang through the window. . . ."

"You mean to say," gasped Cap'n Hosey, "he reco'nized Barker?"

Ellery smiled wanly. "Who knows? I don't give dogs credit for human intelligence, although they do startling enough things at times. If he did, then he must have lain paralyzed from Barker's blow on the night of Gillette's murder, but still conscious enough to witness Barker's burial of the body under the floor of the cabin. Either that, or it was merely that an alien hand was desecrating his master's grave. In any event, I knew Barker must have murdered Gillette; the juxtaposition of his sample trunks with its contents and the use of quicklime on the body was too significant."

"But why did Barker come back, Mr. Queen?" whispered Jenny. "That was stupid—ghoulish." She shivered.

"The answer to that, I fancy," murmured Ellery, "is simplicity itself. I have a notion—" They were in the alcove. He went out into the living room where Benson and his men were squatting over the hole in the floor, raking in the mess below with hammers and chisels. "Well, Benson?"

"Got it, by Christopher!" roared Benson, leaping to his feet and dropping a hammer. "You were dead right. Mr. Queen!" In his hand there was an enormous raw diamond.

"I thought so," murmured Ellery. "If Barker deliberately came back it could only have been for one reason, since the body was well buried and Gillette was considered to be alive. That was— the loot. But he must have taken what he thought to be the loot when he murdered Gillette. Therefore he had been fooled— Gillette, the lapidary, had cleverly made a paste replica of the diamond before he skipped, and it was the replica that Barker had stolen. When he discovered his error after leaving here in July it was too late. So he had to wait until his next sales trip to New Bedford and dig back under the floor. That was why he was crouched over that spot on the rug when the dog jumped him."

There was a little silence. Then Jenny said softly: "I think y— it's perfectly wonderful, Mr. Queen." She patted her hair.

Ellery shuffled to the door. "Wonderful? There's only one wonderful thing about this case, aside from the unorthodox identity of the murderer, my dear. Some day I shall write a monograph on the phenomenon of coincidence."

"What's that?" demanded Jenny.

He opened the door and sniffed the crisp morning air, its invigorating fillip of salt, with grateful nostrils. The first streaks of dawn were visible in the cold black sky. "The name," he chuckled, "of the inn."

The Adventure of
THE GLASS-DOMED CLOCK

OF ALL the hundreds of criminal cases in the solution of which Mr. Ellery Queen participated by virtue of his self-imposed authority as son of the famous Inspector Queen of the New York Detective Bureau, he has steadfastly maintained that none offered a simpler diagnosis than the case which he has designated as "The Adventure of the Glass-Domed Clock." "So simple," he likes to say—sincerely!—"that a sophomore student in high school with the most elementary knowledge of algebraic mathematics would find it as easy to solve as the merest equation." He has been asked, as a result of such remarks, what a poor untutored first-grade detective on the regular police force—whose training in algebra might be something less than elementary— could be expected to make of such a "simple" case. His invariably serious response has been: "Amendment accepted. The resolution now reads: Anybody with common sense could have solved that crime. It's as basic as five minus four leaves one."

This was a little cruel, when it is noted that among those who had opportunity—and certainly wishfulness—to solve the crime was Mr. Ellery Queen's own father, the Inspector, certainly not the most stupid of criminal investigators. But then Mr. Ellery Queen, for all his mental prowess, is sometimes prone to confuse his definitions: *viz.*, his uncanny capacity for strict logic is far from the average citizen's common sense. Certainly one would not be inclined to term elementary a problem in which such components as the following figured: a pure purple amethyst, a somewhat bedraggled expatriate from Czarist Russia, a silver loving-cup, a poker game, five birthday encomiums, and of course that peculiarly ugly relic of early Americana catalogued as "the glass-domed clock"—among others! On the surface the thing seems too utterly fantastic, a maniac's howling nightmare. Anybody with Ellery's cherished "common sense" would have said so. Yet when he arranged those weird elements in their proper order and pointed out the "obvious" answer to the riddle—with that almost monastic intellectual innocence of his, as if everybody possessed his genius for piercing the veil of complexities!—Inspector Queen, good Sergeant Velie, and the others figuratively rubbed their eyes, the thing was so clear.

It began, as murders do, with a corpse. From the first the eeriness of the whole business struck those who stood about in the faintly musked atmosphere of Martin Orr's curio shop and stared down at the shambles that had been Martin Orr. Inspector Queen, for one, refused to credit the evidence of his old senses; and it was not the gory nature of the crime that gave him pause, for he was as familiar with scenes of carnage as a butcher and blood no longer made him squeamish. That Martin Orr, the celebrated little Fifth Avenue curio dealer whose establishment was a treasure-house of authentic rarities, had had his shiny little bald head bashed to red ruin—this was an indifferent if practical detail; the bludgeon, a heavy paperweight spattered with blood but wiped clean of fingerprints, lay not far from the body; so *that* much was clear. No, it was not the assault on Orr that opened their eyes, but what Orr had apparently done, as he lay gasping out his life on the cold cement floor of his shop, *after* the assault.

The reconstruction of events after Orr's assailant had fled the shop, leaving the curio dealer for dead, seemed perfectly legible: having been struck down in the main chamber of his establishment, toward the rear, Martin Orr had dragged his broken body six feet along a counter—the red trail told the story plainly—had by super-human effort raised himself to a case of precious and semi-precious stones, had smashed the thin glass with a feeble fist, had groped about among the gem-trays, grasped a large unset amethyst, fallen back to the floor with the stone tightly clutched in his left hand, had then crawled on a tangent five feet past a table of antique clocks to a stone pedestal, raised himself again, and deliberately dragged off the pedestal the object it supported—an old clock with a glass dome over it—so that the clock fell to the floor by his side, shattering its fragile case into a thousand pieces. And there Martin Orr had died, in his left fist the amethyst, his bleeding right hand resting on the clock as if in benediction. By some miracle the clock's machinery had not been injured by the fall; it had been one of Martin Orr's fetishes to keep all his magnificent timepieces running; and to the bewildered ears of the little knot of men surrounding Martin Orr's corpse that gray Sunday morning came the pleasant *tick-tick-tick* of the no longer glass-domed clock.

Weird? It was insane!

"There ought to be a law against it," growled Sergeant Velie.

Dr. Samuel Prouty, Assistant Medical Examiner of New York County, rose from his examination of the body and prodded Martin Orr's dead buttocks—the curio dealer was lying face down—with his foot.

"Now here's an old coot," he said grumpily, "sixty if he's a day, with more real stamina than many a youngster. Marvelous powers of resistance! He took a fearful beating about the head and shoulders, his assailant left him for dead, and the old monkey clung to life long enough to make a tour about the place! Many a younger man would have died in his tracks."

"Your professional admiration leaves me cold," said Ellery. He had been awakened out of a pleasantly warm bed not a half-hour before to find Djuna, the Queens' gypsy boy-of-all-work, shaking him. The Inspector had already gone, leaving word for Ellery, if he should be so minded, to follow. Ellery was always so minded when his nose sniffed crime, but he had not had breakfast and he was thoroughly out of temper. So his taxicab had rushed through Fifth Avenue to Martin Orr's shop, and he had found the Inspector and Sergeant Velie already on the fluttered scene interrogating a grief-stunned old woman—Martin Orr's aged widow—and a badly frightened Slavic giant who introduced himself in garbled English as the "ex-Duke Paul." The ex-Duke Paul, it developed, had been one of Nicholas Romanov's innumerable cousins caught in the whirlpool of the Russian revolution who had managed to flee the homeland and was eking out a none too fastidious living in New York as a sort of social curiosity. This was in 1926, when royal Russian expatriates were still something of a novelty in the land of democracy.

As Ellery pointed out much later, this was not only 1926, but precisely Sunday, March the seventh, 1926, although at the time it seemed ridiculous to consider the specific date of any importance whatever.

"Who found the body?" demanded Ellery, puffing at his first cigarette of the day.

"His Nibs here," said Sergeant Velie, hunching his colossal shoulders. "*And* the lady. Seems like the Dook or whatever he is has been workin' a racket—been a kind of stooge for the old duck that was murdered. Orr used to give him commissions on the customers he brought in—and I understand he brought in plenty. Anyway, Mrs. Orr here got sort of worried when her hubby didn't come home last night from the poker game. . . ."

"Poker game?"

The Russian's dark face lighted up. "Yuss. Yuss. It is remarkable game. I have learned it since my sojourn in your so amazing country. Meester Orr, myself, and some others here play each week. Yuss." His face fell, and some of his fright returned. He looked fleetingly at the corpse and began to edge away.

"You played last night?" asked Ellery in a savage voice.

The Russian nodded. Inspector Queen said: "We're rounding 'em up: It seems that Orr, the Duke, and four other men had a sort of poker club, and met in Orr's back room there every Saturday night and played till all hours. Looked over that back room, but there's nothing there except the cards and chips. When Orr didn't come home Mrs. Orr got frightened and called up the Duke—he lives at some squirty little hotel in the Forties—the Duke called for her, they came down here this morning. . . . This is what they found." The Inspector eyed Martin Orr's corpse and the debris of glass surrounding him with gloom, almost with resentment. "Crazy, isn't it?"

Ellery glanced at Mrs. Orr; she was leaning against a counter, frozen-faced, tearless, staring down at her husband's body as if she could not believe her eyes. Actually, there was little to see: for Dr. Prouty had flung outspread sheets of a Sunday newspaper over the body, and only the left hand—still clutching the amethyst—was visible.

"Unbelievably so," said Ellery dryly. "I suppose there's a desk in the back room where Orr kept his accounts?"

"Sure."

"Any paper on Orr's body?"

"Paper?" repeated the Inspector in bewilderment. "Why, no."

"Pencil or pen?"

"No. Why, for heaven's sake?"

Before Ellery could reply, a little old man with a face like wrinkled brown papyrus pushed past a detective at the front door; he walked like a man in a dream. His gaze fixed on the shapeless bulk and the bloodstains. Then, incredibly, he blinked four times and began to cry. His weazened frame jerked with sobs. Mrs. Orr awoke from her trance; she cried: "Oh, Sam, Sam!" and, putting her arms around the newcomer's racked shoulders, began to weep with him.

Ellery and the Inspector looked at each other, and Sergeant Velie belched his disgust. Then the Inspector grasped the crying man's little arm and shook him. "Here, stop that!" he said gruffly. "Who are you?"

The man raised his tear-stained face from Mrs. Orr's shoulder; he blubbered: "S-Sam Mingo, S-Sam Mingo, Mr. Orr's assistant. Who—who—Oh, I can't believe it!" and he buried his face in Mrs. Orr's shoulder again.

"Got to let him cry himself out, I guess," said the Inspector, shrugging. "Ellery, what the deuce do you make of it? I'm stymied."

Ellery raised his eyebrows eloquently. A detective appeared in the street-door escorting a pale, trembling man. "Here's Arnold Pike, Chief. Dug him out of bed just now."

Pike was a man of powerful physique and jutting jaw; but he was thoroughly unnerved and, somehow, bewildered. He fastened his eyes on the heap which represented Martin Orr's mortal remains and kept mechanically buttoning and unbuttoning his overcoat. The Inspector said: "I understand you and a few others played poker in the back room here last night. With Orr. What time did you break up?"

"Twelve-thirty." Pike's voice wabbled drunkenly.

"What time did you start?"

"Around eleven."

"Cripes," said Inspector Queen, "that's not a poker game, that's a game of tiddledywinks. . . . Who killed Orr, Mr. Pike?"

Arnold Pike tore his eyes from the corpse. "God, sir, I don't know."

"You don't, hey? All friends, were you?"

"Yes. Oh, yes."

"What's your business, Mr. Pike?"

"I'm a stock-broker."

"Why—" began Ellery, and stopped. Under the urging of two detectives, three men advanced into the shop—all frightened, all exhibiting evidences of hasty awakening and hasty dressing, all fixing their eyes at once on the paper-covered bundle on the floor, the streaks of blood, the shattered glass. The three, like the incredible ex-Duke Paul, who was straight and stiff and somehow ridiculous, seemed petrified; men crushed by a sudden blow.

A small fat man with brilliant eyes muttered that he was Stanley Oxman, jeweler. Martin Orr's oldest, closest friend. He could not believe it. It was frightful, unheard of. Martin murdered! No, he could offer no explanation. Martin had been a peculiar man, perhaps, but as far as he, Oxman, knew the curio dealer had not had an enemy in the world. And so on, and so on, as the other two stood by, frozen, waiting their turn.

One was a lean, debauched fellow with the mark of the ex-athlete about him. His slight paunch and yellowed eyeballs could not conceal the signs of a vigorous prime. This was, said Oxman, their mutual friend, Leo Gurney, the newspaper feature-writer. The other was J. D. Vincent, said Oxman—developing an unexpected streak of talkativeness which the Inspector fanned gently—who, like Arnold Pike, was in Wall Street—"a manipulator," whatever that was. Vincent, a stocky man with the gambler's tight face, seemed incapable of speech; as for Gurney, he seemed glad that Oxman had constituted himself spokesman and kept staring at the body on the cement floor.

Ellery sighed, thought of his warm bed, put down the rebellion in his breakfastless stomach, and went to work—keeping an ear cocked for the Inspector's sharp questions and the halting replies. Ellery followed the streaks of blood to the spot where Orr had ravished the case of gems. The case, its glass front smashed, little frazzled splinters framing the orifice, contained more than a dozen metal trays floored with black velvet, set in two rows. Each held scores of gems—a brilliant array of semi-precious and precious stones beautifully variegated in color. Two trays in the center of the front row attracted his eye particularly—one containing highly polished stones of red, brown, yellow, and green; the other a single variety, all of a sub-translucent quality, leek-green in color, and covered with small red spots. Ellery noted that both these trays were in direct line with the place where Orr's hand had smashed the glass case.

He went over to the trembling little assistant, Sam Mingo, who had quieted down and was standing by Mrs. Orr, clutching her hand like a child. "Mingo," he said, touching the man. Mingo started with a leap of his stringy muscles. "Don't be alarmed, Mingo. Just step over here with me for a moment." Ellery smiled reassuringly, took the man's arm, and led him to the shattered case.

And Ellery said: "How is it that Martin Orr bothered with such trifles as these? I see rubies here, and emeralds, but the others. . . . Was he a jeweler as well as a curio dealer?"

Orr's assistant mumbled: "No. N-no, he was not. But he always liked the baubles. The baubles, he called them. Kept them for love. Most of them are birth-stones. He sold a few. This is a complete line."

"What are those green stones with the red spots?"

"Bloodstones."

"And this tray of red, brown, yellow, and green ones?"

"All jaspers. The common ones are red, brown, and yellow. The few green ones in the tray are more valuable. . . . The bloodstone is itself a variety of jasper. Beautiful! And. . ."

"Yes, yes," said Ellery hastily. "From which tray did the amethyst in Orr's hand come, Mingo?"

Mingo shivered and pointed a crinkled forefinger to a tray in the rear row, at the corner of the case.

"*All* the amethysts are kept in this one tray?"

"Yes. You can see for yourself—"

"Here!" growled the Inspector, approaching. "Mingo! I want you to look over the stock. Check everything. See if anything's been stolen."

"Yes, sir," said Orr's assistant timidly, and began to potter about the shop with lagging steps. Ellery looked about. The door to the back room was twenty-five feet from the spot where Orr had been assaulted. No desk in the shop itself, he observed, no paper about. . . .

"Well, son," said the Inspector in troubled tones, "it looks as if we're on the trail of something. I don't like it. . . . Finally dragged it out of these birds. I *thought* it was funny, this business of breaking up a weekly Saturday night poker game at half-past twelve. They had a fight!"

"Who engaged in fisticuffs with whom?"

"Oh, don't be funny. It's this Pike feller, the stockbroker. Seems they all had something to drink during the game. They played stud, and Orr, with an ace-king-queen-jack showing, raised the roof off the play. Everybody dropped out except Pike; he had three sixes. Well, Orr gave it everything he had and when Pike threw his cards away on a big over-raise, Orr cackled, showed his hole-card—a deuce!—and raked in the pot. Pike, who'd lost his pile on the hand, began to grumble; he and Orr had words— you know how those things start. They were all pie-eyed, anyway, says the Duke. Almost a fist-fight. The others interfered, but it broke up the game."

"They all left together?"

"Yes. Orr stayed behind to clean up the mess in the back room. The five others went out together and separated a few blocks away. Any one of 'em could have come back and pulled off the job before Orr shut up shop!"

"And what does Pike say?"

"What the deuce would you expect him to say? That he went right home and to bed, of course."

"The others?"

"They deny any knowledge of what happened after they left here last night. . . . Well, Mingo? Anything missing?"

Mingo said helplessly: "Everything seems all right."

"I thought so," said the Inspector with satisfaction. "This is a grudge kill, son. Well, I want to talk to these fellers some more. . . . What's eating you?"

Ellery lighted a cigarette. "A few random thoughts. Have you decided in your own mind why Orr dragged himself about the shop when he was three-quarters dead, broke the glass-domed clock, pulled an amethyst out of the gem-case?"

"That," said the Inspector, the troubled look returning, "is what I'm all foggy about. I can't—'Scuse me." He returned hastily to the waiting group of men.

Ellery took Mingo's lax arm. "Get a grip on yourself, man. I want you to look at that smashed clock for a moment. Don't be afraid of Orr—dead men don't bite, Mingo." He pushed the little assistant toward the paper-covered corpse. "Now tell me something about that clock. Has it a history?"

"Not much of one. It's a h-hundred and sixty-nine years old. Not especially valuable. Curious piece because of the glass dome over it. Happens to be the only glass-domed clock we have. That's all."

Ellery polished the lenses of his *pince-nez,* set the glasses firmly on his nose, and bent over to examine the fallen clock. It had a black wooden base, circular, about nine inches deep, and scarified with age. On this the clock was set—ticking away cosily. The dome of glass had fitted into a groove around the top of the black base, sheathing the clock completely. With the dome unshattered, the entire piece must have stood about two feet high.

Ellery rose, and his lean face was thoughtful. Mingo looked

at him in a sort of stupid anxiety. "Did Pike, Oxman, Vincent, Gurney, or Paul ever own this piece?"

Mingo shook his head. "No, sir. We've had it for many years. We couldn't get rid of it. Certainly *those* gentlemen didn't want it."

"Then none of the five ever tried to purchase the clock?"

"Of course not."

"Admirable," said Ellery. "Thank you." Mingo felt that he had been dismissed; he hesitated, shuffled his feet, and finally went over to the silent widow and stood by her side. Ellery knelt on the cement floor and with difficulty loosened the grip of the dead man's fingers about the amethyst. He saw that the stone was a clear glowing purple in color, shook his head as if in perplexity, and rose.

Vincent, the stocky Wall Street gambler with the tight face, was saying to the Inspector in a rusty voice: "—can't see why you suspect any of us. Pike particularly. What's in a little quarrel? We've always been good friends, all of us. Last night we were pickled—"

"Sure," said the Inspector gently. "Last night you were pickled. A drunk sort of forgets himself at times, Vincent. Liquor affects a man's morals as well as his head."

"Nuts!" said the yellow-eyeballed Gurney suddenly. "Stop sleuthing, Inspector. You're barking up the wrong tree. Vincent's right. We're all friends. It was Pike's birthday last week." Ellery stood very still. "We all sent him gifts. Had a celebration, and Orr was the cockiest of us all. Does that look like the preparation for a pay-off?"

Ellery stepped forward, and his eyes were shining. All his temper had fled by now, and his nostrils were quivering with the scent of the chase. "And when was this celebration held, gentlemen?" he asked softly.

Stanley Oxman puffed out his cheeks. "Now they're going to suspect a birthday blowout! Last Monday, mister. This past Monday. What of it?"

"This past Monday," said Ellery. "How nice. Mr. Pike, your gifts—"

"For God's sake. . . ." Pike's eyes were tortured.

"When did you receive them?"

"After the party, during the week. Boys sent them up to me. I didn't see any of them until last night, at the poker game."

The others nodded their heads in concert; the Inspector was looking at Ellery with puzzlement. Ellery grinned, adjusted his *pince-nez*, and spoke to his father aside. The weight of the Inspector's puzzlement, if his face was a scale, increased. But he said quietly to the white-haired broker: "Mr. Pike, you're going to take a little trip with Mr. Queen and Sergeant Velie. Just for a few moments. The others of you stay here with me. Mr. Pike, please remember not to try anything—foolish."

Pike was incapable of speech; his head twitched side-wise and he buttoned his coat for the twentieth time. Nobody said anything. Sergeant Velie took Pike's arm, and Ellery preceded them into the early-morning peace of Fifth Avenue. On the sidewalk he asked Pike his address, the broker dreamily gave him a street-and-number, Ellery hailed a taxicab, and the three men were driven in silence to an apartment-building a mile farther uptown. They took a self-service elevator to the seventh floor, marched a few steps to a door, Pike fumbled with a key, and they went into his apartment.

"Let me see your gifts, please," said Ellery without expression—the first words uttered since they had stepped into the taxicab. Pike led them to a den-like room. On a table stood four boxes of different shapes, and a handsome silver cup. "There," he said in a cracked voice.

Ellery went swiftly to the table. He picked up the silver cup. On it was engraved the sentimental legend:

To a True Friend
ARNOLD PIKE
March 1, 1876, to ——
J. D. Vincent

"Rather macabre humor, Mr. Pike," said Ellery, setting the cup down, "since Vincent has had space left for the date of your demise." Pike began to speak, then shivered and clamped his pale lips together.

Ellery removed the lid of a tiny black box. Inside, imbedded in a cleft between two pieces of purple velvet, there was a man's signet-ring, a magnificent and heavy circlet the signet of which revealed the coat-of-arms of royalist Russia. "The tattered old eagle," murmured Ellery. "Let's see what our friend the ex-Duke has to say." On a card in the box, inscribed in minute script, the following was written in French:

To my good friend Arnold Pike on his 50th birthday. March the first ever makes me sad. I remember that day in 1917—two weeks before the Czar's abdication—the quiet, then the storm. . . . But be merry, Arnold! Accept this signet-ring, given to me by my royal Cousin, as a to-ken of my esteem. Long life!

Paul

Ellery did not comment. He restored ring and card to the box, and picked up another, a large flat packet. Inside there was a gold-tipped Morocco-leather wallet. The card tucked into one of the pockets said:

> *"Twenty-one years of life's rattle*
> *And men are no longer boys,*
> *They gird their loins for the battle*
> *And throw away their toys—*
>
> *"But here's a cheerful plaything*
> *For a white-haired old mooncalf,*
> *Who may act like any May-thing*
> *For nine years more and a half!"*

"Charming verse," chuckled Ellery. "Another misbegotten poet. Only a newspaper man would indite such nonsense. This is Gurney's?"

"Yes," muttered Pike. "It's nice, isn't it?"

"If you'll pardon me," said Ellery, "it's rotten." He threw aside the wallet and seized a larger carton. Inside there was a glittering pair of patent-leather carpet slippers; the card attached read:

> Happy Birthday, Arnold! May We Be All Together On as Pleasant a March First to Celebrate Your 100th Anniversary!
>
> *Martin*

"A poor prophet," said Ellery dryly. "And what's this?" He laid the shoebox down and picked up a small flat box. In it he saw a gold-plated cigarette-case, with the initials *A. P.* engraved on the lid. The accompanying card read:

Good luck on your fiftieth birthday. I look forward to your sixtieth on March first, 1936, for another bout of whoopee!

Stanley Oxman

"And Mr. Stanley Oxman," remarked Ellery, putting down the cigarette-case, "was a little less sanguine than Martin Orr. His imagination reached no farther than sixty, Mr. Pike. A significant point."

"I can't see—" began the broker in a stubborn little mutter, "why you have, to bring my friends into it—"

Sergeant Velie gripped his elbow, and he winced. Ellery shook his head disapprovingly at the man-mountain. "And now, Mr. Pike, I think we may return to Martin Orr's shop. Or, as the Sergeant might fastidiously phrase it, the scene of the crime. . . . Very interesting. *Very* interesting. It almost compensates for an empty belly."

"You got something?" whispered Sergeant Velie hoarsely as Pike preceded them into a taxicab downstairs.

"Cyclops," said Ellery, "all God's chillun got something. But *I* got everything."

Sergeant Velie disappeared somewhere *en route* to the curio shop, and Arnold Pike's spirits lifted at once. Ellery eyed him quizzically. "One thing, Mr. Pike," he said as the taxicab turned into Fifth Avenue, "before we disembark. How long have you six men been acquainted?"

The broker sighed. "It's complicated. *My* only friend of considerable duration is Leo; Gurney, you know. Known each other for fifteen years. But then Orr and the Duke have been friends since 1918, I understand, and of course Stan Oxman and Orr have known each other—knew each other—for many years. I met Vincent about a year ago through my business affiliations and introduced him into our little clique."

"Had you yourself and the others—Oxman, Orr, Paul—been acquainted before this time two years ago?"

Pike looked puzzled. "I don't see . . . Why, no. I met Oxman and the Duke a year and a half ago through Orr."

"And that," murmured Ellery, "is so perfect that I don't care if I *never* have breakfast. Here we are, Mr. Pike."

They found a glum group awaiting their return—nothing had changed, except that Orr's body had disappeared, Dr. Prouty was gone, and some attempt at sweeping up the glass fragments of the domed clock had been made. The Inspector was in a fever of impatience, demanded to know where Sergeant Velie was, what Ellery had sought in Pike's apartment. . . . Ellery whispered something to him, and the old man looked startled. Then he dipped his fingers into his brown snuff-box and partook with grim relish.

The regal expatriate cleared his bull throat. "You have mystery re-solved?" he rumbled. "Yuss?"

"Your Highness," said Ellery gravely, "I have indeed mystery re-solved." He whirled and clapped his palms together; they jumped. "Attention, please! Piggott," he said to a detective, "stand at that door and don't let any one in but Sergeant Velie."

The detective nodded. Ellery studied the faces about him. If one of them was apprehensive, he had ample control of his physiognomy. They all seemed merely interested, now that the first shock of the tragedy had passed them by. Mrs. Orr clung to Mingo's fragile hand; her eyes did not once leave Ellery's face. The fat little jeweler, the journalist, the two Wall Street men, the Russian ex-duke. . .

"An absorbing affair," grinned Ellery, "and quite elementary, despite its points of interest. Follow me closely." He went over to the counter and picked up the purple amethyst which had been clutched in the dead man's hand. He looked at it and smiled. Then he glanced at the other object on the counter—the round-based clock, with the fragments of its glass dome protruding from the circular groove.

"Consider the situation. Martin Orr, brutally beaten about the head, manages in a last desperate living action to crawl to the jewel-case on the counter, pick out this gem, then go to the stone pedestal and pull the glass-domed clock from it. Whereupon, his mysterious mission accomplished, he dies.

"Why should a dying man engage in such a baffling procedure? There can be only one general explanation. He knows his assailant and is endeavoring to leave clues to his assailant's identity." At this point the Inspector nodded, and Ellery grinned again behind the curling smoke of his cigarette. "But such clues! Why? Well, what would you expect a dying man to do if he wished to leave behind him the name of his murderer? The answer is obvious: he would write it. But on Orr's body we find no paper, pen, or pencil; and no paper in the immediate vicinity. Where else might he secure writing materials? Well, you will observe that Martin Orr was assaulted at a spot twenty-five feet from the door of the back room. The distance, Orr must have felt, was too great for his failing strength. Then Orr couldn't write the name of his murderer except by the somewhat fantastic method of dipping his finger into his own blood and using the floor as a slate. Such an expedient probably didn't occur to him.

"He must have reasoned, with rapidity, life ebbing out of him at every breath. Then—he crawled to the case, broke the glass, took out the amethyst. Then—he crawled to the pedestal and dragged off the glass-domed clock. Then—he died. So the amethyst and the clock were Martin Orr's bequest to the police. You can almost hear him say: 'Don't fail me. This is clear, simple, easy. Punish my murderer.'"

Mrs. Orr gasped, but the expression on her wrinkled face did not alter. Mingo began to sniffle. The others waited in total silence.

"The clock first," said Ellery lazily. "The first thing one thinks of in connection with a timepiece is time. Was Orr trying, then, by dragging the clock off the pedestal, to smash the works and, stopping the clock, so fix the time of his murder? Offhand a possibility, it is true; but if this was his purpose, it failed, because the clock didn't stop running after all. While this circumstance does not invalidate the time-interpretation, further consideration of the whole problem does. For you five gentlemen had left Orr in a body. The time of the assault could not possibly be so checked against your return to your several residences as to point inescapably to one of you as the murderer. Orr must have realized this, if he thought of it at all; in other words, there wouldn't be any particular *point* to such a purpose on Orr's part.

"And there is still another—and more conclusive—consideration that invalidates the time-interpretation; and that is, that Orr crawled *past* a table full of running clocks to get to this glass-domed one. If it had been time he was intending to indicate, he could have preserved his energies by stopping at this table and pulling down one of the many clocks upon it. But no— he deliberately passed that table to get to the *glass-domed* clock. So it wasn't time.

"Very well. Now, since the glass-domed clock is *the only one* of its kind in the shop, it must have been not time in the general sense but this particular timepiece in the specific sense by which Martin Orr was motivated. But what could this particular timepiece possibly indicate? In itself, as Mr. Mingo has informed me, it has no personal connotation with any one connected with Orr. The idea that Orr was leaving a clue to a clock-maker is unsound; none of you gentlemen follows that delightful craft, and certainly Mr. Oxman, the jeweler, could not have been indicated, when so many things in the gem-case would have served."

Oxman began to perspire; he fixed his eyes on the jewel in Ellery's hand.

"Then it wasn't a professional meaning from the clock, as a clock," continued Ellery equably, "that Orr was trying to convey. But what is there about this particular clock which is different from the other clocks in the shop?" Ellery shot his forefinger forward. "This particular clock has a glass dome over it!" He straightened slowly. "Can any of you gentlemen think of a fairly common object almost perfectly suggested by a glass-domed clock?"

No one answered, but Vincent and Pike began to lick their lips. "I see signs of intelligence," said Ellery. "Let me be more specific. What is it—I feel like Sam Lloyd!—that has a base, a glass dome, and ticking machinery inside the dome?" Still no answer. "Well," said Ellery, "I suppose I should have expected reticence. Of course, *it's a stock-ticker!*"

They stared at him, and then all eyes turned to examine the whitening faces of J. D. Vincent and Arnold Pike. "Yes," said Ellery, "you may well gaze upon the countenances of the *Messieurs* Vincent and Pike. For they are the only two of our little cast who are connected with stock-tickers: Mr. Vincent is a Wall Street operator, Mr. Pike is a broker." Quietly two detectives left a wall and approached the two men.

"Whereupon," said Ellery, "we lay aside the glass-domed clock and take up this very fascinating little bauble in my hand." He held up the amethyst. "A purple amethyst—there are bluish violet ones, you know. What could this purple amethyst have signified to Martin Orr's frantic brain? The obvious thing is that it is a jewel. Mr. Oxman looked disturbed a moment ago; you needn't be, sir. The jewelry significance of this amethyst is eliminated on two counts. The first is that the tray on which the amethysts lie is in a corner at the rear of the shattered case. It was necessary for Orr to reach far into the case. If it was a jewel he sought, why didn't he pick any one of the stones nearer to his palsied hand? For any single one of them would connote 'jeweler.' But no; Orr went to the excruciating trouble of ignoring what was close at hand—as in the business of the clock—and deliberately selected something from an inconvenient place. Then the amethyst did not signify a jeweler, but something else.

"The second is this, Mr. Oxman: certainly Orr knew that the stock-ticker clue would not fix guilt on *one* person; for two of his cronies are connected with stocks. On the other hand, did Orr have two assailants, rather than one? Not likely. For if by the amethyst he meant to connote you, Mr. Oxman, and by the glass-domed clock he meant to connote either Mr. Pike or Mr. Vincent, he was still leaving a wabbly trail; for we still would not know whether Mr. Pike or Mr. Vincent was meant. Did he have *three* assailants, then? You see, we are already in the realm of fantasy. No, the major probability is that, since the glass-domed clock cut the possibilities down to two persons, the amethyst was meant to single out one of those two.

"How does the amethyst pin one of these gentlemen down? What significance besides the obvious one of jewelry does the amethyst suggest? Well, it is a rich purple in color. Ah, but one of your coterie fits here: His Highness the ex-Duke is certainly one born to the royal purple, even if it is an ex-ducal purple, as it were. . . ."

The soldierly Russian growled: "I am *not* Highness. You know nothing of royal address!" His dark face became suffused with blood, and he broke into a volley of guttural Russian.

Ellery grinned. "Don't excite yourself—Your Grace, is it? *You* weren't meant. For if we postulate you, we again drag in a third person and leave unsettled the question of which Wall Street man Orr meant to accuse; we're no better off than before. Avaunt, royalty!

"Other possible significances? Yes. There is a species of humming-bird for instance, known as the amethyst. Out! We have no aviarists here. For another thing, the amethyst was connected with ancient Hebrew ritual—an Orientalist told me this once—breastplate decoration of the high-priest, or some such thing. Obviously inapplicable here. No, there is only one other possible application." Ellery turned to the stocky gambler. "Mr. Vincent, what is your birthdate?" Vincent stammered: "November s-second."

"Splendid. That eliminates *you*." Ellery stopped abruptly. There was a stir at the door and Sergeant Velie barged in with a very grim face. Ellery smiled. "Well, Sergeant, was my hunch about motive correct?"

Velie said: "And how. He forged Orr's signature to a big check. Money-trouble, all right. Orr hushed the matter up, paid, and said he'd collect from the forger. The banker doesn't even know who the forger is."

"Congratulations are in order, Sergeant. Our murderer evidently wished to evade repayment. Murders have been committed for less vital reasons." Ellery flourished his *pince-nez*. "I said, Mr. Vincent, that you are eliminated. Eliminated because the only other significance of the amethyst left to us is that it is a *birth-stone*. But the November birth-stone is a topaz. On the other hand, Mr. Pike has just celebrated a birthday which. . ."

And with these words, as Pike gagged and the others broke into excited gabble, Ellery made a little sign to Sergeant Velie, and himself leaped forward. But it was not Arnold Pike who found himself in the crushing grip of Velie and staring into Ellery's amused eyes. It was the newspaper man, Leo Gurney.

"As I said," explained Ellery later, in the privacy of the Queens' living-room and after his belly had been comfortably filled with food, "this has been a ridiculously elementary problem." The Inspector toasted his stockinged feet before the fire, and grunted. Sergeant Velie scratched his head. "You don't think so?

"But look. It was evident, when I decided what the clues of the clock and the amethyst were intended to convey, that Arnold Pike was the man meant to be indicated. For what is the month of which the amethyst is the birth-stone? *February*—in both the Polish and Jewish birth-stone systems, the two almost universally recognized. Of the two men indicated by the clock-clue, Vincent was eliminated because his birth-stone is a topaz. Was Pike's birthday then in February? Seemingly not, for he celebrated it—this year, 1926—in March! March first, observe. What could this mean? Only one thing: since Pike was the sole remaining possibility, then his birthday *was* in February, but on the *twenty-ninth*, on Leap Day, as it's called, and 1926 not being a Leap Year, Pike chose to celebrate his birthday on the day on which it would ordinarily fall, March first.

"But this meant that Martin Orr, to have left the amethyst, must have known Pike's birthday to be in February, since he seemingly left the February birth-stone as a clue. Yet what did I find on the card accompanying Orr's gift of carpet-slippers to Pike last week? 'May we all be together on as pleasant a *March first* to celebrate your hundredth anniversary.' But if Pike is fifty years old in 1926, he was born in 1876—a Leap Year—and his hundredth anniversary would be 1976, also a Leap Year. They *wouldn't* celebrate Pike's birthday on his hundredth anniversary on March first! Then Orr *didn't* know Pike's real birthday was February twenty-ninth, or he would have said so on the card. He thought it was March.

"But the person who left the amethyst sign *did* know Pike's birth-month was February, since he left February's birth-stone. We've just established that Martin Orr didn't know Pike's birth-month was February, but thought it was March. Therefore Martin Orr was not the one who selected the amethyst.

"Any confirmation? Yes. The birth-stone for March in the Polish system is the bloodstone; in the Jewish it's the jasper. But both these stones were nearer a groping hand than the amethysts, which lay in a tray at the back of the case. In other words, whoever selected the amethyst deliberately ignored the March stones in favor of the February stone, and therefore knew that Pike was born in February, not in March. But had Orr selected a stone, it would have been bloodstone or jasper, since he believed Pike *was* born in March. Orr eliminated again.

"But if Orr did not select the amethyst, as I've shown, then what have we? Palpably, a frame-up. Some one arranged matters to make us believe that Orr himself had selected the amethyst and smashed the clock. You can see the murderer dragging poor old Orr's dead body around, leaving the blood-trail on purpose. . . ."

Ellery sighed. "I never did believe Orr left those signs. It was all too pat, too slick, too weirdly unreal. It is conceivable that a dying man will leave one clue to his murderer's identity, but *two*. . . ." Ellery shook his head.

"If Orr didn't leave the clues, who did? Obviously the murderer. But the clues deliberately led to Arnold Pike. Then Pike couldn't be the murderer, for certainly he would not leave a trail to himself had he killed Orr.

"Who else? Well, one thing stood out. Whoever killed Orr, framed Pike, and really selected that amethyst, knew Pike's birthday to be in February. Orr and Pike we have eliminated. Vincent didn't know Pike's birthday was in February, as witness his inscription on the silver cup. Nor did our friend the ex-Duke, who also wrote 'March the first,' on his card. Oxman didn't— he said they'd celebrate Pike's sixtieth birthday on March first, 1936—a Leap Year, observe, when Pike's birthday would be celebrated on February twenty-ninth. . . . Don't forget that we may accept these cards' evidence as valid; the cards were sent before the crime, and the crime would have no connection in the murderer's mind with Pike's five birthday-cards. The flaw in the murderer's plot was that he assumed—a natural error—that Orr and perhaps the others, too, knew Pike's birthday really fell on Leap Day. And he never did see the cards which proved the others didn't know, because Pike himself told us that after the party Monday night he did not see any of the others until last night, the night of the murder."

"I'll be fried in lard," muttered Sergeant Velie, shaking his head.

"No doubt," grinned Ellery. "But we've left some one out. How about Leo Gurney, the newspaper feature-writer? His stick o' doggerel said that Pike wouldn't reach the age of twenty-one for another nine and a half years. Interesting? Yes, and damning. For this means he considered facetiously that Pike was at the time of writing eleven and a half years old. But how is this possible, even in humorous verse? It's possible only if Gurney knew that Pike's birthday falls on February twenty-ninth, which occurs only once in four years! Fifty divided by four is twelve and a half. But since the year 1900 for some reason I've never been able to discover, was not a Leap Year, Gurney was right, and actually Pike had celebrated only 'eleven and a half' birthdays."

And Ellery drawled: "Being the only one who knew Pike's birthday to be in February, then Gurney was the only one who could have selected the amethyst. Then Gurney arranged matters to make it seem that Orr was accusing Pike. Then Gurney was the murderer of Orr. . . .

"Simple? As a child's sum!"

The Adventure of

THE SEVEN BLACK CATS

THE TINKLY bell quavered over the door of Miss Curleigh's Pet Shoppe on Amsterdam Avenue, and Mr. Ellery Queen wrinkled his nose and went in. The instant he crossed the threshold he was thankful it was not a large nose, and that he had taken the elementary precaution of wrinkling it. The extent and variety of the little shop's odors would not have shamed the New York Zoological Park itself. And yet it housed only creatures, he was amazed to find, of the puniest proportions; who, upon the micrometrically split second of his entrance, set up such a chorus of howls, yelps, snarls, yawps, grunts, squeaks, caterwauls, croaks, screeches, chirrups, hisses, and growls that it was a miracle the roof did not come down.

"Good afternoon," said a crisp voice. "I'm Miss Curleigh. What can I do for you, please?"

In the midst of raging bedlam Mr. Ellery Queen found himself gazing into a pair of mercurial eyes. There were other details—she was a trim young piece, for example, with masses of titian hair and curves and at least one dimple—but for the moment her eyes engaged his earnest attention. Miss Curleigh, blushing, repeated herself.

"I beg your pardon," said Ellery hastily, returning to the matter at hand. "Apparently in the animal kingdom there is no decent ratio between lung-power and—ah—aroma on the one hand and size on the other. We live and learn! Miss Curleigh, would it be possible to purchase a comparatively noiseless and sweet-smelling canine with frizzy brown hair, inquisitive ears at the half-cock, and crooked hind-legs?"

Miss Curleigh frowned. Unfortunately, she was out of Irish terriers. The last litter had been gobbled up. Perhaps a Scottie—?

Mr. Queen frowned. No, he had been specifically enjoined by Djuna, the martinet, to procure an Irish terrier; no doleful-looking, sawed-off substitute, he was sure, would do.

"I expect," said Miss Curleigh professionally, "to hear from our Long Island kennels tomorrow. If you'll leave your name and address?"

Mr. Queen, gazing into the young woman's eyes, would be delighted to. Mr. Queen, provided with pencil and pad, hastened to indulge his delight.

As Miss Curleigh read what he had written the mask of business fell away. "You're not Mr. *Ellery* Queen!" she exclaimed with animation. "Well, I declare. I've heard *so* much about you, Mr. Queen. And you live practically around the corner, on Eighty-seventh Street! This is really thrilling. I never expected to meet—"

"Nor I," murmured Mr. Queen. "Nor I."

Miss Curleigh blushed again and automatically prodded her hair. "One of my best customers lives right across the street from you, Mr. Queen. I should say one of my most *frequent* customers. Perhaps you know her? A Miss Tarkle—Euphemia Tarkle? She's in that large apartment house, you know."

"I've never had the pleasure," said Mr. Queen absently. "What extraordinary eyes you have! I mean—Euphemia Tarkle? Dear, dear, this is a world of sudden wonders. Is she as improbable as her name?"

"That's unkind," said Miss Curleigh severely, "although she *is* something of a character, the poor creature. A squirrely-faced old lady, *and* an invalid. Paralytic, you know. The queerest, frailest, tiniest little thing. Really, she's quite mad."

"Somebody's grandmother, no doubt," said Mr. Queen whimsically, picking up his stick from the counter. "Cats?"

"Why, Mr. Queen, however did you guess?"

"It always is," he said in a gloomy voice, "cats."

"*You'd* find her interesting, I'm sure," said Miss Curleigh with eagerness.

"And why I, Diana?"

"The name," said Miss Curleigh shyly, "is Marie. Well, she's *so* strange, Mr. Queen. And I've always understood that strange people interest you."

"At present," said Mr. Queen hurriedly, taking a firmer grip on his stick, "I am enjoying the fruits of idleness."

"But do you know what Miss Tarkle's been doing, the mad thing?"

"I haven't the ghost of a notion," said Mr. Queen with truth.

"She's been buying cats from me at the rate of about one a week for weeks now!"

Mr. Queen sighed. "I see no special cause for suspicion. An ancient and invalid lady, a passion for cats—oh, they go together, I assure you. I once had an aunt like that."

"That's what's so strange about it," said Miss Curleigh trium-phantly. "She doesn't *like* cats!"

Mr. Queen blinked twice. He looked at Miss Curleigh's pleasant little nose. Then he rather absently set his stick on the counter again. "And how do you know that, pray?"

Miss Curleigh beamed. "Her sister told me.—Hush, Ginger! You see, Miss Tarkle is absolutely helpless with her paralysis and all, and her sister Sarah-Ann keeps house for her; they're both of an age, I should say, and they look so much alike. Dried-up little apples of old ladies, with the same tiny features and faces like squirrels. Well, Mr. Queen, about a year ago Miss Sarah-Ann came into my shop and bought a black male cat—she hadn't much money, she said, couldn't buy a really expensive one; so I got just a—well, just a cat for her, you see."

"Did she ask for a black tomcat?" asked Mr. Queen intently.

"No. Any kind at all, she said; she liked them all. Then only a few days later she came back. She wanted to know if she could return him and get her money back. Because, she said, her sister Euphemia couldn't stand having a cat about her; Euphemia just *detested* cats, she said with a sigh, and since she was more or less living off Euphemia's bounty she couldn't very well cross her, you see. I felt a little sorry for her and told her I'd take the cat back; but I suppose she changed her mind, or else her sister changed *her* mind, because Sarah-Ann Tarkle never came back. Anyway, that's how I know Miss Euphemia doesn't like cats."

Mr. Queen gnawed a fingernail. "Odd," he muttered. "A ver-itable saga of oddness. You say this Euphemia creature has been buying 'em at the rate of one a week? What kind of cats, Miss Curleigh?"

Miss Curleigh sighed. "Not very good ones. Of course, since

she has pots of money—that's what her sister Sarah-Ann said, anyway—I tried to sell her an Angora—I had a beauty—and a Maltese that took a ribbon at one of the shows. But she wanted just cats, she said, like the one I sold her sister. Black ones."

"Black. . . . It's possible that—"

"Oh, she's not at all superstitious, Mr. Queen. In some ways she's a very weird old lady. Black tomcats with green eyes, all the same size. I thought it very queer."

Mr. Ellery Queen's nostrils quivered a little, and not from the racy odor in Miss Curleigh's Pet Shoppe, either. An old invalid lady named Tarkle who bought a black tomcat with green eyes every week!

"Very queer indeed," he murmured; and his gray eyes narrowed. "And how long has this remarkable business been going on?"

"You *are* interested! Five weeks now, Mr. Queen. I delivered the sixth one myself only the other day."

"Yourself? Is she totally paralyzed?"

"Oh, yes. She never leaves her bed; can't walk a step. It's been that way, she told me, for ten years now. She and Sarah-Ann hadn't lived together up to the time she had her stroke. Now she's absolutely dependent on her sister for everything—meals, baths, bedp . . . all sorts of attention."

"Then why," demanded Ellery, "hasn't she sent her sister for the cats?"

Miss Curleigh's mercurial eyes wavered. "I don't know," she said slowly. "Sometimes I get the shivers. You see, she's always telephoned me—she has a 'phone by her bed and can use her arms sufficiently to reach for it—the day she wanted the cat. It would always be the same order—black, male, green eyes, the same size as before, and as cheap as possible." Miss Curleigh's pleasant features hardened. "She's something of a haggler, Miss Euphemia Tarkle is."

"Fantastic," said Ellery thoughtfully. "Utterly fantastic. There's something in the basic situation that smacks of lavenderish tragedy. Tell me: how has her sister acted on the occasions when you've delivered the cats?"

"*Hush*, Ginger! I can't tell you, Mr. Queen, because she hasn't been there."

Ellery started. "Hasn't been there! What do you mean? I thought you said the Euphemia woman is helpless—"

"She is, but Sarah-Ann goes out every afternoon for some air, I suppose, or to a movie, and her sister is left alone for a few hours. It's been at such times, I think, that she's called me. Then, too, she always warned me to come at a certain time, and since I've never seen Sarah-Ann when I made the delivery I imagine she's planned to keep her purchases a secret from her sister. I've been able to get in because Sarah-Ann leaves the door unlocked when she goes out. Euphemia has told me time and time again not to breathe a word about the cats to any one."

Ellery took his *pince-nez* off his nose and began to polish the shining lenses—an unfailing sign of emotion. "More and more muddled," he muttered. "Miss Curleigh, you've stumbled on something—well, morbid."

Miss Curleigh blanched. "You don't think—"

"Insults already? I *do* think; and that's why I'm disturbed. For instance, how on earth could she have hoped to keep knowledge of the cats she's bought from her sister? Sarah-Ann isn't blind, is she?"

"Blind? Why, of course not. And Euphemia's sight is all right, too."

"I was only joking. It doesn't make sense, Miss Curleigh."

"Well," said Miss Curleigh brightly, "at least I've given the great Mr. Queen something to think about. . . . I'll call you the moment an Ir—"

Mr. Ellery Queen replaced the glasses on his nose, threw back his square shoulders, and picked up the stick again.

"Miss Curleigh, I'm an incurable meddler in the affairs of others. How would you like to help me meddle in the affairs of the mysterious Tarkle sisters?"

Scarlet spots appeared in Miss Curleigh's cheeks. "You're not serious?" she cried.

"Quite."

"I'd love to! What am I to do?"

"Suppose you take me up to the Tarkle apartment and introduce me as a customer. Let's say that the cat you sold Miss Tarkle the other day had really been promised to me, that as a stubborn fancier of felines I won't take any other, and that you'll have to have hers back and give her another. Anything to permit me to see and talk to her. It's mid-afternoon, so Sarah-Ann is probably in a movie theatre somewhere languishing after Clark Gable. What do you say?"

Miss Curleigh flung him a ravishing smile. "I say it's—it's too magnificent for words. One minute while I powder my nose and get some one to tend the shop, Mr. Queen. I wouldn't miss this for *anything!*"

Ten minutes later they stood before the front door to Apartment 5-C of the *Amsterdam Arms,* a rather faded building, gazing in silence at two full quart-bottles of milk on the corridor floor. Miss Curleigh looked troubled, and Mr. Queen stooped. When he straightened he looked troubled, too.

"Yesterday's and today's," he muttered, and he put his hand on the doorknob and turned. The door was locked. "I thought you said her sister leaves the door unlocked when she goes out?"

"Perhaps she's in," said Miss Curleigh uncertainly. "Or, if she's out, that she's forgotten to take the latch off."

Ellery pressed the bell-button. There was no reply. He rang again. Then he called loudly: "Miss Tarkle, are you there?"

"I can't understand it," said Miss Curleigh with a nervous laugh. "She really should hear you. It's only a three-room apartment, and both the bedroom and the living room are directly off the sides of a little foyer on the other side of the door. The kitchen's straight ahead."

Ellery called again, shouting. After a while he put his ear to the door. The rather dilapidated hall, the ill-painted door. . .

Miss Curleigh's extraordinary eyes were frightened silver lamps. She said in the queerest voice: "Oh, Mr. Queen. Something dreadful's happened."

"Let's hunt up the superintendent," said Ellery quietly.

They found *Potter, Sup't* in a metal frame before a door on the ground floor. Miss Curleigh was breathing in little gusts. Ellery rang the bell.

A short fat woman with enormous forearms flecked with suds opened the door. She wiped her red hands on a dirty apron sad brushed a strand of bedraggled gray hair from her sagging face. "Well?" she demanded stolidly.

"Mrs. Potter?"

"That's right. We ain't got no empty apartments. The doorman could 'a' told you—"

Miss Curleigh reddened. Ellery said hastily: "Oh, We're not apartment hunting, Mrs. Potter. Is the superintendent in?"

"No, he's not," she said suspiciously, "He's got a part time job at the chemical works in Long Island City and he never gets home till ha'-past three. What you want?"

"I'm sure you'll do nicely, Mrs. Potter, This young lady and I can't seem to get an answer from Apartment 5-C. We're calling on Miss Tarkle, you see."

The fat woman scowled. "Ain't the door open? Generally is this time o' day. The spry one's out, but the paralysed one—"

"It's locked, Mrs. Potter, and there's no answer to the bell or to our cries."

"Now ain't that funny," shrilled the fat woman, staring at Miss Curleigh. "I can't see—Miss Euphemia's a cripple; she *never* goes out. Maybe the poor thing's threw a fit!"

"I trust not. When did you see Miss Sarah-Ann last?"

"The spry one? Let's see, now. Why, two days ago. And, come to think of it, I ain't seen the cripple for two days, neither."

"Heavens," whispered Miss Curleigh, thinking of the two milk-bottles. "Two days!"

"Oh, you do see Miss Euphemia occasionally?" asked Ellery grimly.

"Yes, sir." Mrs. Potter began to wring her red hands as if she were still over the tub. "Every once in a while she calls me up by 'phone in the afternoon if her sister's out to take somethin' out to the incinerator, or do somethin' for her. The other day it was to mail a letter for her. She—she gives me somethin' once in a while. But it's been two days now. . . . ."

Ellery pulled something out of his pocket and cupped it in his palm before the fat woman's tired eyes. "Mrs. Potter," he said sternly, "I want to get into that apartment. There's something wrong. Give me your master-key."

"P-p-police!" she stammered, staring at the shield. Then suddenly she fluttered off and returned to thrust a key into Ellery's hand. "Oh, I wish Mr. Potter was home!" she wailed. You won't—"

"Not a word about this to any one, Mrs. Potter."

They left the woman gaping loose-tongued and frightened after them, and took the self-service elevator back to the fifth floor. Miss Curleigh was white to the lips; she looked a little sick.

"Perhaps," said Ellery kindly, inserting the key into the lock, "you had better not come in with me, Miss Curleigh. It might be unpleasant. I—" He stopped abruptly, his figure crouching.

Somebody was on the other side of the door.

There was the unmistakable sound of running feet, accompanied by an uneven scraping, as if something were being dragged. Ellery twisted the key and turned the knob in a flash, Miss Curleigh panting at his shoulder. The door moved a half-inch and stuck. The feet retreated.

"Barricaded the door," growled Ellery. "Stand back; Miss Curleigh." He flung himself sidewise at the door. There was a splintering crash and the door shot inward, a broken chair toppling over backward. "Too late—"

"The fire-escape!" screamed Miss Curleigh. "In the bedroom. To the left!"

He darted into a large narrow room with twin beds and an air of disorder and made for an open window. But there was no one to be seen on the fire-escape. He looked up: an iron ladder curved and vanished a few feet overhead.

"Whoever it is got away by the roof, I'm afraid," he muttered, pulling his head back and lighting a cigarette. "Smoke? Now, then, let's have a look about. No bloodshed, apparently. This may be a pig-in-the-poke after all. See anything interesting?"

Miss Curleigh pointed a shaking finger. "That's her—her bed. The messy one. But where is she?"

The other bed was neatly made up, its lace spread undisturbed. But Miss Euphemia Tarkle's was in a state of turmoil. The sheets had been ripped away and its mattress slashed open; some of the ticking was on the floor. The pillows had been torn to pieces. A depression in the center of the mattress indicated where the missing invalid had lain.

Ellery stood still, studying the bed. Then he made the rounds of the closets, opening doors, poking about, and closing them again. Followed closely by Miss Curleigh, who had developed an alarming habit of looking over her right shoulder, he glanced briefly into the living room, the kitchen, and the bathroom. But there was no one in the apartment. And, except for Miss Tarkle's bed, nothing apparently had been disturbed. The place was ghastly, somehow. It was as if violence had visited it in the midst of a cloistered silence; a tray full of dishes, cutlery, and half-finished food lay on the floor, almost under the bed.

Miss Curleigh shivered and edged closer to Ellery. "It's so—so deserted here," she said, moistening her lips. "Where's Miss Euphemia? And her sister? And who was that—that creature who barred the door?"

"What's more to the point," murmured Ellery, gazing at the tray of food, "where are the seven black cats?"

"Sev—"

"Sarah-Ann's lone beauty, and Euphemia's six. Where are they?"

"Perhaps," said Miss Curleigh hopefully, "they jumped out the window when that man—"

"Perhaps. And don't say 'man.' We just don't know." He

looked irritably about. "If they did, it was a moment ago, because the catch on the window has been forced, indicating that the window has been closed and consequently that the cats might have—" He stopped short. "Who's there?" he called sharply, whirling.

"It's me," said a timid voice, and Mrs. Potter appeared hesitantly in the foyer. Her tired eyes were luminous with fear and curiosity. "Where's—"

"Gone," He stared at the slovenly woman. "You're sure you didn't see Miss Euphemia or her sister today?"

"Nor yesterday. I—"

"There was no ambulance in this neighborhood within the past two days?"

Mrs. Potter went chalky. "Oh, no, sir I can't understand how she got *out*. She couldn't walk a step. If she'd been carried, *some one* would have noticed. The doorman, sure. I just asked him. But nobody did. I know everythin' goes on—"

"Is it possible your husband may have seen one or both of them within the past two days?"

"Not Potter. He saw 'em night before last. Harry's been makin' a little side-money, sort of, see, sir. Miss Euphemia wanted the landlord to do some decoratin' and paperin', and a little carpentry, and they wouldn't do it. So, more'n a month ago, she asked Harry if he wouldn't do it on the sly, and she said she'd pay him, although less than if a reg'lar decorator did it. So he's been doin' it spare time, mostly late afternoons and nights—he's handy, Potter is. He's most done with the job. It's pretty paper, ain't it? So he saw Miss Euphemia night before last." A calamitous thought struck her, apparently, for her eyes rolled and she uttered a faint shriek. "I just thought if—if anythin's happened to the cripple, we won't get paid! All that work . . . And the landlord—"

"Yes, yes," said Ellery impatiently. "Mrs. Potter, are there mice or rats in this house?"

Both women looked blank. "Why, not a one of 'em," began Mrs. Potter slowly. "The exterminator comes—" when they all spun about at a sound from the foyer. Some one was opening the door.

"Come in," snapped Ellery, and strode forward; only to halt in his tracks as an anxious face poked timidly into the bedroom.

"Excuse me," said the newcomer nervously, starting at sight of Ellery and the two women. "I guess I must be in the wrong apartment. Does Miss Euphemia Tarkle live here?" He was a tall needle-thin young man with a scared, horsy face and stiff tan hair. He wore a rather rusty suit of old-fashioned cut and carried a small handbag.

"Yes, indeed," said Ellery with a friendly smile. "Come in, come in. May I ask who you are?"

The young man blinked. "But where's Aunt Euphemia? I'm Elias Morton, Junior. Isn't she here?" His reddish little eyes blinked from Ellery to Miss Curleigh in a puzzled, worried way.

"Did you say 'Aunt' Euphemia, Mr. Morton?"

"I'm her nephew. I come from out of town—Albany. Where—"

Ellery murmured: "An unexpected visit, Mr. Morton?"

The young man blinked again; he was still holding his bag. Then he dumped it on the floor and eagerly fumbled in his pockets until he produced a much-soiled and wrinkled letter. "I—I got this only a few days ago," he faltered. "I'd have come sooner, only my father went off somewhere on a—I don't understand this."

Ellery snatched the letter from his lax fingers. It was scrawled painfully on a piece of ordinary brown wrapping paper; the en-

222121

22111121

velope was a cheap one. The pencilled scribble, in the crabbed hand of age, said:

Dear Elias:—You have not heard from your Auntie for so many years, but now I need you, Elias, for you are my only blood kin to whom I can turn in my Dire Distress! I am in great danger, my dear boy. You must help your poor Invalid Aunt who is so helpless. *Come at once.* Do not tell your Father or any one, Elias! When you get here make believe you have come just for a Visit. Remember. Please, please do not fail me. Help me, please! Your Loving Aunt—

Euphemia

"Remarkable missive," frowned Ellery. "Written under stress, Miss Curleigh. Genuine enough. Don't tell any one, eh? Well, Mr. Morton, I'm afraid you're too late."

"Too—But—" The young man's horse-face whitened. "I tried to come right off, b-but my father had gone off somewhere on a—on one of his drunken spells and I couldn't find him. I didn't know what to do. Then I came. T-t-to think—" His buck teeth were chattering.

"This *is* your aunt's handwriting?"

"Oh, yes. Oh, yes."

"Your father, I gather, is not a brother of the Tarkle sisters?"

"No, sir. My dear mother w-was their sister, God rest her." Morton groped for a chair-back. "Is Aunt Euphemia—d-dead? And where's Aunt Sarah?"

"They're both gone." Ellery related tersely what he had found. The young visitor from Albany looked as if he might faint. "I'm—er—unofficially investigating this business, Mr. Morton. Tell me all you know about your two aunts."

"I don't know m-much," mumbled Morton. "Haven't seen them for about fifteen years, since I was a kid. I heard from my Aunt Sarah-Ann once in a while, and only twice from Aunt Euphemia. They never—I never expected—I do know that Aunt Euphemia since her stroke became . . . funny. Aunt Sarah wrote me that. She had some money—I don't know how much—left her by my grandfather, and Aunt Sarah said she was a real miser about it. Aunt Sarah didn't have anything; she had to live with Aunt Euphemia and take care of her. She wouldn't trust banks, Aunt Sarah said, and had hidden the money somewhere about her, Aunt Sarah didn't know where. She wouldn't even have doctors after her stroke, she was—is so stingy. They didn't get along; they were always fighting, Aunt Sarah wrote me, and Aunt Euphemia was always accusing her of trying to steal her money, and she didn't know how she stood it. That—that's about all I know, sir."

"The poor things," murmured Miss Curleigh with moist eyes. "What a wretched existence! Miss Tarkle can't be responsible for—"

"Tell me, Mr. Morton," drawled Ellery, "it's true that your Aunt Euphemia detested cats?"

The lantern-jaw dropped. "Why, how'd you know? She hates them. Aunt Sarah wrote me that many times. It hurt her a lot, because *she's* so crazy about them she treats her own like a child, you see, and that makes Aunt Euphemia jealous, or angry, or something. I guess they just didn't—don't get along."

"We seem to be having a pardonable difficulty with our tenses," said Ellery. "After all, Mr. Morton, there's no evidence to show that your aunts aren't merely off somewhere on a vacation, or a visit, perhaps." But the glint in his eyes remained. "Why don't you stop at a hotel somewhere nearby? I'll keep you informed." He scribbled the name and address of a hotel in the Seventies on the page of a notebook, and thrust it into Morton's damp palm. "Don't worry. You'll hear from me." And he hustled the bewildered young man out of the apartment. They heard the click of the elevator-door a moment later.

Ellery said slowly: "The country cousin in full panoply. Miss Curleigh, let me look at your refreshing loveliness. People with faces like that should be legislated against." He patted her cheek with a frown, hesitated, and then made for the bathroom. Miss Curleigh blushed once more and followed him quickly, casting another apprehensive glance over her shoulder.

"What's this?" she heard Ellery say sharply. "Mrs. Potter, come out of that—By George!"

"What's the matter now?" cried Miss Curleigh, dashing into the bathroom behind him.

Mrs. Potter, the flesh of her powerful forearms crawling with goose-pimples, her tired eyes stricken, was glaring with open mouth into the tub. The woman made a few inarticulate sounds, rolled her eyes alarmingly, and then fled from the apartment.

Miss Curleigh said: "Oh, my God," and put her hand to her breast. "Isn't that—isn't that *horrible!*"

"Horrible," said Ellery grimly and slowly, "and illuminating. I overlooked it when I glanced in here before. I think. . ." He stopped and bent over the tub. There was no humor in his eyes or voice now; only a sick watchfulness. They were both very quiet. Death lay over them.

A black tomcat, limp and stiff and boneless, lay in a welter and smear of blood in the tub. He was large, glossy black, green-eyed, and indubitably dead. His head was smashed in and his body seemed broken in several places. His blood had clotted in splashes on the porcelain sides of the tub. The weapon, hurled by a callous hand, lay beside him: a blood-splattered bathbrush with a heavy handle.

"That solves the mystery of the disappearance of at least one of the seven," murmured Ellery, straightening. "Battered to death with the brush. He hasn't been dead more than a day or so, either, from the looks of him. Miss Curleigh, we're engaged in a tragic business."

But Miss Curleigh, her first shock of horror swept away by rage, was crying: "Any one who would kill a puss so brutally is— is a monster!" Her silvery eyes were blazing. "That terrible old woman—"

"Don't forget," sighed Ellery, "she can't walk."

"Now this," said Mr. Ellery Queen some time later, putting away his cunning and compact little pocket-kit, "is growing more and more curious, Miss Curleigh. Have you any notion what I've found here?"

They were back in the bedroom again, stooped over the bedtray which he had picked up from the floor and deposited on the night-table between the missing sisters' beds. Miss Curleigh had recalled that on all her previous visits she had found the tray on Miss Tarkle's bed or on the table, the invalid explaining with a tightening of her pale lips that she had taken to eating alone of late, implying that she and the long-suffering Sarah-Ann had reached a tragic parting of the ways.

"I saw you mess about with powder and things, but—"

"Fingerprint test." Ellery stared enigmatically down at the knife, fork, and spoon lying awry in the tray. "My kit's a handy gadget at times. You saw me test this cutlery, Miss Curleigh. You would say that these implements had been used by Euphemia in the process of eating her last meal here?"

"Why, of course," frowned Miss Curleigh. "You can still see the dried food clinging to the knife and fork."

"Exactly. The handles of knife, fork, and spoon are not engraved, as you see—simple silver surfaces. They should bear fingerprints." He shrugged. "But they don't."

"What do you mean, Mr. Queen? How is that possible?"

"I mean that some one has wiped this cutlery free of prints. Odd, eh?" Ellery lit a cigarette absently. "Examine it, however. This is Euphemia Tarkle's bedtray, her food, her dishes, her cutlery. She is known to eat in bed, and alone. But if only Euphemia handled the cutlery, who wiped off the prints? She? Why should she? Some one else? But surely there would be no sense in some one else's wiping off *Euphemia's* prints. Her fingerprints have a right to be there. Then, while Euphemia's prints were probably on these implements, some one else's prints were also on them, which accounts for their having been wiped off. Some one else, therefore, handled Euphemia's cutlery. Why? I begin," said Ellery in the grimmest of voices, "to see daylight. Miss Curleigh, would you like to serve as handmaiden to Justice?" Miss Curleigh, overwhelmed, could only nod. Ellery began to wrap the cold food leftovers from the invalid's tray. "Take this truck down to Dr. Samuel Prouty—here's his address—and ask him to analyze it for me. Wait there, get his report, and meet me back here. Try to get in here without being observed."

"The *food?*"

"The food."

"Then you think it's been—"

"The time for thinking," said Mr. Ellery Queen evenly, "is almost over."

When Miss Curleigh had gone, he took a final look around,

even to the extent of examining some empty cupboards which had a look of newness about them, set his lips firmly, locked the front door behind him—pocketing the master-key which Mrs. Potter had given him—took the elevator to the ground floor, and rang the bell of the Potter apartment.

A short thickset man with heavy, coarse features opened the door; his hat was pushed back on his head. Ellery saw the agitated figure of Mrs. Potter hovering in the background.

"That's the policeman!" shrilled Mrs. Potter. "Harry, don't get mixed up in—"

"Oh, so you're the dick," growled the thickset man, ignoring the fat woman. "I'm the super here—Harry Potter. I just got home from the plant and my wife tells me there's somethin' wrong up in the Tarkle flat. What's up, for God's sake?"

"Now, now, there's no cause for panic, Potter," murmured Ellery. "Glad you're home, though; I'm in dire need of information which you can probably provide. Has either of you found anywhere on the premises recently—*any dead cats?*"

Potter's jaw dropped, and his wife gurgled with surprise. "Now that's damn' funny. We sure have. Mrs. Potter says one of 'em's dead up in 5-C now—I never thought *those* two old dames might be the ones—"

"Where did you find them, and how many?" snapped Ellery.

"Why, down in the incinerator. Basement."

Ellery smacked his thigh. "Of course! What a stupid idiot I am. I see it all now. The incinerator, eh? There were six, Potter, weren't there?"

Mrs. Potter gasped: "How'd you know that, for mercy's sake?"

"Incinerator," muttered Ellery, sucking his lower lip. "The bones, I suppose—the skulls?"

"That's right," exclaimed Potter; he seemed distressed: "I

found 'em myself. Empty out the incinerator every mornin' for ash-removal. Six cats' skulls and a mess o' little bones. I raised hell around here with the tenants lookin' for the damn' fool who threw 'em down the chute but they all played dumb. Didn't all come down the same time. It's been goin' now maybe four-five weeks. One a week, almost. The damn' fools. I'd like to get my paws on—"

"You're certain you found six?"

"Sure."

"And nothing else of a suspicious nature?"

"No, *sir.*"

"Thanks. I don't believe there will be any more trouble. Just forget the whole business." And Ellery pressed a bill into the man's hand and strolled out of the lobby.

He did not stroll far. He strolled, in fact, only to the sidewalk steps leading down into the basement and cellar. Five minutes later he quietly let himself into Apartment 5-C again.

When Miss Curleigh stopped before the door to Apartment 5-C in late afternoon, she found it locked. She could hear Ellery's voice murmuring inside and a moment later the click of a telephone receiver. Reassured, she pressed the bell-button; he appeared instantly, pulled her inside, noiselessly shut the door again, and led her to the bedroom, where she slumped into a rosewood chair, an expression of bitter disappointment on her pleasant little face.

"Back from the wars, I see," he grinned. "Well, sister, what luck?"

"You'll be dreadfully put out," said Miss Curleigh with a scowl. "I'm sorry I haven't been more helpful—"

"What did good Dr. Prouty say?"

"Nothing encouraging. I like your Dr. Prouty, even if he *is* the Medical Examiner or something and wears a horrible little peaked hat in the presence of a lady; but I can't say I'm keen about his reports. He says there's not a thing wrong with that food you sent by me! It's a little putrefied from standing, but otherwise it's pure enough."

"Now isn't that too bad?" said Ellery cheerfully. "Come, come, Diana, perk up. It's the best news you could have brought me."

"Best n—" began Miss Curleigh with a gasp.

"It substitutes fact for theory very nicely. Fits, lassie, like a *brassière* on Mae West. We have," and he pulled over a chair and sat down facing her, "arrived. By the way, did any one see you enter this apartment?"

"I slipped in by the basement and took the elevator from there. No one saw me, I'm sure. But I don't underst—"

"Commendable efficiency. I believe we have some time for expatiation. I've had an hour or so here alone for thought, and it's been a satisfactory if morbid business." Ellery lit a cigarette and crossed his legs lazily. "Miss Curleigh, you have sense, plus the advantage of an innate feminine shrewdness, I'm sure. Tell me: Why should a wealthy old lady who is almost completely paralyzed stealthily purchase six cats within a period of five weeks?"

Miss Curleigh shrugged. "I told you I couldn't make it out. It's a deep, dark mystery to me." Her eyes were fixed on his lips.

"Pshaw, it can't be as completely baffling as all that. Very well, I'll give you a rough idea. For example, so many cats purchased by an eccentric in so short a period suggests—vivisection. But neither of the Tarkle ladies is anything like a scientist. So that's out. You see?"

"Oh, yes," said Miss Curleigh breathlessly. "I see now what

you mean. Euphemia couldn't have wanted them for companionship, either, because she hates cats!"

"Precisely. Let's wander. For extermination of mice? No, this is from Mrs. Potter's report a pest-free building. For mating? Scarcely; Sarah-Ann's cat was a male, and Euphemia also bought only males. Besides, they were nondescript tabbies, and people don't play Cupid to nameless animals."

"She might have bought them for gifts," said Miss Curleigh with a frown. "That's possible."

"Possible, but I think not," said Ellery dryly. "Not when you know the facts. The superintendent found the skeletal remains of six cats in the ashes of the incinerator downstairs, and the other one lies, a very dead pussy, in the bathtub yonder." Miss Curleigh stared at him, speechless. "We seem to have covered the more plausible theories. Can you think of some wilder ones?"

Miss Curleigh paled. "Not—not for their *fur?*"

"*Brava,*" said Ellery with a laugh. "There's a wild one among wild ones. No, not for their fur; I haven't found any fur in the apartment. And besides, no matter who killed Master Tom in the tub, he remains bloody but unskinned. I think, too, that we can discard the even wilder food theory; to civilized people killing cats for food smacks of cannibalism. To frighten Sister Sarah-Ann? Hardly; Sarah is used to cats and loves them. To scratch Sister-Ann to death? That suggests poisoned claws. But in that case there would be as much danger to Euphemia as to Sarah-Ann; and why *six* cats? As—er—guides in eternal dark? But Euphemia is not blind, and besides she never leaves her bed. Can you think of any others?"

"But those things are *ridiculous!*"

"Don't call my logical meanderings names. Ridiculous, perhaps, but you can't ignore even apparent nonsense in an elimination."

"Well, I've got one that isn't nonsense," said Miss Curleigh suddenly. "Pure hatred. Euphemia loathed cats. So, since she's cracked, I suppose, she's bought them just for the pleasure of exterminating them."

"All black tomcats with green eyes and identical dimensions?" Ellery shook his head. "Her mania could scarcely have been so exclusive. Besides, she loathed cats even before Sarah-Ann bought her distinctive tom from you. No, there's only one left that I can think of, Miss Curleigh." He sprang from the chair and began to pace the floor. "It's not only the sole remaining possibility, but it's confirmed by several things . . . *Protection.*"

"Protection!" Miss Curleigh's devastating eyes widened. "Why, Mr. Queen. How could that be? People buy dogs for protection, not cats."

"I don't mean that kind of protection," said Ellery impatiently. "I'm referring to a compound of desire to remain alive and an incidental hatred for felines that makes them the ideal instrument toward that end. This is a truly horrifying business, Marie. From every angle. Euphemia Tarkle was afraid. Of what? Of being murdered for her money. That's borne out amply by the letter she wrote to Morton, her nephew; and it's bolstered by her reputed miserliness, her distrust of banks, and her dislike for her own sister. How would a cat be protection against intended murder?"

"Poison!" cried Miss Curleigh.

"Exactly. *As a food-taster.* There's a reversion to mediœvalism for you! Are there confirming data? A-plenty. Euphemia had taken to eating alone of late; that suggests some secret activity. Then she reordered cats five, times within a short period. Why?

Obviously, because each time her cat, purchased from you, had acted in his official capacity, tasted her food, and gone the way of all enslaved flesh. The cats were poisoned, poisoned by food intended for Euphemia. So she had to re-order. Final confirmation: the six feline skeletons in the incinerator."

"But she can't walk," protested Miss Curleigh. "So how could she dispose of the bodies?"

"I fancy Mrs. Potter innocently disposed of them for her. You'll recall that Mrs. Potter said she was often called here to take garbage to the incinerator for Euphemia when Sarah-Ann was out. The 'garbage,' wrapped up, I suppose, was a cat's dead body."

"But why all the black, green-eyed tomcats of the same size?"

"Self-evident. Why? Obviously, again, *to fool Sarah-Ann*. Because Sarah-Ann had a black tomcat of a certain size with green eyes, Euphemia purchased from you identical animals. Her only reason for this could have been, then, to fool Sarah-Ann into believing that the black tom she saw about the apartment at any given time was her own, the original one. That suggests, of course, that Euphemia used Sarah-Ann's cat to foil the first attempt, and Sarah-Ann's cat was the first poison-victim. When he died, Euphemia bought another from you—without her sister's knowledge.

"How Euphemia suspected she was slated to be poisoned, of course, at the very time in which the poisoner got busy, we'll never know. It was probably the merest coincidence, something psychic—you never know about slightly mad old ladies."

"But if she was trying to fool Sarah-Ann about the cats," whispered Miss Curleigh, aghast, "then she suspected—"

"Precisely. She suspected her sister of trying to poison her."

Miss Curleigh bit her lip. "Would you mind giving me a—a

cigarette? I'm—" Ellery silently complied. "It's the most terrible thing I've ever heard of. Two old women, sisters, practically alone in the world, one dependent on the other for attention, the other for subsistence, living at cross-purposes—the invalid helpless to defend herself against attacks. . . ." She shuddered. "What's *happened* to those poor creatures, Mr. Queen?"

"Well, let's see. Euphemia is missing. We know that there were at least six attempts to poison her, all unsuccessful. It's logical to assume that there was a seventh attempt, then, and that—since Euphemia is gone under mysterious circumstances—*the seventh attempt was successful.*"

"But how can you *know* she's—she's dead?"

"Where is she?" asked Ellery dryly. "The only other possibility is that she fled. But she's helpless, can't walk, can't stir from bed without assistance. Who can assist her? Only Sarah-Ann, the very one she suspects of trying to poison her. The letter to her nephew shows that she wouldn't turn to Sarah-Ann. So flight is out and, since she's missing, she must be dead. Now, follow. Euphemia knew she was the target of poisoning attacks via her food, and took precautions against them; then how did the poisoner finally penetrate her defenses—the seventh cat? Well, we may assume that Euphemia made the seventh cat taste the food we found on the tray. We know that food was not poisoned, from Dr. Prouty's report. The cat, then, didn't die of poisoning from the food itself—confirmed by the fact that he was beaten to death. But if the cat didn't die of poisoned *food,* neither did Euphemia. Yet all the indications are that she must have died of poisoning. Then there's only one answer: she died of poisoning not in eating but *in the process of* eating."

"I don't understand," said Miss Curleigh intently.

"The cutlery!" cried Ellery. "I showed you earlier this afternoon that some one other than Euphemia had handled her knife, spoon, and fork. Doesn't this suggest that the poisoner had *poisoned the cutlery* on his seventh attempt? If, for example, the fork had been coated with a colorless odorless poison which dried, Euphemia would have been fooled. The cat, flung bits of food by hand—for no one feeds an animal with cutlery would live; Euphemia, eating the food with the poisoned cutlery, would die. Psychologically, too, it rings true. It stood to reason that the poisoner, after six unsuccessful attempts one way, should in desperation try a seventh with a variation. The variation worked and Euphemia, my dear, is dead."

"But her body— Where—"

Ellery's face changed as he whirled noiselessly toward the door. He stood in an attitude of tense attention for an instant and then, without a word, laid violent hands upon the petrified figure of Miss Curleigh and thrust her rudely into one of the bedroom closets, shutting the door behind her. Miss Curleigh, half-smothered by a soft sea of musty-smelling feminine garments, held her breath. She had heard that faint scratching of metal upon metal at the front door. It must be—if Mr. Queen acted so quickly—the poisoner. Why had he come back? she thought wildly. The key he was using—easy—a duplicate. Earlier when they had surprised him and he had barricaded the door, he must have entered the apartment by the roof and fire-escape window because he couldn't use the key . . . some one may have been standing in the hall. . . .

She choked back a scream, her thoughts snapping off as if a switch had been turned. A hoarse, harsh voice—the sounds of a struggle—a crash . . . they were fighting!

Miss Curleigh saw red. She flung open the door of the closet and plunged out. Ellery was on the floor in a tangle of threshing arms and legs. A hand came up with a knife. . . . Miss Curleigh sprang and kicked in an instantaneous reflex action. Something snapped sharply, and she fell back, sickened, as the knife dropped from a broken hand.

"Miss Curleigh—the door!" panted Ellery, pressing his knee viciously downward. Through a dim roaring in her ears Miss Curleigh heard pounding on the door, and tottered toward it. The last thing she remembered before she fainted was a weird boiling of blue-clad bodies as police poured past her to fall upon the struggling figures.

"It's all right now," said a faraway voice, and Miss Curleigh opened her eyes to find Mr. Ellery Queen, cool and immaculate, stooping over her. She moved her head dazedly. The fireplace, the crossed swords on the wall. . ."Don't be alarmed, Marie," grinned Ellery; "this isn't an abduction. You have achieved Valhalla. It's all over, and you're reclining on the divan in my apartment."

"Oh," said Miss Curleigh, and she swung her feet unsteadily to the floor. "I—I must look a sight. What happened?"

"We caught the bogey very satisfactorily. Now you rest, young lady, while I rustle a dish of tea—"

"Nonsense!" said Miss Curleigh with asperity. "I want to know how you performed that miracle. Come on, now, don't be irritating!"

"Yours to command. Just what do you want to know?"

"Did you *know* that awful creature was coming back?"

Ellery shrugged. "It was a likely possibility. Euphemia had been poisoned, patently, for her hidden money. She must have been murdered at the very latest yesterday—you recall yesterday's milk-bottle—perhaps the night before last. Had the murderer found the money after killing her? Then who was the prowler whom we surprised this afternoon and who made his escape out the window after barricading the door? It must have been the murderer. But if he came back *after* the crime, then he had not found the money when he committed the crime. Perhaps he had so much to do immediately after the commission of the crime that he had no time to search. At any rate, on his return we surprised him—probably just after he had made a mess of the bed. It was quite possible that he had still not found the money. If he had not, I knew he would come back—after all, he had committed the crime for it. So I took the chance that he would return when he thought the coast was clear, and he did. I 'phoned for police assistance while you were out seeing Dr. Prouty."

"Did you *know* who it was?"

"Oh, yes. It was demonstrable. The first qualification of the poisoner was availability; that is, in order to make those repeated poisoning attempts, the poisoner had to be near Euphemia or near her food at least since the attempts began, which was presumably five weeks ago. The obvious suspect was her sister. Sarah-Ann had motive—hatred and possibly cupidity; and certainly opportunity, since she prepared the food herself. But Sarah-Ann I eliminated on the soundest basis in the world.

"For who had brutally beaten to death the seventh black tomcat? Palpably, either the victim or the murderer in a general sense. But it couldn't have been Euphemia, since the cat was killed in the bathroom and Euphemia lay paralyzed in the bedroom, unable to walk. Then it must have been the murderer who killed the cat. But if Sarah-Ann were the murderer, would she have clubbed to death a cat—she, who loved cats? Utterly inconceivable. Therefore Sarah-Ann was not the murderer."

"Then what—"

"I know. What happened to Sarah-Ann?" Ellery grimaced.

"Sarah-Ann, it is to be feared, went the way of the cat and her sister. It must have been the poisoner's plan to kill Euphemia and have it appear that Sarah-Ann had killed her—the obvious suspect. Sarah-Ann, then, should be on the scene. But she isn't. Well, her disappearance tends to show—I think the confession will bear me out—that she was accidentally a witness to the murder and was killed by the poisoner on the spot to eliminate a witness to the crime. He wouldn't have killed her under any other circumstances."

"Did you find the money?"

"Yes. Lying quite loosely," shrugged Ellery, "between the pages of a Bible Euphemia always kept in her bed. The Poe touch, no doubt."

"And," quavered Miss Curleigh, "the bodies. . . ."

"Surely," drawled Ellery, "the incinerator? It would have been the most logical means of disposal. Fire is virtually all-consuming. What bones there were could have been disposed of more easily than . . . Well, there's no point in being literal. You know what I mean."

"But that means—Who was that fiend on the floor? I never saw him before. It couldn't have been Mr. Morton's f-father. . . ?"

"No, indeed. Fiend, Miss Curleigh?" Ellery raised his eyebrows. "There's only a thin wall between sanity and—"

"You called me," said Miss Curleigh, "Marie before."

Ellery said hastily: "No one but Sarah-Ann and Euphemia lived in the apartment, yet the poisoner had access to the invalid's food for over a month—apparently without suspicion. Who could have had such access? Only one person: the man who had been decorating the apartment in late afternoons and evenings—around dinner-time—for over a month; the man who worked in a chemical plant and therefore, better than any one, had knowl-

edge of and access to poisons; the man who tended the incinerator and therefore could dispose of the bones of his human
victims without danger to himself. In a word," said Ellery, "the
superintendent of the building, Harry Potter."

The Adventure of
THE MAD TEA-PARTY

THE TALL young man in the dun raincoat thought that he had never seen such a downpour. It gushed out of the black sky in a roaring flood, gray-gleaming in the feeble yellow of the station lamps. The red tails of the local from Jamaica had just been drowned out in the west. It was very dark beyond the ragged blur of light surrounding the little railroad station, and unquestionably very wet. The tall young man shivered under the eaves of the platform roof and wondered what insanity had moved him to venture into the Long Island hinterland in such wretched weather. And where, damn it all, was Owen?

He had just miserably made up his mind to seek out a booth, telephone his regrets, and take the next train back to the City, when a lowslung coupé came splashing and snuffling out of the darkness, squealed to a stop, and a man in chauffeur's livery leaped out and dashed across the gravel for the protection of the eaves.

"Mr. Ellery Queen?" he panted, shaking out his cap. He was a blond young man with a ruddy face and sun-squinted eyes.

"Yes," said Ellery with a sigh. Too late now.

"I'm Millan, Mr. Owen's chauffeur, sir," said the man. "Mr. Owen's sorry he couldn't come down to meet you himself. Some guests—This way, Mr. Queen."

He picked up Ellery's bag and the two of them ran for the coupé. Ellery collapsed against the mohair in an indigo mood. Damn Owen and his invitations! Should have known better. Mere acquaintance, when it came to that. One of J.J.'s questionable friends. People were always pushing so. Put him up on exhibition, like a trained seal. Come, come, Rollo; here's a juicy little fish for you! . . . Got vicarious thrills out of listening to crime yarns. Made a man feel like a curiosity. Well, he'd be drawn and quartered if they got him to mention crime once! But then Owen had said Emmy Willowes would be there, and he'd always wanted to meet Emmy. Curious woman, Emmy, from all the reports. Daughter of some blueblood diplomat who had gone to the dogs—in this case, the stage. Stuffed shirts, her tribe, probably. Atavi! There were some people who still lived in mediœval . . . Hmm. Owen wanted him to see "the house." Just taken a month ago. Ducky, he'd said. "Ducky!" The big brute . . .

The coupé splashed along in the darkness, its head-lights revealing only remorseless sheets of speckled water and occasionally a tree, a house, a hedge.

Millan cleared his throat. "Rotten weather, isn't it, sir. Worst this spring. The rain, I mean."

Ah, the conversational chauffeur! thought Ellery with an inward groan. "Pity the poor sailor on a night like this," he said piously.

"Ha, ha," said Millan. "Isn't it the truth, though? You're a little late, aren't you, sir? That was the eleven-fifty. Mr. Owen told me this morning you were expected tonight on the nine-twenty."

"Detained," murmured Ellery, wishing he were dead.

"A case, Mr. Queen?" asked Millan eagerly, rolling his squinty eyes.

Even he, O Lord. . . . "No, no. My father had his annual attack of elephantiasis. Poor dad! We thought for a bad hour there that it was the end."

The chauffeur gaped. Then, looking puzzled, he returned his attention to the soggy pelted road. Ellery closed his eyes with a sigh of relief.

But Millan's was a persevering soul, for after a moment of silence he grinned—true, a trifle dubiously—and said: "Lots of excitement at Mr. Owen's tonight, sir. You see, Master Jonathan—"

"Ah," said Ellery, starting a little. Master Jonathan, eh? Ellery recalled him as a stringy, hot-eyed brat in the indeterminate years between seven and ten who possessed a perfectly fiendish ingenuity for making a nuisance of himself. Master Jonathan. . . . He shivered again, this time from apprehension. He had quite forgotten Master Jonathan.

"Yes, sir, Jonathan's having a birthday party tomorrow, sir—ninth, I think—and Mr. and Mrs. Owen've rigged up something special." Millan grinned again, mysteriously. "Something very special, sir. It's a secret, y'see. The kid—Master Jonathan doesn't know about it yet. Will he be surprised!"

"I doubt it, Millan," groaned Ellery, and lapsed into a dismal silence which not even the chauffeur's companionable blandishments were able to shatter.

Richard Owen's "ducky" house was a large rambling affair of gables and ells and colored stones and bright shutters, set at the terminal of a winding driveway flanked by soldierly trees. It blazed with light and the front door stood ajar.

"Here we are, Mr. Queen!" cried Millan cheerfully, jumping out and holding the door open. "It's only a hop to the porch; you won't get wet, sir."

Ellery descended and obediently hopped to the porch. Millan fished his bag out of the car and bounded up the steps. "Door open 'n' everything," he grinned. "Guess the help are all watchin' the show."

"Show?" gasped Ellery with a sick feeling at the pit of his stomach.

Millan pushed the door wide open. "Step in, step in, Mr. Queen. I'll go get Mr. Owen. . . . They're rehearsing, y'see. Couldn't do it while Jonathan was up, so they had to wait till he'd gone to bed. It's for tomorrow, y'see. And he was very suspicious; they had an awful time with him—"

"I can well believe that," mumbled Ellery. Damn Jonathan and all his tribe! He stood in a small foyer looking upon a wide brisk living room, warm and attractive. "So they're putting on a play. Hmm. . . . Don't bother, Millan; I'll just wander in and wait until they've finished. Who am I to clog the wheels of Drama?"

"Yes, sir," said Millan with a vague disappointment; and he set down the bag and touched his cap and vanished in the darkness outside. The door closed with a click curiously final, shutting out both rain and night.

Ellery reluctantly divested himself of his drenched hat and raincoat, hung them dutifully in the foyer-closet, kicked his bag into a corner, and sauntered into the living room to warm his chilled hands at the good fire. He stood before the flames soaking in heat, only half-conscious of the voices which floated through one of the two open door ways beyond the fireplace.

A woman's voice was saying in odd childish tones: "No, please go on! I won't interrupt you again. I dare say there may be *one*."

"Emmy," thought Ellery, becoming conscious very abruptly. "What's going on here?" He went to the first doorway and leaned against the jamb.

An astonishing sight met him. They were all—as far as he could determine—there. It was apparently a library, a large bookish room done in the modern manner. The farther side had been cleared and a homemade curtain, manufactured out of starchy sheets and a pulley, stretched across the room. The curtain was open, and in the cleared space there was a long table covered with a white cloth and with cups and saucers and things on it. In an armchair at the head of the table sat Emmy Willowes, whimsically girlish in a pinafore, her gold-brown hair streaming down her back, her slim legs sheathed in white stockings, and black pumps with low heels on her feet. Beside her sat an apparition, no less: a rabbity creature the size of a man, his huge ears stiffly up, an enormous bow-tie at his furry neck, his mouth clacking open and shut as human sounds came from his throat. Beside the hare there was another apparition: a creature with an amiably rodent little face and slow sleepy movements. And beyond the little one, who looked unaccountably like a dormouse, sat the most remarkable of the quartet—a curious creature with shaggy eyebrows and features reminiscent of George Arliss', at his throat a dotted bow-tie, dressed Victorianishly in a quaint waistcoat, on his head an extraordinary tall cloth hat in the band of which was stuck a placard reading: "For This Style 10/6."

The audience was composed of two women: an old lady with pure white hair and the stubbornly sweet facial expression which more often than not conceals a chronic acerbity; and a very beautiful young woman with full breasts, red hair, and green eyes. Then Ellery noticed that two domestic heads were stuck in another doorway, gaping and giggling decorously.

"The mad tea-party," thought Ellery, grinning. "I might have known, with Emmy in the house. Too good for that merciless brat!"

"They were learning to draw," said the little dormouse in a high-pitched voice, yawning and rubbing its eyes, "and they drew all manner of things—everything that begins with an M—"

"Why with an M?" demanded the woman-child.

"Why not?" snapped the hare, flapping his ears indignantly.

The dormouse began to doze and was instantly beset by the top-hatted gentleman, who pinched him so roundly that he awoke with a shriek and said: "—that begins with an M, such as mousetraps, and the moon, and memory, and muchness—you know you say things are 'much of a muchness'—did you ever see such a thing as a drawing of a muchness?"

"Really, now you ask me," said the girl, quite confused, "I don't think—"

"Then you shouldn't talk," said the Hatter tartly.

The girl rose in open disgust and began to walk away, her white legs twinkling. The dormouse fell asleep and the hare and the Hatter stood up and grasped the dormouse's little head and tried very earnestly to push it into the mouth of a monstrous teapot on the table.

And the little girl cried, stamping her right foot: "At any rate I'll never go *there* again. It's the stupidest tea-party I was ever at in all my life!"

And she vanished behind the curtain; an instant later it swayed and came together as she operated the rope of the pulley.

"Superb," drawled Ellery, clapping his hands. "*Brava*, Alice. And a couple of *bravi* for the zoological characters, Messrs.

Dormouse and March Hare, not to speak of my good friend the Mad Hatter."

The Mad Hatter goggled at him, tore off his hat, and came running across the room. His vulturine features under the make-up were both good-humored and crafty; he was a stoutish man in his prime, a faintly cynical and ruthless prime. "Queen! When on earth did you come? Darned if I hadn't completely forgotten about you. What held you up?"

"Family matter. Millan did the honors. Owen, that's your natural costume, I'll swear. I don't know what ever possessed you to go into Wall Street. You were born to be the Hatter."

"Think so?" chuckled Owen, pleased. "I guess I always did have a yen for the stage; that's why I backed Emmy Willowes' *Alice* show. Here, I want you to meet the gang. Mother," he said to the white-haired old lady, "may I present Mr. Ellery Queen. Laura's mother, Queen—Mrs. Mansfield." The old lady smiled a sweet, sweet smile; but Ellery noticed that her eyes were very sharp. "Mrs. Gardner," continued Owen, indicating the buxom young woman with the red hair and green eyes. "Believe it or not, she's the wife of that hairy Hare over there. Ho, ho, ho!"

There was something a little brutal in Owen's laughter. Ellery bowed to the beautiful woman and said quickly: "Gardner? You're not the wife of Paul Gardner, the architect?"

"Guilty," said the March Hare in a cavernous voice; and he removed his head and disclosed a lean face with twinkling eyes. "How are you, Queen? I haven't seen you since I testified for your father in that Schultz murder case in the Village."

They shook hands. "Surprise," said Ellery. "This *is* nice. Mrs. Gardner, you have a clever husband. He set the defense by their respective ears with his expert testimony in that case."

"Oh, I've always said Paul is a genius," smiled the red-haired woman. She had a queer husky voice. "But he won't believe me. He thinks I'm the only one in the world who doesn't appreciate him."

"Now, Carolyn," protested Gardner with a laugh; but the twinkle had gone out of his eyes and for some odd reason he glanced at Richard Owen.

"Of course you remember Laura," boomed Owen, taking Ellery forcibly by the arm. "That's the Dormouse. Charming little rat, isn't she?"

Mrs. Mansfield lost her sweet expression for a fleeting instant; very fleeting indeed. What the Dormouse thought about being publicly characterized as a rodent, however charming, by her husband was concealed by the furry little head; when she took it off she was smiling. She was a wan little woman with tired eyes and cheeks that had already begun to sag.

"And this," continued Owen with the pride of a stock-raiser exhibiting a prize milch-cow, "is the one and only Emmy. Emmy, meet Mr. Queen, that murder-smelling chap I've been telling you about. Miss Willowes."

"You see us, Mr. Queen," murmured the actress, "in character. I hope you aren't here on a professional visit? Because if you are, we'll get into mufti at once and let you go to work. I know *I've* a vicariously guilty conscience. If I were to be convicted of every mental murder I've committed, I'd need the nine lives of the Cheshire Cat. Those damn' critics—"

"The costume," said Ellery, not looking at her legs, "is most fetching. And I think I like you better as Alice." She made a charming Alice; she was curved in her slimness, half-boy, half-girl. "Whose idea was this, anyway?"

"I suppose you think we're fools or nuts," chuckled Owen. "Here, sit down, Queen. Maud!" he roared. "A cocktail for Mr.

Queen. Bring some more fixin's." A frightened domestic head vanished. "We're having a dress-rehearsal for Johnny's birthday party tomorrow; we've invited all the kids of the neighborhood. Emmy's brilliant idea; she brought the costumes down from the theatre. You know we closed Saturday night."

"I hadn't heard. I thought *Alice* was playing to S.R.O."

"So it was. But our lease at the *Odeon* ran out and we've our engagements on the road to keep. We open in Boston next Wednesday."

Slim-legged Maud set a pinkish liquid concoction before Ellery. He sipped slowly, succeeding in not making a face.

"Sorry to have to break this up," said Paul Gardner, beginning to take off his costume. "But Carolyn and I have a bad trip before us. And then tomorrow . . . The road must be an absolute washout."

"Pretty bad," said Ellery politely, setting down his three-quarters'-full glass.

"I won't hear of it," said Laura Owen. Her pudgy little Dormouse's stomach gave her a peculiar appearance, tiny and fat and sexless. "Driving home in this storm! Carolyn, you and Paul must stay over."

"It's only four miles, Laura," murmured Mrs. Gardner.

"Nonsense, Carolyn! More like forty on a night like this," boomed Owen. His cheeks were curiously pale and damp under the make-up. "That's settled! We've got more room than we know what to do with. Paul saw to that when he designed this development."

"That's the insidious part of knowing architects socially," said Emmy Willowes with a grimace. She flung herself in a chair and tucked her long legs under her. "You can't fool 'em about the number of available guest-rooms."

"Don't mind Emmy," grinned Owen. "She's the Peck's Bad Girl of show business: no manners at all. Well, well! This is great. How's about a drink, Paul?"

"No, thanks."

"You'll have one, won't you, Carolyn? Only good sport in the crowd." Ellery realized with a furious embarrassment that his host was, under the red jovial glaze of the exterior, vilely drunk.

She raised her heavily-lidded green eyes to his. "I'd love it, Dick." They stared with peculiar hunger at each other. Mrs. Owen suddenly smiled and turned her back, struggling with her cumbersome costume.

And, just as suddenly, Mrs. Mansfield rose and smiled her unconvincing sweet smile and said in her sugary voice to no one in particular: "*Will* you all excuse me? It's been a trying day, and I'm an old woman. . . . Laura, my darling." She went to her daughter and kissed the lined, averted forehead.

Everybody murmured something; including Ellery, who had a headache, a slow pinkish fire in his vitals, and a consuming wishfulness to be far, far away.

Mr. Ellery Queen came to with a start and a groan. He turned over in bed, feeling very poorly. He had dozed in fits since one o'clock, annoyed rather than soothed by the splash of the rain against the bedroom windows. And now he was miserably awake, inexplicably sleepless, attacked by a rather surprising insomnia. He sat up and reached for his wrist-watch, which was ticking thunderously away on the night-table beside his bed. By the radium hands he saw that it was five past two.

He lay back, crossing his palms behind his head, and stared into the half-darkness. The mattress was deep and downy, as one had a right to expect of the mattress of a plutocrat, but it did not rest his tired bones. The house was cozy, but it did not comfort him. His hostess was thoughtful, but uncomfortably woebegone. His host was a disturbing force, like the storm. His fellow-guests; Master Jonathan snuffling away in his junior bed—Ellery was positive that Master Jonathan snuffled. . . .

At two-fifteen he gave up the battle and, rising, turned on the light and got into his dressing-gown and slippers. That there was no book or magazine on or in the night-table he had ascertained before retiring. Shocking hospitality! Sighing, he went to the door and opened it and peered out. A small night-light glimmered at the landing down the hall. Everything was quiet.

And suddenly he was attacked by the strangest diffidence. He definitely did not want to leave the bedroom.

Analyzing the fugitive fear, and arriving nowhere, Ellery sternly reproached himself for an imaginative fool and stepped out into the hall. He was not habitually a creature of nerves, nor was he psychic; he laid the blame to lowered physical resistance due to fatigue, lack of sleep. This was a nice house with nice people in it. It was like a man, he thought, saying: "Nice doggie, nice doggie," to a particularly fearsome beast with slavering jaws. That woman with the sea-green eyes. Put to sea in a sea-green boat. Or was it pea-green. . . . "No room! No room!". . ."There's *plenty* of room," said Alice indignantly. . . . And Mrs. Mansfield's smile did make you shiver.

Berating himself bitterly for the ferment his imagination was in, he went down the carpeted stairs to the living room.

It was pitch-dark and he did not know where the light-switch was. He stumbled over a hassock and stubbed his toe and cursed silently. The library should be across from the stairs, next to the fireplace. He strained his eyes toward the fireplace, but the last embers had died. Stepping warily, he finally reached the fireplace-wall. He groped about in the rain-splattered silence, searching for the library door. His hand met a cold knob, and he turned the knob rather noisily and swung the door open. His eyes were oriented to the darkness now and he had already begun to make out in the mistiest black haze the unrecognizable outlines of still objects.

The darkness from beyond the door however struck him like a blow. It was darker darkness. . . . He was about to step across the sill when he stopped. It was the wrong room. Not the library at all. How he knew he could not say, but he was sure he had pushed open the door of the wrong room. Must have wandered orbitally to the right. Lost men in the dark forest. . . . He stared intently straight before him into the absolute, unrelieved blackness, sighed, and retreated. The door shut noisily again.

He groped along the wall to the left. A few feet. . . . There it was! The very next door. He paused to test his psychic faculties. No, all's well. Grinning, he pushed open the door, entered boldly, fumbled on the nearest wall for the switch, found it, pressed. The light flooded on to reveal, triumphantly, the library.

The curtain was closed, the room in disorder as he had last seen it before being conducted upstairs by his host.

He went to the built-in bookcases, scanned several shelves, hesitated between two volumes, finally selected *Huckleberry Finn* as good reading on a dour night, put out the light, and felt his way back across the living room to the stairway. Book tucked under his arm, he began to climb the stairs. There was a footfall from the landing above. He looked up. A man's dark form was silhouetted below the tiny landing light.

"Owen?" whispered a dubious male voice.

Ellery laughed. "It's Queen, Gardner. Can't you sleep, either?"

He heard the man sigh with relief. "Lord, no! I was just coming downstairs for something to read. Carolyn—my wife's asleep, I guess, in the room adjoining mine. How she can sleep—! There's something in the air tonight."

"Or else you drank too much," said Ellery cheerfully, mounting the stairs.

Gardner was in pajamas and dressing-gown, his hair mussed. "Didn't drink at all to speak of. Must be this confounded rain. My nerves are all shot."

"Something in that. Hardy believed, anyway, in the Greek unities. . . . If you can't sleep, you might join me for a smoke in my room, Gardner."

"You're sure I won't be—"

"Keeping me up? Nonsense. The only reason I fished about downstairs for a book was to occupy my mind with something. Talk's infinitely better than Huck Finn, though he does help at times. Come on."

They went to Ellery's room and Ellery produced cigarettes and they relaxed in chairs and chatted and smoked until the early dawn began struggling to emerge from behind the fine gray wet bars of the rain outside. Then Gardner went yawning back to his room and Ellery fell into a heavy, uneasy slumber.

He was on the rack in a tall room of the Inquisition and his left arm was being torn out of his shoulder-socket. The pain was almost pleasant. Then he awoke to find Millan's ruddy face in broad daylight above him, his blond hair tragically dishevelled. He was jerking at Ellery's arm for all he was worth.

"Mr. Queen!" he was crying. "Mr. Queen! For God's sake, wake up!"

Ellery sat up quickly, startled. "What's the matter, Millan?"

"Mr. Owen, sir. He's—he's gone!"

Ellery sprang out of bed. "What d'ye mean, man?"

"Disappeared, Mr. Queen. We—we can't find him. Just gone. Mrs. Owen is all—"

"You go downstairs, Millan," said Ellery calmly, stripping off his pajama-coat, "and pour yourself a drink. Please tell Mrs. Owen not to do anything until I come down. And nobody's to leave or telephone. You understand?"

"Yes, sir," said Millan in a low voice, and blundered off.

Ellery dressed like a fireman, splashed his face, spat water, adjusted his necktie, and ran downstairs. He found Laura Owen in a crumpled négligé on the sofa, sobbing. Mrs. Mansfield was patting her daughter's shoulder. Master Jonathan Owen was scowling at his grandmother, Emmy Willowes silently smoked a cigarette, and the Gardners were pale and quiet by the gray-washed windows.

"Mr. Queen," said the actress quickly. "It's a drama, hot off the script. At least Laura Owen thinks so. Won't you assure her that it's all probably nothing?"

"I can't do that," smiled Ellery, "until I learn the facts. Owen's gone? How? When?"

"Oh, Mr. Queen," choked Mrs. Owen, raising a tear-stained face. "I know something—something dreadful's happened. I had a feeling—You remember last night, after Richard showed you to your room?"

"Yes."

"Then he came back downstairs and said he had some work to do in his den for Monday, and told me to go to bed. Everybody else had gone upstairs. The servants, too. I warned him not to stay up too late and I went up to bed. I—I was exhausted, and I fell right asleep—"

"You occupy one bedroom, Mrs. Owen?"

"Yes. Twin beds. I fell asleep and didn't wake up until a half-hour ago. Then I saw—" She shuddered and began to sob again. Her mother looked helpless and angry. "His bed hadn't been slept in. His clothes—the ones he'd taken off when he got into the costume—were still where he had left them on the chair by his bed. I was shocked, and ran downstairs; but he was gone. . . ."

"Ah," said Ellery queerly. "Then, as far as you know, he's still in that Mad Hatter's rig? Have you looked over his wardrobe? Are any of his regular clothes missing?"

"No, no; they're all there. Oh, he's dead. I know he's dead."

"Laura, dear, please," said Mrs. Mansfield in a tight quavery voice.

"Oh, mother, it's too horrible—"

"Here, here," said Ellery. "No hysterics. Was he worried about anything? Business, for instance?"

"No, I'm sure he wasn't. In fact, he said only yesterday things were picking up beautifully. And he isn't—isn't the type to worry, anyway."

"Then it probably isn't amnesia. He hasn't had a shock of some sort recently?"

"No, no."

"No possibility, despite the costume, that he went to his office?"

"No. He never goes down Saturdays."

Master Jonathan jammed his fists into the pockets of his Eton jacket and said bitterly: "I bet he's drunk again. Makin' mamma cry. I hope he *never* comes back."

"Jonathan!" screamed Mrs. Mansfield. "You go up to your room this very minute, do you hear, you nasty boy? This minute!"

No one said anything; Mrs. Owen continued to sob; so Master Jonathan thrust out his lower lip, scowled at his grandmother with unashamed dislike, and stamped upstairs.

"Where," said Ellery with a frown, "was your husband when you last saw him, Mrs. Owen? In this room?"

"In his den," she said with difficulty. "He went in just as I went upstairs. I saw him go in. That door, there." She pointed to the door at the right of the library door. Ellery started; it was the door to the room he had almost blundered into during the night in his hunt for the library.

"Do you think—" began Carolyn Gardner in her husky voice, and stopped. Her lips were dry, and in the gray morning light her hair did not seem so red and her eyes did not seem so green. There was, in fact, a washed-out look about her, as if all the fierce vitality within her had been quenched by what had happened.

"Keep out of this, Carolyn," said Paul Gardner harshly. His eyes were red-rimmed from lack of sleep.

"Come, come," murmured Ellery, "we may be, as Miss Willowes has said, making a fuss over nothing at all. If you'll excuse me . . . I'll have a peep at the den."

He went into the den, closing the door behind him, and stood with his back squarely against the door. It was a small room, so narrow that it looked long by contrast; it was sparsely furnished and seemed a business-like place. There was a simple neatness about its desk, a modern severity about its furnishings that were reflections of the direct, brutal character of Richard Owen. The room was as trim as a pin; it was almost ludicrous to conceive of its having served as the scene of a crime.

Ellery gazed long and thoughtfully. Nothing out of place, so far as he could see; and nothing, at least perceptible to a stranger, added. Then his eyes wavered and fixed themselves upon what stood straight before him. That *was* odd. . . . Facing him as he leaned against the door there was a bold naked mirror set flush into the opposite wall and reaching from floor to ceiling—a startling feature of the room's decorations. Ellery's lean figure, and the door behind him, were perfectly reflected in the sparkling glass. And there, above . . . In the mirror he saw, above the reflection of the door against which he was leaning, the reflection of the face of a modern electric clock. In the dingy grayness of the light there was a curious lambent quality about its dial. . . . He pushed away from the door and turned and stared up. It was a chromium-and-onyx clock, about a foot in diameter, round and simple and startling.

He opened the door and beckoned Millan, who had joined the silent group in the living room. "Have you a step-ladder?"

Millan brought one. Ellery smiled, shut the door firmly, mounted the ladder, and examined the clock. Its electric outlet was behind, concealed from view. The plug was in the socket, as he saw at once. The clock was going; the time—he consulted his wrist-watch—was reasonably accurate. But then he cupped his hands as best he could to shut out what light there was and stared hard and saw that the numerals and the hands, as he had suspected, were radium-painted. They glowed faintly.

He descended, opened the door, gave the ladder into Millan's keeping, and sauntered into the living room. They looked up at him trustfully.

"Well," said Emmy Willowes with a light shrug, "has the Master Mind discovered the all-important clue? Don't tell us that Dickie Owen is out playing golf at the Meadowbrook links in that Mad Hatter's get-up!"

"Well, Mr. Queen?" asked Mrs. Owen anxiously.

Ellery sank into an armchair and lighted a cigarette. "There's something curious in there. Mrs. Owen, did you get this house furnished?"

She was puzzled. "Furnished? Oh, no. We bought it, you know; brought all our own things."

"Then the electric clock above the door in the den is yours?"

"The clock?" They all stared at him. "Why, of course. What has that—"

"Hmm," said Ellery. "That clock has a disappearing quality, like the Cheshire Cat—since we may as well continue being Carrollish, Miss Willowes."

"But what can the clock possibly have to do with Richard's—being gone?" asked Mrs. Mansfield with asperity.

Ellery shrugged. "*Je n' sais.* The point is that a little after two this morning, being unable to sleep, I ambled downstairs to look for a book. In the dark I blundered to the door of the den, mistaking it for the library door. I opened it and looked in. But I saw nothing, you see."

"But how could you, Mr. Queen?" said Mrs. Gardner in a small voice; her breasts heaved. "If it was dark—"

"That's the curious part of it," drawled Ellery. "I *should* have seen something *because* it was so dark, Mrs. Gardner."

"But—"

"The clock over the door."

"Did you go in?" murmured Emmy Willowes, frowning. "I can't say I understand. The clock's above the door, isn't it?"

"There is a mirror facing the door," explained Ellery absently, "and the fact that it was so dark makes my seeing nothing quite remarkable. Because that clock has luminous hands and numerals. Consequently I should have seen their reflected glow very clearly indeed in that pitch-darkness. But I didn't, you see. I saw literally nothing at all."

They were silent, bewildered. Then Gardner muttered: "I still don't see—You mean something, somebody was standing in front of the mirror, obscuring the reflection of the clock?"

"Oh, no. The clock's above the door—a good seven feet or more from the floor. The mirror reaches to the ceiling. There isn't a piece of furniture in that room seven feet high, and certainly we may dismiss the possibility of an intruder seven feet or more tall. No, no, Gardner. It does seem as if the clock wasn't above the door at all when I looked in."

"Are you sure, young man," snapped Mrs. Mansfield, "that you know what you're talking about? I thought we were concerned with my son-in-law's absence. And how on earth could the clock not have been there?"

Ellery closed his eyes. "Fundamental. *It was moved from its position.* Wasn't above the door when I looked in. After I left, it was returned."

"But why on earth," murmured the actress, "should any one want to move a mere clock from a wall, Mr. Queen? That's almost as nonsensical as some of the things in *Alice*."

"That," said Ellery, "is the question I'm propounding to myself. Frankly I don't know." Then he opened his eyes. "By the way, has any one seen the Mad Hatter's hat?"

Mrs. Owen shivered. "No, that—that's gone, too."

"You've looked for it?"

"Yes. Would you like to look yours—"

"No, no, I'll take your word for it, Mrs. Owen. Oh, yes. Your husband has no enemies?" He smiled. "That's the routine question, Miss Willowes. I'm afraid I can't offer you anything startling in the way of technique."

"Enemies? Oh, I'm sure not," quavered Mrs. Owen. "Richard was—is strong and—and sometimes rather curt and contemptuous, but I'm sure no one would hate him enough to—to kill him." She shivered again and drew the silk of her négligé closer about her plump shoulders.

"Don't say that, Laura," said Mrs. Mansfield sharply. "I do declare, you people are like children! It probably has the simplest explanation."

"Quite possible," said Ellery in a cheerful voice. "It's the depressing weather, I suppose. . . . There! I believe the rain's stopped." They dully looked out the windows. The rain had perversely ceased, and the sky was growing brighter. "Of course," continued Ellery, "there are certain possibilities. It's conceivable—I say conceivable, Mrs. Owen—that your husband has been . . . well, kidnaped. Now, now, don't look so frightened. It's a theory only. The fact that he has disappeared in the costume does seem to point to a very abrupt—and therefore possibly enforced—departure. You haven't found a note of some kind? Nothing in your letter-box? The morning mail—"

"Kidnaped," whispered Mrs. Owen feebly.

"Kidnaped?" breathed Mrs. Gardner, and bit her lip. But there was a brightness in her eye, like the brightness of the sky outdoors.

"No note, no mail," snapped Mrs. Mansfield. "Personally, I think this is ridiculous. Laura, this is your house, but I think I have a duty. . . . You should do one of two things. Either take this seriously and telephone the *regular* police, or forget all about it. *I'm* inclined to believe Richard got befuddled—he *had* a lot to drink last night, dear—and wandered off drunk somewhere. He's probably sleeping it off in a field somewhere and won't come back with anything worse than a bad cold."

"Excellent suggestion," drawled Ellery. "All except for the summoning of the *regular* police, Mrs. Mansfield. I assure you I possess—er—*ex officio* qualifications. Let's not call the police and say we did. If there's any explaining to do—afterward—I'll do it. Meanwhile, I suggest we try to forget all this unpleasantness and wait. If Mr. Owen hasn't returned by nightfall, we can go into conference and decide what measures to take. Agreed?"

"Sounds reasonable," said Gardner disconsolately. "May I—" he smiled and shrugged—"this *is* exciting!—telephone my office, Queen?"

"Lord, yes."

Mrs. Owen shrieked suddenly, rising and tottering toward the stairs. "Jonathan's birthday party! I forgot all about it! And all those children invited—What *will* I say?"

"I suggest," said Ellery in a sad voice, "that Master Jonathan is indisposed, Mrs. Owen. Harsh, but necessary. You might 'phone all the potential spectators of the mad tea-party and voice your regrets." And Ellery rose and wandered into the library.

It was a depressing day for all the lightening skies and the crisp sun. The morning wore on and nothing whatever happened. Mrs. Mansfield firmly tucked her daughter into bed, made her swallow a small dose of luminol from a big bottle in the medicine-chest, and remained with her until she dropped off to exhausted sleep. Then the old lady telephoned to all and sundry the collective Owen regrets over the unfortunate turn of events. Jonathan *would* have to run a fever when . . . Master Jonathan, apprised later by his grandmother of the *débâcle,* sent up an ululating howl of surprisingly healthy anguish that caused Ellery, poking about downstairs in the library, to feel prickles slither up and down his spine. It took the combined labors of Mrs. Mansfield, Millan, the maid, and the cook to pacify the Owen hope. A five-dollar bill ultimately restored a rather strained *entente*. . . . Emmy Willowes spent the day serenely in reading. The Gardners listlessly played two-handed bridge.

Luncheon was a dismal affair. No one spoke in more than monosyllables, and the strained atmosphere grew positively taut.

During the afternoon they wandered about, restless ghosts. Even the actress began to show signs of tension: she consumed innumerable cigarettes and cocktails and lapsed into almost sullen silence. No word came; the telephone rang only once, and then it was merely the local confectioner protesting the cancellation of the ice-cream order. Ellery spent most of the afternoon in mysterious activity in the library and den. What he was looking for remained his secret. At five o'clock he emerged from the den, rather gray of face. There was a deep crease between his brows. He went out onto the porch and leaned against a pillar, sunk in thought. The gravel was dry; the sun had quickly sopped up the rain. When he went back into the house it was already dusk and growing darker each moment with the swiftness of the country nightfall.

There was no one about; the house was quiet, its miserable occupants having retired to their rooms. Ellery sought a chair. He buried his face in his hands and thought for long minutes, completely still.

And then at last something happened to his face and he went to the foot of the stairs and listened. No sound. He tiptoed back, reached for the telephone, and spent the next fifteen minutes in low-voiced, earnest conversation with some one in New York. When he had finished, he went upstairs to his room.

An hour later, while the others were downstairs gathering for dinner, he slipped down the rear stairway and out of the house unobserved even by the cook in the kitchen. He spent some time in the thick darkness of the grounds.

How it happened Ellery never knew. He felt its effects soon after dinner; and on retrospection he recalled that the others, too, had seemed drowsy at approximately the same time. It was a late dinner and a cold one, Owen's disappearance apparently having disrupted the culinary organization as well; so that it was not until a little after eight that the coffee—Ellery was certain later it had been the coffee—was served by the trim-legged maid. The drowsiness came on less than half an hour later. They were seated in the living room, chatting dully about nothing at all. Mrs. Owen, pale and silent, had gulped her coffee thirstily; had called for a second cup, in fact. Only Mrs. Mansfield had been belligerent. She had been definitely of a mind, it appeared, to telephone the police. She had great faith in the local constabulary of Long Island, particularly in one Chief Naughton, the local prefect; and she left no doubt in Ellery's mind of *his* incompetency. Gardner had been restless and a little rebellious; he had tinkered with the piano in the alcove. Emmy Willowes had drawn herself into a slant-eyed shell, no longer amused and very, very quiet. Mrs. Gardner had been nervous. Jonathan, packed off screaming to bed. . . .

It came over their senses like a soft insidious blanket of snow. Just a pleasant sleepiness. The room was warm, too, and Ellery rather hazily felt beads of perspiration on his forehead. He was half-gone before his dulled brain sounded a warning note. And then, trying in panic to rise; to use his muscles, he felt himself slipping, slipping into unconsciousness, his body as leaden and remote as Vega. His last conscious thought, as the room whirled dizzily before his eyes and he saw blearily the expressions of his companions, was that they had all been drugged. . . .

The dizziness seemed merely to have taken up where it had left off, almost without hiatus. Specks danced before his closed eyes and somebody was hammering petulantly at his temples. Then he opened his eyes and saw glittering sun fixed upon the floor at his feet. Good God, all night. . . .

He sat up groaning and feeling his head. The others were sprawled in various attitudes of labored-breathing coma about him—without exception. Some one—his aching brain took it in dully; it was Emmy Willowes—stirred and sighed. He got to his feet and stumbled toward a portable bar and poured himself a stiff, nasty drink of Scotch. Then, with his throat burning, he felt unaccountably better; and he went to the actress and pummeled her gently until she opened her eyes and gave him a sick, dazed, troubled look.

"What—when—"

"Drugged," croaked Ellery. "The crew of us. Try to revive these people, Miss Willowes, while I scout about a bit. And see if any one's shamming."

He wove his way a little uncertainly, but with purpose, toward the rear of the house. Groping, he found the kitchen. And there were the trim-legged maid and Millan and the cook unconscious in chairs about the kitchen table over cold cups of coffee. He made his way back to the living room, nodded at Miss Willowes working over Gardner at the piano, and staggered upstairs. He discovered Master Jonathan's bedroom after a short search; the boy was still sleeping—a deep natural sleep punctuated by nasal snuffles. Lord, he *did* snuffle! Groaning, Ellery visited the lavatory adjoining the master-bedroom. After a little while he went downstairs and into the den. He came out almost at once, haggard and wild-eyed. He took his hat from the foyer-closet and hurried outdoors into the warm sunshine. He spent fifteen minutes poking about the grounds; the Owen house was shallowly surrounded by timber and seemed isolated as a Western ranch. . . . When he returned to the house, looking grim and disappointed, the others were all conscious, making mewing little sounds and holding their heads like scared children.

"Queen, for God's sake," began Gardner hoarsely.

"Whoever it was used that luminol in the lavatory upstairs," said Ellery, flinging his hat away and wincing at a sudden pain in his head. "The stuff Mrs. Mansfield gave Mrs. Owen yesterday to make her sleep. Except that almost the whole of that large bottle was used. Swell sleeping draught! Make yourselves comfortable while I conduct a little investigation in the kitchen. I think it was the java." But when he returned he was grimacing. "No luck. *Madame la Cuisinière*, it seems, had to visit the bathroom at one period; Millan was out in the garage looking at the cars; and the maid was off somewhere, doubtless primping. Result: our friend the luminolist had an opportunity to pour most of the powder from the bottle into the coffeepot. Damn!"

"I *am* going to call the police!" cried Mrs. Mansfield hysterically, striving to rise. "We'll be murdered in our beds, next thing we know! Laura, I positively insist—"

"Please, please, Mrs. Mansfield," said, Ellery wearily. "No heroics. And you would be of greater service if you went into the kitchen and checked the insurrection that's brewing there. The two females are on the verge of packing, I'll swear."

Mrs. Mansfield bit her lip and flounced off. They heard her no longer sweet voice raised in remonstrance a moment later.

"But, Queen," protested Gardner, "we can't go unprotected—"

"What I want to know in my infantile way," drawled Emmy Willowes from pale lips, "is who did it, and why. That bottle upstairs . . . It looks unconscionably like one of us, doesn't it?"

Mrs. Gardner gave a little shriek. Mrs. Owen sank back into her chair.

"One of us?" whispered the red-haired woman.

Ellery smiled without humor. Then his smile faded and he cocked his head toward the foyer. "What was that?" he snapped suddenly.

They turned, terror-stricken, and looked. But there was nothing to see. Ellery strode toward the front door.

"What is it now, for heaven's sake?" faltered Mrs. Owen.

"I thought I heard a sound—" He flung the door open. The early morning sun streamed in. Then they saw him stoop and pick up something from the porch and rise and look swiftly about outside. But he shook his head and stepped back, closing the door.

"Package," he said with a frown. "I *thought* some one. . ."

They looked blankly at the brown-paper bundle in his hands. "Package?" asked Mrs. Owen. Her face lit up. "Oh, it may be from Richard!" And then the light went out, to be replaced by fearful pallor. "Oh, do you think—?"

"It's addressed," said Ellery slowly, "to you, Mrs. Owen. No stamp, no postmark, written in pencil in disguised block-letters. I think I'll take the liberty of opening this, Mrs. Owen." He broke the feeble twine and tore away the wrapping of the crude parcel. And then he frowned even more deeply. For the package contained only a pair of large men's shoes, worn at the heels and soles—sport oxfords in tan and white.

Mrs. Owen rolled her eyes, her nostrils quivering with nausea. "Richard's!" she gasped. And she sank back, half-fainting.

"Indeed?" murmured Ellery. "How interesting. Not, of course, the shoes he wore Friday night. You're positive they're his, Mrs. Owen?"

"Oh, he *has* been kidnaped!" quavered Mrs. Mansfield "from the rear doorway. "Isn't there a note, b-blood. . ."

"Nothing but the shoes. I doubt the kidnap theory now, Mrs. Mansfield. These weren't the shoes Owen wore Friday night. When did you see these last, Mrs. Owen?"

She moaned: "In his wardrobe closet upstairs only yesterday afternoon. Oh—"

"There. You see?" said Ellery cheerfully. "Probably stolen from the closet while we were all unconscious last night. And now returned rather spectacularly. So far, you know, there's been no harm done. I'm afraid," he said with severity, "we're nursing a viper at our bosoms."

But they did not laugh. Miss Willowes said strangely: "Very odd. In fact, insane Mr. Queen. I can't see the slightest purpose in it."

"Nor I, at the moment. Somebody's either playing a monstrous prank, or there's a devilishly clever and warped mentality behind all this." He retrieved his hat and made for the door.

"Wherever are you going?" gasped Mrs. Gardner.

"Oh, out for a thinking spell under God's blue canopy. But remember," he added quietly, "that's a privilege reserved to detectives. No one is to set foot outside this house."

He returned an hour later without explanation.

At noon they found the second package. It was a squarish parcel wrapped in the same brown paper. Inside there was a cardboard carton, and in the carton, packed in crumpled tissue-paper, there were two magnificent toy sailing-boats such as children race on summer lakes. The package was addressed to Miss Willowes.

"This is getting dreadful," murmured Mrs. Gardner, her full lips trembling. "I'm all goose-pimples."

"I'd feel better," muttered Miss Willowes, "if it was a bloody dagger, or something. Toy boats!" She stepped back and her eyes narrowed. "Now, look here, good people, I'm as much a sport as anybody, but a joke's a joke and I'm just a bit fed up on this particular one. Who's manœuvring these monkeyshines?"

"Joke," snarled Gardner. He was white as death. "It's the work of a madman, I tell you!"

"Now, now," murmured Ellery, staring at the green-and-cream boats. "We shan't get anywhere this way. Mrs. Owen, have you ever seen these before?"

Mrs. Owen, on the verge of collapse, mumbled: "Oh, my good dear God. Mr. Queen, I don't—Why, they're—they're Jonathan's!"

Ellery blinked. Then he went to the foot of the stairway and yelled: "Johnny! Come down here a minute."

Master Jonathan descended sluggishly, sulkily. "What you want?" he asked in a cold voice.

"Come here, son." Master Jonathan came with dragging feet. "When did you see these boats of yours last?"

"Boats!" shrieked Master Jonathan, springing into life. He pounced on them and snatched them away, glaring at Ellery. "My boats! Never seen such a place. My boats! You stole 'em!"

"Come, come," said Ellery, flushing, "be a good little man. When did you see them last?"

"Yest'day! In my toy-chest! My boats! Scan'lous," hissed Master Jonathan, and fled upstairs, hugging his boats to his scrawny breast.

"Stolen at the same time," said Ellery helplessly. "By thunder, Miss Willowes, I'm almost inclined to agree with you. By the way, who bought those boats for your son, Mrs. Owen?"

"H-his father."

"Damn," said Ellery for the second time that impious Sunday, and he sent them all on a search of the house to ascertain if anything else were missing. But no one could find that anything had been taken.

It was when they came down from upstairs that they found Ellery regarding a small white envelope with puzzlement.

"Now what?" demanded Gardner wildly.

"Stuck in the door," he said thoughtfully. "Hadn't noticed it before. This *is* a queer one."

It was a rich piece of stationery, sealed with blue wax on the back and bearing the same pencilled scrawl, this time addressed to Mrs. Mansfield.

The old lady collapsed in the nearest chair, holding her hand to her heart. She was speechless with fear.

"Well," said Mrs. Gardner huskily, "open it."

Ellery tore open the envelope. His frown deepened. "Why," he muttered, "there's nothing at all inside!"

Gardner gnawed his fingers and turned away, mumbling. Mrs. Gardner shook her head like a dazed pugilist and stumbled toward the bar for the fifth time that day. Emmy Willowes' brow was dark as thunder.

"You know," said Mrs. Owen almost quietly, "that's mother's stationery." And there was another silence.

Ellery muttered: "Queerer and queerer. I *must* get this organized. . . . The shoes are a puzzler. The toy boats might be construed as a gift; yesterday was Jonathan's birthday; the boats are his—a distorted practical joke. . . ." He shook his head. "Doesn't wash. And this third—an envelope without a letter in it. That would seem to point to the envelope as the important thing. But the envelope's the property of Mrs. Mansfield. The only other thing—ah, the wax!" He scanned the blue blob on the back narrowly, but it bore no seal-insignia of any kind.

"That," said Mrs. Owen again in the quiet unnatural voice, "looks like our wax, too, Mr. Queen, from the library."

Ellery dashed away, followed by a troubled company. Mrs. Owen went to the library desk and opened the top drawer.

"Was it here?" asked Ellery quickly.

"Yes," she said, and then her voice quivered. "I used it only Friday when I wrote a letter. Oh, good. . ."

There was no stick of wax in the drawer.

And while they stared at the drawer, the front doorbell rang.

It was a market-basket this time, lying innocently on the porch. In it, nestling crisp and green, were two large cabbages.

Ellery shouted for Gardner and Millan, himself led the charge down the steps. They scattered, searching wildly through the brush and woods surrounding the house. But they found nothing. No sign of the bell-ringer, no sign of the ghost who had cheerfully left a basket of cabbages at the door as his fourth odd gift. It was as if he were made of smoke and materialized only for the instant he needed to press his impalpable finger to the bell.

They found the women huddled in a corner of the living room, shivering and white-lipped. Mrs. Mansfield, shaking like an aspen, was at the telephone ringing for the local police. Ellery started to protest, shrugged, set his lips, and stooped over the basket.

There was a slip of paper tied by string to the handle of the basket. The same crude pencil-scrawl. . . . "Mr. Paul Gardner."

"Looks," muttered Ellery, "as if you're elected, old fellow, this time."

Gardner stared as if he could not believe his eyes. "Cabbages!"

"Excuse me," said Ellery curtly. He went away. When he returned he was shrugging. "From the vegetable-bin in the outside pantry, says Cook. She hadn't thought to look for missing *vegetables*, she told me with scorn."

Mrs. Mansfield was babbling excitedly over the telephone to a sorely puzzled officer of the law. When she hung up she was red as a newborn baby. "That will be *quite* enough of this crazy nonsense, Mr. Queen!" she snarled. And then she collapsed in a chair and laughed hysterically and shrieked: "Oh, I knew you were making the mistake of your life when you married that beast, Laura!" and laughed again like a madwoman.

The law arrived in fifteen minutes, accompanied by a howling siren and personified by a stocky brick-faced man in chief's stripes and a gangling young policeman.

"I'm Naughton," he said shortly. "What the devil's goin' on here?"

Ellery said: "Ah, Chief Naughton. I'm Queen's son—Inspector Richard Queen of Centre Street. How d'ye do?"

"Oh!" said Naughton. He turned on Mrs. Mansfield sternly. "Why didn't you say Mr. Queen was here, Mrs. Mansfield? You ought to know—"

"Oh, I'm sick of the lot of you!" screamed the old lady. "Nonsense, nonsense, nonsense from the instant this weekend began! First that awful actress-woman there, in her short skirt and legs and things, and then this—this—"

Naughton rubbed his chin. "Come over here, Mr. Queen,

where we can talk like human beings. What the deuce happened?"

Ellery with a sigh told him. As he spoke, the Chief's face grew redder and redder. "You mean you're serious about this business?" he rumbled at last. "It sounds plain crazy to me. Mr. Owen's gone off his nut and he's playing jokes on you people. Good God, you can't take this thing serious!"

"I'm afraid," murmured Ellery, "we must. . . . What's that? By heaven, if that's another manifestation of our playful ghost—!" And he dashed toward the door while Naughton gaped and pulled it open, to be struck by a wave of dusk. On the porch lay the fifth parcel, a tiny one this time.

The two officers darted out of the house, flashlights blinking and probing. Ellery picked up the packet with eager fingers. It was addressed in the now familiar scrawl to Mrs. Paul Gardner. Inside were two identically shaped objects: chessmen, kings. One was white and the other was black.

"Who plays chess here?" he drawled.

"Richard," shrieked Mrs. Owen. "Oh, my God, I'm going mad!"

Investigation proved that the two kings from Richard Owen's chess-set were gone.

The local officers came back, rather pale and panting. They had found no one outside. Ellery was silently studying the two chessmen.

"Well?" said Naughton, drooping his shoulders.

"Well," said Ellery quietly. "I have the most brilliant notion, Naughton. Come here a moment." He drew Naughton aside and began to speak rapidly in a low voice. The others stood limply about, twitching with nervousness. There was no longer any pretense of self-control. If this was a joke, it was a ghastly one indeed. And Richard Owen looming in the background. . .

The Chief blinked and nodded. "You people," he said shortly, turning to them, "get into that library there." They gaped. "I mean it! The lot of you. This tomfoolery is going to stop right now."

"But, Naughton," gasped Mrs. Mansfield, "it couldn't be any of us who sent those things. Mr. Queen will tell you we weren't out of his sight today—"

"Do as I say, Mrs. Mansfield," snapped the officer.

They trooped, puzzled, into the library. The policeman rounded up Millan, the cook, the maid, and went with them. Nobody said anything; nobody looked at any one else. Minutes passed; a half-hour; an hour. There was the silence of the grave from beyond the door to the living room. They strained their ears. . . .

At seven-thirty the door was jerked open and Ellery and the Chief glowered in on them. "Everybody out," said Naughton shortly. "Come on, step on it."

"Out?" whispered Mrs. Owen. "Where? Where is Richard? What—"

The policeman herded them out. Ellery stepped to the door of the den and pushed it open and switched on the light and stood aside.

"Will you please come in here and take seats," he said dryly; there was a tense look on his face and he seemed exhausted.

Silently, slowly, they obeyed. The policeman dragged in extra chairs from the living room. They sat down. Naughton drew the shades. The policeman closed the door and set his back against it.

Ellery said tonelessly: "In a way this has been one of the most remarkable cases in my experience. It's been unorthodox from every angle. Utterly nonconforming. I think, Miss Willowes, the wish you expressed Friday night has come true. You're about to witness a slightly cock-eyed exercise in criminal ingenuity."

"Crim—" Mrs. Gardner's full lips quivered. "You mean—there's been a crime?"

"Quiet," said Naughton harshly.

"Yes," said Ellery in gentle tones, "there has been a crime. I might say—I'm sorry to say, Mrs. Owen—a major crime."

"Richard's d—"

"I'm sorry." There was a little silence. Mrs. Owen did not weep; she seemed dried out of tears. "Fantastic," said Ellery at last. "Look here." He sighed. "The crux of the problem was the clock. The Clock That Wasn't Where It Should Have Been, the clock with the invisible face. You remember I pointed out that, since I hadn't seen the reflection of the luminous hands in that mirror there, the clock must have been moved. That was a tenable theory. But it wasn't the *only* theory."

"Richard's dead," said Mrs. Owen, in a wondering voice.

"Mr. Gardner," continued Ellery quickly, "pointed out one possibility: that the clock may still have been over this door, but that something or some one may have been standing in front of the mirror. I told you why that was impossible. But," and he went suddenly to the tall mirror, "there was still another theory which accounted for the fact that I hadn't seen the luminous hands' reflection. And that was: that when I opened the door in the dark and peered in and saw nothing, the clock was still there but the *mirror* wasn't!"

Miss Willowes said with a curious dryness: "But how could that be, Mr. Queen? That—that's silly."

"Nothing is silly, dear lady, until it is proved so. I said to myself: How could it be that the mirror wasn't there at that instant? It's apparently a solid part of the wall, a built-in section in this modern room." Something glimmered in Miss Willowes' eyes. Mrs. Mansfield was staring straight before her, hands clasped tightly in her lap. Mrs. Owen was looking at Ellery with glazed eyes, blind and deaf. "Then," said Ellery with another sigh, "there was the very odd nature of the packages which have been descending upon us all day like manna from heaven. I said this was a fantastic affair. Of course it must have occurred to you that some one was trying desperately to call our attention to the secret of the crime."

"Call our at—" began Gardner, frowning.

"Precisely. Now, Mrs. Owen," murmured Ellery softly, "The first package was addressed to you. What did it contain?" She stared at him without expression. There was a dreadful silence. Mrs. Mansfield suddenly shook her, as if she had been a child. She started, smiled vaguely; Ellery repeated the question.

And she said, almost brightly: "A pair of Richard's sport oxfords."

He winced. "In a word, *shoes*. Miss Willowes," and despite her nonchalance she stiffened a little, "you were the recipient of the second package. And what did that contain?"

"Jonathan's toy boats," she murmured.

"In a word, again—*ships*. Mrs. Mansfield, the third package was sent to you. It contained what, precisely?"

"Nothing." She tossed her head. "I still think this is the purest drivel. Can't you see you're driving my daughter—all of us—insane? Naughton, are you going to permit this farce to continue? If you know what's happened to Richard, for goodness' sake tell us!"

"Answer the question," said Naughton with a scowl.

"Well," she said defiantly, "a silly envelope, empty, and sealed with our own wax."

"And again in a word," drawled Ellery, "*sealing-wax*. Now, Gardner, to you fell the really whimsical fourth bequest. It was—?"

"Cabbage," said Gardner with an uncertain grin.

"Cabbages, my dear chap; there were two of them. And finally, Mrs. Gardner, you received what?"

"Two chessmen," she whispered.

"No, no. Not just two chessmen, Mrs. Gardner. Two *kings*." Ellery's gray eyes glittered. "In other words, in the order named we were bombarded with gifts. . ." he paused and looked at them, and continued softly, "'*of shoes and ships and sealing-wax, of cabbages and kings.*'"

There was the most extraordinary silence. Then Emmy Willowes gasped: "The Walrus and the Carpenter. *Alice's Adventures in Wonderland!*"

"I'm ashamed of you, Miss Willowes. Where precisely does Tweedledee's Walrus speech come in Carroll's duology?"

A great light broke over her eager features. "*Through the Looking Glass!*"

"*Through the Looking Glass*," murmured Ellery in the crackling silence that followed. "And do you know what the subtitle of *Through the Looking Glass* is?"

She said in an awed voice: "*And What Alice Found There.*"

"A perfect recitation, Miss Willowes. We were instructed, then, to go through the looking glass and, by inference, find something on the other side connected with the disappearance of Richard Owen. Quaint idea, eh?" He leaned forward and said brusquely: "Let me revert to my original chain of reasoning. I said that a likely theory was that the mirror didn't reflect the luminous hands because the mirror wasn't there. But since the wall at any rate is solid, the mirror itself must be movable to have been shifted out of place. How was this possible? Yesterday I sought for two hours to find the secret of that mirror—or should I say . . . looking glass?" Their eyes went with horror to the tall mirror set in the wall, winking back at them in the glitter of the bulbs. "And when I discovered the secret, I looked *through the looking glass* and what do you suppose I—a clumsy Alice, indeed!—found there?"

No one replied.

Ellery went swiftly to the mirror, stood on tiptoe, touched something, and something happened to the whole glass. It moved forward as if on hinges. He hooked his fingers in the crack and pulled. The mirror, like a door, swung out and away, revealing a shallow closet-like cavity.

The women with one breath screamed and covered their eyes.

The stiff figure of the Mad Hatter, with Richard Owen's unmistakable features, glared out at them—a dead, horrible, baleful glare.

Paul Gardner stumbled to his feet, choking and jerking at his collar. His eyes bugged out of his head. "O-O-Owen," he gasped. "Owen. He *can't* be here. I b-b-buried him myself under the big rock behind the house in the woods. Oh, my God." And he smiled a dreadful smile and his eyes turned over and he collapsed in a faint on the floor.

Ellery sighed. "It's all right now, De Vere," and the Mad Hatter moved and his features ceased to resemble Richard Owen's magically. "You may come out now. Admirable bit of statuary histrionics. And it turned the trick, as I thought it would. There's your man, Mr. Naughton. And if you'll question Mrs. Gardner, I believe you'll find that she's been Owen's mistress for some time. Gardner obviously found it out and killed him. Look out—there *she* goes, too!"

"What I can't understand," murmured Emmy Willowes after a long silence late that night, as she and Mr. Ellery Queen sat side by side in the local bound for Jamaica and the express for Pennsylvania Station, "is—" She stopped helplessly. "I can't understand so many things, Mr. Queen."

"It was simple enough," said Ellery wearily, staring out the window at the rushing dark countryside.

"But who is that man—that De Vere?"

"Oh, he! A Thespian acquaintance of mine temporarily 'at liberty.' He's an actor—does character bits. You wouldn't know him, I suppose. You see, when my deductions had led me to the looking glass and I examined it and finally discovered its secret and opened it, I found Owen's body lying there in the Hatter costume—"

She shuddered. "Much too realistic drama to my taste. Why didn't you announce your discovery at once?"

"And gain what? There wasn't a shred of evidence against the murderer. I wanted time to think out a plan to make the murderer give himself away. I left the body there—"

"You mean to sit there and say you knew Gardner did it all the time?" she demanded, frankly skeptical.

He shrugged. "Of course. The Owens had lived in that house barely a month. The spring on that compartment is remarkably well concealed; it probably would never be discovered unless you knew it existed and were looking for it. But I recalled that Owen himself remarked Friday night that Gardner had designed 'this development.' I had it then, naturally. Who more likely than the architect to know the secret of such a hidden closet? Why he designed and had built a secret panel I don't know; I suppose it fitted into some architectural whim of his. So it had to be Gardner, you see." He gazed thoughtfully at the dusty ceiling of the car. "I reconstructed the crime easily enough. After we retired Friday night Gardner came down to have it out with Owen about Mrs. Gardner—a lusty wench, if I ever saw one. They had words; Gardner killed him. It must have been an unpremeditated crime. His first impulse was to hide the body. He couldn't take it out Friday night in that awful rain without leaving traces on his night-clothes. Then he remembered the panel behind the mirror. The body would be safe enough there, he felt, until he could remove it when the rain stopped and the ground dried to a permanent hiding-place; dig a grave, or whatnot. . . . He was stowing the body away in the closet when I opened the door of the den; that was why I didn't see the reflection of the clock. Then, while I was in the library, he closed the mirror-door and dodged upstairs. I came out quickly, though, and he decided to brazen it out; even pretended he thought I might be 'Owen' coming up.

"At any rate, Saturday night he drugged us all, took the body out, buried it, and came back and dosed himself with the drug to make his part as natural as possible. He didn't know I had found the body behind the mirror Saturday afternoon. When, Sunday morning, I found the body gone, I knew of course the reason for the drugging. Gardner by burying the body in a place unknown to anyone—without leaving, as far as he knew, even a clue to the fact that murder had been committed at all—was naturally doing away with the primary piece of evidence in any murder-case . . . the *corpus delicti*. . . . Well, I found the opportunity to telephone De Vere and instruct him in what he had to do. He dug up the Hatter's costume somewhere, managed to get a photo of Owen from a theatrical office, came down here. . . . We put him in the closet while Naughton's man was detaining you people in the library. You see, I had to build up suspense, make Gardner give himself away, break down his moral resistance. He had to be forced to disclose where he had buried the body; and he was the only one who could tell us. It worked."

The actress regarded him sidewise out of her clever eyes. Ellery sighed moodily, glancing away from her slim legs outstretched to the opposite seat. "But the most puzzling thing of all," she said with a pretty frown. "Those perfectly fiendish and fantastic packages. Who sent them, for heaven's sake?"

Ellery did not reply for a long time. Then he said drowsily, barely audible above the clatter of the train: "You did, really."

"*I?*" She was so startled that her mouth flew open.

"Only in a manner of speaking," murmured Ellery, closing his eyes. "Your idea about running a mad tea-party out of *Alice* for Master Jonathan's delectation—the whole pervading spirit of the Reverend Dodgson—started a chain of fantasy in my own brain, you see. Just opening the closet and saying that Owen's body had been there, or even getting De Vere to act as Owen, wasn't enough. I had to prepare Gardner's mind psychologically, fill him with puzzlement first, get him to realize after a while where the gifts with their implications were leading. . . . Had to torture him, I suppose. It's a weakness of mine. At any rate, it was an easy matter to telephone my father, the Inspector; and he sent Sergeant Velie down and I managed to smuggle all those things I'd filched from the house out into the woods behind and hand good Velie what I had. . . . He did the rest, packaging and all."

She sat up and measured him with a severe glance. "Mr. Queen! Is that cricket in the best detective circles?"

He grinned sleepily. "I had to do it, you see. Drama, Miss Willowes. You ought to be able to understand that. Surround a murderer with things he doesn't understand, bewilder him, get him mentally punch-drunk, and then spring the knock-out blow, the crusher. . . . Oh, it was devilish clever of me, I admit."

She regarded him for so long and in such silence and with such supple twisting of her boyish figure that he stirred uncomfortably, feeling an unwilling flush come to his cheeks. "And what, if I may ask," he said lightly, "brings that positively lewd expression to your Peter Pannish face, my dear? Feel all right? Anything wrong? By George, how *do* you feel?"

"As Alice would say," she said softly, leaning a little toward him, "curiouser and curiouser."

THE END

DISCUSSION QUESTIONS

- What sort of detective is Ellery Queen? What qualities make him appealing to readers? What qualities make him an effective crime-solver?

- How did the cultural history of the era play into these stories? Did anything help date them for you?

- Were you able to solve any of the mysteries before the solution was given? If so, which ones?

- Which story had the most dazzling solution?

- Did any stories surprise you in terms of subject, character, or setting? If so, which ones?

- Did the stories remind you of anything else you've read?

- If you have read Ellery Queen's novels, how do they compare with the short stories?

MORE ELLERY QUEEN FROM
AMERICAN MYSTERY CLASSICS

The Spanish
Cape Mystery

—

ELLERY
QUEEN

"One of the best of the Ellery Queen stories."
—*New York Times*

The Siamese
Twin Mystery

—

ELLERY
QUEEN

"The most baffling and most dramatic of all the
Ellery Queen yarns."—*New York Times*

The Chinese
Orange Mystery

—

ELLERY
QUEEN

"Ellery Queen *is* the American detective story"
—Anthony Boucher, *The New York Times*

The Egyptian
Cross Mystery

—

ELLERY
QUEEN

"A genre giant."—*Publishers Weekly*

All titles are available in hardcover and in trade paperback.

Order from your favorite bookstore or from
The Mysterious Bookshop, 58 Warren Street, New York, N.Y. 10007
(www.mysteriousbookshop.com).

Charlotte Armstrong, *The Chocolate Cobweb*. When Amanda Garth was born, a mix-up caused the hospital to briefly hand her over to the prestigious Garrison family instead of to her birth parents. The error was quickly fixed, Amanda was never told, and the secret was forgotten for twenty-three years … until her aunt revealed it in casual conversation. But what if the initial switch never actually occurred? **Introduction by A. J. Finn.**

Charlotte Armstrong, *The Unsuspected*. First published in 1946, this suspenseful novel opens with a young woman who has ostensibly hanged herself, leaving a suicide note. Her friend doesn't believe it and begins an investigation that puts her own life in jeopardy. It was filmed in 1947 by Warner Brothers, starring Claude Rains and Joan Caulfield. **Introduction by Otto Penzler.**

Anthony Boucher, *The Case of the Baker Street Irregulars*. When a studio announces a new hard-boiled Sherlock Holmes film, the Baker Street Irregulars begin a campaign to discredit it. Attempting to mollify them, the producers invite members to the set, where threats are received, each referring to one of the original Holmes tales, followed by murder. Fortunately, the amateur sleuths use Holmesian lessons to solve the crime. **Introduction by Otto Penzler.**

Anthony Boucher, *Rocket to the Morgue*. Hilary Foulkes has made so many enemies that it is difficult to speculate who was responsible for stabbing him nearly to death in a room with only one door through which no one was seen entering or leaving. This classic locked room mystery is populated by such thinly disguised science fiction legends as Robert Heinlein, L. Ron Hubbard, and John W. Campbell. **Introduction by F. Paul Wilson.**

Fredric Brown, *The Fabulous Clipjoint*. Brown's outstanding mystery won an Edgar as the best first novel of the year (1947). When Wallace Hunter is found dead in an alley after a long night of drinking, the police don't really care. But his teenage son Ed and his uncle Am, the carnival worker, are convinced that some things don't add up and the crime isn't what it seems to be. **Introduction by Lawrence Block.**

John Dickson Carr, *The Crooked Hinge*. Selected by a group of mystery experts as one of the 15 best impossible crime novels ever written, this is one of Gideon Fell's greatest challenges. Estranged from his family for 25 years, Sir John Farnleigh returns to England from America to claim his inheritance but another person turns up claiming that he can prove he is the real Sir John. Inevitably, one of them is murdered. **Introduction by Charles Todd.**

John Dickson Carr, *The Eight of Swords*. When Gideon Fell arrives at a crime scene, it appears to be straightforward enough. A man has been shot to death in an unlocked room and the likely perpetrator was a recent visitor. But Fell discovers inconsistencies and his investigations are complicated by an apparent poltergeist, some American gangsters, and two meddling amateur sleuths. **Introduction by Otto Penzler.**

John Dickson Carr, *The Mad Hatter Mystery*. A prankster has been stealing top hats all around London. Gideon Fell suspects that the same person may be responsible for the theft of a manuscript of a long-lost story by Edgar Allan Poe. The hats reappear in unexpected but conspicuous places but, when one is found on the head of a corpse by the Tower of London, it is evident that the thefts are more than pranks. **Introduction by Otto Penzler.**

John Dickson Carr, *The Plague Court Murders*. When murder occurs in a locked hut on Plague Court, an estate haunted by the ghost of a hangman's assistant who died a victim of the black death, Sir Henry Merrivale seeks a logical solution to a ghostly crime. A spiritual medium employed to rid the house of his spirit is found stabbed to death in a locked stone hut on the grounds, surrounded by an untouched circle of mud. **Introduction by Michael Dirda.**

John Dickson Carr, *The Red Widow Murders.* In a "haunted" mansion, the room known as the Red Widow's Chamber proves lethal to all who spend the night. Eight people investigate and the one who draws the ace of spades must sleep in it. The room is locked from the inside and watched all night by the others. When the door is unlocked, the victim has been poisoned. Enter Sir Henry Merrivale to solve the crime. **Introduction by Tom Mead.**

Frances Crane, *The Turquoise Shop.* In an arty little New Mexico town, Mona Brandon has arrived from the East and becomes the subject of gossip about her money, her influence, and the corpse in the nearby desert who may be her husband. Pat Holly, who runs the local gift shop, is as interested as anyone in the goings on—but even more in Pat Abbott, the detective investigating the possible murder. **Introduction by Anne Hillerman.**

Todd Downing, *Vultures in the Sky.* There is no end to the series of terrifying events that befall a luxury train bound for Mexico. First, a man dies when the train passes through a dark tunnel, then it comes to an abrupt stop in the middle of the desert. More deaths occur when night falls and the passengers panic when they realize they are trapped with a murderer on the loose. **Introduction by James Sallis.**

Mignon G. Eberhart, *Murder by an Aristocrat.* Nurse Keate is called to help a man who has been "accidentally" shot in the shoulder. When he is murdered while convalescing, it is clear that there was no accident. Although a killer is loose in the mansion, the family seems more concerned that news of the murder will leave their circle. *The New Yorker* wrote than "Eberhart can weave an almost flawless mystery." **Introduction by Nancy Pickard.**

Erle Stanley Gardner, *The Case of the Baited Hook.* Perry Mason gets a phone call in the middle of the night and his potential client says it's urgent, that he has two one-thousand-dollar bills that he will give him as a retainer, with an additional ten-thousand whenever he is called on to represent him. When Mason takes the case, it is not for the caller but for a beautiful woman whose identity is hidden behind a mask. **Introduction by Otto Penzler.**

Erle Stanley Gardner, *The Case of the Borrowed Brunette.* A mysterious man named Mr. Hines has advertised a job for a woman who has to fulfill very specific physical requirements. Eva Martell, pretty but struggling in her career as a model, takes the job but her aunt smells a rat and hires Perry Mason to investigate. Her fears are realized when Hines turns up in the apartment with a bullet hole in his head. **Introduction by Otto Penzler.**

Erle Stanley Gardner, *The Case of the Careless Kitten.* Helen Kendal receives a mysterious phone call from her vanished uncle Franklin, long presumed dead, who urges her to contact Perry Mason. Soon, she finds herself the main suspect in the murder of an unfamiliar man. Her kitten has just survived a poisoning attempt—as has her aunt Matilda. What is the connection between Franklin's return and the murder attempts? **Introduction by Otto Penzler.**

Erle Stanley Gardner, *The Case of the Rolling Bones.* One of Gardner's most successful Perry Mason novels opens with a clear case of blackmail, though the person being blackmailed claims he isn't. It is not long before the police are searching for someone wanted for killing the same man in two different states—thirty-three years apart. The confounding puzzle of what happened to the dead man's toes is a challenge. **Introduction by Otto Penzler.**

Erle Stanley Gardner, *The Case of the Shoplifter's Shoe.* Most cases for Perry Mason involve murder but here he is hired because a young woman fears her aunt is a kleptomaniac. Sarah may not have been precisely the best guardian for a collection of valuable diamonds and, sure enough, they go missing. When the jeweler is found shot dead, Sarah is spotted leaving the murder scene with a bundle of gems stuffed in her purse. **Introduction by Otto Penzler.**

Erle Stanley Gardner, *The Bigger They Come.* Gardner's first novel using the pseudonym A.A. Fair starts off a series featuring the large and loud Bertha Cool and her employee, the small and meek Donald Lam. Given the job of delivering divorce papers to an evident crook,

Lam can't find him—but neither can the police. The *Los Angeles Times* called this book: "Breathlessly dramatic ... an original." Introduction by Otto Penzler.

Frances Noyes Hart, *The Bellamy Trial*. Inspired by the real-life Hall-Mills case, the most sensational trial of its day, this is the story of Stephen Bellamy and Susan Ives, accused of murdering Bellamy's wife Madeleine. Eight days of dynamic testimony, some true, some not, make headlines for an enthralled public. Rex Stout called this historic courtroom thriller one of the ten best mysteries of all time. **Introduction by Hank Phillippi Ryan.**

H. F. Heard, *A Taste for Honey*. The elderly Mr. Mycroft quietly keeps bees in Sussex, where he is approached by the reclusive and somewhat misanthropic Mr. Silchester, whose honey supplier was found dead, stung to death by her bees. Mycroft, who shares many traits with Sherlock Holmes, sets out to find the vicious killer. Rex Stout described it as "sinister ... a tale well and truly told." **Introduction by Otto Penzler.**

Dolores Hitchens, *The Alarm of the Black Cat*. Detective fiction aficionado Rachel Murdock has a peculiar meeting with a little girl and a dead toad, sparking her curiosity about a love triangle that has sparked anger. When the girl's great grandmother is found dead, Rachel and her cat Samantha work with a friend in the Los Angeles Police Department to get to the bottom of things. **Introduction by David Handler.**

Dolores Hitchens, *The Cat Saw Murder*. Miss Rachel Murdock, the highly intelligent 70-year-old amateur sleuth, is not entirely heartbroken when her slovenly, unattractive, bridge-cheating niece is murdered. Miss Rachel is happy to help the socially maladroit and somewhat bumbling Detective Lieutenant Stephen Mayhew, retaining her composure when a second brutal murder occurs. **Introduction by Joyce Carol Oates.**

Dorothy B. Hughes, *Dread Journey*. A bigshot Hollywood producer has worked on his magnum opus for years, hiring and firing one beautiful starlet after another. But Kitten Agnew's contract won't allow her to be fired, so she fears she might be terminated more permanently. Together with the producer on a train journey from Hollywood to Chicago, Kitten becomes more terrified with each passing mile. **Introduction by Sarah Weinman.**

Dorothy B. Hughes, *Ride the Pink Horse*. When Sailor met Willis Douglass, he was just a poor kid who Douglass groomed to work as a confidential secretary. As the senator became increasingly corrupt, he knew he could count on Sailor to clean up his messes. No longer a senator, Douglass flees Chicago for Santa Fe, leaving behind a murder rap and Sailor as the prime suspect. Seeking vengeance, Sailor follows. **Introduction by Sara Paretsky.**

Dorothy B. Hughes, *The So Blue Marble*. Set in the glamorous world of New York high society, this novel became a suspense classic as twins from Europe try to steal a rare and beautiful gem owned by an aristocrat whose sister is an even more menacing presence. *The New Yorker* called it "Extraordinary ... [Hughes'] brilliant descriptive powers make and unmake reality." **Introduction by Otto Penzler.**

W. Bolingbroke Johnson, *The Widening Stain*. After a cocktail party, the attractive Lucie Coindreau, a "black-eyed, black-haired Frenchwoman" visits the rare books wing of the library and apparently takes a head-first fall from an upper gallery. Dismissed as a horrible accident, it seems dubious when Professor Hyett is strangled while reading a priceless 12th-century manuscript, which has gone missing. **Introduction by Nicholas A. Basbanes**

Baynard Kendrick, *Blind Man's Bluff*. Blinded in World War II, Duncan Maclain forms a successful private detective agency, aided by his two dogs. Here, he is called on to solve the case of a blind man who plummets from the top of an eight-story building, apparently with no one present except his dead-drunk son. **Introduction by Otto Penzler.**

Baynard Kendrick, *The Odor of Violets*. Duncan Maclain, a blind former intelligence officer, is asked to investigate the murder of an actor in his Greenwich Village apartment. This would cause a stir at any time but, when the actor possesses secret government plans that then go missing, it's enough to interest the local police as well as the American government and Maclain, who suspects a German spy plot. **Introduction by Otto Penzler.**

C. Daly King, *Obelists at Sea*. On a cruise ship traveling from New York to Paris, the lights of the smoking room briefly go out, a gunshot crashes through the night, and a man is dead. Two detectives are on board but so are four psychiatrists who believe their professional knowledge can solve the case by understanding the psyche of the killer—each with a different theory. **Introduction by Martin Edwards.**

Jonathan Latimer, *Headed for a Hearse*. Featuring Bill Crane, the booze-soaked Chicago private detective, this humorous hard-boiled novel was filmed as *The Westland Case* in 1937 starring Preston Foster. Robert Westland has been framed for the grisly murder of his wife in a room with doors and windows locked from the inside. As the day of his execution nears, he relies on Crane to find the real murderer. **Introduction by Max Allan Collins**

Lange Lewis, *The Birthday Murder*. Victoria is a successful novelist and screenwriter and her husband is a movie director so their marriage seems almost too good to be true. Then, on her birthday, her happy new life comes crashing down when her husband is murdered using a method of poisoning that was described in one of her books. She quickly becomes the leading suspect. **Introduction by Randal S. Brandt.**

Frances and Richard Lockridge, *Death on the Aisle*. In one of the most beloved books to feature Mr. and Mrs. North, the body of a wealthy backer of a play is found dead in a seat of the 45th Street Theater. Pam is thrilled to engage in her favorite pastime—playing amateur sleuth—much to the annoyance of Jerry, her publisher husband. The Norths inspired a stage play, a film, and long-running radio and TV series. **Introduction by Otto Penzler.**

John P. Marquand, *Your Turn, Mr. Moto*. The first novel about Mr. Moto, originally titled *No Hero*, is the story of a World War I hero pilot who finds himself jobless during the Depression. In Tokyo for a big opportunity that falls apart, he meets a Japanese agent and his Russian colleague and the pilot suddenly finds himself caught in a web of intrigue. Peter Lorre played Mr. Moto in a series of popular films. **Introduction by Lawrence Block.**

Stuart Palmer, *The Penguin Pool Murder*. The

first adventure of schoolteacher and dedicated amateur sleuth Hildegarde Withers occurs at the New York Aquarium when she and her young students notice a corpse in one of the tanks. It was published in 1931 and filmed the next year, starring Edna May Oliver as the American Miss Marple—though much funnier than her English counterpart. **Introduction by Otto Penzler.**

Stuart Palmer, *The Puzzle of the Happy Hooligan*. New York City schoolteacher Hildegarde Withers cannot resist "assisting" homicide detective Oliver Piper. In this novel, she is on vacation in Hollywood and on the set of a movie about Lizzie Borden when the screenwriter is found dead. Six comic films about Withers appeared in the 1930s, most successfully starring Edna May Oliver. **Introduction by Otto Penzler.**

Otto Penzler, ed., *Golden Age Bibliomysteries*. Stories of murder, theft, and suspense occur with alarming regularity in the unlikely world of books and bibliophiles, including bookshops, libraries, and private rare book collections, written by such giants of the mystery genre as Ellery Queen, Cornell Woolrich, Lawrence G. Blochman, Vincent Starrett, and Anthony Boucher. **Introduction by Otto Penzler.**

Otto Penzler, ed., *Golden Age Detective Stories*. The history of American mystery fiction has its pantheon of authors who have influenced and entertained readers for nearly a century, reaching its peak during the Golden Age, and this collection pays homage to the work of the most acclaimed: Cornell Woolrich, Erle Stanley Gardner, Craig Rice, Ellery Queen, Dorothy B. Hughes, Mary Roberts Rinehart, and more. **Introduction by Otto Penzler.**

Otto Penzler, ed., *Golden Age Locked Room Mysteries*. The so-called impossible crime category reached its zenith during the 1920s, 1930s, and 1940s, and this volume includes the greatest of the great authors who mastered the form: John Dickson Carr, Ellery Queen, C. Daly King, Clayton Rawson, and Erle Stanley Gardner. Like great magicians, these literary conjurors will baffle and delight readers. **Introduction by Otto Penzler.**

Ellery Queen, *The Adventures of Ellery Queen*. These stories are the earliest short works to feature Queen as a detective and are among the best of the author's fair-play mysteries. So many of the elements that comprise the gestalt of Queen may be found in these tales: alternate solutions, the dying clue, a bizarre crime, and the author's ability to find fresh variations of works by other authors. **Introduction by Otto Penzler.**

Ellery Queen, *The American Gun Mystery*. A rodeo comes to New York City at the Colosseum. The headliner is Buck Horne, the once popular film cowboy who opens the show leading a charge of forty whooping cowboys until they pull out their guns and fire into the air. Buck falls to the ground, shot dead. The police instantly lock the doors to search everyone but the offending weapon has completely vanished. **Introduction by Otto Penzler.**

Ellery Queen, *The Chinese Orange Mystery*. The offices of publisher Donald Kirk have seen strange events but nothing like this. A strange man is found dead with two long spears alongside his back. And, though no one was seen entering or leaving the room, everything has been turned backwards or upside down: pictures face the wall, the victim's clothes are worn backwards, the rug upside down. Why in the world? **Introduction by Otto Penzler.**

Ellery Queen, *The Dutch Shoe Mystery*. Millionaire philanthropist Abagail Doorn falls into a coma and she is rushed to the hospital she funds for an emergency operation by one of the leading surgeons on the East Coast. When she is wheeled into the operating theater, the sheet covering her body is pulled back to reveal her garroted corpse—the first of a series of murders **Introduction by Otto Penzler.**

Ellery Queen, *The Egyptian Cross Mystery*. A small-town schoolteacher is found dead, headed, and tied to a T-shaped cross on December 25th, inspiring such sensational headlines as "Crucifixion on Christmas Day." Amateur sleuth Ellery Queen is so intrigued he travels to Virginia but fails to solve the crime. Then a similar murder takes place on New York's Long Island—and then another. **Introduction by Otto Penzler.**

Ellery Queen, *The Siamese Twin Mystery*. When Ellery and his father encounter a raging forest fire on a mountain, their only hope is to drive up to an isolated hillside manor owned by a secretive surgeon and his strange guests. While playing solitaire in the middle of the night, the doctor is shot. The only clue is a torn playing card. Suspects include a society beauty, a valet, and conjoined twins. **Introduction by Otto Penzler.**

Ellery Queen, *The Spanish Cape Mystery*. Amateur detective Ellery Queen arrives in the resort town of Spanish Cape soon after a young woman and her uncle are abducted by a gun-toting, one-eyed giant. The next day, the woman's somewhat dicey boyfriend is found murdered—totally naked under a black fedora and opera cloak. **Introduction by Otto Penzler.**

Patrick Quentin, *A Puzzle for Fools*. Broadway producer Peter Duluth takes to the bottle when his wife dies but enters a sanitarium to dry out. Malevolent events plague the hospital, including when Peter hears his own voice intone, "There will be murder." And there is. He investigates, aided by a young woman who is also a patient. This is the first of nine mysteries featuring Peter and Iris Duluth. **Introduction by Otto Penzler.**

Clayton Rawson, *Death from a Top Hat*. When the New York City Police Department is baffled by an apparently impossible crime, they call on The Great Merlini, a retired stage magician who now runs a Times Square magic shop. In his first case, two occultists have been murdered in a room locked from the inside, their bodies positioned to form a pentagram. **Introduction by Otto Penzler.**

Craig Rice, *Eight Faces at Three*. Gin-soaked John J. Malone, defender of the guilty, is notorious for getting his culpable clients off. It's the innocent ones who are problems. Like Holly Inglehart, accused of piercing the black heart of her well-heeled aunt Alexandria with a lovely Florentine paper cutter. No one who knew the old battle-ax liked her, but Holly's prints were found on the murder weapon. **Introduction by Lisa Lutz.**

Craig Rice, *Home Sweet Homicide*. Known as the Dorothy Parker of mystery fiction for her memorable wit, Craig Rice was the first detective writer to appear on the cover of *Time* magazine. This comic mystery features two kids who are trying to find a husband for their widowed mother while she's engaged in sleuthing. Filmed with the same title in 1946 with Peggy Ann Garner and Randolph Scott. **Introduction by Otto Penzler.**

Mary Roberts Rinehart, *The Album*. Crescent Place is a quiet enclave of wealthy people in which nothing ever happens—until a bedridden old woman is attacked by an intruder with an ax. *The New York Times* stated: "All Mary Roberts Rinehart mystery stories are good, but this one is better." **Introduction by Otto Penzler.**

Mary Roberts Rinehart, *The Haunted Lady*. The arsenic in her sugar bowl was wealthy widow Eliza Fairbanks' first clue that somebody wanted her dead. Nightly visits of bats, birds, and rats, obviously aimed at scaring the dowager to death, was the second. Eliza calls the police, who send nurse Hilda Adams, the amateur sleuth they refer to as "Miss Pinkerton," to work undercover to discover the culprit. **Introduction by Otto Penzler.**

Mary Roberts Rinehart, *Miss Pinkerton*. Hilda Adams is a nurse, not a detective, but she is observant and smart and so it is common for Inspector Patton to call on her for help. Her success results in his calling her "Miss Pinkerton." *The New Republic* wrote: "From thousands of hearts and homes the cry will go up: Thank God for Mary Roberts Rinehart." **Introduction by Carolyn Hart.**

Mary Roberts Rinehart, *The Red Lamp*. Professor William Porter refuses to believe that the seaside manor he's just inherited is haunted but he has to convince his wife to move in. However, he soon sees evidence of the occult phenomena of which the townspeople speak. Whether it is a spirit or a human being, Porter accepts that there is a connection to the rash of murders that have terrorized the countryside. **Introduction by Otto Penzler.**

Mary Roberts Rinehart, *The Wall*. For two decades, Mary Roberts Rinehart was the second-best-selling author in America (only Sinclair Lewis outsold her) and was beloved for her tales of suspense. In a magnificent mansion, the ex-wife of one of the owners turns up making demands and is found dead the next day. And there are more dark secrets lying behind the walls of the estate. **Introduction by Otto Penzler.**

Joel Townsley Rogers, *The Red Right Hand*. This extraordinary whodunnit that is as puzzling as it is terrifying was identified by crime fiction scholar Jack Adrian as "one of the dozen or so finest mystery novels of the 20th century." A deranged killer sends a doctor on a quest for the truth—deep into the recesses of his own mind—when he and his bride-to-be elope but pick up a terrifying sharp-toothed hitch-hiker. **Introduction by Joe R. Lansdale.**

Roger Scarlett, *Cat's Paw*. The family of the wealthy old bachelor Martin Greenough cares far more about his money than they do about him. For his birthday, he invites all his potential heirs to his mansion to tell them what they hope to hear. Before he can disburse funds, however, he is murdered, and the Boston Police Department's big problem is that there are too many suspects. **Introduction by Curtis Evans**

Vincent Starrett, *Dead Man Inside*. 1930s Chicago is a tough town but some crimes are more bizarre than others. Customers arrive at a haberdasher to find a corpse in the window and a sign on the door: *Dead Man Inside! I am Dead. The store will not open today.* This is just one of a series of odd murders that terrorizes the city. Reluctant detective Walter Ghost leaps into action to learn what is behind the plague. **Introduction by Otto Penzler.**

Vincent Starrett, *The Great Hotel Murder*. Theater critic and amateur sleuth Riley Blackwood investigates a murder in a Chicago hotel where the dead man had changed rooms with a stranger who had registered under a fake name. *The New York Times* described it as "an ingenious plot with enough complications to keep the reader guessing." **Introduction by Lyndsay Faye.**

Vincent Starrett, *Murder on 'B' Deck*. Walter Ghost, a psychologist, scientist, explorer, and former intelligence officer, is on a cruise ship and his friend novelist Dunsten Mollock, a Nigel Bruce-like Watson whose role is to offer occasional comic relief, accommodates when he fails to leave the ship before it takes off. Although they make mistakes along the way, the amateur sleuths solve the shipboard murders. **Introduction by Ray Betzner.**

Phoebe Atwood Taylor, *The Cape Cod Mystery*. Vacationers have flocked to Cape Cod to avoid the heat wave that hit the Northeast and find their holiday unpleasant when the area is flooded with police trying to find the murderer of a muckraking journalist who took a cottage for the season. Finding a solution falls to Asey Mayo, "the Cape Cod Sherlock," known for his worldly wisdom, folksy humor, and common sense. **Introduction by Otto Penzler.**

S. S. Van Dine, *The Benson Murder Case*. The first of 12 novels to feature Philo Vance, the most popular and influential detective character of the early part of the 20th century. When wealthy stockbroker Alvin Benson is found shot to death in a locked room in his mansion, the police are baffled until the erudite flaneur and art collector arrives on the scene. Paramount filmed it in 1930 with William Powell as Vance. **Introduction by Ragnar Jónasson.**

Cornell Woolrich, *The Bride Wore Black*. The first suspense novel by one of the greatest of all noir authors opens with a bride and her new husband walking out of the church. A car speeds by, shots ring out, and he falls dead at her feet. Determined to avenge his death, she tracks down everyone in the car, concluding with a shocking surprise. It was filmed by Francois Truffaut in 1968, starring Jeanne Moreau. **Introduction by Eddie Muller.**

Cornell Woolrich, *Deadline at Dawn*. Quinn is overcome with guilt about having robbed a stranger's home. He meets Bricky, a dime-a-dance girl, and they fall for each other. When they return to the crime scene, they discover a dead body. Knowing Quinn will be accused of the crime, they race to find the true killer before he's arrested. A 1946 film starring Susan Hayward was loosely based on the plot. **Introduction by David Gordon.**

Cornell Woolrich, *Waltz into Darkness*. A New Orleans businessman successfully courts a woman through the mail but he is shocked to find when she arrives that she is not the plain brunette whose picture he'd received but a radiant blond beauty. She soon absconds with his fortune. Wracked with disappointment and loneliness, he vows to track her down. When he finds her, the real nightmare begins. **Introduction by Wallace Stroby.**